FACING CALGARY'S DREAM
Published by Anne Stone

Cover Design, Editing, and Interior Format

BLACK GOLD
MANAGEMENT AGENCY
The Ferguson's

FACING
Calgary's
DREAM

Anne Stone

Anne
Stone
BOOKS

Dedication:

To my grandmother, Gega, who lived to the age of 95. You were strong, independent and wanted to do everything your way. It's hard to believe you've been gone for over thirty years. Here's to Charlotte Russe and Snow Pudding! Miss you today and every day.

I'd like to thank my ever patient editor, Barb, from the Killion Group. My writing is so much better because of you!

To my sister, Isabel, who never let me give up hope that my dream could become a reality.

And as always, to you Dad. I wouldn't be on this journey without your encouragement.

this meeting and my presence." Ryne nodded, running his hand through his damp hair. He took a deep breath, waiting for the words. "You're being traded to the Generals." He clenched his fists and his heart dropped. Ryne saw Adam's lips move but didn't hear everything he said. He was shocked by the news. *What the...why? Traded.* "Did you hear what I said? You're headed to the Generals."

Ryne held his expression in check. He didn't want to overreact with the news, but he was stunned. He took one, then a second calming breath and dropped into the chair beside him.

"I'd like to thank you for everything you did for the team," Beck said. "You've been a role model to everyone." Beck stopped, pausing as if he didn't know what to say to his captain and star player. Albeit ex-player now. "This is a business, Ryne. The Generals need you." Beck didn't know what to say. He started to ramble when Ryne raised his hand.

"I fully understand that this is a business. I guess I'm done for the night."

"You are."

"At least I ended on a high note, then." Ryne stood and started to leave the room. Adam blocked his exit. "I need to change, Adam. Pack my things."

"Yeah, I know. When you're done, stop back by, and we'll conference in Jacob Niles, the GM for the Generals."

Ryne ducked his head and pushed past Adam. He felt dejected. The hat trick he'd fought for was the farthest thing from his mind. He'd felt his blood pressure rise as his future changed right before his eyes. His jaw throbbed from clenching it so tightly.

He was leaving the team that drafted him into the NHL. He'd known this could be a possibility at some point in his career, but he was totally taken aback after recently signing a three-year extension. After an early season injury, he'd fought hard rehabbing, returning to the team earlier than expected. All the hard work and dedication he'd given this team would be pushed aside. He didn't think he deserved being traded. But what did he know? It was a business.

Ryne returned to the locker room after the team returned to the ice. He didn't want them to lose focus on a win. He packed his stuff and returned to the adjacent room where Adam was waiting. Ryne glared at his agent. Running his hand across his face, he shook his head, then began to pace about the room. "You could have given me a heads-up."

"It all came down in a matter of hours." Ryne stopped mid-step and glanced over his shoulder at Adam. "I was lucky to make it to the arena before Beck pulled you in. If I'd had an inkling you were on the trading block, I would have prepared you."

Ryne spun towards Adam and looked him directly in the eyes. "I know. It's just a shock, that's all."

Chapter One

"HAVE FUN AT THE GAME, Ms. Steele," Jeremy said as he slung his backpack over his shoulder and headed out of the classroom. Stopping in his tracks he called back, "Maybe you'll see Ferguson tonight. I still can't believe we got him in that trade." She smiled and waved as her fourth-grade student ran to catch his bus. Jennifer Steele had taught at Lakeview a private school since graduating from college. It catered to the wealthier families in the St. Louis area.

She zipped her backpack closed and smiled. She was a season ticket holder and loved the game of hockey. Generals fans were all a buzz with the unexpected trade that led to Ryne Ferguson joining the team.

Jennifer was running behind. She often met her best friend, Lauren Masters, for a quick pregame bite to eat at Faceoff's located inside the Generaldome; then, they'd have an after-game celebration at Union Central, the local hangout frequented by the players. As she hurried from her classroom, Lakeview's principal, Johnston O'Bryan, called to her. "Are you in a rush, Jennifer?"

She stopped dead in her tracks. She hadn't heard Johnston approach. "I'm meeting a friend before the game. Do you need something?"

"I won't keep you, but tomorrow stop by my office. I'd like to discuss something with you. Don't fret while you're at the game, I just want to run an idea past you, that's all. Have a nice evening."

Jennifer hurried home, changed, and jumped right back into her car. The Generaldome was about a half hour from her house. She preferred to get there early so she could park close to the gates.

Jennifer was still running late and was stuck in stop and go traffic. *If I know Lauren, she'll worry about me...* She pulled out her cell phone and punched in her friend's number. Focused on making sure the call went through, she wasn't paying attention as she drove through the entrance to the parking lot. That's when she heard the loud voice and felt her car jolt.

She wasn't exactly sure what had happened, then she heard someone yelling at her. She glanced up and threw her car in park. There, standing beside her car, was a man who didn't look too happy.

She rolled down her window. "Is there a problem?"

"There most certainly is," he stated. "You almost ran over me."

"I don't know how that could have happened. I didn't see you."

"I guess you didn't as you were looking at your phone."

Jennifer wasn't sure what she could say to deny the true fact that she was focused more on her phone. "Sorry about that. You're right. I wasn't paying attention. Are you alright? I didn't hurt you, did

I?"

"I'm fine but promise me that you will stop using your cell when you drive."

"I don't use my phone when I drive." The man looked at her with a half-smirk. "I don't."

"Fine. I've gotta go. I'm already late," he called over his shoulder before he jogged off in the direction of the players' entrance.

She had no idea who he was. *What just happened?* She sighed. *Thank goodness he's okay.* She raised her hand to her chest, doing the best to slow her speeding heart.

Jennifer parked, took a calming breath, and rushed into the dome. She'd been to Faceoff's often over the years and could find the restaurant with her eyes closed. As she rushed through the doors, she spotted Lauren standing at the bar, tapping her foot.

Lauren pulled her into a tight hug. "Hey, what's wrong? You're shaking."

Looking down at her phone, Jennifer said, "I was trying to call you and ran into a man on the parking lot."

"He didn't hurt you, did he? Let's call the police before he can get away."

"No, I almost ran into him with my car."

"You what?"

"You heard me. I was trying to phone you to let you know I was on the way when I glanced down to make sure the call was going through. I lost focus and the next thing I knew I heard someone yell out."

"Was he injured?"

"He said he wasn't. At least I don't think he was."

"Where'd he go?"

She sighed. "Funny thing, he headed towards the players' entrance." Gripping the countertop to still her shaking hands, she added. "I could sure use a drink."

"Yep, I'm sure you can."

They seated themselves at their usual table.

"What's new outside of almost running someone down in the parking lot?" Lauren asked as she sipped her water waiting for the waitress to take their order.

"Not much. Johnston stopped me on my way out the door. He wants to see me in his office tomorrow. He wouldn't tell me what he wanted, but that's not unusual for him. He likes to keep us in suspense. What about you?"

"Same old, same old. We're pretty slow right now. I'm thinking about taking a trip to some warmer climate. I can't wait for spring. I thought Punxsutawney Phil didn't see his shadow and winter was supposed to end sooner rather than later. I guess he got that wrong."

"Yeah, I think so. I still don't understand why we rely on a ground hog to tell us how much longer we're going to endure the winter months. That's crazy!"

Jennifer had barely finished her thought when they were greeted by Wanda, their longtime waitress. "Hey there ladies, how goes it? What can I get for you this evening?"

"After the day I've had, I'll just take a glass of water with lemon."

"Must've been pretty bad— you never drink water."

"I know but after almost running someone down,

I need to keep my wits about me."

"Oh honey, was anyone injured?"

"No, but it scared the living daylights out of me. I'm still recovering." She raised her shaking hands.

"I'm sure it did. What about you, Lauren?"

"You know, I think I'll have the same. I don't want my friend here enjoying her drink too much." They laughed as Wanda headed off to get their waters.

Jennifer was still rattled and had lost her appetite. So instead of ordering a burger like she usually did, she chose a bowl of French onion soup instead. Lauren decided on a chef salad. They ate their meals then headed out to the rink where they could watch the Generals warm-up.

Their seats were Club Level, just high enough so they could enjoy watching the players move the puck across the ice. They took their places as the Generals skated out. Jennifer became distracted and didn't notice the team members standing along the boards.

"Jen, do you know that guy?"

Jennifer wasn't paying attention to where Lauren nodded and perused the stands. "Not over there silly, down there. See, one of the players is gesturing at you."

Jennifer followed Lauren's gaze to the men standing below them. Gasping, she said, "That's him. That's the guy I ran into."

"Jen?" she asked questioningly. "Do you know who that is?"

"He looks familiar but you know me, I'm really not good at putting faces to names."

"Well, my dear, I think you almost upended our new star player."

"That can't be. Why would he be walking across the parking lot? He should have been here hours ago."

"Can't say, but I'm sure that's him." As they discussed the player, he smiled at her.

"Yep, that's got to be him. He's smiling at you like he knows you."

"He doesn't know me." And then he waved.

"He thinks he does. See? Look at him waving at you. You need to wave back."

"I can't. I'm embarrassed." She covered her face with her hand.

"You have nothing to be embarrassed about. It was an accident, and it looks like he's forgiven you." Lauren grabbed ahold of Jen's arm and raised it, forcing her to return Ryne's wave. He pointed back at her then returned to his warm-up skate.

"I can't believe that's him," Jen muttered while searching through her purse.

"Yeah, well it is. I think he likes you."

"How can you say that when I almost killed him?"

"You didn't and he looks perfectly well to me."

The game passed in a blur for Jennifer. She still couldn't believe that she almost ran over the Generals' new star player.

"That was a fantastic game," Lauren said as they headed down the escalator towards the parking lot. "I'm thinking a beer sounds good right about now, how about it?"

"Even though I know I shouldn't, I have to agree. I need something to calm me." They took their time exiting the dome and agreed to meet at Union Central.

The bar was located a few miles from the Generaldome and often drew fans coming home from the game. She was surprised when she pulled into an almost-empty parking lot. Then she realized it was a school night and attributed the lack of cars to that.

She jumped from her car and met Lauren at the door. "Where is everyone?" Lauren asked as they were greeted by the hostess.

Shrugging her shoulders, she said, "It's been slow all night."

They headed to their usual table and were greeted by their waitress. They both ordered a beer. Their attention was drawn to the television monitor over the bar where Kelly Rhodes was interviewing Ryne Ferguson.

"How does it feel being a General?"

"Great."

"The fans certainly seem to be excited by the trade. Any thoughts?"

"I'm happy to be here. I'm looking forward to learning the city, and I hope to make an impact on the team."

"I hear you barely made the game tonight."

Jen's eyes grew wide waiting for his response.

"Yeah, my plane was delayed coming out of Vancouver. Then I got lost on my way to the dome. I was nearly run over by an anxious fan."

"Anxious? Did he just say that I was anxious?'

"He did."

Jen drew her lips in and shook her head.

"I was not anxious. I was trying to call you."

"Better he say that than what you were really doing."

"I guess you're right." Both of them cheered when the waitress delivered their beers to the table. "I've needed this all night." Jen raised hers to Lauren's and clinked her bottle. "To another win."

As she took a swig, she looked up. Her eyes grew wider by the second. She started coughing uncontrollably, and Lauren smacked her hard on the back. Jen pointed towards the bar. Before either of them could react, they heard a loud voice. It belonged to none other than Ryne Ferguson and he was coming straight towards them.

Chapter Two

A S SOON AS THE GAME ended, Ryne's new teammates suggested he join them at Union Central for dinner. He was tired after a long day traveling but agreed. He wanted to start off right and having a beer with the guys was the best way to get to know them.

As he was leaving the rink, Derek Pfeil, the team captain, told him to meet them in the back of the bar. Ryne, being unfamiliar with the town, got lost on his way, arriving later than the rest of the guys. He made his way through the doors and discovered that Union Central was much larger than he originally thought.

He stopped at the bar and ordered a cola. He wasn't in the mood for an alcoholic beverage. His head was still foggy from everything that had transpired in the last twenty-four hours. Yesterday, he thought he'd be in Vancouver for the remainder of the week, but instead he found himself in St. Louis. In a city that he'd only traveled in and out of with the Eagles. Now it would be his home. For how long, he hadn't a clue. He thought he'd been secure in Vancouver for another three years, but he'd definitely read those tea leaves wrong. Now he knew he was ripe for trade no matter how effective he was for his team.

Ryne sipped his cola as he meandered through the bar looking for Derek, and that's when he saw her. She was sitting with the same girl he'd seen her with at the game. He'd never forget her. She had long, flowing brown hair and, in the moments he'd spoken to her, he'd noticed her gorgeous brown eyes and the honey color that surrounded the iris. They glowed. He wasn't good with age but guessed she was in her mid to late twenties.

He headed straight for her table, deciding his teammates could wait a little longer. As he approached, he knew the exact moment she noticed him. She'd been raising her beer to her lips. He watched as she tipped the bottle, and that's when she realized his presence. A look of panic crossed her face, and then she began to choke. She wildly pointed in his direction while her friend beat her across the back.

He neared the table and spoke. "Are you okay?" And that's when her friend realized she'd been trying to get her attention. He knew immediately that she'd recognized him as her mouth dropped open. A look of fear appeared as she flung her hands across her face.

He rushed to the brunette's side and hit her squarely across the shoulder blades. Miraculously she stopped coughing.

Gasping for air she sputtered, "It's you."

"Yep, it's me in the flesh. Since I didn't have the chance to introduce myself earlier, I will now. I'm..."

"Ryne Ferguson," her friend called out exuberantly.

"Indeed I am. And you are?" he asked, looking at Jen.

"My name is Lauren Masters."

Turning towards her friend he reached out his hand. "Nice to meet you," he said, not making eye contact with her at all. Instead he kept his eyes focused solely on the other one. She cleared her throat. He paused and then he finally heard the name he'd been waiting for all night.

"My name is Jennifer Steele," she shyly said, doing her best to not look at him. Ryne reached out his hand and held it eye level until she took it. He firmly grasped it and shook it.

"It's my pleasure to meet you," she practically whispered. Ryne took a step closer as she spoke. She cleared her throat again and said with a little more vigor, "You played well tonight."

Ryne pulled out a chair and sat beside her. "It was an off night for me. My legs just didn't seem to have it. I barely got an hour's sleep as I rushed here after my game last night. We were delayed in Boston, and I barely made it to the dome in time. But you already know that, don't you, Jennifer?" He teasingly winked at her.

"Ah, yeah. That's right." She reached for a strand of hair, curling it around her finger. He knew she was nervous especially with the way she kept gnawing on her lower lip. He wanted to ease her nervousness and turned to Lauren.

"So Lauren, what do you do?" Laughing at himself he said, "You already know what I do."

"I, ah, yeah, well I'm a tax attorney. I specialize in trust and estates."

"I bet you're pretty busy these days with everyone trying to avoid paying taxes."

"We're always busy making sure our clients are protected."

Turning back towards the woman that had gotten under his skin, he sipped his cola. "So Jennifer, what's your profession?"

She stopped spinning her hair and began toying with the napkin that sat in front of her. He reached for her hand, stopping her actions. It felt natural to him and surprisingly she didn't pull her hand back. She finally raised her eyes to him and began to speak. "I'm a fourth grade teacher at Lakeview."

"My mom's a teacher, too. I sympathize for what you have to put up with these days. My mom loves her students, but she has her issues with the parents."

"On good days they can be trying, that's for sure."

They were interrupted when he heard his name being called. "Ryne, there you are. I was wondering if you got lost."

Ryne turned to see Derek ambling towards him. "I did get lost. But then I spied someone I knew, so I had to stop and say hello." He introduced them to Derek.

"The guys are waiting for you in the back."

"About that, where exactly is the back?" He watched as Derek pointed out the room that was hidden off to the side. "That's not really the back."

"It is to me. Ladies, would you like to join us?"

"Thank you, no," Jennifer snapped. Ryne knew she was uncomfortable around him. It was up to him to calm her, and he would, in time.

"Hey man, I've got to use the little boys' room.

That's where I was headed when I saw you. Nice meeting you, ladies." He watched as Derek made his way towards the restrooms behind the bar.

"I guess I'd better head off. It was a pleasure meeting you, Lauren. And you too, Jennifer." Ryne stood and said his goodbyes.

He wanted to get to know Jennifer. He wasn't sure if she realized it or not, but he remembered where she worked. He'd committed Lakeview to his memory. He'd seek her out sooner rather than later.

He found his way through the door and was warmly greeted by what looked like the entire team. He was even more surprised when their coach, Trevor Lampkins, approached with an outstretched hand. "Welcome to the team, Ferguson. You were a little tardy today for me to formally introduce myself." Shaking his hand he added, "Let's not let that happen again."

"No sir, I won't. I got lost on my way to the dome and then was almost run over in the parking lot."

The coach shook his head. "That's one story you have there... Almost run over."

Ryne decided not to challenge the coach. Before he knew it, he was surrounded by his teammates. Each took their time introducing themselves. Nicknames were thrown about. Perry Zaney chimed in. "You can call me Zaney."

"Well, that is your name, isn't it?" Ryne slapped him on the shoulder. Carson Tucker was the last to approach him. What struck Ryne was the fact that Tucker was married, his wife was a teacher, and she taught at Lakeview. Immediately, Ryne knew he had an in at Jennifer's school. He'd find a way to see her again.

Chapter Three

JENNIFER HAD GOTTEN TO BED late the evening before after rushing out of Union Central when Ryne went to meet his teammates. She knew Lauren wanted to stay longer, but Jennifer feigned a headache and fled the bar.

When she got home, she changed into her pajamas, scrubbed her face clean of make-up, and headed off to bed. Sleep eluded her. She tossed and turned for hours. She remembered glancing at the clock at five, and the next thing she was aware of was her alarm clock bellowing. It seemed louder than normal, but she attributed it to her lack of sleep. She knew it had nothing to do with alcohol since she'd barely had one sip of her beer the night before.

She pried her left eye open and noticed it was almost six o'clock. She'd barely slept forty-five minutes. Groaning, she launched herself from bed and headed off to take a hot shower. Less than a half hour later, she jumped into her car and drove directly to the nearest gas station where she filled up the tank and grabbed a much-needed coffee. "Rough morning?" the clerk asked.

"You could say that," she answered, pouring creamer into her cup.

"Sorry to hear it," the chipper clerk responded. "I

hope you have a better day."

"Thanks." Jennifer groaned as she walked through the doors.

She took a sip from her cup as she started her car. The warm coffee eased down her throat, jolting her awake, and that's when she remembered she was supposed to meet with Johnston at some point during the day. She hadn't a clue what he wanted, and she hoped she hadn't ticked off a parent. She had a few challenging students in her classroom, and in fact, she'd sent one of them to the office the day before. She decided she wouldn't worry about what he wanted. Her mind was on the night before. She still couldn't believe she'd almost run down the Generals' new star player. And to top it all off, she was even more surprised when he recognized her and sought her out at the bar. In the short time she was around him, she'd realized how handsome he truly was.

Ryne Ferguson was well over six feet tall. He definitely towered over her five feet two inches. She'd had to look way up to find his face after almost hitting him. His height became even more apparent at the bar. She remembered his darkish colored hair brushed the collar of his coat. His hazel eyes intrigued her. She'd never seen eyes the color of his.

She pulled into her parking place, realizing she didn't remember driving the rest of the way to school. Her mind had been focused on Ryne Ferguson. She grabbed her backpack from the backseat and reached for her coffee. "I'm definitely going to need you today," she said as she took a swig from her cup. The caffeine hadn't begun to hit her system, and she hoped she wouldn't fall asleep standing up.

She made her way to her classroom and was imme-diately greeted by Johnston. "Jennifer, you're late." She looked at her watch. The bell hadn't rung, and her classroom wasn't filled with her students yet.

"It's just a little after seven. In fact, I think I'm early for the day."

"Don't you normally arrive before seven? Late night, was it?"

She glared at Johnston, not sure what he was implying. "Is there something you needed before I begin my day?"

"I'd like to meet with you during your break. Ten o'clock, my office." With that, he spun around and exited her classroom. She was in a mood with her lack of sleep. *He'd better not push me today.*

Before she knew it, she was dropping her class off for music and was on her way to Johnston's office. Her headache that had appeared once he'd left her classroom had intensified. She knew it was from lack of both sleep and caffeine. She prayed she'd get through the meeting.

Johnston's door was closed, so Jennifer knocked. Just as she was ready to walk away, he threw open the door. She took one look at his face and thought she was in trouble. "Come in," he said as he made his way to his desk. "Please, close the door behind you."

He used the word please; maybe I'm not in trouble. Jen-nifer sat down and waited for him to speak. She became more nervous by the second as she sat in the utter quiet of the room.

He took a deep breath and blew it out. Pursing his

lips, he looked her directly in the eyes. "Jennifer, I need your help with a special project that's near and dear to my heart." He paused. "I'm not sure if you are aware or not, but this is my second marriage."

She was surprised by his comment. She didn't say a word, listening as he spoke.

"My first wife was killed in a hit and run accident."

"I'm so sorry. I had no idea."

"Thank you. It was a long time ago. She loved this school. In fact, she helped me come up with the concept. Her father was a professional hockey player, and she was forced to transfer schools several times when he'd been traded. She wanted to create an environment that helped a student when they were forced to transfer. Help them discover ways to make friends and adjust to their new surroundings."

"Wow, that's remarkable that she felt that way and wanted to help others."

"Yeah, that was my Helen. She always focused on the youngsters. She died a few weeks before Lakeview opened and never got to see it filled with students." He paused momentarily. "Anyway, this fall will be our fifteenth year in operation, and I want to have a fundraiser. Not a typical one but something different. I know you could be a professional photographer."

She'd given up her dream of working in her father's profession when her parents were killed. A little embarrassed by his comment, she flipped her hair behind her ear. "Not really."

"Oh yes, you can. I've seen your work. I know your father was well known before his passing.

Anyway, I thought about doing a showing of some kind, maybe an auction. One thing for sure, I want to showcase some of the photographs we've had throughout the years, and I'd like you to coordinate it. A book of memories."

"I'm not sure about that."

"I am and I'd like you to take photographs at all the special events the remainder of the year. I want you to have a camera glued to your neck. You have an eye and I want you to use it. I plan on using your photographs along with some I have in the archives for the showing. In fact, I want to make them available for purchase. I think this would be a fantastic fundraiser. We could have a dinner, auction; the sky's the limit. I want to celebrate Lakeview, but I also want to celebrate Helen and her brilliance behind the school. We've had many professional athletes walk through these doors, and I hope some of them will be able to attend the event. So, what do you have to say?"

"Um…I'm not sure about my talents as a photographer, but I will help in whatever capacity I can. When do you plan on having this event?"

"I'm thinking in the fall, maybe around Halloween. I haven't narrowed that down yet, but for sure before the holidays."

"May I ask who else you've asked to be on this project?'

"No one, yet. I wanted to speak with you first. Maybe we can get a member of the Generals to co-chair."

"That's a thought."

"Any suggestions?"

"Ah, I don't."

"We have some time to figure that out. I wanted to run this past you. Think about it over the weekend, and maybe we can meet again the first of next week. I'd like to announce it before Spring Break, if possible."

"That's just around the corner."

"It is, but I think it's doable."

"I have to say I'm shocked that you asked me to participate in this."

"Yesterday was Helen's birthday, and my mind was on her." He stopped and smiled. "Don't get me wrong...I love my wife and my life today, but I still miss Helen."

"I understand. I still grieve for my parents, and they died almost eight years ago. No matter how hard you try to move on, it's still difficult. The pain may lessen but it's always there."

"It is," Johnston said as he stood. "It's almost time for you to get your class. Thank you again for agreeing to do this, Jennifer." She smiled at him and opened the door.

As she walked down the hallway to get her students, she thought of her parents and how their loss affected her day after day. They'd been killed the night of her high school graduation.

The day flew by after meeting with Johnston. She drove home in a blur and spent the night on the couch. Her parents had been on her mind off and on since her earlier meeting. She missed them so much and believed the ache would never fully go away. She replayed her conversation and decided to pull out some of her father's albums. He'd had volumes of his work, and she took inspiration in reviewing it.

The more she thought about the project, the more excited she became, especially after going through her father's photographs. Since several of the parents at Lakeview had ties to the Generals, she decided that she'd focus many of the photographs on the Generals' players. She'd contact Ed Talent, the owner of the team. He was a friend of her father's, and she still remained close with him.

She texted Ed, and before she knew it, her phone rang. She looked at the caller ID and was surprised that he was returning her call so quickly. "Hey, Jen, is everything alright?"

"I'm doing well, Ed. I wanted to run something past you."

"Okay, shoot."

"Johnston met with me today. Did you know he was married before Alana?"

"I did. Helen, in fact, was the driving force behind Lakeview."

"That's what I learned. Anyway, he wants to have a celebration in honor of the fifteenth anniversary of the school, and he's asked me to have a showing."

"A showing? Of your dad's stuff?"

"No, mine."

"Jen, are you sure you want to go there? I know you haven't been behind the lens much these days."

"I haven't and I really don't know how he discovered that I was a photographer alongside my dad, but he did. He thinks my work is good enough to auction off."

"No question, it is."

"Thanks, but Ed, I don't know."

"I think it's a fantastic idea. Stop worrying. You need to jump right in. Now, what do you need other than my words of encouragement?"

"I was thinking of focusing on the Generals. Since several of the players, along with members of the management team, have children at Lakeview, I thought I could showcase them. I could take photographs at practice, games, and the like… I know I'm rambling."

"I think that's a great idea. And no, you aren't rambling. When the team returns from their road trip, I'll speak with Jacob and his management team. Sound good to you?"

"Yeah, thanks, Ed. You don't know what this means to me."

"I think I do. And Jen."

"Yeah."

"Your dad would be proud."

"Thanks," she muttered as tears formed in the back of her throat.

Jennifer hadn't taken her photography seriously in a long, long time. Not since her dad passed away. She really had no idea how Johnston knew about her photography, but she was taking his interest as a sign. Maybe this was a sign that she needed to put the sadness behind her, pick up her camera again and make a change in her life.

Chapter Four

RYNE PREPARED TO BOARD THE return flight home. It had been his first road trip as a General, and he wasn't the only exhausted player. As he headed along the jetway, Trevor stopped him.

"Ryne, after we level off, come see me, okay?"

Ryne nodded and continued down the aisle. He stowed his bag and dropped into his seat. As the attendants prepared the cabin for departure, he ticked off all the injuries that had occurred during their trip.

Just last night, Derek, their captain, injured his shoulder. He'd be out a few games. It was a blow to the team, especially since they were entering the home stretch of the season.

When the bell chimed indicating they could move about the cabin, Ryne scrubbed his hand across this face, stood, and headed to the front where Trevor sat. He wasn't sure what he'd done to deserve this meeting with the coach. He thought he'd played well, having made few mistakes, and had spent no time in the penalty box.

Ryne cleared his throat, notifying Trevor of his presence. He'd gestured to Ryne to have a seat.

"You looked good out there, Ferguson."

"Thanks, Coach." He was a little nervous as he sat

beside Trevor, clenching and unclenching his fists.

"Derek's going to be out a few games."

"That's what I heard."

"We have a few more injuries too."

"I know."

"Is there a problem?"

"Ah, no why would you think that?"

"You're being a little quiet." He chuckled shaking his head. At least his comment broke the ice and Ryne relaxed a little. "So, how do you feel about stepping it up a little?"

Ryne looked at him, shocked. He was a newbie with the team and was still learning the players' personalities and skills.

"I know your background. You were a leader on the Eagles, and I need you to be the same kind of leader here. I think we have a great chance to make the playoffs, but with our injuries mounting, I need your experience out there on the ice. I need you to lead the rookies while Derek sits out."

Ryne listened intently and nodded often. "I can do that. I don't want to overstep myself with being new and all."

"You won't, that's for sure. I know everyone respects you and what you did before your trade. I feel like you've been here all year and not just a few weeks. You're fitting in nicely, jelling with the guys."

Ryne smiled broadly. "I have to say, I feel the same way. It's a great group of guys, and they all have one another's backs."

"They do. So you understand my expectations."

"Yes, sir I do."

"Good. Now one more thing."

"Shoot."

"Derek was supposed to speak at an assembly, Wednesday morning. I'd like you to fill in."

"Okay."

"It's at Lakeview Private School." Ryne eyebrows shot up. *Lakeview. Maybe I'll see Jennifer.* "We regularly help out with assemblies. Derek was going to talk to the students about attaining a good education. With your record, I think you'll be perfect to represent the Generals."

"I can do that."

"The assembly is at ten. I'll email you the information. I know Jacob will be pleased that you are attending. I think Ed may be there as well, speaking from the perspective of an owner." They spoke about various other subjects until it was time for the plane to land. Ryne returned to his seat and started making notes of some of the points he'd discuss.

He realized he'd had nothing to be nervous about. From all signs, he was adjusting well to his teammates and management better than he thought possible. He was surprised that he'd been asked to fill in for Derek both on and off the ice. He planned on doing his best; he had no intentions of being traded again. The only way he'd change teams would be to go home. Home to his Calgary Storm.

They arrived in St. Louis late Monday evening. Their next game wasn't scheduled until Thursday, and the players didn't have to report to practice until Wednesday afternoon. Ryne took the time to settle into his extended-stay hotel room. He wouldn't begin to find a place to live permanently until after the season.

He slept in later than normal and when he woke, powered up his laptop. As promised, Trevor had emailed him the information he needed for the assembly the following morning. He pulled out his cell phone and located Carson's number. He decided to check in with him to gain further background on Lakeview.

Carson groggily answered. "Yeah," he grumbled into the phone.

"Carson, it's Ryne. Ryne Ferguson."

"What do you want? Didn't I just leave your presence?"

"You did." Ryne held on waiting for Carson to further respond. "Carson, are you there?"

"I'm here." Dead silence. "Sorry about that, Ferguson. I'm here. I didn't get much sleep. My daughter cried through what was left of the night. My wife says she has an ear infection."

"Sorry to hear that. I know what that's like. My youngest sister gets them all the time."

"What do you need?"

"Coach asked me to speak at an assembly tomorrow, and I thought I'd ask you a few questions."

"Me, why me?"

"I'm going to Lakeview, and I wanted a little insight into the school. And since your wife works there, I thought you'd be the perfect person to fill me in." Ryne waited a moment, giving Carson some time to get himself together.

"Okay, shoot."

Ryne went through his list of questions. Carson told him how the school came to be and ticked off several current and former famous names who attended. He expressed what he saw were the positives and negatives of a school such as Lakeview. "First of all, even though they try not to, many of our kids seem to have an attitude as though they are superior since we play a professional sport. I know the coaches address that but just so you know."

"I get that. I had the same issue growing up, especially with my dad playing for the Storm. I tried not to have that attitude, but I know I did. My dad worked with me. He wanted all of us to be regular guys. I think he had a rougher time with me and my twin, Etienne. Since Philippe's the oldest, I'm sure he was perfect. I know my parents learned a lot with us, so when Rafael and Jules were going through school, they knew what to expect and how to handle them. My sisters, Olivia and Emma, are still in school. They're playing hockey too, and I'm sure my parents will be faced with totally different dilemmas than they were with us boys."

"I forgot that you were a twin."

"Yeah, Etienne was drafted right out of high school. He played four years with the Boston Ice before being traded to the Storm. He's played the last five years with Philippe, who has played his entire career in Calgary. Rafael plays for the Arizona Tide, while Jules followed in my footsteps and is playing for the University of Wisconsin."

"Your mom must have gone batty dealing with your dad traveling and all of your hockey schedules."

"My mom's the best. She's a teacher, too. Looking back, I have no idea how she kept it all together, but she did. We were never late for a game or a

practice." They spoke for a few minutes longer and
then Ryne could hear Carson's daughter crying in
the background. "I'll let you go so you can deal
with your daughter. Thanks for the info."

"Anytime. Have fun tomorrow."

"I will." Ryne groaned and said his goodbyes.

That evening, he prepared his notes. He liked to
speak extemporaneously and from the heart, but he
did have a few points he wanted to stress in his presentation. He wanted to make sure that whether the
kids were into sports or not, a good education was
paramount in life. They weren't always going to be
able to play baseball, hockey, football, or whatever
their sport was. These kids needed to know just one
injury could sideline them for the remainder of their
lives, and a back-up plan was necessary to survive.

Ryne always arrived at an event early. He was
never late and prided himself on that quality,
engrained in him from childhood. He still wondered how his mom did it when he was a kid. She'd
had seven children who now ranged in age from
twenty-nine to ten. He hadn't a clue how she kept
everyone organized. She often had a baby in tow
too. Ryne always remembered his mom was upbeat
and never got angry or upset with them. Every day
she had a smile on her face, and he would always
remember that about her.

Ryne dressed casually for himself. Normally he
wore a suit when he spoke at events. Since he was
speaking with students, he chose dark colored pants,
a long-sleeved white shirt and a striped tie. He left
his suit coat at home. He was greeted at the front
doors by Ed and Johnston. Ed introduced him

and explained that he was replacing Derek for the assembly.

"I heard about his injury," Johnston said.

"Second time this year he's been out with that shoulder. Luck certainly hasn't been on his side," Ed stated.

Johnston extended his hand in a greeting and explained that Ryne would be presenting to the middle grades. He was almost assured that Jennifer's class would be there. *Didn't she teach fourth grade?*

Johnston led both Ed and Ryne to the back of the stage. The students knew that one of the Generals was speaking, but they had no idea who it was. Johnston addressed the assembly and then introduced Ed.

"Some of you may remember me and, well, some may not," he said to a round of laughter. "My name is Ed Talent and I'm the owner of your Generals." A round of applause followed. "I know many of you were hoping that Derek Pfeil would be here today. Unfortunately, he was injured Monday night and is undergoing therapy as we speak. Hopefully, he'll be back on the ice in the near future. So instead of Derek, I thought I'd introduce you to a new player— someone you know very little about." Ed held their attention as he touted Ryne's background.

"Let me tell you a little bit about him. He's from Calgary, Alberta, Canada. He's one of seven children, all who play hockey in some regard. He has four brothers of which three play in the NHL. So I'd have to say not only did he grow up in the hockey profession with his dad playing for the Calgary Storm, he's surrounded by it as well. He knows what many of you experience when your dad goes on a long road trip." Ed heard the groans from the audience.

"What I want you to take from his speech is that he didn't go straight into the NHL from high school. He attended the University of Wisconsin where he played for the Badgers. As a Badger, he won several awards graduating with honors. He's a born leader, was captain of the Eagles and is a mentor to all. So please listen to what he has to say. I think each of you can learn a lot from him. So without further boring you, I'd like to introduce our newest General, Ryne Ferguson."

Ryne walked from the back of the stage to roaring applause. As he approached the podium, he reached for the microphone and his eyes searched the audience. There, sitting in the third row, was Jennifer. By the expression on her face and the way she threw her hand across her mouth, he could tell she was shocked by his presence. He smiled broadly in her direction and began to thank the audience. "Thank you for the warm welcome. I am so happy to be here. I'm sure most of you were expecting Derek. Let's keep him in our thoughts as he works to return to the ice." He received another round of applause.

"Many of you probably have never heard of me before. I'll give you a short history of my background. As Ed said, I'm one of seven children. My dad played for the Calgary Storm while my mom was a teacher who raised seven kids practically alone a good part of the year since my dad traveled so much. She dealt with all of our crazy schedules and did it every day with a smile on her face. I never can remember my mom without her effervescent smile.

"Now that my dad's retired and running our ranch, she has a little help getting my two sisters to school and hockey practice. I have an older brother, Philippe, a younger brother, Rafael, and my twin brother, Etienne, who all play in the NHL. My youngest brother followed me and is attending the University of Wisconsin and plays for the Badgers. My sisters are still in school and as I said, both play hockey."

Ryne hated to stand behind a podium, so he walked about the stage. He could feel Jennifer's eyes following him. He paused, looked down and then spoke. "Who here likes school?" Ryne chuckled as he heard the loud groans. "I guess I know the answer to that question." He moved across the stage and paused again. "Raise your hand if you play a sport." Nearly everyone's hands were raised. "Who hopes to become a pro in their sport?" Cheers rang out as hands flailed in the audience. "Who thinks they'll be a professional their entire life?" A few hands fell but many stayed raised.

Ryne walked from the stage and went down to the audience. "Keep your hands raised now." He approached a boy that had a Generals shirt on. "I guess you play hockey?"

"I do," the boy quickly answered.

"And I guess you want to play for the Generals too?"

"You got that."

"That's a good goal. Let me ask you this…what do you want to do with your life?"

"I told you, play hockey."

"Let me rephrase my question...What are your plans if you can't play hockey?"

"I'll play. I'm the best." Everyone laughed at his comment.

"I'm sure you are good, but what if you become injured liked Derek did. What if you can't come back from your injury, or worse yet, what if you've set your goals on making the NHL and aren't drafted or signed to a team? Have you thought about that?"

"Ah, no."

Ryne returned to the stage. "I'd like all of you to think about what you want to do when you grow up and take your sport out of the equation. I was drafted by the Eagles at the age of seventeen, but I chose instead to go to the UW and get an education. And why do you think I did that?"

"In case you got injured."

"Bingo," he said pointing to the girl in the back of the audience who answered his question. "I worked hard, got my degree. I graduated in the top of my class. I even attended graduate school online too. I had a plan and I followed through with my plan. I'm prepared for life after hockey. I have a career when I retire from the game, and God forbid I get injured, I have that same career. Do you see how important it is to study hard now and why it's important to go to school?

"I have a plan to fall back on if something happens that I didn't foresee. My dad, when he played hockey, had a fallback plan. He runs our family ranch. My brothers were drafted into the NHL and didn't attend college. Instead, they chose to play hockey. I think they've each learned a little something from me. Now, all three of them are taking classes online. They're not going about it the same way I did, but at least they've decided to create a fallback plan too."

Ryne had no worries when he retired from the game he loved having carefully mapped out his life. All was going according to plan. That had worked well for him just like his brothers' decision to play right out of school had worked for them.

As Ryne spoke, he often caught Jennifer's eye. He saw her smiles as he addressed the need for education. He hoped she saw a different person than the one she almost ran down. He was not your typical hockey player. He'd excelled in school and had a solid future after playing the game he loved.

He spoke a few more minutes and then took questions. "What's your degree in?"

"I have a degree in finance along with a master's in business."

He saw another hand raised. "I'm sure it's difficult studying, practicing, and traveling. What kind of grades did you get?"

"I did pretty well."

Another student raised his hand, "Did you just pass or what?"

"Actually, I graduated summa cum laude with a 4.0 grade point average. I worked hard and that's what this assembly is all about— working hard, setting goals, and achieving those goals."

While he stood there and listened to Johnston end the assembly, Ryne caught Jennifer's eye and smiled at her. He decided right there and then, he was going to speak with her before leaving. He moved to the doors so he could thank each of the students as they returned to their classrooms. As Jennifer made her way towards him, he reached for her hand. "I'd like to speak to you."

"Not right now. I need to get my students back to class. Later."

Later. She didn't even have his number. How would she get ahold of him? Ryne stood in the doorway until all of the students had left the auditorium.

"Do you have a minute? I'd like to run an idea past you," Johnston asked.

"I do." Ryne followed him to his office. There he listened as Johnston pitched the idea that he said came to him as Ryne spoke with the students. Ryne realized it was masterful and he couldn't wait for Johnston to share it with Jennifer.

Chapter Five

JENNIFER RETURNED TO HER CLASSROOM just in time for her students to head off to lunch. *Perfect timing.* She needed a few moments to sit back and take in what Ryne had shared. She'd never taken him to be a summa cum laude graduate from one of the toughest universities in the country, especially earning it while playing hockey at such a high level. She'd realized he definitely wasn't one to brag about himself after discovering he'd been recognized on several All-American teams and won various awards for his playing abilities. She'd been clueless to all his accomplishments.

She sat at her desk, staring out the window when she heard a soft knock. She often ate in her class-room so she could grade papers and prepare for her afternoon classes. She turned towards the door and in walked Johnston and Ryne. She was taken aback by their visit; she'd thought Ryne had left right after his presentation.

"Jennifer, Ryne here tells me you know one another."

"Ah, I can't say we know one another but we have met." Ryne smiled broadly. She was getting accus-tomed to his winsome smile. His eyes lit up as he looked at her. He seemed comfortable in his surroundings.

"I was thinking." *Oh boy, this doesn't sound good.* "The fundraiser that I was speaking to you about."

"Yes."

"Well, I think you need a co-chair. So as Ryne stood up there telling us all about himself it hit me. What better person to help highlight Lakeview and our striving for a sound fundamental education than Ryne here," Johnston said motioning to him. "I think he'd make a fantastic spokesperson and co-chair. What do you say?"

"Ahh, I think it's a good idea. I had no idea you were so well educated."

"I don't really like to talk about it. I feel like I'm bragging about my successes, but I knew I had to today." He shrugged. "Are you sure you're okay with me being your assistant?"

"Not assistant. Co-chair."

"Whatever. I just want to make sure you're comfortable with me helping out. I've never done this before. You're definitely going to have to show me the ropes."

"To be honest with you, I haven't either, so it looks like we're going to learn together."

"Well, then, I guess I'll leave you two alone." Johnston spun on his heel and headed out the door, softly closing it behind him.

Jennifer looked at Ryne as he swept his hand across his face. They both started to speak at the same time, then he deferred to her. "The floor's all yours."

She gestured to him to take the chair directly across from her. "Wow. I'm certainly surprised by this."

"Yeah, I am too. I had no idea filling in for Derek would lead me to hosting an auction, or whatever it is."

"I'm not too sure what Johnston is calling this shindig. All I know is that I'm supposed to have a showing."

"A showing?" He looked perplexed at her as she spun a pencil on her desk.

"That's right. He wants me to have a showing of my work. He thinks I have all these photographs lined up just waiting to be displayed and I don't."

"I'm a little unclear what you're talking about." Jennifer began to fill Ryne in on Johnston's expectations. As she spoke, his eyes never left her face. "You're a photographer?"

"Not really anymore, but Johnston thinks that I am."

"From what I know, once a photographer, always a photographer."

"I guess you could say that, but I don't feel like one. I haven't picked up a camera in that capacity in a really long time. I did speak with Ed yesterday about taking shots of you all as you warmed up and played, but that's the extent of where I've gone with this."

"Ed? You mean Ed Talent, the owner of the Generals?" She raised her brow at him. "You know Ed?"

She lowered her eyes. "Yeah, I know Ed. We go back a long way. He was a good friend of my father's. He checks in on me now and again. I see him all the time at the dome. I have season tickets."

"So our meeting wasn't necessarily happenstance?"

"I'd say the way we met on the parking lot was, but more than likely our paths would have crossed at one time or another."

"That's good to know. So where do we go from here? In fact, when is this soiree?"

"I'm not sure the exact date. Sometime this fall."

She could tell he was pondering the date. "I hope we're in town and not on the road. I'm going to have to check out when training camp begins. Normally, it starts-up the middle of September with preseason games that run through the first week or so of October. The season officially begins mid-month. I better get on this. I need to tell everyone: Ed, Jacob, Trevor…"

She reached across her desk for his hands that were perched on top of her planner. "You can take a breath." He looked at her stupefied. "I don't think you've taken a breath in the last minute or so. Relax. We have plenty of time."

He squeezed her hands.

"I guess we do. This is all so much for me. Between the trade and running into you— literally, and now this. I'm still trying to get my feet wet in the city. Johnston's request certainly has done that for me."

"I guess it has. So where should we begin?"

"I think by you giving me your phone number." She cracked a smile at him.

"That's a good start." She reached for her phone while he pulled his from his pocket. Exchanging phone numbers, she glanced at the clock. "Oh wow, I need to go. I have to pick my kids up from recess. Sorry," she called as she headed out the door.

She could tell he was shocked by the time himself. "Yeah, as it is I'm going to be late for practice.
Coach will not be too kind, I'm sure." She quirked
her brow again. "He wasn't happy when I was late
the night we first met. In fact, I don't think he
bought my story about being almost run down in
the parking lot, either." She smirked as she headed
out the door.

"I'll have to fix that one for you."

"No worries," he claimed as he followed her down
the hallway. She turned right towards the stairway
while he kept on his path for the front door.

Jennifer was going to be late. She hated being
late to anything. She flew around the corner and
ran smack into Johnston. "Oh my," she called out
reaching for the wall to prevent herself from falling.

"Ms. Steele, are you alright?"

Catching her breath, she breathed, "I am, Mr.
O'Bryan. You surprised me that's all. I'm sorry I
was late picking up my students." The staff always
formally referred to one another when in the presence of the students.

"No worries. You weren't late. I thought I'd give
you and Ryne a chance to speak, so I decided to
meet your class."

"Thank you," she replied as they returned to her
classroom. "I had no idea you were considering
him."

"I wasn't until I heard him speak. I explained to
him that I thought he was perfect for the job. I sold
it as a way for him to donate his time to a worthy
cause. He agreed hook, line, and sinker. I'm pretty
proud of myself." He stoically stood beside her as

her students entered the classroom. "I'm going to get my thoughts together, check in with Ed, and then set-up a meeting with the two of you to discuss my goals for the event."

"Just let me know when."

"Sure thing, and thanks again for agreeing to chair this with him. I think this fundraiser will be quite successful."

"I hope so," she said turning to reenter her classroom. *I certainly hope so.*

Jennifer's day ended on a low note. One of her students tripped down the stairs breaking his ankle. She was upset the remainder of the day and didn't check her phone until she got home when she discovered several missed calls—all from Ryne.

Tapping her finger on the side of her phone, she contemplated what she should do since he hadn't left a message. She wasn't in the best frame of mind, but she decided to return his call anyway. She knew he had practice and wasn't sure if it had ended.

When he didn't answer, she kicked off her shoes and dove into her slippers that sat right inside the kitchen. It felt exquisite to be able to wiggle her toes back and forth in the softness. She hated wearing heels to school and often wondered why she did. She was tired and just wanted to relax. She grabbed a bottle of water, her phone, and her backpack and headed off to her home office. She had a few papers to grade and wanted to finish them before dinner. Reaching into her bag, her hand got stuck as she pulled out the papers causing them to fly about the floor. *What else can go wrong?* She sorted them back into their respective piles and reached for her red pen. Opening her water, she threw back a swallow and started at the task in hand. Her phone sat beside her. She reached for her water, and her phone slid against her leg, and that's when she felt it vibrate. Glancing down, she discovered she's missed his call again.

Quickly she reached for the phone and redialed. Ryne answered immediately. "Hey there, I've been trying to call you."

"I know. Sorry about that. We had a little excitement this afternoon, and I've been trying to catch up since."

"What happened?"

"One of my students missed a step, fell, and broke his ankle."

"Ouch!"

"Yeah, ouch. It's had me a little rattled since."

"So, what are you doing right now?"

"Grading papers."

"Another ouch!"

"It's not that bad. It actually relaxes me. I know that sounds crazy but it does. What about you? What are you up to?"

"We just finished practice. I was wondering if you'd like to get together and have a bite to eat. Brainstorm a little."

"Ah, Ryne, I'm a little tired."

"I understand if you don't want to go out. How about I grab us something to eat and come over. That way you can put on your pj's and relax a little."

"Pj's?"

"Well, whatever it is your wear when you relax. I haven't a clue what that may be. I know what I wear when I relax— sweats and a t-shirt."

She knew he was smiling as she could hear it in his voice. "To be honest, I have on my lounge pants. They're pretty comfortable." She paused not knowing where that thought came from.

"So how about it? Are you game?"

"I am. Thank you."

"What are you in the mood for?"

"Whatever. In fact, I'm starved. I didn't get a chance to eat lunch today—you know, with our meeting and all."

"Sorry about that. I didn't realize you missed lunch. I'll make it up to you." He paused. "Oh, by the way I need your address."

"I'll text it along with directions."

"Great. How about an hour? Is that good?"

"That works."

"Well, okay then, I'll see you in an hour." She hung up the phone smiling. It actually felt good to smile after the day she'd had. She hurried to finish grading the last of the papers. She didn't want any distractions. In fact, she was looking forward to seeing him again. Twice in one day— maybe luck was on her side.

Chapter Six

RYNE HADN'T A CLUE WHERE to go for dinner. As he hurried from the locker room, he stopped Derek, who'd attended practice just to skate about so he could keep his legs strong while he recuperated. His shoulder was still a work in progress. He hoped to return to the team in the next couple of days. "Can you recommend a restaurant that does take out?"

"Sure thing. Try Vigliano's Pizzeria. It's right around the corner. They have fabulous lasagna, cavatelli, and they make the best thin crust pizza. If you like salad, it's a good choice too. And their cheesecake is one of the best I've ever eaten."

"Thanks, man. I'm still learning the city." Derek gave him directions. Ryne accessed their on-line menu, selecting a few choices. As promised, his order was ready when he walked through the doors. He was impressed with the quickness and how they'd separated their salad, dessert, rolls and butter into a separate bag to keep them from getting hot.

Ryne programmed Jennifer's address into his GPS and before he knew it was pulling up in front of her huge, Victorian-styled home. The outside of her house was ablaze in light that illuminated its grandeur. As he took in its beauty, he noticed the turret that sat at the corner. The exterior of the home was gorgeous, and he couldn't wait to see the inside. As he walked up the steps, he took in the wrap-around porch. It was welcoming. He knew she spent a lot of time sitting outside as he noticed the outdoor furniture that graced it.

As he approached the door, he saw her through the window. She waved then threw open the door. He immediately recognized her tiredness. Her shoulders were slumped, and she had dark circles beneath her eyes that hadn't been there earlier in the day. "Dinner," he called as he raised two shopping bags.

"Did you buy out the restaurant?" She noticed the restaurant logo. "Ooh, Vigliano's. I love their food."

"Good choice then. You need to thank Derek since he recommended it."

She moved aside and ushered him into her foyer. Immediately, he took in the magnificence of her home. "This is beautiful! I love old Victorians!"

"Thanks. I've lived here all my life. How about a tour?"

Her stomach grumbled. Knowing she hadn't eaten, he said, "Let's eat first. I know you're starving," he said pointing to her stomach. Then his chimed in tune with hers. "And I am too." He grinned at her while she led him towards the kitchen.

"I hope it's okay if we eat in here."

He looked around the room. It was beautiful. All stainless-steel appliances, a quartz countertop. It was spotless, like she never used it. "This is fine. Do you even use it?"

"Of course, I do. I love to cook."

"Just wondering. It's spotless." She reached into a cabinet, grabbing plates and glassware. He moved to her side, taking the plates from her.

"Wine?" she asked as she moved to her wine refrigerator where she retrieved a bottle.

"That sounds nice." She grabbed the opener and handed it to him while she reached for their utensils and napkins. He opened it and set it on the table, waiting for her to join him. As she approached, he surprised her by pulling out her chair. He waited for her to take her seat, then sat beside her.

"Wow, this smells good. Did I say I was hungry?"

"You did," he claimed as he poured their wine. "Shall we toast?"

"Sure, what to?"

"How about to a successful fundraiser? Yep, that's what I'll call it— fundraiser." Taking a sip of her wine, she agreed with his terminology.

"So what do you have in here?" she asked as she reached into the bag.

"Let's see…On high recommendation there's lasagna, cavatelli, spaghetti and meatballs, a vegetable of some kind— actually I think it's broccoli." He grabbed the other bag. "In here is salad, rolls and dessert."

"Oh boy, dessert, too."

"Yep. I heard they have a one-of-a kind cheesecake."

"They do."

Ryne pulled out their salads along with the rolls and butter. He watched her as she broke her roll in half and spread a pat of butter across it, taking a large bite.

"Oh my gosh, this is so good."

"When you're that hungry, I think you could eat chalk and it would taste wonderful." He couldn't take his eyes off her as she took another bite of salad. As he ate his, he rested his head on his hand. He was enamored by her. The more he was in her presence, the more he felt a connection. What, he didn't know, but he certainly couldn't get enough of her. Her eyes shined brightly as she took a swallow of her wine.

"Is there something wrong?"

"Why would you think that?"

"You haven't taken your eyes off me since you sat down."

"Ahh, sorry about that." He looked away and took another bite of his salad. He felt her hand reach for his. He cocked his head and wasn't sure where he should take the conversation so he went with the truth. "I think you're beautiful."

"Ryne."

"Well, I do and I enjoy being in your company."

"After I almost ran you over."

"Yeah, even after that." He grinned and clasped her hand in his. "I don't want to be presumptuous here, but will you go on a date with me? I have to be honest. I haven't been able to get you out of my mind since we first met. I want you to know that I'm a little nervous assisting you in the fundraiser since I've never done anything like that before, but I'm also overjoyed because I'll be able to spend time with you."

He thought she'd turned a little shy as she became quiet. "Did I overstep myself here? Was I misreading this," he said pointing back and forth between them. "I feel something here between us, what about you?"

She squeezed his hand. "Yeah, I feel it too. And yes, I'd love to go out with you."

"Good. On that note, let's try the rest of our dinner. I can't wait to cut into that cheesecake." He withdrew his hand, smiling at her as he pulled out their meals and opened the containers. He glanced up and saw her bright smile. Thankfully, he'd read her mannerisms well enough and didn't think that he'd said the wrong thing.

After dinner, he followed her through the house as she gave him the complete tour. It was a gorgeous home. It had five bedrooms, a formal living room and dining room, a game room, media room, and more bathrooms than he could count. "You live here all by yourself." She nodded and pulled away. "Did I say something wrong?"

"Of course not. It's just hard sometimes. My parents..." A look of despair crossed her face, and he pulled her into his arms. He hoped he didn't misread her need for a hug. It took her a moment before she wrapped her arms around his waist. He held her until she pulled away. He could see the tears in her eyes.

Ryne reached his hand up and caressed the side of her face. "Hey, forget that I asked, okay? I don't want to bring sadness into this evening."

She inhaled deeply and blew out a breath through her mouth. "No, it's okay. I don't know why I get this way, but sometimes the memories are just too much." She grabbed his hand, and he followed her into the family room where she sat down on the sofa. She pulled in close to him and clasped her hands around his forearm. "I need to tell you this so it might as well be right now." Ryne watched her hand as she fiddled with the cuff of his shirt. "It was the night of my high school graduation. My dad was running late. He'd had a photo shoot that ran long, and my mom decided to wait for him. I had to be at the auditorium for pictures, and I can't remember what else, but I had to be there like two hours before."

"I can't imagine pictures taking that long..."

"Well, they did," she said, smiling at him, remembering the day. "I was ecstatic to graduate and move on with my life. I couldn't wait to head off to college. I was taking every minute in, burning it to memory, knowing this would be the last time I'd be in the same room with some of my classmates. I remember laughing at something trivial one of my friends said, and then I saw the look on the administrator's face. I knew something was wrong, especially when he approached me. My heart dropped. I imagined the worst and, in fact, it came true." She stopped speaking and grasped his hand tightly in hers. He knew she was reliving that night and didn't want to push her, so he sat silently waiting for her to continue. Several minutes passed before she spoke again.

"I vividly recall the way he approached me, reaching out his hand. The look in his eyes, the expression on his face. I can hear every word as he asked to speak with me. I remember being escorted into a room, and there before me were my grandparents.

Tears were pouring down my grandmother's face. I didn't know what happened or why she was crying. Then my grandfather Steele approached me. They live in the northeast and had come to town for my graduation.

"He reached for my hand and led me to a chair. I can still hear the leather as it creaked and groaned as I sat down. I felt like the chair consumed me. My grandfather kneeled down in front of me and grasped my hands. A horrible look crossed his face, and then he broke the news. My parents had been killed in a car accident."

Ryne sat still, not moving or speaking. She was his focus, and he wanted her to know she had his full attention. A tear careened down her face, then another and another. He couldn't sit still any longer. He pulled her into his arms, wanting to comfort her anyway that he could. Take the sadness away. He knew he couldn't do that, but he wanted to lessen her pain, if possible.

He pulled back slightly and wiped each tear that fell from her eyes. No words were needed. He felt her never-ending pain and loss. Silence ensued until she finally gathered her emotions and began to speak again. "After they died, I pretty much went to pieces. After the funeral, I spent the summer with my grandparents. Being away helped but when I returned home for college, I had a rough go of it. My dad had some wonderful friends— Ed being one of them. He jumped in and became my support and still is to this day. My maternal grandparents were here, too, taking care of me. They are close by and check on me regularly. It was difficult at first, rambling around this house all by myself, but eventually I got used to it. Now, I can't imagine not living here."

"Jen, I'm so sorry this happened to you."

"Thank you. It seems like a long time ago and then it seems like only yesterday. It'll be eight years soon. There are days when I can't remember the sound of their voices or what it felt like to be in their arms. What I learned was never take a day for granted. If you love someone, don't hesitate to tell them. Bad things can happen in the blink of an eye, and you can't get back a feeling or a time or sometimes even a remembrance. Time passes too quickly. You need to embrace each and every moment because you never know when that'll be the last time you can tell someone how you feel."

He didn't know what came over him, but he reached down and placed a gentle kiss on her lips. He wanted her to know that she was turning into someone special in his life, and he was taking that moment in time to tell her that with his kiss.

As he pulled away, a surprised look crossed her face. "Sorry if I overstepped myself. I listened to what you said and I wanted you to know that you're someone special in my life."

Her lips curved upward as she smiled back at him through her remaining tears. "I feel the same way," and then she reciprocated with a kiss herself.

Chapter Seven

A WEEK HAD PASSED SINCE RYNE and Jennifer had shared their special moment. He'd gone on the road for two games which the Generals easily won. He'd texted and left her several messages since leaving but they hadn't had a chance to talk. They had an unusual Saturday afternoon game. He was thankful for that since he had plans. He wanted to take Jen out for dinner, brainstorm about the fundraiser, and spend time getting to know her.

He phoned her bright and early right before he walked over to the dome. Since his hotel was just blocks away, he liked to clear his mind and get in the zone before hitting the ice.

Surprisingly, she answered right away. Her voice sounded gravelly.

"Did I wake you?" he asked as he walked out of the hotel.

Clearing her voice she croaked, "No, I've got a cold, that's all."

"Sorry to hear that. Are you coming to the game today?"

"As of this moment I am. I never miss a game, but I'll have to see how I feel."

"I have a proposition for you."

"I'm all ears."

"If you feel up to it, I'd like to take you out. Remember, you promised me a date."

"How could I forget," she said, sighing. "In fact, I couldn't wait for you to return from your road trip. I'd hoped you'd call. But this cold…"

"Let's play it by ear. If you feel up to it we can go out. Otherwise, maybe you'd feel up to just having dinner at your place where you can take it easy. In all honesty, I just really want to see you."

"I hate to admit it, but I missed you while you were gone. I apologize that we couldn't connect. It seems like it's been forever since I last saw you."

"I feel that same way. As I said, let's play it by ear. If I see you at the game, great. If not, I'll plan on stopping by with dinner shortly thereafter."

"Sounds like a plan. And Ryne, I can't wait to see you."

"Right back at you, Jen." He picked up his step as he turned the corner. Crossing his fingers, he hoped he'd see her in the stands, cheering him on.

Ryne went through his normal pregame ritual. He was excited to see Derek's name on the list of available players. He'd missed having him as his line mate. He walked into the locker room. Carson sat in front of his locker hanging his head. "Hey Carson, what's up? Looks like you had a rough night."

"You could say that a thousand times over, and it wouldn't even begin to touch the night I had."

"Your daughter?" He nodded trying to suppress a yawn.

"Right on. She still has that earache," he grumbled. "I told my wife I can't go through another night like that."

"I can imagine, but think of her and what she's endured while you've been on the road."

"You've got a point there. Thanks. I think I need to apologize. I wasn't the nicest when I walked out of the house today."

Remembering Jen's story about her parents he added, "You need to call her and apologize right away. Don't let the last words you said to her be something you'll regret." Carson rolled his eyes at Ryne, not quite understanding the underlying meaning. "Just do it, okay?" He didn't want to get into any specifics so he added, "You know the saying 'don't go to bed mad.' Well, treat this episode like that— don't leave without telling her you love her." He walked away as Carson reached for his phone.

"Thanks, man. I know and I get it."

He'd learned a lot from Jen and knew that he would never walk away from her, especially with words left unspoken. He wasn't one to proclaim openly how he felt in a relationship, but after his conversation with her he definitely learned a lesson.

Ryne sat staring into his locker and thought about Whitney, his ex-fiancée. He wrung his hands remembering but also trying to forget their brief relationship. She was Derek's sister. They'd met while he played with the Eagles and hadn't dated long before becoming engaged. She was beautiful and had sought him out several times before he broke down and went out with her. He didn't know how it happened, but in the blink of an eye he'd found himself engaged.

When he thought back to that six-month period

in his life, he realized he'd never loved her. She'd been the one to push their relationship, and she'd been the one to push the engagement. Thankfully, he'd come around before he'd broken the news to his family. He'd found her in the arms of another man, and that did it for him. When he'd confronted her, she batted her hand in mid-air, indicating that she'd been playing him for a fool and knew that he'd eventually figure out that they weren't meant to be together.

When Derek discovered what his sister had done, he was livid. He'd known she'd been a player but thought she'd settled down when she began dating Ryne. Derek was so disgusted with his sister that they hadn't spoken in years.

When Ryne had first joined the Generals, he'd been unsure how welcoming Derek would be, being captain and all. Derek had been traded away from the Eagles shortly after Ryne's breakup with Whitney and they'd lost touch. He'd surprised Ryne and acted as though the incident with his sister had never happened. Ryne knew at some point they'd need to discuss it, especially if he and Jen became an item.

After the break-up with Whitney, he'd elected not to do the relationship thing again. There was the possibility of being traded and he used that as his excuse. Now, he didn't know what he'd do. From out of nowhere, he'd started having feelings for Jen. Feelings that he needed to put aside but wasn't sure he could. He'd already told her she meant something to him. He didn't know why or how that had slipped out, but it had. *Maybe she's different. Maybe all women aren't like Whitney.*

Ryne heard a voice and realized it was Trevor's, indicating it was time to take the ice for their pre-game warm-up. He slipped on his protective gear, grabbed his stick, and headed down the tunnel towards the rink. Jen's face was all he saw as he hit the ice. He hoped he'd see her hovering in the stands.

He skated around the rink, warming his legs before taking part in the pre-game drills. He gazed towards the stands and didn't see her. In fact, her seats were empty. *I guess she's not coming.* He practiced his passing and slap shots and before leaving the ice took another glance towards her seats. Still no Jen. He was dismayed. In the few games he'd played at the dome since being traded, she'd always cheered him on. He'd felt energized with her presence, knowing he had a cheering section. He was sorry to hear she was ill, especially since he was looking forward to their first real date. *In time.*

The Generals took the ice as did the Eagles. It was the first game he'd played against them since being traded. He had good friends on the team, but he also knew he had a game to play, and he couldn't let their friendship affect it. And it didn't. Almost as soon as the puck was dropped, Ryne was upended, flying feet first into the boards. He was stunned momentarily and when he got his wits about himself made his way from the ice shouting a not-so-friendly reminder to his former teammates.

Trevor recognized that he needed a few moments and stopped him from returning to the ice "I'm going to have you sit out a few," he called to him as he watched Derek fly into the boards.

"You played for them?" Trevor shouted as they watched Derek limp from the ice.

"Hey man, what's with it? I thought they'd take it a little easier on us," Derek exclaimed as he fell onto the bench beside him.

Laughing, Ryne smacked Derek on the back. "Ya think? They want to show us who's boss, but I say we return the favor."

Ryne returned with a vengeance. He wasn't going to let his friends play him for a fool. Before he knew it, he was being sent to the penalty box after slashing one of his 'so-called' friends.

While he sat in the box, he took a second to look up into the stands. They were already half-way through the first period, and Jen was still a no-show. His mind quickly returned to the game. Carson went to retrieve the puck in front of him and was knocked hard into the plexiglass. Ryne heard the loud grunt that accompanied it. He hoped Carson had made things right with his wife. He didn't need to get injured and have that hanging over his head.

Ryne's two minutes were up. The doors opened and he flew back onto the ice. Derek had played it just right, and as Ryne skated out, he passed the puck to him. He had a break-away. Raising his stick high above his head, he slapped the puck which flew past the goalie. He was surrounded by his teammates as they celebrated Ryne's goal.

The game became more physical as the minutes passed. They were well into the third period and the score was tied. Ryne had become so focused on the game; he hadn't had a chance to glance towards the stands. That is until he found himself lying flat on the ice. He didn't know how it happened but he was circling the net behind his goal. He broke out with the puck past the blue line and headed into Eagles territory. He remembered passing the puck to Carson and then everything went black.

Next thing he realized, Stafford Beck, the Generals' trainer, was leaning over him. Ryne blinked several times at first unsure where he was. Then he felt the cold of the ice against his back and Stafford calling his name. He tried to sit up and Stafford held him down. "Take a moment."

Ryne lay there listening to the hush of the crowd. Something caught his attention, and he turned his head towards the stands. Raising his eyes, he saw her. On the edge of her seat with her hand covering her mouth sat Jen. He knew he needed to move— let her know he was alright. He took a deep breath, blowing it out through his mouth. "I'm okay."

He sat up and then took a hand from Perry Zaney, another of his line mates. Between Perry and Stafford, Ryne was standing and being helped from the ice. With less than five minutes remaining in the third period, Stafford escorted him back to the locker room to examine him and check for concussion.

As he skated off, he nodded towards Jen who acknowledged him. Thankfully, Stafford ruled out a concussion. He was sore from the hit that had come out of nowhere. He had no clue as to who upended him.

After Stafford cleared him, he showered and changed. He texted Jen that he was okay, and asked for her to meet him outside the locker room. He'd assumed she was feeling better since she'd chosen to attend the game. Just as he finished texting her message, he heard the crowd erupt. He knew they'd broken the tie and had won in the final seconds of the game, especially when he heard the buzzer sound moments later. He congratulated his team mates and left the room. As he walked through the doorway, he saw her. He took one look at her, knowing that she wasn't feeling well but also knowing that he wanted to take care of her.

Ryne strolled to her side, reached down and kissed her forehead. "Feeling better?"

"I am but what about you? That was some hit you took."

"Yeah, I didn't see it coming either, so I couldn't prepare myself. Next thing I knew I was looking up at Stafford. I guess I blacked out for a few seconds."

"Do you have a concussion?"

"Nope. Not sure what happened although I am sore— that's for sure."

"Since we're both not feeling our best, let's put this date on hold."

He reached down and ran his hand along her jawline. "I want to spend time with you. I've missed you." He waited for her to react. He saw her take a breath, but she didn't say a word. "Let's get something to eat and go back to your house. That way we both can relax for the night."

"That sounds nice. I, ah, took a cab here…"

He smiled at her, realizing that she planned on spending the night with him. "Don't worry, I've got you covered." He reached for her hand and led her out of the dome. "My hotel's just a short walk.

We can get room service, or we can grab carryout and go back to your place."

She looked up at him. "You know room service sounds pretty good right about now." He squeezed her hand and led her down the sidewalk towards his home.

Chapter Eight

JENNIFER DIDN'T KNOW WHAT CAME over her, but she was bolder than she'd ever been in her entire life. She barely knew him, and she was going with him to his hotel room. She still didn't feel well and, in the end, hadn't wanted to disappoint him, so she showed up at the game. A chill hit her as she walked beside him. She knew he felt her body tremble when he drew her close.

As they walked along, she felt protected, cared for. She hadn't really felt that way since her parents died. Yes, her grandparents had been there for her but this was different. As they walked through the revolving door of the hotel, a large photograph of the city skyline stood before her. She took one look at it and realized it was one her father had taken right before his death. She'd forgotten he'd sold it to the hotel. A feeling of sadness overcame her. She'd never really dated since her parents died, and as she made her way with Ryne towards the elevator bay, she wondered if her parents would approve of him. From what she knew, he seemed kind, protective, and gentle off the ice. She decided not to go there right now. She'd contemplate that another time.

"You feel okay?" he asked as he called for the elevator.

"I'm okay right now. I just wish I could get rid of this cold." The elevator opened as she finished her thought. Ryne, being a gentleman, held the doors open as she entered. He reached for her hand and squeezed it as the elevator began to move.

When the doors opened, she started to step off and was hit with a sneezing fit. She sneezed several times. "Maybe this wasn't such a bright idea. You can't afford to get sick," she choked out around another sneeze.

"Let me worry about that." He smiled at her as he slipped his arm about her waist and led her to his room. He inserted the key card into the door, and she swayed. His hold on her tightened as he led her through the doorway. "It's early yet, unless you're hungry, how about you lie down and take a rest? Maybe you'll feel better…"

"I didn't come here to fall asleep on you."

"I realize that, but I think that would be the best medicine for you. You rest while I take care of a few things. The bedroom's right through that door. We'll figure out dinner later."

She quirked a smile at him and reached in, placing a soft kiss on his cheek. "Thank you."

"You know, you didn't need to come to the game today. I completely understood you were under the weather. We could have gotten together another day." He pulled her into his arms hugging her. "I'm glad you came, though. I missed seeing you." He led her to the doorway and opened the door to his bedroom. "Rest and I'll see you shortly." He dropped a kiss atop her head and eased her towards the bed where he drew down the covers. She sat on the side of the bed and curled onto her side. He covered her, placing one last kiss on her cheek and walked away. "Sweet dreams," she heard as she drifted off to sleep.

Ryne grabbed a bottle of water and his laptop. He'd seen the look that overcame her when she walked through the revolving doors and was greeted by that photograph. He wasn't mistaken when she'd tensed. The photographer's name was proudly displayed beside it. Marcus Steele. Ryne hadn't put two and two together until he saw her reaction.

He waited while his laptop booted up. He needed to learn more about her life before he met her. He knew her father was rather well known in the area but wasn't fully aware of the impact he had on the community until he searched for Marcus Steele. The wealth of information available shocked him.

Her father was from a well-known family that resided in the Northeast. He'd relocated to the St. Louis area when he attended a local university. By happenstance, he'd picked up photography and had never looked back. He'd won several awards and had been featured in quite a few magazines for his landscape photography. He also was known for his sports photography where he'd had many of his action shots featured in the sporting magazines. Ryne understood why Johnston asked her to have a showing of her work. Jennifer had been mentioned in several articles for her knack for photography as well. She was described as a natural who followed in her father's footsteps.

Ryne speculated why at the age of seventeen she'd given up what would have been a promising career. She'd been touted as the next big photographer in the area. As he researched her further, he noticed that all articles regarding her and photography stopped without another mention eight years earlier. He paused and thought back to their earlier conversation. Eight years. That's when her parents had been killed and when she must have ended her career as a photographer. *Why?*

As he perused the examples of her work he found on the internet, he was captivated with her style. She'd had a showing at one of the local galleries. He'd come across the catalog of the pieces she displayed and had been amazed with her talent. In time he hoped to uncover why she walked away from such a promising career.

He closed his eyes and let his mind wander. With her talent and his connections, he knew they'd be able to raise quite a sum for Lakeview. As he sat there his muscles relaxed and his eyes drifted shut.

The next thing he knew, he felt a presence. He cracked open an eye and discovered her standing before him. A smile broke across his lips as he fully opened his eyes and reached out his hand. She tentatively grasped it and slid down beside him. "Did I wake you?"

"I was just resting my eyes."

"Sure you were, right along with that snore." She giggled.

Groaning, he forced himself to sit upright. "Are you in pain?" she asked.

He pulled his lips in, trying not to let her know how much pain he was actually in.

"What can I do for you? Do you need ice, a heating pad?" She started to rise but he squeezed her hand.

"I'm okay. It's nothing new. Let me catch my breath for a second." He felt her eyes as they scanned his face. Reaching her free hand upwards, she smoothed it along his forehead and then moved towards his cheek.

"Please tell me what I can do for you. I know you must be in tremendous pain after taking that hit earlier." She carefully ran her hand across his shoulder and along his chest. "I want to help you. Let me."

"I'll be fine, I promise. I'll meet with the trainers tomorrow, and they'll see to my aches and pains. It's you I'm worried about. How's that cold?"

Sniffling she raised her eyes to his. "About the same. I probably should have stayed home, but I couldn't go another day without seeing you. Ryne, I missed you while you were gone. Really missed you."

"Same goes here," he said pulling her close. He glanced at his laptop. Thankfully it had gone to sleep since the last thing he remembered was looking at the catalog of her gallery showing. He needed to uncover a little more about her past before he raised the subject again. He didn't want to cause her any undue upset. She'd been through a lot with her parents' death. He wanted to get to know her inside out, and the more he could to minimize her anguish, he would. Since Ed was a friend of hers, he'd speak with him and maybe get the answers he was searching for.

She curled herself into his side. They were getting more and more comfortable with one another. He felt her breathing slow. "Going to sleep on me?" he asked nudging her side.

"Nope just warming myself and getting comfortable." With that her stomach growled.

"Hungry?"

"I guess you heard that." She snickered into his side.

Nodding he said, "Sure did." He tried not to jolt her as he reached for the room service menu that sat on the table in front of him. "I already know what I want." Handing her the menu he added, "The food's pretty good. I've tried practically everything. I'm having the grilled chicken and a salad. Choose whatever you want."

"Soup's about all I can handle."

"I can't vouch for that since I normally get a meal of some sorts." She decided on a cup of tomato soup and a grilled cheese sandwich.

While they waited for their order, he brought up the fundraiser. "Has Johnston set a date yet?"

"Not that I know of, but I did inform him of your concern about it being around training camp and the start of the season. He said he was going to speak with Ed and set a date."

"Good. At least Ed will know what will work for everyone." She looked at him funny. "It's not about just me. I want everyone involved from the Generals and whoever else from the other local teams we can recruit to participate. Anything I put my name on is a success, and this will be a success, too."

Their food arrived in short order. "How's that tomato soup?"

"Since I can't taste a thing, I have to say it's great." She raised her sandwich to her mouth. "Mmm, this grilled cheese is the best," she claimed as she chewed and smiled at him.

"Not that you would know," he returned as he took a bite of his chicken.

By the time they finished their meal, it was getting late and Jen could barely keep her eyes open. "Come on, let's get you home." He stood reaching for her hand.

Pulling her from the couch, he grabbed their coats and led her from the room. When they reached the lobby, he requested his car be brought around. He held her close as they waited for the valet. "I'm sorry you're not feeling well. Next time, we're going out on the town. No more tomato soup and grilled cheese sandwiches for you, my lady."

She looked up at him and smiled. "Thanks for understanding. I just don't think I could have gone out tonight."

"Hey," he said placing his finger underneath her chin raising it so he could look her squarely in the eyes. He winked at her adding, "Don't worry. We have plenty of time to have a redo."

"Yes, we will have a redo. Sooner rather than later." She leaned over and kissed his cheek.

Chapter Nine

A WEEK HAD PASSED SINCE THEY last saw one another. Ryne was still feeling the after affects from the hit that knocked him out. The morning after their quasi date he caught a cab for the short distance to the dome. He'd barely been able to move when he woke, and phoned Stafford after catching his bearings.

The phone had scarcely rung on his end when Stafford answered. "I guess you're feeling it right about now."

Groaning Ryne told him his status. "Yeah, you could say I'm definitely feeling that hit. In fact, I plan on calling my good friend that sent me to the ice to thank him for the welcoming."

"I'm headed over to the dome," Stafford said. "Think you can meet me in, say, an hour?"

"Yeah, I'll be there." He disconnected the call and threw his arm over his eyes. Just that small movement caused him pain. He hoped it wasn't something serious. He'd encountered numerous injuries over the years, but for some reason he was really feeling this one.

He eased off the bed and made his way to the shower. Even standing under the hot spray did nothing to allay his pain. In fact, as he dressed, he had to sit down to catch his breath. He was worried. He didn't need a season-ending injury.

His eye caught something lying on the floor. It was small and he wasn't quite sure what it was. He had a devil of a time leaning over to discover that it was an earring. Smiling to himself he realized Jen must have lost it the night before. He wanted to call her but elected to wait until he met with Stafford to see what fate would be dealing him. Running his hand through his hair, he already knew that his fate had been sealed. He was almost sure he'd injured his hip again. It had been a nagging injury off and on for years, but this time he knew it was more serious than in the past. The night before he'd ignored the throbbing, thinking it would go away, but deep down he knew better.

He phoned the front desk and requested a cab. He'd never be able to walk the few short blocks to the dome. Limping through the lobby, he made his way to the waiting taxi. He didn't know where he got the strength, but somehow, he was able to make it to the trainer's room. Stafford took one look at him and was by Ryne's side in a heartbeat, "What'd you do now?"

"You tell me. I haven't been in this much pain since..." he gutted out through clenched teeth. "Since, I don't know!" He lay there as Stafford examined him, knowing all along what his conclusion would be.

"I'm going to send you for X-rays and an MRI. When did it start hurting? And why didn't you call me sooner?"

He racked his hand across his face not liking the

news Stafford had delivered. "Last night."

"Last night?"

"When I went back to my room, I started stiff-ening up but didn't think anything of it. I thought after a good night's sleep it would disappear. When I woke up this morning, I could hardly move and called you right away."

Ryne feared by the look on Stafford's face he'd be out the remainder of the season. His previous inju-ries were openly disclosed to the team when he'd been traded. Yes, he'd recovered quickly but he was older now, and he had awkwardly landed on his side. His hip had been the farthest thing from his mind after having blacked out. He'd worried more about a concussion.

Ryne lay on the table and listened as Stafford made the arrangements. He also heard him phone the team orthopedic surgeon, and knew he'd definitely reached the end of his season. With less than three weeks remaining, even if his injury wasn't too bad, he still wouldn't make it back in time even for the playoffs. He took a long deep breath, easing it out slowly from his lungs. *Yep, my season's over.*

His tests were scheduled later that morning. Staf-ford drove him to the hospital and waited. All the while Ryne knew what the outcome would be.

It almost felt like the end of the world. His thoughts immediately went to Jen. If he were out for the sea-son, he'd have plenty of time to begin planning the fundraiser. He'd at least have something productive to keep his mind off his injury while he recuperated.

"I'm afraid you're going to be out for the sea-son." Ryne heard the words that he knew had been coming since he first woke that morning. "You've injured this hip before."

"I have."

"You need to stay off that leg. This is a pretty severe injury this time, especially with its recurrence. I'm putting you on crutches for the next couple of weeks, but ultimately you need to take it easy. Then, we'll work on muscle strengthening exercises."

He lay there listening to the doctor. He'd been through this before, although his season hadn't been put on hold. He'd returned to the ice pretty quickly then, but this time was different. The blow he'd taken had been one of the hardest of his career. Still, he was thankful he hadn't received a concussion.

Stafford shook his head as Ryne hobbled out on the crutches. "Couldn't you have wheeled me to the car?"

"You need your practice, that's for sure," Stafford claimed as he opened the car door. Ryne stumbled into the car, calling out in pain. "See, what did I tell you?" He pointed to the crutches that Ryne held out to him. "Will you be okay at the hotel all by yourself?"

"It's not like I haven't been on crutches before, but yeah I'll be fine."

By the time he returned to his room, Ryne was exhausted. He fell into bed and didn't wake until the next day. He spent the next several days undergoing treatment only to return to his hotel room completely worn out where sleep claimed him.

He'd thought of Jen often but hadn't found the strength to phone her. He didn't want her to know the extent of his injury. The team had kept it pretty quiet and on game nights scratched him from the lineup of available players. They'd kept him out of the media eyes, and he was more than agreeable to their tactics.

Jacob was doing his best to keep his injury from the public. The players knew he was done for the season, but they didn't want to add any fuel for possible further injury when he returned. Hockey players were a breed unlike any other. If they knew of a nagging injury, many would wreak havoc trying to cause reinjury. Ryne didn't want or need any further damage to that hip.

He hobbled through the doors to his room and rested against the doorframe. He was tired and wasn't bouncing back as quickly as he once did. He made his way to the couch. Throwing his crutches beside him, he noticed Jen's earring sitting on the table. He'd forgotten about it. Running his hands across his face, he reached for his phone. He missed her and, in all honesty, needed to see her. The Generals were on the road. He had his daily therapy but other than that had nothing on his calendar.

It was almost five o'clock and he hoped she'd answer. He knew the school day ended around three o'clock. Her phone rang several times. Just as he was ready to leave a message, she answered. She was out breath as though she'd run to the phone. "Hello."

"Jen, hey it's me, Ryne."

"Oh, hi there. Shouldn't you be on a plane right about now?" He needed to be honest and tell her about his injury. She followed the team too closely not to realize they'd been protecting him.

"About that. Are you busy tonight? I found something of yours, and I want to return it. If you haven't eaten yet, what do you say about coming over for dinner?"

"No, I haven't eaten. It's still a little early for me." She paused as though she were pondering his question. "Umm, are you sure?"

"I wouldn't have asked if I didn't want you to join me. How about seven? Is that too late?"

"Ah no, that's just fine."

"See you then." He stared at his phone when he ended the conversation. He wasn't sure how he would address his injury with her, but he'd find a way. He hadn't intended to nap until he heard a pounding on his door and was jolted awake.

"Ryne, are you in there?"

He had a difficult time getting up, so he called out that he'd be right there. He reached for his crutches and lost his balance falling to the floor. He knew she heard him yell out in pain.

"Coming," he called as he slowly stood and gimped towards the door opening it. Her eyes flew from his face to the crutches that precariously kept him upright. A fine sheen had broken out on his brow. He was in pain—a lot of pain—after his fall.

Before he knew it, he felt her arm close around his waist. "Here let me help you." She shut the door and eased him toward the couch. "What happened to you?"

"First off, how's the cold?"

"Cold, my cold? You're concerned about me and my cold? Forget about that, what happened to you?"

Pointing to his hip. "Hip pointer injury."

"That sounds painful." She scrunched her face.

"It is. And I don't think it's gotten much better."

"When did this happen?"

"Last week when I was upended."

"You mean you've been hurt this entire time and haven't bothered calling me?"

He knew he was in trouble. Cocking his head, he drew in his lips and nodded.

"Why didn't you call? I would have been here in a heartbeat."

"I know. We've been trying to keep my injury under wraps."

"And who would I tell?"

"Jen, I'm sorry. I didn't mean to insinuate that you'd tell anyone. We're trying to keep my injury out of the news."

"Why?"

"So I won't be a target when I return."

"A target?"

"Yeah. Some guys don't let you live down certain injuries. This isn't my first hip injury and may not be my last..."

"So that's why you've been scratched from the lineup? When are you planning to return? From the looks of it, you can hardly walk let alone get up on skates."

"It's going to be awhile."

"So you'll be on the playoff team." She caught the far off look in his eyes. "Well, won't you?" He shook his head. "You are returning, right?"

"Honey, not this year."

"Ryne. Is it that serious?"

"Doc says it is and unfortunately I have to agree. He thinks it's going to take a couple of months to fully recover. On the bright side, I have some time on my hands, so we can jump right in on the fundraiser."

"Seriously?"

"Yeah. I need something to do, so what better way to spend my time. Right?"

She nodded and reached for his hands. "I'm so sorry."

"I know, but injuries are a part of the game. You learn to deal with them." He squeezed her hands. "Oh, I forgot, I have something for you." He reached for her earring and handed it to her.

"I was wondering where I lost this."

"I found it on the carpeting. You must have lost it went you went to lie down."

"Thanks," she said smiling up at him. "My mom gave these to me as an early graduation gift. I was worried that I'd never find it. Thanks."

He caught the faraway look in her eyes again but decided not to comment. Instead he asked, "So what's for dinner?"

They ordered room service, but this time she was able to enjoy her meal. She took the last bite of her grilled salmon. "This beats a grilled cheese sandwich hands down."

"Glad to hear," he said, reaching for his glass of wine. Taking a sip her eyes glimmered in the light. She looked happy.

Just as he was ready to comment further on the fundraiser, his napkin fell from his lap. As he reached for it an intense pain seared through his hip.

Gasping, he grabbed his side. She jumped from her seat, knocking her water glass over in the process. His eyes were tightly closed as he dealt with the throbbing. He felt her hand tease the side of his face. "What happened?"

He drew his lips in and shook his head. "Just my hip," he said, sighing through the unpleasantness. It took a moment for the twinge to pass when he opened his eyes. She was kneeling beside him with her hand draped across the back of his chair, her look of happiness replaced with one of concern. "I'm okay now."

He raised his hand and cupped the side of her face. As he moved in, he saw her eyes change color. He ran his lips across hers and felt her warm to his kiss. She wrapped her arms around his neck as he drew her closer. He was enjoying the kiss when she pulled away for no apparent reason. "Did I do something wrong?"

"No," she said as she grabbed his napkin from the floor dabbing up the spilt water. "Look what I did. I'm such a klutz."

"You're not a klutz." He reached for her hand. Taking it in his, he smiled up at her. "You were reacting to my cry of pain."

"Are you better?"

"Much, especially after that kiss." He watched the red blush creep into her face. She started to pull away, but instead he pulled her hand and she fell hard onto his lap. He cried out again.

She jumped up all excited. "Oh my," she exclaimed. "Now I really hurt you."

"You didn't hurt me." He pulled her close and

she rested her head against his chest. "I'm fine."
He tightened his hold. Rubbing his thumb against
her cheek, he leaned in and softly kissed her lips.
"Relax."

They sat in the quiet of the room for a few seconds
before he spoke again. "I was reaching to pick up
my napkin and that's when I felt the twinge."

"Twinge, it seemed more than a twinge. You
groaned in pain."

"You have me there. It felt like a lightning bolt
searing through my side. I don't know what that
was all about, but it's better now. Enough about me
and my injury. Let's discuss the fundraiser."

She described everything she'd done so far. Then
he told her he'd spoken with Ed and had his full
support. They could use the team any way they
needed. Not only did they discuss her showing of
photographs, they decided on an auction and dinner
too. By the time they hashed out the details, it was
well past midnight, and they'd long since forgotten
the episode with his hip.

Jen tried to suppress a yawn and that's when he
decided to call it a night. He led her to the door.
Smoothing her hair from her face, he leaned in and
gave her one last kiss. "Thanks for everything— I
had a great time. I think we got a lot accomplished,"
he said while running his forefinger across her brow.
"I'll phone Ed tomorrow. I have several ideas, and
I'm sure he'll support them. I'll call you."

She smiled and the effervescence of her eyes
glowed. At this moment, she seemed happy. "You
look beautiful and I hate to let you go." Teasing
her lower lip with his thumb, he kissed her one last

time. "But I must," he exclaimed as he opened the door. "Call me when you get home."

"I'll be fine," she said as she turned away.

"It's late and I'd feel better if you did."

"Fine," she called over her shoulder as she started down the hallway.

"Don't forget to call...Careful driving home," he proclaimed louder than he intended. She was definitely making an impact on his life. He'd been hurt by Whitney and her ways. He closed the door and leaned against it. *Jen's different. She just might be the one for me.* He made his way to the couch where he wrote down several ideas he intended to discuss with Ed the following morning. He got lost in his thoughts and heard the ringing of his cell.

"I'm home," he heard her say.

"Glad to hear. Sweet dreams."

Chapter Ten

JENNIFER KNEW IF SHE WAS going to have a showing of her photographs, she needed to get busy. Luckily, she was on spring break for the next ten days, so she phoned Ed and was given full access to the team. Fortunately for her, the Generals played the remainder of their scheduled games at home. The downside was Ryne was still hobbling around on crutches and she wouldn't be able to capture any photographs of him playing. They'd figure out something once he was able to return to the ice.

One of the upsides was she had Ryne's full attention once he completed his therapy for the day. He did attend team meetings but practice wasn't a requirement since his 'practice' was the grueling therapy he endured.

She witnessed his pain one day. She'd been at the dome, photographing the team's workout when she heard a loud commotion. She wasn't quite sure what was happening until she heard Derek. "I guess he's having a bad day," he'd said as he skated past her. She wasn't aware he was talking to her until he sprayed her with ice as he approached the boards. "Hey, what was that for?" she hollered as she flung ice crystals from her sweater.

"Did you hear me?"

"I heard you, but I haven't a clue who you are referring to. Everyone looks like they're having a tremendous practice."

"Not us, silly. Ryne."

She looked at him in surprise. "I don't know what you're talking about. How is he having a bad day?"

"Didn't you just hear him as he walked from the trainer's room?"

"That was him?"

"Sure thing. I'd know that voice anywhere." She'd forgotten that they'd played together before he was traded to the Generals. "I've known him long enough, and I definitely know when he's not having a good day."

"Maybe you should go check on him. After all, you are his friend."

"And so are you," he said, waggling his eyebrows.

"Yes, I am, but I think you know him a little better than I do."

"You sure about that?" he questioned as he skated away.

She didn't know what to do, so she did nothing other than take another round of shots as the players partook in practice. When they left the ice, she packed up her equipment and headed towards the hallway that led to the locker room. She wasn't sure if she'd see Ryne.

One by one, each player left the locker room. She thought she'd missed him when she heard the thunk, thunk of the rubber as his crutches met the floor. Not sure of the emotion she'd capture, she raised her camera and began clicking away. She caught him just as he walked through the doorway with a pensive expression on his face.

Lowering her camera, she held his eyes. Immediately, she knew he wasn't in the mood for a photograph. He hopped his way towards her, never losing eye contact. "I wasn't sure you were here today." He stopped and rested his arms on his crutches.

"I'm trying to finish up a few shots with the season ending and all."

"Did you get anything noteworthy?"

"In fact, I did. Derek sprayed me as he approached the boards, and I think I was able to capture the ice flying through the air. I'm really excited about that one if it turns out like I think it will."

"Any plans for the rest of the day?"

"Nope. Just waiting for you." She caught a smile along with a grimace as he raised himself from his crutches. She knew about his mood and hoped she could brighten it somewhat.

"Well, let's get out of here." She reached for her bag and tripod and noticed him as he shook his head. "I wish I could be a gentleman and carry that for you."

"Hey, you are a gentleman, but I think I can carry my own equipment. I have for years before now." She placed her hand on his arm halting his movement. She reached up placing a kiss on his cheek.

"What's that for?"

"For being you."

She smiled at him. She wanted to do whatever she could to take his pain away. If that peck on the cheek helped his mood in any way, she'd be happy. "My car's right inside the garage, where would you like to go?"

He swallowed deeply. "What I'd really like to do is go back to my room and take a long nap." She held the door open for him as they made their way to her car. "I'm not in the best of moods today."

"Is that so?" she asked, trying to suppress her grin. She wanted to laugh at him for no reason other than to cheer him up.

"What's so funny," he queried as he made his way alongside her. "I know you're trying not to laugh at me. Do I have something on the bottom of my shoe?"

Scrunching her face at him they reached her car, "Why would you say that?"

"I can tell something's up. Each day I get to know you a little better, and that look on your face says it all. So what is it?"

"Just something Derek said to me, that's all. Now, get in the car." She waited while he eased himself into her car and then grabbed his crutches, storing them in the backseat. He groaned as he reached to lock his seatbelt. She jumped into the driver's seat and stuck her key in the ignition. He'd been staring out the window when she sat down beside him. She dropped her hand from the key and turned. "You know you can be honest with me." He didn't respond. Instead, he continued to stare through the window, at what she didn't know. His hands lay clasped in his lap.

She reached over and laid her hand atop his. "Ryne, what is it?" He clenched his jaw all the while she grew more concerned as the seconds ticked away. "You can tell me, you know. I want to help you."

He began to gnaw on his lower lip. He turned with what appeared to be unshed tears in his eyes. "I'm not getting any better. My hip," he stopped and shook his head. "Hurt like hell today and I don't know why."

"What does Stafford have to say? Should you see the doctor again?"

"You know I really don't know what he said. I remember tuning him out... Actually, I lost it in there today. Something I normally don't do." He shook his head again. "I don't know what's come over me. I'm afraid I'm..."

She reached up and smoothed her hand across his jaw. Edging closer to him, she forced him to look at her. "It's one day at a time. Remember? You're going to have your good days and bad ones. It's all a part of the healing process. Enough of feeling sorry for yourself; let's do something fun."

She knew he'd heard her because she saw the light return to his eyes. "Thank you," he uttered. He leaned in and placed a gentle kiss on her lips. "You know just what I need. Where have you been all my life?" She felt the tension leave his body as he kissed her one more time. "I really need to change." He pointed at his clothes.

"You look fine to me," she grinned and started the car. She knew he was in pain and didn't want to stress him more than he already was. She started to back away from her parking space when she came up with a plan. She grabbed her phone and called in a carryout order from the bar just around the corner from her home. Dixon's Bar & Grille had the best toasted ravioli and hot wings in town. At least that was her opinion. She ordered that along with two cheeseburgers and fries. She was hungry and knew Ryne was too. He always seemed to be starved when they were together.

"It'll be ready in twenty minutes." She started up the car and headed out of the garage.

"What did you just do?"

"Ordered us a snack."

"That sounded like more than a snack. If fact, I think you ordered enough food to feed the team."

"I'm hungry." She sheepishly looked at him. "And I know you're always hungry." He burst out laughing as she pulled from the garage.

"You could say that," he chuckled. They entered the highway and headed towards her home.

"What are your plans?"

"I thought we'd take it easy at my house. I think you'll be more comfortable there than in your cramped hotel room. We can watch a movie, play a game, or take a peek at my photos."

"Ooh, I like that idea. I haven't seen any of your photography."

"Yeah, well, don't get too excited. It's been a while since I've taken it seriously. I'm excited to look at the pics from today, though. I think I got some really nice shots that could earn a good price at the fundraiser."

"Well, Grandma, put the pedal to the metal— I can't wait to see them."

"Did you just call me Grandma?"

"I did. You drive like one."

"Hey," she yelled. "I drive the speed limit. No tickets here." She pointed to herself.

"I can't confess either way…" The air in the car was much more relaxed as they drove along.

She pulled up in front of Dixon's and parked in the spot reserved for carryout. "I'll be right back."

"I'm not going anywhere." He smiled when she opened the door.

Jennifer ran into the bar and waited for their food. She'd made it there in less than fifteen minutes. *Grandma! I am not a grandma driver.* She thanked the bartender and hurried back to the car where she discovered Ryne had drifted off to sleep. She wondered if he'd taken a pain killer as that seemed to throw him over the edge every time. She hated to wake him. So instead of going straight home, she set their food on the floor of the back seat, hopped into the car, and started to drive. She knew rest was the best medicine for him, and he needed that after his difficult therapy session.

Almost an hour had passed since she'd picked up their food. Just as she pulled into her driveway, he started to wake. She saw him brush the sleep from his eyes and stroke his jaw with his hand. "Sorry about that. I don't know what happened. One minute you were getting our food and the next…"

"You were asleep."

"Yeah, not sure what quite happened."

"I do." He looked surprised by her words. "You took a pain pill."

He nodded his head. "I did."

"And you did it on an empty stomach."

"That too." She pulled her car into the garage, and he reached to open his door. "Thanks."

"For what?"

"For being here for me." He reached behind the seats and grabbed ahold of his crutches. She listened for him to call out in pain, but he didn't. She jumped from the car, grabbed their food and her camera case, and met him at her door. She opened it.

"You don't lock your doors?" he asked.

"You think I should?"

"I do. You never know when someone can break into your garage."

"Thanks for the lesson." She held the door for him as he hopped through the doorway towards the bar stools.

"You know, I don't believe you use this kitchen. Every time I'm in here it's cleaner than…"

"Stop, will you. I cook and I'll prove it to you some day."

"Promise?"

"I promise." Turning, she started to pull their food from the bag. "I'm starving. I've driven around for almost an hour, smelling this greasy bar food while you slept."

She turned around to grab the plates and he stopped her. Placing his hands on her hips her drew he close. She closed her eyes as he brushed her hair behind her ears. He ran his finger along her cheek, and she waited for his kiss. When it came, it felt so right. She felt cared for, protected, and most of all loved. She caught herself when she thought about that. She hadn't felt that way in a long, long time. Not since that fateful day eight years ago when she left her home for her graduation only to return to a home filled with loneliness and sadness.

In the weeks since she'd known Ryne, those feelings had waned. She wasn't as lonely and definitely didn't feel the sadness that always seemed to follow her. Today, she felt a sense of hope. She'd found someone to help change a life that was once filled with darkness into one filled with hope and maybe even love, too.

She felt his hand on hers, and that's when she realized he'd been speaking to her. "Hey, where'd you just go?" She looked at him and knew where her mind had drifted off. "I was asking you…"

"What'd ya say?"

"Nothing. It wasn't important. Let's eat." She'd reheated their food since it had grown cold and placed the toasted ravioli in front of him. He reached for one and dipped it into the marinara sauce. "These are really good. I always tried to have an order when I traveled through the city. There's nothing like a St. Louis toasted ravioli." He tossed the remainder into his mouth. "Um, mmm, good." With a smile on his face, he reached for another and she fell instantly back under his spell. A moment passed before she indulged in the tasty appetizer as well.

Out of nowhere Ryne brought up his family. "I think my brothers are going to go all the way and win the cup." He took a huge bite of his hamburger, wiping the ketchup from his lips. "Etienne and Philippe both play for the Storm, and I think they're going to win the Stanley Cup."

"How lucky for them, although they do have to make it through the playoffs that have yet to begin."

"I realize that, but I really do believe they have the perfect team." He paused and she watched the light dim from his eyes.

"Hey, what's wrong?"

"Nothing, really. I should be thankful that I am a player in the NHL."

"What is it then?"

"My brothers both have had their dreams come true, that's all."

"And what's your dream?"

"My dream. That's easy. I've always wanted to play for the hometown team, but since being traded to the Generals, I'm not sure that'll ever become my reality."

"So you want to play for the Calgary Storm?" Nodding his head, he looked down at his burger. "Has your agent spoken with them?"

He ignored her question. "It was always in the back of my mind that I wanted to play for the Storm. I was happy playing for the Eagles. Vancouver drafted me and allowed me to go to college. I even renegotiated my contract with them earlier this year, and then I was traded. So much for franchise loyalty."

"Do you not like it here?"

"Oh no, don't get me wrong. The Generals is a first-class team. Ed runs a well-oiled machine. It's just when I think about it... If I have a chance, I want to do it—play for the Storm. It's in the family. My dad played for the team too." He stopped, drew in his lips, and shook his head. "My dream is to play for Calgary, maybe someday before I get old and am forced to retire." She knew his thoughts went immediately to his hip as he began massaging it.

"Keep the faith; maybe one day it'll happen."

"Unless I'm traded, I have what's left of a three-year contract with the Generals."

She took a bite of her burger and felt his demeanor change before her eyes.

He surprised her with how quickly he could go from being happy to sad. She watched him finish his sandwich and take a sip of his cola. "Ready?"

"Ready for what?" she asked.

"To look at your work."

"Oh, yeah. Let me finish my snack first," she teasingly said as she dropped the last bite of her burger into her mouth. They'd arrived at a comfort level that brought tears to her eyes. She didn't know where they'd come from, but she'd gotten a little emotional listening to him as he shared his dream with her. He had a dream that if he could, he would fulfill. That dream— playing for his Calgary Storm.

She closed her eyes briefly. She knew he'd do his best to fulfill it, but she'd given up on her dream all those years ago. Her dream once had been to work beside her father, bringing their art to life. Johnston had given her a second chance. She was discovering a life she never thought she'd find again. Being behind the lens gave her a sense of calm that she hadn't felt since walking into her high school graduation. She decided to follow her own advice and take one day at a time. And then she'd make the all-important decision on whether to end her teaching career and pick back up the one thing that had meant the world to her— her love of photography.

Chapter Eleven

THAT EVENING THEY SAT SIDE by side at her computer while she loaded her photographs. He looked at each picture with awe. She'd captured the intensity on Carson's face as he'd passed a puck to Jasper Allis. She caught the determination on Perry's face as he raised his stick to drive a slap shot towards the net. She'd found a smile on Adam's face as he took a tumble to the ice. And lastly, she netted the shot that she'd hoped for— Derek spraying her with ice as he approached the boards.

Ryne was amazed with her talent and sat quietly as she moved from one photo to the next. She'd just hit upon Derek's picture when he placed his hand atop hers. "Wow, you got it. I feel like the ice is coming right towards me."

He saw a brief smile cross her lips and then be replaced with a look of sadness. "What's wrong?"

"Nothing," she tersely said and moved onto the next photograph.

"Come on now, Jen. What's bothering you?" He watched the emotions play out on her face. He didn't know if he should let it go or push her to share what was troubling her. For once, he decided to let it go. In time, he hoped she'd feel comfortable enough with him to share whatever was on her mind.

She'd moved on to the next shot. It was of him exiting the locker room. She'd caught the insecure look as he'd come through the door. At that moment he wasn't sure where his career was going. He was in tremendous pain and just wanted to get out of the building. Then the next photo of him had the glimmer of a smile as he'd seen her and knew his day would improve.

"Outside of the shots of me, I'm impressed with your talent. You captured everything." He watched her eyes as she examined the picture on her screen. He'd seen the briefest of smile but then it disappeared.

"Jen," he said, reaching for her face. He turned her head so she was looking him directly in the eyes. She lowered her gaze and began fumbling with her mouse. He laid his hand atop hers, stopping her anxiousness. They sat for a moment before he added, "You can trust me."

She began to sniffle and that's when he noticed the tear on her face. He reached in, wiping it aside. "Honey, what's got you so troubled?" She chewed on her lower lip, obviously contemplating what she wanted to say. "Don't edit your words for me. Just say whatever's on your mind."

He knew she was struggling and then she turned and thrust herself into his arms. He held her tight against his chest as she cried, running his hand up and down her back to soothe her. His attempt at calming her didn't work; she cried harder and harder. When he'd finally had the chance to calm her, his shirt was drenched in her tears.

She'd relaxed somewhat when she pulled away from him. He placed his hands on either side of her face and touched his forehead to hers. She took a calming breath, and then he felt her lips against his. It was the first time she'd reached out to him in that way. He sensed an immediate change in her as she smiled winsomely at him. A soft thank you escaped her lips before she pulled him towards her again, holding him close to her heart. He'd been sitting awkwardly in his chair while she held him against her body.

Out of nowhere, he groaned and reached for his side. "Are you in pain?"

He pulled away and closed his eyes, nodding his head in the process. "Just a little. I guess I was sitting a little funny in the chair." He chewed on his lip as though he was pondering his next words. "I'm okay now— just a little twinge."

"It had to have been more than a little with the way you groaned."

"Sorry about that, as I said, I'm okay now." He turned back to her computer. "I'd like to see more of your work."

He knew by the look on her face that she was through for the day. "You've seen it all," she claimed as she closed down her program. He sensed her withdrawal as she stood and moved about the room.

She was hiding something but he decided not to press her. With as close as they'd become in the last several weeks, he believed, in time, she'd share with him whatever was on her mind.

"Jen, I think I'm going to call a cab and head on home."

"Why don't you stay here? I have a guest bed-room."

"I appreciate the offer..."

"What's wrong?"

"My painkillers are back in my room and my hip is starting to call for one."

A look of panic struck her face. "I'll drive you."

"Jen, hey, it's not that bad. I want to head off the pain before it gets too bad. Don't worry about me. It's getting late and I don't want you driving this time of night." He picked up his phone, and she paced the room while he gave the cab company her address. "They'll be here in fifteen minutes," he said.

He pulled her into his arms and rested his chin on the top of her head. "I had a really nice time today. You have fabulous talent. That photo you took of Derek? The spray of ice? All I can say is you are definitely working in the wrong profession..."

He knew he'd said the wrong thing when she pulled away with that look of pain on her face. "I'm sorry if I said something to upset you."

"You didn't," she claimed, all the while he knew that he did. Before either of them could comment further, he heard the honk of his awaiting cab.

"That was fast," she said as she looked out the window.

"Yeah, I don't know what happened to fifteen minutes. It was more like fifteen seconds." He leaned in dropping a kiss on her cheek, turned, and headed towards the door. "I'll phone you tomor-row. Have a pleasant evening."

With that Ryne walked out. He felt her eyes on

him as he made his way to the cab. He was sore and tired and tense. He knew how to explain his first two maladies but not the third. He assumed the tension came from not knowing what had upset her. He hoped she'd open up to him soon.

As he got into the cab, he turned and discovered she hadn't moved. She still stood in the doorway, watching him as he left. If he wasn't mistaken, she wiped a tear from her face. Something had caused her angst, and in due time he'd uncover what it was.

When the taillights of the cab disappeared around the corner, Jennifer turned back into her house and closed the door. Leaning against it, she wiped away tears. She needed to get ahold of herself.

Listening to Ryne comment on her talent brought the memories right back up in front of her. She hadn't thought about all the times she'd spent with her dad in the darkroom or even at his computer in a long, long time. He'd just started getting into digital photography when he was killed.

Flashbacks to their times together overwhelmed her as she fell to the floor. She could still remember the smell of the chemicals and the bright red light from the darkroom as they processed the many rolls of film and developed the multitude of photographs that hung across many of the buildings in the St. Louis area. She'd been reminded of the cityscape when she visited Ryne's hotel. It was a time in her life that she'd buried. Just like the career she'd turned her back on... Instead, she'd found herself becoming a teacher rather than following her heart's dream of being the photographer her father would be proud of. She sobbed at the memories.

It took her a few minutes before she was able to calm herself. She ran her hands across her face, wiping the remaining tears from her eyes. She sat on the floor, wondering what her father would expect her to do. Should she even consider what her heart was telling her?

Sitting there, she made a decision— one that she'd been hiding from for eight years now. She'd been given a chance to reclaim her dream. She'd take it and see if she still had the talent to survive. And if she did, she was going to embrace it with both hands and recover the career she'd thrown away. In the end if she didn't make it, she had a fallback career. She had over a year to develop a portfolio before she'd have to give her decision to Johnston. *One more year of teaching*, and maybe she could salvage her dream and her father's dream as well. Except this time, she'd be fulfilling it alone. Without her father beside her.

Chapter Twelve

THEY TOOK EACH DAY ONE at a time as Ryne's hip improved ever so slowly, and Jennifer continued snapping photographs. Unfortunately, the team missed the playoffs, losing the last game of the season in a shootout. Everyone had had such high expectations, but between Ryne's season-ending injury and a flu outbreak running throughout the locker room, it just wasn't in the cards.

Ryne was bothered that he couldn't contribute and push the team on, but Jen was by his side, encouraging him that they'd have the next season. By then he'd be healthy, and the Generals would have a fresh start.

The two of them worked on the fundraiser several times a week. Ryne often met her after school and would join her as she sought new sites to photograph. With the baseball season in full swing, she'd also obtained access to the St. Louis Rivermen since their general manager's children attended Lakeview. She'd been able to attend batting practice, capturing one-of-a-kind images as the players goofed around on the field.

Ryne watched Jen work and recognized her passion as she took shot after shot. Often times, a broad smile would cross her face after catching a special moment. He loved seeing her shine. She was in her element and he knew that's where she needed to be.

The school year was coming to an end, and he'd planned on traveling back to Calgary to visit his family. But first, he had to attend a gala in Greenwich, Connecticut. Black Gold Management was having a huge party celebrating the recent victories of its married star tennis players, Tony and Ashley Regada. For the first time a married couple had won the Grand Slam of tennis. Winning this title was an incredible feat, but a married couple doing it as single tennis players was unheard of.

Ryne knew Jen had planned on returning to Greenwich to visit her grandparents and decided to invite her as his date. They'd been growing closer by the day and he thought it was the next step as they meandered their way through the dating process. He'd been taking it slow since he knew she hadn't dated much and was going through a little bit of a rough patch remembering her parents, even more so of late. He'd realized the extent of her sadness several times and decided to confront her on the matter.

They'd been to a festival at the Botanical Gardens. They were on the pathway heading from the rose garden to the exit when she stopped abruptly in front of the last of the greenhouses. A look crossed her face —one he'd often seen when she was concentrating while flipping through her photographs on the computer. Yet this time, there was no computer. All that stood before them was a greenhouse built in the late 1800's. It was a brick structure with a glass roof. He stood watching her, unsure what he should say or do.

It was a beautiful day so he decided to confront her. He knew, as a couple, they needed to get out into the open whatever seemed to be bothering her. So instead of leaving the gardens, he grabbed her hand and pulled her onto a pathway. He ushered her towards a bench in a private setting surrounded by trees. He slid her camera bag from her shoulder, set it on the ground beside the bench, then pulled on her hand and sat down.

He was surprised she hadn't asked what he was doing as he led her towards the alcove. But she'd fallen back into her own world, and he hoped that he could discover whatever seemed to trouble her at the strangest of times.

He squeezed her hand as he looked into her eyes that had grown misty with tears. "Hey, what's wrong? What's troubling you?"

He knew she was contemplating what to say. A lone tear escaped her eye and trickled down her cheek. He reached in, wiping it aside. She scrunched her face, trying to prevent another tear from falling, but she wasn't successful. One tear became two and before he knew it, she was in his arms. Her sobs were muffled by his chest. He hadn't a clue what had overcome her, but knew it had something to do with the old-styled greenhouse she'd halted in front of.

Ryne rubbed his hand up and down her back, softly speaking words of encouragement he hoped would calm her. Eventually, her sobs waned and she pulled away from him. "Better?" he asked.

"Yeah, thanks for that. I'm not sure what happened…"

"Jen, I think you know."

Again, he watched her face. He saw the look of sadness and then caught the slight nod of her head. He waited for her to speak, knowing that she was attempting to put her thoughts and feelings in order. He couldn't wait another minute and then he spoke. "It's the photography, isn't it?"

Surprise crossed her face. He'd hit the nail on the head. Again, she nodded, pulling herself ever further away. He continued to wait, wanting her to take the lead on their discussion. And then she cleared her throat. Scraping her hands across her face, she took a deep breath and sighed. "You know me too well."

He smiled and didn't speak. Instead, he let her. "Yeah, it's the photography."

He reached out to her again, and this time she drew near and slipped her arms around his waist. She laid her head in the crook of his neck and started sharing her dreams.

"My dad and I were inseparable. I spent every waking minute with him at his studio. I helped him on his photo shoots, processed film, printed photographs. I did it all and I loved every minute of it. I was his protégé and I'd planned to follow in his footsteps. We had plans. I'd dreamed of being a photographer from the time I could hold a camera and take a half-way decent photo.

"Then, my world came crashing down around me. When he died, it was as though the world had come to a halt. I'd lost my passion. I put my camera away and rarely took it out again. When Johnston asked me to head up the fundraiser and feature my own photography, I about lost it. I didn't want to, but then I thought of my dad, and I wanted to make him proud. So I agreed.

"Ever since the moment I took my first photograph again, my thoughts have been on my parents, especially my dad. It's hard doing this. I want my gallery showing to be successful for Lakeview, but every time I pick up my camera, I see his eyes. I see him standing behind his lens snapping away. I see the happy baby having his first photographs taken. I see the high school graduate having their senior picture taken before they embark on a new life. And then, the last images of him. Of him standing there, watching me head off for my graduation not knowing that it would be the last time I saw him happily smiling at me. Telling me how proud he was of me knowing that I'd decided to follow in his footsteps.

"I'd intended on getting my business degree and then an MBA. My dream was to take over his business when he retired. But then, it faded when my grandfather broke the news of their accident. I decided I couldn't follow the dream because, as I look back, it was his dream. He wanted me to run the business and always reminded me of it. For some reason, I got my degree in education. Don't get me wrong. I love teaching but now that I've picked up my camera again, I have to wonder if that's where I need to be."

Ryne listened, all the while knowing she was coming to a realization that what she needed more than anything was to become that photographer she'd once dreamed of becoming. He held her tightly as she came to grips with her own dreams.

"I've had way too many flashback memories since I started down this path. Often times, they come out of nowhere. Like today...We came out of the rose garden and walked towards the greenhouse. My dad loved that specific spot in the garden. The way the light gleamed off the glass roof. The smell of the blooming roses. And then I saw a man looking at the signage at the edge of the garden. At first glance, I thought it was my dad. The way he held his daughter's hand. His posture. Everything about him made me believe it was my dad just out taking a leisurely stroll. And then he turned towards us, and I realized it wasn't him. That moment took my breath away. Then I looked down at my hand. I was holding a camera. I looked up again and he was gone. Just as my dad was. Gone and never coming back."

Ryne ran his finger along the side of her face, causing her to look up at him. "I completely understand what you're experiencing. What can I do to help you through this?"

"Just do what you're doing. Be there by my side. When I have that moment where I'm not quite sure whether I am in the present or past—just hold my hand and I'll be okay." She eased her hand up to the side of his face. "You're becoming my everything. You always seem to know what to say and when not to say anything. You listen and don't seem to judge me either. You let me be who I am, and I appreciate that more than you'll ever know."

He squeezed her hand. "Jen, will you come home with me?"

"Tonight?"

"No silly. Home. Home to Calgary so you can meet my family." He felt her tense momentarily, and then he heard the words he'd hoped to hear.

"When?"

"In a couple of weeks, but first I have to go to Greenwich and attend a soiree for Black Gold. I want you to go with me. Be my date. Meet the management team that's behind me."

Her eyes brightened when he asked her to go to Greenwich. "I'll go with you if you'll go with me."

"I'd follow you anywhere." He leaned in and placed a soft kiss on her lips. "Where am I going?"

"To meet my grandparents. They also live in Greenwich." He nodded at her request.

"Of course, I'd love to."

Before they knew it, the sun was starting to set on their day. They'd made significant strides in their relationship. Jen had opened up and shared the pain that she'd been facing since agreeing to take part in the fundraiser. Ryne was thrilled with her decision to reveal what she'd been going through.

That one conversation had opened the doors for him. He now understood the memories she'd been facing and carrying on her shoulders. He noticed the sense of calm that came over her once she shared her memories.

He was excited to introduce her to even more of his world. She'd meet Adam and everyone affiliated with his success. His parents, brothers, and sisters.

Ryne had a huge smile on his face. "Let's go. We need to plan our trip."

"Now? Can't we do that tomorrow?"

"I want to do it now. I can't wait for you to meet my family. I feel like we made a huge step in our relationship today, and I can't wait to see where it takes us. Come on. It's getting late, and the garden is getting ready to close. In fact, let's go Skype with my parents. I know they're just as excited to meet you as I am for you to meet them."

He reached for her hand. He didn't want to over-whelm her with family especially after she'd further shared with him her story, but he was excited for them as a couple. "Ya know, it's okay if you don't want to Skype. I understand that I've thrown a lot at you today... I'm excited, that's all."

She smiled. For once in the last several weeks, he believed she was happy. Her eyes glittered in the waning sun. "Thank you."

"For what?"

"For everything you did for me today. You made me face my past, and I'm forever grateful for that. So, I'm game. Let's call your parents, let's make those reservations. For once in a long, long time, I feel free. I want to move on. Make new memories and maybe even decide on my career path." She loudly smacked her lips on his cheek and rose, grab-bing her camera bag. "Come on, let's go. I can't wait to meet your family."

Ryne reached for her hand, raising it to his lips. Brushing a kiss across her palm, he pulled her down the pathway towards the exit.

He was thankful he'd taken that moment in time and led her to the alcove where she'd finally con-fessed the reason behind her sadness. They'd come a long way in their few short weeks together.   Right there, in that moment, he realized the truth. He'd fallen in love with her and couldn't wait to share her with both his professional family and his true family.

Ryne knew she'd fit in without issue. She was so different from Whitney. She was loving, caring, and had a heart of gold. She was true to herself and her friends, whereas Whitney was all about herself. He was grateful he'd never introduced Whitney to his family. But now, he couldn't wait to take Jen home. Skype was not the wisest of ways to introduce her, but he couldn't contain himself any longer. He needed to share her right now with his family, and he hoped and prayed she'd love them as much as he knew they would love her.

Chapter Thirteen

THEY HURRIED BACK TO RYNE'S car. Just as they started to pull away from the parking lot, Jen's phone rang. She looked down at an unfamiliar number. She hesitated answering because she didn't want to interrupt the moment, but she answered anyway.

"Jennifer," she heard in a shaking unsteady voice.

"Gram? Is that you?"

"Yes, honey, it's me."

"What's wrong? You sound upset. Where are you calling from because this certainly isn't your number?"

"It's your grandfather."

"What happened? Where are you?" she asked anxiously, causing Ryne to pull over. He knew by the tone in her questioning voice that something was seriously wrong.

"We're at the hospital. Your grandfather wasn't feeling well…"

"Don't tell me… Is he dead?" Gasping, she tried to take in air but with her heart pounding so fast she wasn't able to. She was starting to hyperventilate. She felt Ryne's hand on her leg as she listened to her grandmother. She felt his comfort immediately and found a way to slow her breathing although her heart kept pounding away.

"Oh no, sweetheart, he's still with us. The doctors believe he is having a gall bladder attack. I wanted you to know."

"Where are you? What hospital?"

"Sweetheart, you don't need to come. I just wanted you to know."

"Where are you?" she adamantly asked. She listened to her grandmother, discovering that he was at a hospital not far from where they were. "I'm on my way." She looked at Ryne and he nodded. "I'll be there in a little while."

Within minutes of taking her grandmother's call, Jen found herself in her grandmother's loving arms. Ryne had dropped her off at the Emergency Room entrance while he parked the car.

Jen draped an arm around her grandmother's shoulders and led her to a seat near the front door.

Jen was concentrating so intently on her grandmother she didn't notice Ryne standing beside her. It was her grandmother that pointed him out. "Ah dear, do you know this young man?" And that's when she looked up into the handsomest face she knew. His eyes focused on her and in that moment she realized. Realized without a doubt that he was the man for her. She'd had feelings for days, even weeks, but now she knew that what she thought was a deep sense of friendship was more.

Her heart fluttered and she gasped. Ryne saw the look of panic on her face. "Jen are you okay?" he asked as he knelt in front of her. She closed her eyes and reopened them. His eyes said it all to her. "Jen…"

She reached for his hand, squeezing it tightly. "I'm fine." Swallowing, she turned to her grandmother. "Grams, this is Ryne Ferguson, my boyfriend." She glanced over to him and smiled. It was the first time that she'd referred to him as her boyfriend, and it felt good to do so. But at the same time, she knew he was more than just a boyfriend. He'd become her best friend and the man she'd fallen hopelessly in love with. She'd never once shared with anyone her past or her dreams. Her grandparents knew about her change in career, but they didn't know the extent of the turmoil she endured while making that decision.

Ryne was it for her. Her feelings overwhelmed her. Thankfully, her grandmother took over. Jen listened as she told them what had happened earlier. She heard her grandmother's voice but didn't focus on what she was saying. Jen was mesmerized by Ryne's eyes. She knew he was listening and even watched his mouth move as he spoke to her grandmother. Jen was in a fog. She was coming to grips with everything and didn't realize Ryne was speaking to her until she felt his hand upon her leg. That innocuous touch brought her back to the present. She turned back to her grandmother. "I'm sorry, what did you say, Gram?"

"You didn't hear a word, did you?" Her grandmother knew her almost too well. "Where were you just now? I was telling you about our ride in the ambulance."

"I'm sorry, go on." She focused solely on her grandmother's words as she retold her grandfather's trip to the hospital. When she'd finished, a nurse appeared, informing them that they were ready to transfer her grandfather to a room. Additional tests were in the works, and they hoped to release him the following day.

"I'll wait here, Grams," she called out as her grandmother was escorted back to her grandfather.

Ryne took her grandmother's seat and slipped his arm around her. "He's going to be alright," he said, kissing the top of her head.

They sat in the waiting room, watching the hustle and bustle as patients and family members came and went. She'd held tightly onto his hand while she rested her head on his shoulder, waiting for news of her grandfather. She dozed off momentarily. She was safe and secure in Ryne's arms; then, the tightening of his hand woke her.

"They're moving your grandfather to his room," she heard. Wiping the sleep from her eyes, she stood, pulling him up beside her. They made their way through the hospital's halls towards a man that meant the world to her.

They waited in a nearby room while nurses finished the transfer. A soft-spoken nurse interrupted their quiet. "Are you with the Steeles?"

She was paralyzed and heard Ryne immediately speak up. "Yes, we are."

"You can go in to see your grandfather now." She saw Ryne shake his head and felt him tighten his arm about her.

"Come on, I'll walk with you."

"You're not coming in?"

"I'll wait out here. It needs to be family. I can meet him another time when he's feeling better."

She reached up and kissed him on the cheek.

"Thank you for understanding."

"What's there to understand?" He motioned her towards the room. "I'll be waiting right here, I promise." She felt his fingers slip away from hers as he pushed her into the doorway.

A half hour later she found Ryne exactly where he said he would be, waiting right outside her grand-father's room. The wall supported him as he leaned heavily against it.

She took one look at him and knew something wasn't right. The way he leaned against the wall said it all. His hip was bothering him. "Ryne, what are you doing," she called out as she neared his side.

"What do you think I'm doing? I'm waiting for you."

"You shouldn't be standing like this...your hip." As she led him to the waiting room, she felt a hitch to his step and realized he was limping. After all their walking earlier in the day, he shouldn't have continued to stand, especially on the tiled floor without some type of padding. She knew he had to be in pain.

"I'm fine. How's your grandfather?"

"He's still in pain but feels better. They think they're just going to keep him overnight. Enough about him; we need to get you home so you can take your meds."

"Jen, I'm fine. Don't you want to stay here lon-ger?"

"No. My grandparents basically sent me home. My grandmother's best friend is going to take her home. We're free to go."

"You're sure?"

"I am." He gave her the look that she'd become accustomed to of late. The one where he drew his eyebrows in and frowned. She pulled him down the hallway towards the elevators. What she wanted most of all was to take care of him. She knew he was in pain just by the way he held his jaw. She wrapped her arm around his waist while they waited for the doors to open. "Let's go home," she said as they entered the elevator. She felt his arm wrap securely around her when the doors closed.

As they drove towards his hotel, his facial expressions changed. The closer they got to his hotel, the more she became aware of his pain. He clenched his jaw even more and scrunched his eyes. She reached over and patted his leg. "We're almost there."

"Yeah," was the only comment he made as he drove through the entrance to the parking garage. He whipped the car into a space right next to the entrance and threw the car in park. That's when she noticed how tightly he gripped the steering wheel. His knuckles were white, and his temple throbbed as he clenched his jaw.

She threw open her door and made it to his side before he'd even opened his door. Slowly he eased himself from the car. If she hadn't been so focused on him, she might not have heard the groan as it escaped his lips. But she did. She slipped her arm around his waist, led him to the doors, and called for the elevator.

"Lean on me," she said as they stood against the elevator wall. She felt his weight when he followed her request. In fact, she was surprised he'd listened to her. She helped him down the hallway, then grabbed the key card from his hand and opened the door. She helped him to bed and watched as he painfully sat down on the edge and ran his hand through his hair.

She headed towards his bathroom. "Where're your pills?" He motioned towards his bedside safe. He gave her the code and she pulled out the pills so quickly, the bottle flew out of her hand and rolled under the bed.

She dropped to her knees. "I can't reach them…" She scooted further and before she knew it, she was almost all the way under the bed, grunting as she moved across the thick-piled carpeting.

"Got it," she called, then tried to extricate herself. She couldn't move. Frustrated, she cried out, "I'm stuck." She heard his laughter.

"Here, I'll help you," he said as he slid from the bed, groaning in the process.

"I don't need your help. You need to stop. You're in pain."

"I may be in pain, but I can't just leave you stranded under my bed." His hand gripped her ankles and she felt a little tug. The next thing she knew she had been freed and was staring right up at him. He grabbed her hand to help her sit upright.

"Whew, that was close. I thought I was stuck."

"You were but thanks to me…" and that's when she saw the color of his eyes change. They became darker, more intense, then he reached out, sliding his hand up her arm behind her neck. He cupped the back of her head and his lips found hers.

She laid her hands against his chest and pushed

away. "I thought you were in pain."

"I was, I am, but I took one look at you and couldn't stop myself. You're beautiful. The expression on your face when you were freed was priceless."

All of a sudden a pain shot through her backside and that's when she realized she wasn't sure where his pills were. She leaned over and pulled the pill box from underneath her. "I wondered what I was sitting on." She smiled. "Come on, let's get you your pills." She jumped from the floor and reached for his hand.

"I can stand on my own," he claimed as he got to his knees.

"Sure you can." She stood watching him, and when he didn't have the power to stand, she slid her arm about his waist and helped him to the bed. "I'll get you some water." She ran from the room and retrieved a cold bottle of water and handed it to him. He already had the pills in his palm.

He threw back the pills and reached for the water. She couldn't help but watch him as he swallowed. He'd relaxed a little since they'd gotten to his room, but she knew he was waiting for the relief the medicine would provide.

He needed to sleep off the pain, so she pulled back the covers and watched him lie down. "Now that you're settled, I guess I'll leave."

"Please don't go." He held out his hand. "Join me. You look just as tired as I feel." Listening to him describe his tiredness threw her for a moment, and that's when she acknowledged to herself how tired she actually was. On top of the conversation they'd had at the Botanical Gardens, the news of her grandfather's health scare had upset her more than she realized. The happiness that they'd experienced only moments before her grandmother's call had been forgotten.

She latched onto his hand and climbed over his body. Curling up, she laid her head on his chest and placed her hand over his stomach. He pulled her close. "This feels just right," he said as he closed his eyes and drifted off. His pain meds had taken effect almost instantly.

She knew he'd drifted off when she felt the change in his breathing and his arm loosened its hold on her. Her thoughts were all over the place. She was exhausted but sleep eluded her.

"Relax," he murmured. "We'll face it all tomorrow."

She hadn't realized he'd awakened until she heard his words. *Yes, tomorrow is another day.* She was safe and secure in his arms. He'd be there for her just as she was for him. She recalled the smile on his face and the look in his eyes when they'd decided to phone his parents. That was the last thing she remembered before falling to sleep. She'd been happy. Truly happy for the first time in more than eight years.

Chapter Fourteen

RYNE WAS A LIGHT SLEEPER even with having taken the pain killers. He woke with her in his arms; it was barely eleven o'clock. As he lay stroking his hand up and down her back, he replayed the events of the day. She'd been through more than he could ever imagine with the death of her parents and her decision to become a teacher. Then her participation in the fundraiser caused her to reevaluate her life. He'd been down that road before when he elected not to go straight to the NHL, instead heading off to UW. He hoped she'd be able to come to grips with everything and decide on a future that would make her happy.

His eyes focused on the pill bottle he'd thrown onto the end table. He hadn't a clue why his hip had acted up. He'd been pretty much pain-free the last week or so. The painkillers had dulled the discomfort, but he knew he needed to keep a watchful eye on it and maybe revisit Stafford. The season was over for him, but the guys still worked out and kept in touch with the staff. He decided to give it a few days and then decide what to do.

He felt her stir beside him. As she opened her eyes, a smile broke out across her face, then she yawned and pulled away from him.

"Feel better?" he asked as she attempted to sit up. He tightened his hold, and she gave into the pressure, lying back beside him.

"I do. What about you?"

"Painkillers work wonders," he winked. "I don't know what happened today. I'd been feeling pretty much pain-free."

"Too much walking and standing, I guess."

"Yeah, maybe." He tucked a stray hair behind her ear. "So, how about something to eat?"

"What time is it?"

"Just after eleven.'

"I should get going," she said, pulling away and sitting up. "I've got a lot to do with it being the last week of school." She stood.

"We never made that phone call," he said as he ran his hand across his five o'clock shadow.

"No, we didn't."

"Maybe we can call them tomorrow tonight. How about I pick you up and we can visit your grandfather?"

"I first have to see if he comes home. But, yeah, that sounds like a good idea." She eased herself down beside him. He reached up and caressed the side of her face.

"I wish you'd stay." She shyly smiled. "I liked waking with you in my arms." He felt her apprehension and leaned up. Looking her directly in the eyes, he added, "Jen, I think I'm falling for you. I've never felt this way about anyone before." He discounted what he had with Whitney because he'd never had a connection with her like he had with Jen. She'd been all about fame and fortune, while

Jen was the direct opposite. In his heart, he knew she was the one for him. By her wide-eyed expression, he guessed she was surprised by his admission. He'd learned a great deal from his relationship with Whitney. Jen was real and true to herself and her family and that meant more to him. He knew his parents and siblings would fall in love with her just as he had. He just needed to convince her that they had something special. Something real that he'd never experienced before.

Ryne didn't want to scare her. Instead he kissed her forehead and said, "I know you're tired. Go on home and I'll see you tomorrow."

"But Ryne..."

"Think about what I said and we can talk tomorrow, okay?" She leaned over and kissed him; then hurried from his room. He didn't move from the bed.

He didn't want to overwhelm her. She was grappling with so much. Between her career, her grandfather, and now him. He had time. Time to convince her they had something special. And he also had to make travel arrangements. The Black Gold party was soon, and he wanted to treat her to a first-class experience. He wanted her comfortable with his life inside and out of hockey. It could be complicated at times. Training, travel, and the possibility of being traded—all of these factors loomed in the back of his mind, especially after this year's unexpected trade.

While recuperating he'd also made a decision—one that would affect her if they made a go of their relationship. He decided while he was in Greenwich, he was going to have an honest conversation with Adam. He needed him to know that his goal in life was to play for the Storm. Ryne knew this meeting was unheard of, especially with two years remaining on his contract, but he needed Adam to understand that's where he expected to land with his next contract. It was his dream. He would play for Calgary and if he were lucky enough, would end his career with his hometown team.

Ryne hoped he had many years remaining to play, but with his nagging injury, he wasn't sure his hip would hold out. He prayed nightly that he'd over-come it, but in reality, he wasn't assured that he'd be able to, especially after encountering the pain he had that evening. He wanted, no needed, to remain optimistic, but he was also a realist and knew that his career could end sooner rather than later.

The next day dawned with a gorgeous sunrise. He'd had difficulties sleeping and decided to rise and start the day fresh with a new, improved out-look. The night before, he'd felt sorry for himself and wallowed in his uncertainty. With a new day upon him, he was in need of a fresh start and chose to greet Jen before her day began.

Ryne grabbed two coffees and headed off to Lakeview. She began her day early, and judging by the time, he'd never catch her at home. He pulled into Lakeview's parking lot just after six and waited. Like clockwork she pulled in just before six thirty. He caught her surprised look as she reached for her things. He helped her from the car.

"What are you doing here, might I add, this early? I certainly thought you'd sleep in, especially after taking a painkiller."

He extended her coffee cup and leaned in, softly kissing her cheek. "Good morning to you, too, sunshine." He smiled and reached for her bag. "I couldn't sleep and thought I'd start your day off right."

"And how am I starting my day off right?" she teasingly asked.

He scanned the parking lot to make sure they were still alone, cupped her jaw, and softly kissed her lips. She leaned into him, placing her hand against his chest. "That was nice, thank you." She turned and closed her car door. "Follow me." He flung her bag over his shoulder and side by side they walked towards the building.

As they neared the entrance, his hand brushed against hers. He slowed his pace, caught her fingers in his, and smiled at her. He followed her down the hallway towards her classroom. When she went to unlock her classroom door, he noticed a slight tremor in her hand. She had difficulty inserting her key in the lock, became frustrated, and dropped her keys.

They both leaned down to retrieve them. He grabbed them and as they went to stand, they bumped heads. "Ouch," she called and rubbed her forehead.

"Sorry about that." He chose the correct key and unlocked her door.

"School doesn't start until eight, so we have a little time." He set her coffee cup and book bag down and turned. He took one look at her, knowing he made the right decision. She was a breath of fresh air on his day. She grabbed her cup of coffee and took a long sip. "You never answered me; what brings you here today?"

"Why, you, of course."

"Me?" She laughed. "Why would you come out this early to see me? I thought we were getting together this evening."

"We are but I needed to see you. Start my day off right."

"Okay, whatever." She laughed, reaching into her bag.

"How's your grandfather?"

"I spoke with Grams early."

"Shouldn't she be sleeping?"

"Grams?" She scrunched her face. "Never. You think I get up early, she wakes at dawn, every single day." He eased down on the corner of her desk as she prepared for the day. "My grandfather called her early and was feeling much better, so hopefully he can come home sometime today."

"What about us taking them dinner? I'm sure your grandmother's exhausted. It would be the right thing for *us* to do. Text me later in the day and I'll arrange something."

"You'd do that for them?"

He nodded.

"You don't know them. You haven't even met my grandfather."

"So? I want to. They're your family and I want to get to know them."

Ryne watched her flit about her classroom. "Friday's your last school day."

"Yep."

"Then when are you finished here with grades and all?"

"Next week, why?"

He reached out and drew her near. A strand of hair fell in her face. He slid it behind her ear, stroking her face in the process. "I want to make plans for our trip. The event in Greenwich is next Saturday, and then we'd go on to Calgary. Will that work for you?"

A shy smile broke out on her face.

"We can fly up on Thursday, if that works for you. I need to meet with my agent. I hope to schedule that for Friday morning." Her eyes glimmered as she listened to his plans. "Your paternal grandparents live there, right?" She nodded and rested her hand against his chest. "Let's have dinner with them Friday evening. I can't wait to meet them. Can you arrange that?"

"Sure. You really want to meet them?"

"Of course I do. I want to know your entire family." He watched the happiness drain from her face as she drew in her lower lip. Ryne feared he touched a nerve and knew immediately what he said wrong. "Honey, I'm sorry. I shouldn't have said that."

"I'm just a little sentimental these days. It's the end of the school year, and I need to make a few decisions about my future. My parents have been on my mind a lot lately. I just wish they were still alive because I know they'd love you." She pulled away and returned to her desk. "On that note, you better head on out. The bell rings in twenty minutes and I have a weekly meeting I need to get to."

He felt the immediate change in her. He didn't

want her sad, so he made his way to her side and pulled her securely into his arms. "Have a good day. Text me so I know what time to pick you up." He hugged her tightly and walked out the door. He wanted to be there for her and support her in her decision. He thought about reaching out to her grandparents, but thought better of it. He didn't know them and in the excitement from the night before, he wasn't even sure her grandmother remembered he'd been there.

Ryne hurried from the premises somehow avoiding the other teachers. For a day in late May, the morning temperature was still cool, so he decided to take an early morning stroll around the neighborhood. He wanted to test out his hip and see if yesterday's pain was an anomaly.

He took his time as he walked along sipping his coffee and formulating a plan. First, they'd fly into the city. He didn't want to assume anything, so he decided to reserve two rooms at the hotel where the party was being held. That way, they could stay up as late as they wanted and wouldn't have to worry about driving somewhere. As he ticked away on his mental list, he pulled out his cell phone. It was almost nine o'clock in Greenwich and surely Adam should be in the office.

"Black Gold Management."

"Hey Sandy, is Adam in? It's Ryne."

"Hey there Ryne, no he's not. He's in a meeting. Shall I have him call you?"

"That would be great. Just a heads up, tell him I'd like to meet with him next Friday."

"Anything special?"

"I just want to touch base."

"I'll let him know. It'll be good to see you."

"Same here. It's been a while."

Ryne hardly ever made it back to Black Gold's home office. He normally conducted his business via the phone, or Adam would meet him on the road. The last time he'd seen Adam had been the evening of his trade. They'd spoken often, but time hadn't permitted a face to face. Adam also managed Tony and Ashley Regada. They were famous tennis players that encountered tragedy unlike no other. Ashley had lost her first husband, Morgan Cameron, in a car accident and at the same time suffered a miscarriage. Tony had been Morgan's best friend and life-long competitor on the tennis court.

While working through their grief, Tony and Ashley discovered a love like no other and had been together ever since. She was now a mother. Adam had decided to celebrate their one of- a-kind victories— they were both Grand Slam winners, winning all four of the major tennis tournaments in the calendar year. They'd held off on the celebration because she had wanted to step away from the limelight and focus on her pregnancy, especially after suffering multiple miscarriages. Now that she'd successfully delivered her little bundle of joy, the couple and the company decided on the party and also to celebrate the anniversary of Black Gold's founding.

Ashley's father had founded Black Gold Management right after Ashley joined the pro circuit. Organizing her schedule had become more than he or her mother could handle. In addition to managing Ryne and his brothers, Adam also represented a few ice skaters and baseball players. It wasn't a large agency but it was powerful, and Ryne was thankful every day that Adam had reached out to him when he was first drafted. He was a good friend and confidant and Ryne believed he had his best interests at heart. He hoped he wouldn't be offended with their meeting, but he needed him to know he was serious with his quest to play for the Storm.

By the time Ryne had finished his call with Sandy, he'd arrived back at his car. His hip was feeling pretty good, and he chalked up his previous day's pain to being on his feet too much. He'd take it easy the rest of the week and hope for the best.

He planted himself on a bench underneath a tall oak tree. With his planned trip back east, he phoned his best friend, Jim Hollister. Ryne had met Jim in a finance class at the UW, and they'd been friends since. Jim owned his own business, and they rarely saw one another in person. He dialed and his friend immediately answered.

"Ryne, buddy, is that you?"

"Who do you think it is?"

"I'd have to say it's been a while. I heard about the hip. How is it?"

"I have my good and bad days. I'm just thankful the season's over and I can heal properly and not try and force my way back on the ice. Say, I'm coming into town next week, and I was wondering if you'd be available for dinner say Thursday night. I'm bringing my girlfriend too."

"Girlfriend, huh. When did this start?"

"Oh, my first night here. She almost ran me over,

but I'll save that story for another day." He could tell Jim was checking his schedule.

"I think that'll work. Let me check with Holly, and I'll get back to you."

They talked for a few more minutes. Ryne was glad he'd reached out to his friend. Since meeting Jen, he'd realized that life was definitely too short and decided to touch base with his friends and family on a more regular basis. Jen had taught him that lesson if nothing else.

Chapter Fifteen

JEN CHECKED HER PHONE DURING her mid-morning break. Her grandmother had left a message, and surprisingly, her grandfather was being released from the hospital that morning. Relieved with the news, she texted Ryne. *I'll let you know about dinner.*

Having a longer lunch break, she phoned her grandmother, discovering that they'd just arrived home. "Grams, don't worry about dinner. I'll bring it by."

"Oh, honey, you don't have to do that."

"We want to."

"We? Who's we?" she inquired in her meddle-some voice.

"Well, Ryne and I."

"You mean you and that charming young man I met last night?" She snickered.

"One and the same. I want Grandfather to meet him too."

"Okay, dear. We'll see you and your dear man later then."

Jen immediately phoned Ryne, who answered on the first ring. "How's your day since I last saw you?"

"Pretty good, actually better than pretty good. I spoke with Grams and Grandfather came home a little bit ago. She's okay with us bringing dinner by."

"That's good. I'm looking forward to meeting your grandfather. In fact, I'm sure your grandmother doesn't even remember me from last night."

"That's where you're wrong," she laughed. "She remembers you. In fact she called you my 'charming young man.'"

"Did she now?"

"Uh huh. Hey, I've gotta run, my lunch break is almost over. Pick me up at six?"

"See you then."

Jen hung up and started off to her classroom. On the way down the hallway, she was stopped by Alison Tucker, Carson's wife. "You look radiant today. It can't be because this is the last week of school, can it?" Jen kept smiling at her. "Or is it because of a special man in your life?" Jen chuckled at her referral. "I saw him leaving school earlier today."

"You did, did you?"

"Yep, and I'm sure he wasn't here to see Johnston." Jen smiled and continued towards her classroom. "We're onto you two." Calling over her shoulder she added, "Jen, you and Ryne need to come over sometime. Let's set something up." Jen raised her hand, acknowledging her, and entered her classroom. Few knew of their relationship. She was going to have to talk with him about coming out with their friends. It had been new and something sacred to her, but now they needed to let everyone know they were together as a couple— especially with her attending the Black Gold party the following week.

Jen hurried home. She was excited to have dinner with her grandparents. They'd been her rock when her parents died, not that her dad's parents hadn't supported her, but they lived out of town. Grams was always there by her side everyday— all day. On the good and bad days. She was there when Jen couldn't get out of bed, there when she cried herself to sleep, and there on that final day she closed the door for the last time on her dad's studio, holding her for hours as she sobbed uncontrollably. Grams listened when she discussed changing her degree; never once did she try and alter Jen's decision. Her grandparents were always supportive, and now she needed to be there for them.

Jen was lost in thought when she heard a knock on her door that startled her. It was just after five, and she wasn't expecting Ryne until six. She peeked out the door and was pleasantly surprised when his eyes peered back at her. Broadly smiling back, she opened the door. "You're early."

"I am. I couldn't wait to see you." He leaned in kissing her softly on the lips, reached for her hand, and strode through the door. Closing it behind them, she leaned against it.

"Is that your line of the day?"

He squeezed her hand. "I don't do lines. It's just how I feel, and I've missed you more than I thought possible." She raised her hand and smoothed it along his jaw. "I'm being honest here. I missed you."

She pulled on his hand and led him into her family room. She was taken aback with how much he missed her. She didn't know what to say, so she said the first thing that popped into her head. "What's for dinner?"

"Is that all you have to say when I've just expressed how much I missed you?" She pulled away from him and walked across the room. She felt his eyes on her. "Was my honesty too much for you to handle?"

She turned back to him and scrunched her face. "No, it's not. I'm surprised, that's all."

"I'm trying to be truthful with you and at the same time not overwhelm you with my feelings. Like I said last night, this is real to me. You're constantly on my mind, and I've never, ever felt this way before." He crossed the room and clumsily reached for her hand. "I mean what I say. I want to know you and your family. You are becoming more to me than I ever imagined..."

She withdrew her hand from his and placed it on his chest. "I know and you mean a lot to me too. It's just I have a lot going on in here right now." She pointed to her head. "So much. So many memories..."

"I realize that and I want you to know that I'm here for you. Bounce whatever you want off me. Maybe I can help."

"Thanks, I will." Pulling on his shirt, she drew him closer. "So, what's for dinner?" She felt the roar of his laughter in his chest as he pulled her in closely.

"What would you like?"

"What did you do all day? I thought you were arranging it?" Again, he sniggered at her.

They decided on Vigliano's. She knew her grandparents loved everything on the menu including the pizza, but she opted for their various entrees. She sat wrapped in Ryne's arms as she placed their order. "It'll be about twenty minutes."

"Shall we go?" He stood and pulled her up from the couch into his warm embrace. "I meant what I said, you know." He leaned his forehead against hers. "You are becoming very important to me." She nodded. "I can't wait for you to meet my parents; they're gonna love you."

"I don't know about that."

"I do."

"Come on, let's go." She grabbed his hand, reached for her purse, and hurried him out the door. He was getting a little too serious for her especially with her life in flux. She needed to make a decision in the next several weeks if she planned on walking away from teaching and move back into her first love— photography. Her goal was to finish putting her shots together for the gallery presentation. She'd sit back and see how well they were received, and based upon that she'd decide her future. The fundraiser was scheduled for mid-September, right before Ryne started the preseason. She wanted to make her decision early in the school year rather than later because she wanted Johnston to have plenty of time to find her replacement. He'd been good to her and she owed that much to him.

They pulled up at her grandparents' house a little after six. Ryne hopped from the car, grabbing their dinner, and met her as she exited. She took one look at him and knew in that moment that he was the one. He was going out of his way to meet her grandparents. He wanted to get to know them, and that meant the world to her. She reached for his hand and led him in the back door. "Grams, we're here," she called out as she took the food from Ryne and placed it on the kitchen counter.

"In here, dear."

She looked up at him and shyly smiled. "Here goes nothing," she murmured.

He placed his hand on hers stopping her forward motion. "What did you just say?"

"Be prepared because they are going to be non-stop with questions, especially when I tell them I'm going to meet your family."

He chuckled at her, which she loved and had become accustomed to hearing, as he reached in and swept her hair across her shoulders. "Stop being nervous… And anyway, I thought I passed the 'smell test' last night when I met your grandmother at the hospital."

"I'm sure you did. It's my grandfather I'm worried about." She reached for his hand and led him towards the sitting room where her grandparents were watching the news. As soon as her grandfather saw them, he muted the television. He started to stand but Jen rushed to his side. "Grandfather, stay where you are." She leaned in, hugged him, and kissed his cheek. "I'm so happy you're feeling better."

Ryne had stayed where he was just inside the room while her grandfather leaned to the side trying to look around her. "Come here, young man," he said. "Sweetheart, is this your young man your grandmother has been gloating about all day?"

She turned to him with an outstretched hand.

Ryne approached, grabbed her hand and squeezed it tightly. She felt a slight tremor in his hand. Her grandfather could be intimidating at times, and this was definitely one of them. It surprised her since he'd just gotten home from the hospital but then again it didn't. He watched out for her and was continuing to do so in her father's absence.

"Grandfather, this is Ryne Ferguson. He plays for the—"

"Generals. Come here young man. I thought that was you." Ryne approached her grandfather. He still held onto her hand as he reached out his other hand to shake her grandfather's.

"It's a pleasure to meet you, sir. I'm glad you were able to come home."

"Me too. I hate hospitals." Her grandfather turned to Grams. "I can see why you were so excited, Rose. He is a handsome fellow." Jen turned bright red and was even more aware of her blush when Ryne looked at her, smiling at her grandfather's words. "So what's this I hear? You're dating my granddaughter?"

"Yes, sir, I am," Ryne said as he squeezed her hand again.

"And how long has this been going on between you two," he said motioning back and forth between them.

"A few months, sir."

"And may I ask, how did you meet my lovely granddaughter?"

"Ah, well, that's a story in and of itself."

He pointed towards the sofa. "Sit down and stay awhile. I have all night, especially since you brought dinner. You did bring dinner, didn't you?"

"Grandfather, of course we did."

"As I said, we have all night. I'm all ears."

Ryne pulled Jennifer along beside him as they sat down. He continued holding her hand as he recounted the first time they met. "You could have killed him," her grandfather said after hearing how she almost ran him down. "I certainly hope you learned a lesson there."

"I did."

"So Ryne, where are you from? Do you have family?" her grandmother asked.

"Yes ma'am, I do." He told them about his brothers and their ties to the NHL. "My youngest brother plays for my alma mater. My sisters are still in school and also play hockey."

"It runs in the family."

"It certainly does and my father was a professional player for the Calgary Storm."

"What history..." her grandmother added.

They discussed her grandfather's stay in the hospital, and then Ryne's stomach began to grumble. "Someone's hungry," Jen said patting his stomach.

"Shall we eat?" her grandmother said as she made her way to the kitchen.

"Grams, I'll help you." Patting Ryne on the arm she added, "You stay here and keep Grandfather company while we get everything on the table." Jen hurried off to assist her grandmother. She knew her grandfather wanted to interrogate him further.

"So Ryne, when did you arrive in town?"

"I was traded to the Generals in February."

"Ah, that's right. I remember. It was quite a surprise to you, wasn't it?"

"Yes sir, it was."

"And when did you begin seeing my granddaughter?"

"From the moment I arrived. Literally."

"I see. And why are we just learning of your involvement?"

"I guess I've been traveling a lot with the team. I was also injured and had a difficult time getting around..." Ryne didn't know what to say. He hadn't a clue why Jen hadn't shared their relationship with them. He only hoped her grandfather didn't go ballistic when he heard about their trip.

Dinner went well and Jen shared her progress on her showing. "I hope to get some nice shots around town this summer. I can't wait to see what I can shoot in Canada. I'd love to get some wildlife photos. Do you think that's possible?"

With a stern look on his face, her grandfather asked, "Canada. Did I hear you correctly? When are you going to Canada?"

Jen was sitting beside Ryne, and she felt his hand reach for hers underneath the table. The slight squeeze of his hand was all she needed to answer. "Next week Ryne and I are heading up to Greenwich for a party honoring Tony and Ashley Regada. They are represented by the same agency that Ryne uses. I plan on seeing Grandpa Miles and Grandma Rowena." She paused and looked out of the corner of her eye at Ryne. *Here goes nothing...* "Then, Ryne's taking me to visit his family."

"I see," her grandfather said. He set his fork down, scraped his hand across his whiskered jaw, and smiled at her. "So is this serious between you two?"

"Grandfather, we've just started seeing one another."

"I said, is it serious? As you well know, I fell in love and married your grandmother all within a month. So let me ask again, Jennifer, is this serious?"

Ryne drew her hand into his lap, squeezing it more tightly. "Sir, may I speak?"

"Of course you can. It's not like you're not present in this conversation." Her grandfather smiled at them. "Let me say this, I am happy Jennifer has found someone that seems to care for her. I was concerned after her parents died. She spent so much time alone, and now I am happy that she has you in her life. From what I see, you appear to be a stand-up kind of guy." He pointed directly at Ryne. "And don't disappoint me. Now, please answer my question. Is this serious?"

"Sir."

"Will you stop sirring me? Call me Wilford or Grandfather, but please stop the sir." Ryne felt the dam break upon the older man's wanting to be called Wilford or Grandfather. He felt like he'd been accepted by her grandparents.

"Okay, Wilford." Ryne took a deep breath and looked at Jen then turned back to Wilford.

"Sir..." Wilford glared at him. "Sorry, Wilford ...I'm a bit nervous here."

Wilford rested his hand on the table. "There's nothing to be nervous about. Spill your beans..."

"Fine. Wilford, yes, I care a great deal for your granddaughter. Jennifer has been a breath of fresh air to me since I relocated to St. Louis. I care for her deeply. Is it love? I can't say for sure but what I can say is— I think about her all the time. I love being in her presence. She's a remarkable woman and has so many talents."

"That she does," Grams chimed in.

"Only time will tell where this leads, but what I will promise you is I will never hurt Jen. Not in a million years. We came into one another's lives at the right time. I can only hope the near calamity in the Generaldome parking lot was fate playing a hand in our meeting. We're going to take this slowly, one day at a time..."

"That's what I wanted to hear. I don't want my granddaughter hurt in all of this."

Ryne turned back to Jen. "Never. I promise you right here, I will never hurt her. She means too much to me."

Shortly after finishing their dinner, Jen noticed her grandfather begin to tire. He was having a hard time keeping his eyes open and had tried his best to suppress his yawns to no avail. "Grams, I think Ryne and I are going to head on out. Grandfather can't keep his eyes open, and surely you must be exhausted as well."

"That I am, dear," Grams said as she stood.

Jen went to her grandfather's side. She hugged and kissed him and whispered in his ear, "Thank you." She caught the slight tip of his head and the sparkle in his eyes.

Ryne also approached. "Wilford, it was nice meeting you."

"Same here," he said, shaking Ryne's outstretched

hand. "Take care of my girl."

"I will."

Grams followed them to the door. "Thank you for dinner, dear. It was wonderful as always." Grams pulled Jennifer into her arms. "I am happy for you, my dear." Grams pulled Ryne into a hug as well. "Take care of her for me."

As Jennifer and Ryne walked down the sidewalk, Grams remained at the door. Jen turned back as they approached his car. Waving at her she said, "Love you, Grams."

"Love you from here to the moon and back." Jen smiled up at Ryne as she slid into the car. It had been an eventful evening, that's for sure. But in the end, she knew her grandparents supported her and would always be by her side.

"That wasn't so bad," Ryne said. He started up the car and backed out of the driveway. "Your grandfather is wise in his old age."

"That he is, that he is. I know they worry about me. Worry that I'll be alone, but after tonight, I think they won't as much anymore. They liked you."

"How could you tell?"

"I just know it. After all, my grandfather did soften towards the end. He did want you to stop calling him sir, didn't he? And what's with this 'sir', anyway?"

"It's how I was raised. I was trying to show respect."

"And you did."

In the end, Jen thought her grandparents fell in love with Ryne. She knew by the way her grand-

father eyes sparkled back at her. Grams was always
the easy sell but Grandfather took time. And by
the way he responded to Ryne, she knew they had
absolutely nothing to worry about.

Chapter Sixteen

THE WEEK FLEW BY AND before she knew it, they were boarding their flight to Connecticut. School ended on a bittersweet note. She always hated losing her students after a long school year, but she always looked forward to the fall when she could welcome another batch of fourth graders into her world.

Her grandfather was back to his normal self and since their dinner, he'd phoned her more often, checking in on her and Ryne's relationship. She was grateful to have them in her life, but she was also excited to see her father's parents since it had been almost a year since she lasted visited. They always seemed to shed light on her problems and she could use their insight as she sought to change the direction of her life.

Ryne had picked her up at the crack of dawn for their six o'clock flight. She leaned on him as they made their way down the jetway to board the plane. She'd barely slept the night before, excited to not only see her grandparents but also anxious to meet Ryne's family. This was a huge step for her— one she wasn't taking lightly.

They were seated in first class which excited her, especially since they could board almost immediately. Taking their seats, they were greeted by the flight attendant who offered them something to drink before the flight took off. Jen wanted, no needed, a strong cup of coffee if she were going to make it through the day. Ryne instantly reached for her hand while they waited. "This is it," he commented as he looked into her eyes. "I've been waiting for this day..." Before he could finish his thought, their drinks were served.

As they sat waiting for the remaining passengers to board, she laid her head against his shoulder. "I can't wait for you to meet my grandparents."

"Me either, except I hope your grandfather isn't as intense as Wilford." She laughed, listening to him go on about Wilford and all of the questions he asked. "I know how much he loves you and also acknowledge his fierce need to protect but..."

"He was pretty intense, that's for sure. He's phoned me every day wondering what you're up to."

He raised his brow. "He has?"

"Yep, and he always ends the conversation with, 'He's a good man.'"

"So, I guess he likes me." She reached over and slid her hand across his chest and nodded.

"Right now, I don't think you can do anything wrong in his book. As he said, just don't hurt me."

He grabbed her hand squeezing it and then set it in his lap. "Never in a million years would I hurt you," he said pulling her closer.

As the flight attendant provided the rote instructions to the passengers, she fell asleep in his arms.

Ryne had also drifted off to sleep when they were awakened by a bit of turbulence. "Well, that wasn't much fun," she said as she reached for her purse. She pulled out a stick of gum offering him a slice. He shook his head no. "My ears are bothering me a little. Maybe this will help." She popped the gum into her mouth and watched a flight attendant move from the coach section of the plane to first class. When she returned to coach, she stopped at their row.

"Ryne, is that you?" Ryne looked up and took in the svelte woman who had long blonde hair and the bluest of blue eyes Jen had ever seen. She imagined the woman wore contact lenses.

"Oh hey, Darlene, how are you?"

"Great. I heard you were traded."

"Yep, to the Generals. It's been awhile."

"It has. I switched my route. Today, I'm filling in for one of my friends who just lost her parents in a horrific car accident." Jen stiffened. She knew firsthand what Darlene's friend was going through. Ryne's hand reached for hers and she smiled at him.

"I'm sorry to hear that."

"I'll stop by again before we land." Darlene returned to her section of the plane while Jen felt his eyes on hers.

"She used to be the flight attendant when I traveled with the Eagles."

"That's what I figured." He continued holding her hand as they neared their destination.

"I made plans for this evening. I hope that's alright with you. I haven't seen my best friend, Jim Hollister, in some time. I thought we could have dinner with him and his wife, Holly."

"That sounds like fun."

"And tomorrow we're having dinner with your grandparents?"

"That's the plan."

"I'm looking forward to meeting them."

"I told them all about you."

"And?"

"They can't wait to meet you too."

Before they knew it, their plane had landed, and they were on the way to the Towne Square. Ryne had arranged for two separate rooms, but when they arrived, discovered that their reservations had been mixed up. "What do you mean you don't have two rooms available?" Jen stood beside him as he dealt with the hotel staff.

"Sir, I'm sorry. I see where your reservations went through. I don't know what happened, but I can offer you a two-room suite." She saw his eyebrows rise and turned to her.

"Jen, I'm sorry. Are you okay with this? If not, I'll find us something else."

She laid her hand on his arm and smiled at him 'That's fine. I know it's not your fault."

"Mr. Ferguson, I apologize profusely for what happened."

"I understand but why didn't someone contact me?"

"I can't answer that. Again, I'm sorry. Please, follow Alfred and he will show you to your room." Jen could tell Ryne wanted to argue further, but instead she grabbed ahold of his hand and followed the valet to their room.

"Don't worry about it, Ryne. We're adults here. It's not like we haven't shared a bed before." He smirked at her. "Well, you know what I mean."

"I do. It's just the principal of it all."

It was late afternoon by the time they arrived at their room and unpacked. They heard a knock at their door. When Ryne answered, he was surprised to see room service. "Compliments of the hotel." Jen stood alongside Ryne as a huge cart was wheeled into the room filled with appetizers, cheese and crackers, fruit, and freshly squeezed orange juice. Even a bottle of wine was included.

"Wow, I can't believe they did this," she said as Ryne closed the door.

"They needed to do something, that's for sure. They royally messed up my reservations."

"They did, but there's nothing we can do about it. Wipe that grimace off your face and let's enjoy these goodies."

"Nothing seems to bother you, does it?"

"That's where you're wrong. A lot bothers me, but most of it I let roll off my back. It's what I choose to dwell on that sometimes takes me down."

"You never seem bothered by anything."

"Oh, I am, more than you'll ever know."

Ryne confirmed his meeting with Adam the following morning. "Now you're sure you're alright with me leaving you alone?" he asked when he finished.

"I'm sure. I'm going to run by my grandparents and check out their new digs. I haven't seen their new home since they sold their mansion a while ago. The funny thing about that was they continued to live in their home for something like two years before they moved." She shook her head. "That was the craziest thing."

"That does sound a little odd. Shall we just meet back here when we're both done?"

"Yeah. I think that works best since Grandma Rowena can talk your ear off. Be prepared for dinner tomorrow, that's all I can say. I'm going to change. I'm looking forward to meeting your friend."

"Jim's one of a kind. We've been best friends since college although we don't get a chance to see one another often with my schedule and his. Holly, his wife, is a gem too. I think you'll have a lot in common."

Jen took her time changing. She loved the dress she'd chosen for their dinner and believed by Ryne's expression he did too.

She went to his side when he reached his hand out. "Beautiful." He stroked her cheek. She'd chosen a simple black cocktail dress which she'd enhanced with a rose-colored fabric belt. She wore simple jewelry but the look was refined and classic. She knew she took his breath away by the way he gasped when she entered the room. "Jim's going to be jealous with you on my arm."

"Jealous? I thought he's married."

"He is but he, along with every other man in the restaurant, will wish you were on their arm. Jen, you're gorgeous. I'm the lucky one here, that's for sure."

She smiled demurely at him. He was embarrassing her. No one she'd ever dated spoke to her like that. No one had told her how beautiful she was. Ryne was her knight in shining armor.

They were meeting Jim and his wife across town, so Ryne called for a car. "Come on. The car's waiting for us."

Ryne had flown under the radar the entire day except for their flight attendant recognizing him. That was until their driver took one look at him and was in gaga land. He was a huge fan of Ryne's and rambled the entire way to their restaurant about his playing days with the Badgers, Eagles, and now the Generals. "Sorry about your hip."

"Thanks," Ryne said.

"Are you still rehabbing? You know..." Just as the driver started to discuss Ryne's rehab, they pulled up at the restaurant. Both of them couldn't wait to get out of the car.

"I'll phone the service when we're ready to return to the hotel."

"Are you sure? I can wait."

"No, please don't. I'm not sure how long we'll be."

Jen grabbed his hand and started towards the entrance. "Definitely a fan."

"That's for sure. He never stopped. I wondered when he came up for air because I haven't a clue when he took a breath."

They entered the restaurant and were immediately greeted by Jim and his wife. Ryne made the introductions. Jen was pleasantly surprised when Jim pulled her into a hug. "It's nice to see him out and about and dating again." Jen didn't quite understand his reference to Ryne dating again. She made a mental note to ask him about the comment when they returned to the hotel.

Jen really liked Jim and Holly. They were down to earth and she had a blast listening to their children's latest antics. Before she knew it, dinner was over, and they were returning to the hotel.

Hand-in-hand they entered the elevator. She smiled up at him knowing she had to ask the question that had been on her mind since her conversation with Holly. They entered their room and she led him to the sofa where she pulled him down beside her. No sooner had they sat Jen turned to him and asked the question that had been on her mind all evening. "So what did Jim mean about you dating again? Has it been a while? Is there a story there?"

She knew she'd hit upon something by the expression that crossed his face. He immediately looked away and became nervous. He started tapping his fingers against his leg. He couldn't look at her. When he ran his hand through his hair, she knew it was something big that he wasn't thrilled about sharing.

He abruptly stood and walked across the room. He opened the mini-fridge and pulled out a beer. Popping open the bottle, he took a swallow.

She sensed his upset. "It can't be *that* bad, can it?"

He took a deep breath and another swallow from his beer. He returned to the couch and sat, then drew in his lips. All the while she knew he was trying to put into words what he wanted to say. Finally, he said the words that took her breath away. "I was engaged to Derek's sister."

"Derek, as in Derek Pfeil?"

"One and the same."

"Okay," she said, waiting for him to continue.

She knew whatever he had to say troubled him immensely since he'd never had difficulties sharing his thoughts and feelings before. He clenched his jaw. His eyes grew dark and he rapidly blinked as though he were trying to suppress tears. She reached out to him, telling him in her own way that whatever he had to say, it would be alright. She grasped his hand and waited.

A few moments passed before he softly spoke. "Her name is Whitney, and like I said she's Derek's sister. We met when Derek and I played for the Eagles. Now when I think back on our relationship, I wonder what got into me. Why did I lower myself to her standards? She bowled me over. Out of nowhere I was in 'love' with her. But when I look back on it, I wasn't in love with her at all. I guess it was infatuation." He shook his head. "Let's say I was blind and stupid when it came to her. We were engaged in a matter of months. I thought she was it for me. Until I found her in the arms of another man. She couldn't have cared less that I discovered her affair, as it turned out." Jen squeezed his hand in support.

"When I confronted her, not only did I discover she had never loved me, she informed me she'd never considered us exclusive. Can you believe that? We were engaged. She continued to date and, stupid me, I never knew it.

"When Derek discovered what she'd done, he was livid. If she'd been a hockey player on the ice, I'm not sure how far he would have taken it. In fact, he's pretty much turned his back on her. He hasn't spoken to her since our breakup."

"But she's family."

"She threw that away. Whenever he knows she's going to be at a family event, he finds a convenient excuse not to attend. When Whitney and I broke up, we'd just headed into the off-season and shortly thereafter Derek was traded, so I didn't see him again until we played the Generals in a pre-season game. He pulled me aside before the game began and apologized for her behavior. He was disgusted with her and wanted to let me know that what she did would not affect our friendship.

"When I was first traded to the Generals, I wasn't sure how he would react to my presence—seeing me every day. I knew what he'd told me after it first happened but that's been years. All I can say is Derek is a true friend. He accepted me with open arms like nothing happened. We never speak of that time, and to this day I am thankful that my family never knew of Whitney and our engagement."

"Your family never met her?"

He shook his head. "Something always seemed to prevent me from introducing her. Our affair, which is what I like to call it started during preseason and was over in the blink of an eye. I was traveling with the team so much; I didn't know whether I was coming or going. Our schedule was crazy that year. In fact, I didn't even make it home during the holidays. It just didn't work out, and I'm thankful it turned out that way because she was long out of my life when I finally saw my family again."

Ryne drew her near. "I should have told you this before now. I'm sorry I didn't have the courage to share my misfortune with you."

She placed her hand on his chest and felt his strong heart beating wildly. She began to play with the buttons on his shirt, smoothed out the wrinkles, finally moving her hand up to caress his cheek. He sighed while he waited for her to speak. "We all make mistakes and luckily you discovered her wayward ways before you married. It was a learning experience and hopefully you'll never make the same mistake again."

He grabbed her hand, bringing it to his lips. "Never. I know what I want and I've found it. I found it in you, if you'll have me." He smiled down at her. "I guess now's as good a time as any." He paused and smiled the smile she'd grown to love. Placing his hand along the side of her face, he swallowed deeply then said the words he truly meant.

"I've never felt the way I do with anyone including Whitney. In all honesty, I wish I'd never spoken these words to her." He leaned close and touched his forehead to hers. "I love you, Jen. I love you with all of my heart. Please believe that I truly love you with all of my being."

"Wow," she said in a whisper. "I don't know how I can beat that." She looked away briefly. "I don't know how I can outdo your declaration." She chuckled. "So, I'll just say it. I love you too." Winsomely she smiled. "I wouldn't be sitting with you right here, right now, if I didn't believe in you—in us." She leaned over and kissed his lips.

He wrapped his arms around her. As she weaved her hands through his hair he continued, "You're the best thing that's ever happened to me outside of hockey and my family. I can't wait to introduce you to my parents."

"I guess that's a good thing." She chuckled as they snuggled closer. Tonight had been a night of discovery for her, for them, and she knew they could only grow as a couple as they worked towards a future filled with love.

Chapter Seventeen

THE NEXT MORNING WHILE JEN checked out her grandparents' new home, Ryne was scheduled to meet with Adam who had arranged a private room for their meeting.

Ryne had a hard time saying goodbye to Jen after they'd shared their feelings of love the night before. As he stood outside the restaurant, he pulled her close once again before watching her walk away.

His heart beat wildly. If this wasn't love, he didn't know what it was because he'd never once felt this way about Whitney. She looked back and threw him a kiss. A huge smile crossed his face as he waved back.

"I take it she's the one," Adam said as he slapped Ryne on the back.

"Could be," Ryne commented as he shook Adam's hand.

"I look forward to meeting her."

"Enough talk about Jen and me, let's eat."

The hostess led them to their reserved room where a carafe of coffee waited for them.

"Did you come in last night?"

"No, we came in yesterday morning. We had dinner with Jim and Holly and tonight we're having dinner with her grandparents."

"Dinner with the grandparents, huh?"

"Yep! I'm looking forward to it. I've met her maternal grandparents already, and now I get to meet her father's side of the family."

"What are her parents like?"

Ryne flicked the handle on his coffee cup. He pursed his lips, shook his head. "Her parents are both deceased. They were killed in a car accident on the way to her high school graduation."

"How horrible."

"It was a pretty life-altering event for her to the say the least. She's lucky, though, she has phenomenal grandparents. I can't wait to meet her father's parents. Her mother's are a hoot."

The waitress arrived and took their order. Ryne waited to get to the meat of their conversation as he didn't want to be interrupted. "Adam, I wanted to discuss my contract."

"You've still got two years left, have you forgotten?"

"No, that's one thing I'm fully aware of. Let's just say my trade came out of left field. Did you see it coming because I certainly didn't? I know I was injured early in the season, but it still doesn't make sense to me." He tapped his finger on the rim of his cup. "I've been thinking a lot."

"More than normal," Adam asked.

Ryne chuckled at his comment, "Yeah, more than usual." He reached for his cup and took a sip. "I've been thinking a lot lately...You know how loyal I am."

"You are."

"I'm going to come right out and say it. I want..."

He stopped speaking and looked Adam directly in the eyes. "Not I want, I expect to play for the Calgary Storm. With all of the familial ties to the team, I've always wanted to play for them. Between my dad being a stand out star and my brothers... It's always been my dream to play there. I know I'm being a little forward here, but that's what I expect with my next contract, and I thought you should know what my expectations are."

"What if I can get you there before your contract expires?"

"Do it," he claimed as he raised his hand from the table reaching again for his coffee cup. It wasn't the first time he'd expressed his desire to play for the Storm.

"What about Jen? Will she want to live in the cold north?"

"I can't answer that. We haven't really gone there yet with our relationship. We both know there's something special between us, but in all honesty, I don't know what would happen. I know she's in flux right now and is working through a few decisions." Shaking his head, he added, "Time will tell."

Ryne had made his point and that's all that mattered. He only hoped Adam took him seriously.

Jen arrived at her grandparents' and was taken aback with their new home and surrounding grounds. It was large and lavish, something out of a fairytale.

When Jen pulled up, she noticed the huge turret that sat at the front of the house. The entire

front of the home was made of red brick and lime-
stone. She knew it had at least seven bedrooms and
more bathrooms than she could count. The square
footage was larger than their previous home. She
knew this home had an indoor lap pool, a theater,
and a bowling alley. She didn't understand why her
grandparents had upsized instead of downsized at
their age, but she also knew her grandmother still
liked to entertain.

Jen approached the front door and barely hit the
last step when the huge mahogany door flew open.
She guessed Grandma Rowena had seen her as she
drove up. "Jennifer," Rowena said as she pulled her
tightly into her arms. "Honey, it's so good to see
you."

Her grandmother called out for her grandfather.
"Miles come quick. Jennifer is here." Rowena
wrapped her arm around Jennifer and led her
towards the kitchen. "Coffee?" she asked as they
walked into the spacious room.

Out of nowhere, she felt her grandfather wrap
his arms around her. "Jennifer, we're so happy you
finally came to see us."

"Grandpa Miles, you know how hard it is for me
to travel during the school year."

"We understand, sweetheart, it's just that we miss
you so." His comment brought tears to her eyes as
she looked at Miles. He was the splitting image of
her father, and she often had to do a double take
when she looked at him. Her heart always ached
when she first saw him. She missed her father so
much...

"Sit down, honey. We want to hear what you've

been up to." Rowena paused and grasped her hand. "I can't wait to meet your friend too. Tell us all about him." She reached for the coffee pot and filled three cups sitting on the table.

Jen reached for hers, adding a splash of cream. Taking a sip she rolled her eyes. "I miss your coffee. It's always so smooth."

"Honey, it's all in grinding your own beans and pressing it."

"I know. I never seem to quite get it like yours." She took another sip, then set her coffee aside and smiled at her grandparents. "It's just so good to see you both." She looked about the kitchen. "Love the house, but I thought you were downsizing after selling the mansion." Her grandparents referred to their previous house as the 'mansion'.

"You know your grandmother. She always loves to throw a party."

"But really, Grandpa Miles. This house is larger than what you sold."

"It is not," Rowena added as she sat down beside him. She reached for her husband's hand as he quirked his brow. "Okay, the house is a little larger, but we did downsize."

"And where's that, sweetheart?" Miles asked.

"The yard isn't as big."

Jen burst out laughing at her grandmother.

"Who cares about the yard? What? You don't have a tennis court this time?"

"Oh no, honey, we do. We just have a few less trees." Miles shook his head and chuckled at his wife's reasoning. "I'll give you a tour, but first let's talk.

"So tell us about your man." Rowena smiled broadly at her granddaughter. "You've never introduced us before to any of your young men." Jen shyly smiled at her grandmother. "Well, you haven't."

"No, you're right. He plays for the Generals."

"Did Ed introduce you?"

"No, in fact, I practically ran him over." Rowena's eyes grew large listening to Jen. "Grandma, don't look at me like that. It's true. I almost ran him down with my car while he was trying to get to his first game."

"Do tell."

"Let's just say it's not one of my finer moments. After I hit him with my car, we kept running into one another. Then Ryne came and spoke at Lakeview. On top of that, Johnston decided to make him a co-chair of the fundraiser. One thing's led to another and we've grown close."

"Oh honey, I'm so happy for you. I was worried you'd never find anyone." Jen glared at her grandmother. "I'm sorry to say it, but I was. From what I hear from Rose, you never go out."

"I go out."

"Let me finish, dear. You never go out—out with a young man. I know you go out. You're always at a Generals game or a baseball game. It doesn't matter. I can't wait to meet your Ryne."

"Sweetheart, your grandmother told me you're attending a Black Gold Management party honoring Ashley and Tony Regada."

"We are."

"Do you realize who Ashley is?"

She shot a quizzical look at Miles.

"Ashley as in Ashley Hamilton. Morgan Cameron originally bought the mansion."

"On my gosh! I had no idea that Ashley Regada and Ashley Cameron are one in the same. You know I don't follow tennis." Miles laughed. "Well, I don't. Now if I'd have known her maiden name of Hamilton, I would have put two and two together." Jen took another sip of coffee. "That makes attending this party even better. At least I'll know someone— that is other than Ryne. I've never met his agent, Adam."

Rowena changed the subject. "Jennifer, instead of going out to a restaurant for dinner, you and Ryne come over here and I'll cook."

"Oh no, Grandma, that's too much work for you."

Miles tilted his head at her. "Did you forget why we bought this house?" Catching a look at Rowena, "Entertainment purposes."

"How could I forget," Jen stated and chuckled. It felt good to be around her grandparents. She always had a good laugh.

"Honey, we're more relaxed here. It'll just be us, no eyes and ears listening in on our conversation. Didn't you say he's pretty well known?"

She nodded.

"That settles it then. Does six work for you?"

"It does."

"Enough talk about dinner. I want to show you around."

Jen followed her grandmother on a tour of the house. Nothing surprised her especially the huge workout room that sat on the lower level or the indoor tennis court that was built off the workout room. She knew her grandparents had added the tennis court because it fed off the house just like the one did off the mansion. Her grandparents loved the game and played daily.

By the time Jen arrived back at the hotel, she needed a nap. Rowena talked nonstop especially during their tour. One minute she was comparing the house to the mansion and the next she was discussing Ryne. She'd never done so much head flipping in such a short time.

As Jen inserted her key into the door, she came to the conclusion she needed to prepare Ryne for her grandmother. Something had set her off that morning. What? She didn't know. She walked in to discover Ryne fast asleep on the couch. He must have been sleeping for some time with the way his hair was rumpled.

She watched him as he breathed in and out. His face was so relaxed. He looked peaceful and pain free. At off times, like now, she worried about his hip. She knew he was good at hiding his pain and wondered if he'd been keeping it from her. She knew he worried that it wouldn't heal completely and thought that was a portion of why he'd added some fine lines to his face in the last few weeks. Out of nowhere, she'd catch a look of pain cross his face, but always when asked, he brushed her concern aside. She hoped he wasn't hiding it from her, and if he was experiencing a setback, he'd face it head on, do something about it. She decided to wait and see. She'd be around him night and day as they traveled and would confront him with it the next time it concerned her.

She brushed her hand across his forehead, pushing his hair out of his eyes. His eyes slowly opened. He reached for her hand and brushed a kiss against her palm. "You're back already."

"Already? It's almost three." Taking a deep, deep breath, she told him, "I have to warn you, Grandma Rowena is in rare form today. She talked nonstop. I need to take a nap just from listening to her." He pulled on her hand and she fell into his arms. "Ryne, what are you doing?"

"You just told me you needed a nap."

"I do." She felt his arms tighten around her.

"Just lie here with me then. We'll nap together." He nuzzled his head into her shoulder. "What time do we need to meet your grandparents? Isn't the restaurant across town?"

"Plans have changed." She pulled away and ran her hand along the side of his face. "Grandma's decided to cook."

"She doesn't need to go to all that trouble. I had intended on paying for dinner."

"Ryne," she said as she played with the buttons on his shirt. "Don't even bother trying to convince me or her otherwise. She wants to entertain us."

"Entertain?"

"That's what I said." She licked her lips. "She wants to do this. In fact, enjoys it. I tried to talk her out of it, but there was no way around it. It'll make her happy."

"Well, that says it all. We have to keep her happy."

"I don't want you to get the wrong impression of her. She's not that bad— just wound up."

"Why's that?"

"Because it's the first time I've ever brought one of my men friends to visit. She wants to make a good impression."

He smirked at her use of men friends. "So, now I'm relegated to one of your 'men' friends?"

She slapped his chest. "Stop it!"

"Well?"

She continued playing with his shirt. "It's just that they've never met one of my boyfriends before today. In fact, I feel like she's acting as my mother, wanting to approve of you, like I'm sure my parents would have tried to do." She sighed. "She wants to see me happy."

"And are you?"

"Am I what?"

"Happy."

She raised her hand to his face. Brushing her fingertips across his lips, she nodded. "I am," she whispered. He clasped her hand in his. "This is the happiest I've been in a long time."

"Ditto." She looked at him in a quizzical manner. "I'm glad to hear it because I feel the same way. I found you at the right time in my life. Even though you practically killed me in the process."

"Hey, there. It wasn't that bad."

"It could have been," he said, smiling at her. She knew he was joking, but in all honesty, she really could have caused him serious injury.

She wrapped her arms around him and laid her head on his chest. "I think you'll like my grandparents. They mean well."

"I'm sure they do, just as Rose and Wilford do.

They want to see you happy, and I think they'll do anything in their power to see to it."

"They do. I'm forever grateful that I still have them with me. I'd be lost in the world without them." She closed her eyes and lay in his arms. She felt comfortable, but most of all she felt protected. She believed that Ryne was her guiding light, and with him by her side, she knew she'd make the right decision about her future.

Jen wasn't quite sure where she was when she first woke, then realized she was in Ryne's arms. She eased open her eyes and found herself nose to nose with him. He was fast asleep, or so she thought. She watched him breathe in and out. She felt his fingers graze her waist as then move towards her back, and that's when she realized he was teasing her. She looked up into his hazel eyes. "I thought you were asleep."

"Nope. I've been watching you for the last hour." She nestled more into his embrace.

"I hope I didn't drool."

"Nothing like that." She got all anxious, unsure of what she may have done while sleeping. She leaned up, elbowing Ryne in the stomach.

"Ouch," he exclaimed. "What are you doing?"

"Trying to find out what I did and didn't do while sleeping in your arms." He shook his head. "What, you're not going to tell me?" He remained still with a smirk on his face. "Ryne?"

"Nope. Not going there. It's my little secret." He leaned up and swung his legs over the edge of the couch. "It's almost five. What time do we need to be at your grandparents?"

"Six."

"I've gotta get a shower. Can you be ready in a half hour?"

"Of course, I can." Jen watched as Ryne started to his bedroom.

"You better light a light under you if you plan on being ready in thirty minutes."

"You think I can't dress that quickly?"

"I'm betting on it."

"And what's the bet?"

He pursed his lips, shook his head. "I'll let you know when you lose."

"You're not playing fair." She jumped off the couch and hurried to her room. "I'll show you," she claimed as she closed the door behind her.

True to her word, Jen was ready minutes before he was. In fact, she sat waiting for him as he walked from his room. Pointing at her watch, "And who's late?"

He shook his head in disbelief. "I guess I am."

She studied him as he approached, his eyes never leaving her face. "You look stunning." He raised his hand to her face. "You're beautiful, absolutely beautiful." He planted a kiss on her lips. "I'm going to have a hard time keeping my eyes off you." She hugged him tightly. Not only did he look handsome in his suit, but he smelled good, too. She took a deep whiff of his aftershave.

"Like how I smell?" he asked smiling broadly at her. She nodded her head.

"We'd better head on out or we'll be late. And for once I can say I won't be the cause." He grabbed her hand and pulled her towards the door. It was a night of firsts for her, and she planned on enjoying every minute with her knight in shining armor.

Chapter Eighteen

RIGHT AT SIX, THEIR DRIVER pulled up in the circular drive of her grandparents' estate. Ryne wasn't the least bit surprised with their home because she'd described it in explicit detail as they made their way from the hotel.

"I thought they'd downsized, but instead they upsized. My grandmother said they did downsize—they have a few less trees."

He laughed at her grandmother's joke. "I like her sense of humor."

"Yeah, well we'll see how much you like her on the way home."

The car had barely come to a halt when the front door opened, and her grandparents emerged onto the front stoop.

Ryne opened the door and eased out of the car. He reached for her hand as she slid across the seat; all the while he felt her grandparents' eyes on him. Jen emerged from the car with a smile and wave. She reached for the crook of his arm and grasped it tightly. Ryne knew this was a big deal for her and felt her nervousness in the way she held onto his arm. He leaned over and whispered in her ear, "You alright?"

She plastered a smile on her face and with a quiver

in her voice told him she was fine. He knew otherwise.

Rowena welcomed her with open arms, while
Miles extended his hand to Ryne. "Grandma
Rowena, Grandpa Miles, I'd like to introduce Ryne
Ferguson." Rowena moved quickly, throwing her
arms around Ryne. He didn't know what hit him.

"Ryne, it's so good to meet you. I've waited forever for Jen to bring her young man by." She patted
his chest.

He glanced over Rowena's shoulder and caught
Jen's eye. He smiled when she referred to him as
her 'young man'. "It's a pleasure to meet you too,
Mrs. Steele."

"Oh honey, don't call me that. I'm either Grandmother or Grandma Rowena or just Rowena."

"It's a pleasure, Rowena," he said as he pulled
away from her.

"Come this way."

Ryne stretched out his hand toward Jen. Grasping
it tightly, he followed her grandparents as they led
them inside.

He leaned over to Jen as they made their way
across the threshold. "That wasn't so bad."

"Just you wait."

"Jennifer, dear, what was that you said?"

"Ah nothing. I was just clearing my throat."

"Clearing your throat. Ha! That's a good one,"
he whispered as they made their way towards the
formal living room.

Ryne whistled softly as he took in the grandeur of
their home. He looked around, taking in the intri-
cate ceiling, marble floors, and the overall feeling of

their home. It was lavish but all the same felt like it was lived in and full of love.

"Would you care for a cocktail?" Miles asked as he made his way to the bar. After dropping ice cubes into a tumbler, he poured what looked like a whiskey sour into the glass which he handed over to his wife. "Jennifer, glass of wine?"

"Sure thing."

"And Ryne?" Pointing to the pitcher, "Whiskey sour?"

"Ah, no thanks, but a glass of wine sounds good." Miles handed over their wines while Rowena grabbed a tray of appetizers that were sitting on the bar.

Motioning to the settees, "Sit," she said as she laid the tray on the coffee table. "Take a load off," she added as she took her seat.

Ryne glanced at Jen as her grandmother took her seat. "Tell us a little bit about yourself, Ryne. Where are you from? What about your family? How long have you known our granddaughter?"

"Grandmother, enough with the questions."

"Sweetheart, we just want to get to know your beau."

Beau. He suppressed his chuckle as he looked away, taking a large gulp from his glass. *This is going to be some kind of night.*

"Mrs. Steele."

"Rowena."

"Sorry about that, Rowena. Well, let's see if I can remember all of your questions." Ryne caught Jen's sideways glance at him and grinned trying not to laugh at her grandmother. "I'm from Calgary."

"As in Alberta, Canada?" Miles said.

"Yes, sir."

"Isn't it quite cold up there?"

"It can be."

"Don't you get a lot of snow?"

"Not as much as you may think. We average around fifty inches of snow a year."

"Huh, I thought you got feet of snow."

He chuckled listening to Miles.

"Go on, go on," Rowena prodded him.

"I'm from a relatively large family."

"You are, huh?" Rowena added as she sipped her cocktail.

"I'm one of seven children."

"Seven?"

"Yes, ma'am. I have four brothers and two sisters. Three of my brothers play in the NHL while my youngest brother plays for the University of Wisconsin. My two sisters are still in school, but they also play hockey."

"Hockey sure runs in your family."

"It does. My dad also played professional hockey for the Storm."

"That's interesting," said Rowena.

"Yep, hockey runs in the family." Jen must have sensed his nervousness because she reached for his hand. Clasping it tightly, she squeezed it and smiled up at him.

"Go on...did you attend college or were your drafted right out of high school?"

Her grandparents listened intently as Ryne shared with them his path to the NHL. "So you got a degree?"

"Grandmother, enough with the questions. Ryne is not on trial here."

He patted her leg. "It's okay, honey." He looked at Rowena, "Ask away."

He answered all of their questions, and after about an hour Rowena proclaimed it was time for dinner. They started to follow her grandparents from the room when Jen stopped him.

"What?" he asked as he swiped his hand across his face. "Stop fretting, they're just concerned about you."

"This is so much worse than I ever imagined."

He reached down and brushed a soft but simple kiss across her lips. "Come on, they are waiting for us." He slipped his arm around her shoulders and led her in the direction of what he assumed was the kitchen. "Rowena," he called out. "Something sure smells good."

Jen elbowed him in the ribs. "Hey, what was that for?"

"Enough with the brownie points."

He let out a boisterous laugh as they entered the kitchen.

"What's so funny?" Miles asked as he reached for a bottle of wine.

"Ah nothing, Grandfather."

The rest of their meal went off without a hitch. They discussed their trip to visit his parents and the Black Gold party. His thoughts drifted to his parents and wondered how they would treat Jen upon their first meeting. He hadn't heard Jen's question until he felt her hand on his arm. "Hey, you didn't tell me Ashley Regada was Ashley Hamilton and she was married to Morgan Cameron."

"Why?"

"Well, she and her husband bought the mansion from my grandparents."

He was confused. "I'm not quite following you." He listened as Rowena told the story of Morgan buying their home for Ashley. How they'd kept it a secret until they were married.

"We lived in the home right up until they were married." Rowena paused. "Such a shame— a life lost too soon."

Ryne had heard about the death of Morgan Cameron. He'd been rushing back from New York after winning the last leg of the Grand Slam when he'd been killed in an accident. Adam had shared with him the heartfelt story of how Ashley and Tony Regada endured the grief of losing a husband and best friend on the way to finding their own happily ever after.

"Ashley's been through so much in her life. She lost the baby the night of Morgan's death and lived through such tragedy with the death of her father and the constant threats against her life. She's such a strong woman, someone we should all look up to."

He waited for Rowena to finish her thoughts when she abruptly jumped up.

"I thought we'd have after dinner drinks and dessert in the conservatory," she said. "Give me a minute to clear the table."

"Rowena, that meal was phenomenal. Let Jen and

me take charge of clearing the table."

Rowena approached him and laid her hand upon his arm. "You're our guest this evening. Sit right there and I'll be back." He raised his brow at Jen and quirked a smile, not wanting to create a scene. Jen also jumped from her seat, grabbing their plates as she followed her grandmother to the kitchen.

"That was quite a meal, Miles."

"Yes, my Ro loves to entertain." He stood and motioned for Ryne to follow him. "Ro'll know where to find us." Miles led him through a set of French doors into the conservatory. He immediately fell in love with the glassed-in room. His eyes were drawn to the ceiling that was encased in glass. He could image sitting in the darkness, in the comfort of this room, looking out the roof. He was certain they'd be able to stargaze and watch the Perseid Meteor shower along with the Northern lights.

"I always thought conservatories were mainly found in botanical gardens."

"You definitely see them there, but they are becoming popular in homes. Outside of the tennis court, this is my favorite room in the house. I love to relax in here, especially at night when I can stargaze and not have to worry about the cold weather."

Miles took a seat on the rattan couch and motioned for Ryne to join him. He was taken aback when Miles leaned over and whispered, "Don't mind Ro. She's just looking out for our Jennifer. Someone needs to."

He laughed at her grandfather. "That was definitely an inquisition I faced."

"Yep, it was. She loves that girl something fierce

and worries constantly about her. After her parents died, she tried to convince her to move in with us, but Jennifer was adamant about living in her home. I've got to hand it to my granddaughter. She's got spunk and does her best to keep up a front for us, but I know that she still suffers from losing her mother and father." Miles stopped and shook his head. "Her life changed forever that evening. With their loss and then the decision to not follow her father into the business... I often wonder if she made the wrong choice. When I think back on those days, I almost believe she should have taken some time out and not gone to school."

"I would think going to school was good for her. It got her out."

"You're right, it did, but it also convinced her to give up on her dreams. My son was a world class photographer. He had an eye and Jennifer was just like him. I often wonder where she'd be if she followed her heart, took over the business, and did what she loved best. Don't get me wrong, I know how well-loved she is as a teacher, but I just don't get the feeling it's where her heart is these days. It's just a feeling this old man has, but I've seen the light wane in her eyes as she talks about Lakeview. Her passion isn't what it once was."

Ryne listened intently and realized how in tune he was to her. Maybe it was time for her to make the change and follow her heart. He made a mental note to take her to his special place on the ranch. There he hoped to have that conversation with her and convince her to take a chance and follow her dreams.

He was pulled from his thoughts when he heard Rowena calling out. "Who wants coffee? Or would you rather have something stronger?"

"I think that was meant for you, son. Would you care for an after-dinner liqueur? You just might need it." He was referring to his wife and her incessant questioning.

"Coffee's just fine."

"Are you sure about that? She may not be through with her questions for the evening." Miles snickered.

"Don't worry about me. I'm up to the challenge."

They enjoyed a luscious cheesecake that Rowena had made from scratch. "That was some cheesecake. Best I've ever had."

"Thank you, Ryne. It was nothing. I love making them, and I always have one in the freezer for special occasions. Do you have plans for your stay with your parents?"

He caught Jen's eye as her grandmother started back in with him. He knew she was just making idle conversation. "I think we're just going to take it easy. I haven't been home in some time, and all of my family will be there. I hope we don't overwhelm Jen. My family can be a bit much at times."

"I can imagine, with five boys," Miles said. "I guess it's all about hockey?"

"Miles, to answer your question, this time of year it's all about the ranch. My parents own a cattle ranch, so when I'm home I'm usually on horseback, helping out with mending fences, taking care of the cattle, whatever's necessary."

"Huh. That sounds like a tough job."

"It can be, but I really enjoy it. I miss riding through the hills. When I get on horseback, a sense of calm overcomes me. It's just so peaceful out there. It's quiet. I can't explain it, but I love it. I feel like I leave all my troubles behind. We have a stream that runs through the ranch, and my dad's worked with rangeland specialists to insure that we maintain the land. He's planted various shrubs, grasses, wild-flowers...When the flowers are in bloom it's a sight to see. The hillsides are an array of color. Beautiful is all I can say."

"Kind of like driving through South Dakota when the sunflowers are all in bloom. It's a beautiful sight."

"That it is, Rowena. I hope some of the flowers are blooming when we're there. Quite a few of the varieties bloom in June, so I know Jen would do them justice with her camera lens."

"I'm not so sure about that," Jen said.

"I am. You've got an eye, that's for sure." Turning towards Rowena, he said, "You should see some of the photos of the team she's taken for the school's fundraiser. There's this one where she's caught the spray of ice flying through the air."

"Well," Rowena said, "that doesn't surprise me in the least. Her father was one hell of a photographer, and she certainly has his skills."

"Grandmother."

"It's true, dear and I wish you hadn't given up that dream." He caught a sadness flash across her face, and that's when he decided to call it a night. It was getting late and he knew they'd have an even later evening the following day. He waited a moment before he stifled a yawn.

"It's getting late and I need to call for a car. I'm sure it'll be at least an hour before one arrives." He retreated from the room, leaving Jen and her grandparents alone. After Rowena's comment, he knew he needed to get her out of there.

It had been an enlightening evening to say the least. He hadn't been prepared for Rowena and her questions, but as he replayed the night, he believed she'd been interviewing him— much like Jen's father would have been assessing him. He hoped he passed the test because Jen meant the world to him.

Before his thoughts could linger any further, he heard the reservationist asking for his location. Their car would be there shortly, so he hurried towards the conservatory, and that's when he heard Rowena's voice.

"My dear, I think you've got a winner there. He's so polite even when I pushed him with all of my questions."

"That he is."

"And my dear, he is so in love with you. I can tell those things, you know." He heard Miles chuckling at his wife's words. "With the way he looks at you. It's priceless, the emotion I see in him. I approve."

"Ro, you mean we approve. You have our blessings, dear, for whatever may come of this relationship. I can tell he has your best interests at heart."

"That he does, Grandfather. Ryne means the world to me, and thank you for approving of him. I can't wait to meet his family. If they are anything like he is…"

"Then they'll be keepers."

He heard a pause in the conversation, and he called out before entering the room so they'd be sure and not say anything they wouldn't want him to hear. "The car should be here in about ten minutes. A driver was in the area."

"That fast, huh?"

"It's better than waiting hours."

"You're right." She reached for her grandmother's hand. "Thank you for a lovely evening. I don't think we'll have a chance to come by again before we leave. Our plane takes off pretty early Sunday morning."

"That's fine, dear. Just stay in touch like you always do."

"You don't have to worry about that."

Just as they stood, the doorbell rang, signifying their car had arrived. Rowena pulled Jen into her arms.

"I love you, Grandmother."

"Not as much as I love you, dear. Thank you for coming this evening."

While Jen and Rowena were saying their good-byes, Miles approached Ryne with an outstretched hand. "It was good to meet you, Ryne. Take care of our granddaughter."

"Don't you worry, sir, I will," he said shaking his hand.

Then Rowena approached him with outstretched arms. "Come here, you." She wrapped her arms around him. "You're good for my girl." In a stage whisper she said into his ear, "I know you love her. I can see it in your eyes." He nodded and out of the corner of his eye saw Jen depart the room. "Help her find her way. I think she's been lost for a long time and I know you're the one to point her in the right direction. Back to the life she once knew and walked away from." Pulling away from him she added, "She loves you too, so what are you going to do about it?"

He pulled in his lips, preventing his smile and shook his head. Her grandmother was a piece of work who had her granddaughter's best interests at heart. "I'm not quite sure yet, but you will definitely be one of the first to know."

She slapped at his arm.

"We'd better be." And with that the doorbell rang again.

"We'd better head on out of here before we lose our driver. It was definitely nice meeting both of you."

Ryne met up with Jen. Reaching for her hand, he laced their fingers and walked out the door. All in all, it had been a good evening. Questions were asked and answered and a future with her had been approved. When the time came for him to ask her the all-important question, he had no doubts that he'd receive the approval from both sets of grandparents.

Chapter Nineteen

RYNE WOKE THE NEXT MORNING thinking about the night before. He made his way to the kitchenette where he made himself a horrid cup of coffee. He needed half-way decent coffee, so he phoned room service where he ordered two pots and an array of breakfast rolls.

Room service was quick and his first sip was a jolt to his system, and he instantly felt better. He sat down to read the complimentary paper, but he pushed it aside. He couldn't concentrate on the latest box office scores as his mind traveled back to dinner. Even though Rowena asked a boat load of questions, he truly loved Jen's grandparents and left their home feeling accepted.

He recognized their concern over Jen's career and would address it when he spoke with her. In his mind, he could picture the pond where he planned to hold their conversation. It was somewhat removed from the house. In fact, when he thought about it, he couldn't remember how they cleared the snow when they'd played pick-up hockey. That's when he remembered the old tractor his father had retrofitted with a snow blade. *How could I forget that?* Memories of those good times flashed before him, and he didn't realize she'd entered the room until he felt her hair brush his neck as she leaned over his back, placing a kiss along his neck.

"Good morning," she murmured. "Did you sleep well?"

Sleep. How could I sleep when a million and one things were running through my head? "Slept like a log. What about you?"

"I think I had a little too much wine last night."

"Headache?" he asked, turning to pull her onto his lap. She nodded. "Sit tight. I'll get you something for it." He set her in his seat then rushed to his room to retrieve the pain reliever. He returned with a glass of cold water. "Here you go," he said as he dropped two pills into her hand. "I think we should take it easy today. I expect another late night."

Nodding her head, she said. "I would assume so." She reached for his cup of coffee and took a sip. "This is so good."

"It is, especially since you're drinking mine." She raised her brow at his comment. "Don't worry, I have plenty." He pointed to the two huge carafes. "I needed it myself this morning. I guess your grandparents got to me a little more than I thought. I woke up feeling like I'd been run over by a train."

"They can do that to you, especially Grandma Rowena. See, I told you it wasn't going to be easy."

"It definitely wasn't a walk in the park, but I understand why they asked so many questions. They were vetting me, and in the end, I think I passed the test, at least I hope I did."

"You more than passed. I think my grandmother's in love with you."

"I wouldn't go that far, but I think I'm on the right side of the tracks."

She pulled him close and nuzzled his chest.

"Comfortable?" he asked.

"Um hmm. I could sit like this the remainder of the day. Wrapped in your arms I feel so protected." She raised her head, kissing his chin. "So loved."

Before he could say another word, his phone rang. Reaching for it, he saw Philippe's name pop up on the screen. "I've got to get this, okay?"

"Yeah," she climbed off his lap as he answered the call and returned to her room to give him privacy for his conversation.

"Philippe, what's up?" It wasn't unusual for him to call, but Ryne was surprised especially with his pending arrival the next day. He shook his head as he listened. His brother was out of sorts, rambling on and on about nothing in particular. After ten minutes without getting a word in edgewise, Ryne told him he needed to run. "Jen and I arrive on an early morning flight. We're flying out of Newark and should get there around noon. Can we talk then?" He heard his brother grumble a goodbye and the line went dead.

He was concerned about Philippe. Even though he'd had a record season for the Storm, he continued to carry his grief with him. Ryne didn't know how he handled the memories day in and day out. It had been five long years, and he knew his brother still hadn't gotten over the death of his wife. He and Annabelle had been returning from their honeymoon when a wrong way driver hit them head on, killing her instantly. Philippe had sustained lac-

erations and broken ribs. but for the most part he
came out unscathed. He hadn't been the same since
that fateful day. Ryne knew he was the shoulder his
brother leaned on when the memories became too
much.

He was glad he'd arranged their trip for this time
of year as Philippe's wedding anniversary was drawing near, and that brought the memories even closer.
He rarely spoke of Annabelle to anyone but Ryne.
Knowing he was his confidant brought them even
closer. He would definitely carve out some alone
time for them.

"What did your brother have to say?"

"Nothing much. He's just anxious for us to arrive."

"Really?"

"Yeah, he can't wait to meet you."

"I'm not buying that, but whatever."

"Now why would you question Philippe's desire
to meet the woman of my dreams?"

"Because he's a rough and tough defenseman, and
I think he couldn't care less about me."

"You're definitely wrong there." Changing the
subject, he said, "Let's eat, I'm starved."

After they finished their meal, Ryne pulled her to
the couch. "I have something for you."

"And what's that?"

Looking at his watch, he said, "You have a half
hour to get ready."

"Ready for what?"

"You have two appointments."

"I do?"

"Yep, the spa and the beauty salon."

"You didn't?"

"I did. So get ready. I want you to feel relaxed for tonight."

She wrapped her arms around him. "I can't believe you did this for me."

"It's a special night and I want you to..." His thought was interrupted by the ringing of his phone. He knew by the ringtone it was his mother. "Sorry, but I have to take this." He jumped up from the couch and headed straight for his bedroom where he closed the door.

He hated to walk away after sharing his special treat with her, but he feared what his mother wanted. "Hey there, Mom."

"Ryne, have you spoken with your brother?" No helloes, nothing. He knew it must be pretty bad if she didn't ask how he was.

"I just got off the phone with him."

"How do you think he sounded?"

"Just like he always does this time of year. He rambled on and on about nothing, and I had to hang-up. Mom, I plan on spending time with him while I'm home. His season ended too soon."

"It did."

"When he's on the ice, he's focused on the game and doesn't have time to think of her. Now, he's got endless weeks ahead before he returns to the team. He has too much time on his hands and nothing to really focus his attention on. Working on the ranch helps, but when he's alone on the range, I know his mind drifts back to their life together. It has to."

"Son, I wish there was more I could do."

"I think just being there for him when he needs an ear is what he needs. I keep hoping he'll seek a grief counselor. He tells me he's fine, but we all know he's not. Hopefully, our talk will help."

"He's lucky to have you in his corner, Ryne. You've been there for him ever since he arrived at the hospital after the accident."

"I'm glad I was there. Hey Mom, can we talk about this tomorrow?"

"Oh sure. I look forward to meeting Jennifer."

"I can't wait until she meets everyone. I know she's excited."

"I'm glad to hear that. I'll see you tomorrow."

After ending his call, he sat on the edge of his bed. *Philippe must be pretty bad if she called. What can I do that I haven't already done for him? One thing I know for sure is I can't bring Annabelle back.*

He didn't know how long he sat there when he heard Jen's knock. "Come in."

"Everything okay?" she said leaning into the door.

"Yeah, it was my mom." He could tell she didn't believe him. "She's worried about my brother."

"Which one?"

"Philippe."

"I hope he's alright."

"Yeah, me too, but enough of that. We have to get you off to your masseuse."

While Jen enjoyed her day, Ryne spent his time perusing the web, trying to find additional ways to help his brother. Their conversation from earlier bothered him more than normal. He needed to find a way, a way for Philippe to climb out of the hole he'd found himself in after Annabelle's death.

He was enthralled in reading an article on grief when he was startled by a hand on his shoulder.

"Oh, hey there honey, I didn't hear you come in."

"I know. What's that you're reading? I called your name several times, and you didn't hear."

She leaned over his shoulder. He attempted to minimize the window on his computer when she slapped her hand on his. "How to handle grief in a loved one," was splashed across the screen. Her hand trembled on his as she pulled away. He spun around and reached for her.

"Why are you reading that? Do you think I have a problem?"

"No, honey, I don't."

"Then, why are you reading an article on grief?"

He swiped his hand across his face and sighed. *How do I tell her? What do I tell her?* She pulled away and moved to the window. He noticed the tension in her back and shoulders. *So much for the massage.* He walked to her side and ran his hand down her back. Reaching for her hand, he led her to the couch and sat.

"Honey, I need to tell you something. Something about my brother. Something I wanted to keep from you as long as I could, but I realize that I can't, especially with your meeting him tomorrow."

She licked her lips before she spoke. "Ryne, come on now, it can't be that bad."

He shook his head, acknowledging her comment, but what he had to tell her was a nightmare. One that he'd had to endure for the last five years. One that his brother had lived with every day since that fateful night. He grasped her hands and held on for dear life. "I've needed to tell you this for some time, but I held off. In fact, I've tried to forget about this but I can't. It will never, ever go away..."

He jumped off the couch and began to pace. Running his hand through his hair, he didn't know where to begin.

"Just tell me."

He could see the look of panic on her face.

"Honey," he said as he kneeled in front of her. "It's not about us. I love you and I'd never do anything to hurt you."

"I know you love me and I love you, too. So please, tell me." In an almost pleading voice, "You can tell me anything, Ryne."

Breathing hard, he sat down beside her. She grasped his hand. "It's about Annabelle."

"Annabelle? Who's Annabelle?"

"Philippe's wife."

"I didn't know he was married."

"He's not. That is, any longer."

"You're talking in circles. I don't understand."

"I didn't want to tell you about her, but I need to, especially after the state of mind I think Philippe is currently in. I hope I'm wrong, but I need to prepare you."

"Okay."

"Philippe and Annabelle were married five years ago." He stopped and swallowed feeling the pulse of tension that throbbed in his cheek as he tried to keep his emotions in check. "They were high school sweethearts and so in love. I've never seen a couple so perfect. They were— so in tune to one another. She fit right in with the family." The memories flashed before his eyes. "It was a beautiful wedding. They were married on the ranch. It was a gorgeous day. The hillside was full of color. A day any couple would dream of for their wedding. He was happy, so happy. Happier than I'd ever seen him."

Her hand tightened in his as he shared with her that awful night just two weeks later. "I can still remember what I was doing when I received the call. I'd just come off the range after taking a ride to watch the sunset glow off the pond, the end to a gorgeous day. The colors were vivid and lingered in the sky well after sunset. I'd just sat down when my cell phone rang. The caller ID read Philippe. I answered kind of flippantly, but the voice I heard wasn't my brother's. It was someone from the Calgary Police Service. Philippe had thrown his phone at the officer and asked him to phone me. He and Annabelle had been in an accident on the way home from their honeymoon." He heard her gasp and immediately saw the tears form in her eyes.

"Ryne." He pulled in his lips and shook his head.

"They were hit by a wrong-way driver. Philippe couldn't react fast enough. Annabelle was killed on impact."

"Oh no," she cried out and flung herself into his arms. "I'm so sorry. And Philippe, was he injured?"

"He had a few lacerations and broken ribs but otherwise he was okay."

"But he isn't, is he?" He shook his head.

"No, he's not. I'm the only one he seeks comfort with. I was the one to meet the ambulance at the hospital. At the time, he didn't know about Annabelle. He'd been able to exit the vehicle but it took a lot of work to get her out. When he first saw me, he screamed at me to find her. She needed him.

I've never, ever seen my brother so upset. He was frightened for his wife and needed to get to her."

He stood. "I can still see the look on the paramedic's face as Philippe screamed for her. I knew right then and there she had died." He walked over to the mini-fridge and grabbed a bottle of water. Taking a swallow, "I was there when they told him. I can still feel the pain when he learned of Annabelle's death. He lay there, in his own physical pain, sobbing uncontrollably. I remember holding him and feeling his tears as they soaked my shirt. Never have I seen a person so heartbroken. Here a strong defenseman, who never shied away from his fiercest of competitors, lay in a bundle of tears. He was broken to the core, and I'm afraid he remains there to this today. He puts on a good front, but I know he constantly relives that night."

He drew in his lips again, closed his eyes and shook his head. "Losing his heart and the woman of his dreams has forever changed him. I worry about him. Outside of hockey, he's withdrawn and far from the fun-loving man he once was. I don't know what to do to help him."

"I do." He looked at her quizzically. "Let me talk to him."

"I can't let you do that."

"Why? Who would know better than I what he's going through? I lost my parents, but he lost his wife."

"You'd do that for him, for me? You don't even know him."

"But I know you and I can see how this is tearing you up. I can only imagine what he's going through. He lost the love of his life. The one person he'd committed to sharing the rest of his life with. The one person with whom he'd make a family." She went into his arms as his tears began to fall. "I want to help him, or at least try. I've been there and I still am there. I have my good and bad days. I can relate to him, you can't. No one in your family can. So please, let me."

He nodded into her shoulder and held onto her. He loved her more now than he did five minutes earlier. He knew how she still grieved and for her to put all of that out there to help his brother— she was one hell of a woman, and he was lucky to have her in his life.

They sat wrapped in one another's arms until he felt her pull away. "I need to start getting ready if we're going to make the party." As she stood, she remained holding his hand. "Thank you for sharing their story with me."

"I don't want to burden you with his grief."

"You're not. I want to help him. I just hope he'll let me." She leaned over and kissed his cheek. "Come on now, you know how I hate to be late."

He shook his head. "Well?"

"I know all too well. Isn't that how we met in the first place?"

She slapped at his arm. "You need to let that go."

"How can I when that's the moment I fell in love with you?"

"I guess you can't." She laughed as she headed off to her room. He would never let her forget their initial meeting on the Generals' parking lot had forever changed their lives.

As he dressed, he decided he wasn't going to let Philippe's troubles ruin his night. Tonight was about introducing Jen to his world. He took a quick shower, shaved, and donned his tux all the while thinking about what she'd offered to do for him and his family. He knew if anyone would be able to get through to his brother it would be her. Before exiting the room, he reached into the side-pocket of his carryon. He'd wanted tonight to be special.

Sliding the box from his bag, he made his way to the sitting area where she was waiting. One look at her took his breath away. "You look stunning." She'd dressed in a seafoam green dress that hugged her breasts. It was simple, yet elegant. Sequins ran throughout and sparkled as she moved. He caught the back of her dress as she reached for her bag. The sequined lace draped against her back showed a little more skin than he liked. She wore simple diamond stud earrings but no necklace. He knew she'd love his gift as it would add a lovely accessory to her look.

He approached her with a grin on his face. "What?"

"You take my breath away." He reached into his pocket and pulled out the slim box he'd hidden there. "For you."

"What's this?"

"Open it and you'll see."

"You didn't need to get me anything."

"Will you stop it and just open the box?"

"Okay, okay." He watched her face as she slowly removed the jeweler's box. She looked up and gnawed on her lower lip as she flipped open the lid. "Oh Ryne, it's beautiful."

"Here let me help you." He pulled the necklace from the box and swept her hair off her shoulder. He fastened the diamond studded necklace in place; then kissed her shoulder. She lifted the bauble to inspect it. "I can't believe you did this. It's gorgeous. Thank you so much." She spun and put her arms around him.

He placed his hands on either side of her face and rested his forehead against hers. "You're welcome." He brushed his lips against her forehead and pulled away. "Let's go, we can't be late."

"No, we can't."

The party was being held in the second-floor ballroom so they didn't have far to go. He was excited to introduce her to Adam and everyone at Black Gold. If he had his way, she'd be by his side for a long time to come.

They walked through the ballroom doors and were immediately greeted by Adam. He thrust his hand out, welcoming his star player. "Glad you could make it."

"Wouldn't miss it. Adam, I'd like to introduce my girlfriend, Jennifer Steele."

"Finally, I get to meet the girl behind the smile." She looked at him strangely. "He hasn't wiped the smile from his face since you two met."

"I don't know about that."

"I do. Ryne's happier than he's been in a long, long time."

"Well, I'm glad to hear that."

Adam was interrupted by one of the hotel staff, so Ryne reached for her hand and led her towards the bar where he ordered them both a glass of wine.

Moments later, he heard her gasp. "What's wrong?"

"Nothing. There's Ashley. I need to see her." Ryne pressed his hand to her lower back and guided her over to the famous couple. Ashley's back was to her. She took one look at the man at her side and knew it was her husband. He had eyes only for her. He held her fingertips as they spoke to another couple. They approached the Regadas and Jen called out Ashley's name.

Ashley slowly turned and immediately recognized her. "Jen," she exclaimed as she pulled her into a tight embrace. "What are you doing here?"

"I'm with him." She nodded toward Ryne.

"I didn't know you were dating, Jen. Congratulations! I'm so excited to see you. It's been too long."

"It has." Ashley introduced her to her husband.

"How are your grandparents? I just love them. It's been a while since I've seen them. I think I scared them off. They didn't know Tony and I were together."

"They're doing well. I just saw their home for the first time."

"And?"

"I thought they were downsizing."

"They didn't?"

"Not unless you call downsizing a few less trees."

Ashley giggled as she listened to Jen describe in detail her grandparents' new home.

"All I got out of her was, 'I love to entertain.'"

"She does, that's for sure," said Ashley. They were interrupted by Adam who wanted them to take their seats. A special program highlighting both their tennis careers was scheduled before dinner and dancing.

Surprisingly, although most events of this nature dragged on, the evening flew by. Ryne suppressed a yawn and looked at his watch. He couldn't believe the time. It was almost one and they needed to rise early for their flight. Thankfully, the airport was less than a half hour drive. "I think we need to call it a night," he murmured in her ear as they took one last spin on the dance floor.

"I have to agree. I've really enjoyed meeting your friends. I wish we could stay longer."

He looked out across the ballroom. "Yeah, but I think everyone's calling it a night." They'd just said goodnight to Ashley and Tony and several of the partygoers had already left.

"We're one of the last to leave," she said as he pulled her closer.

"We are but at least we don't have far to go." As the song ended, he ushered her off the dance floor. They'd had a fun time albeit he knew his earlier conversation was still fresh on both their minds. Tomorrow, or better yet, today, was upon them. In a few short hours, she'd be meeting his family, and he couldn't wait.

Chapter Twenty

SHE WOKE WHEN THE AIRPLANE began its descent into Calgary. She was tired. They'd left their hotel shortly before four. By the time they returned to their room, it was almost two, and she decided to forego sleep and instead sleep on the plane.

Once awake, she sat with her eyes closed wrapped in Ryne's arms, and her head rested in the crook of his neck. She felt loved. She'd never felt this way before and never wanted the feeling to end. "We should be landing in the next twenty minutes or so," he whispered.

She didn't say a word, just nestled deeper into his embrace. A few minutes elapsed before she pulled away. Wiping the sleep from her eyes, she reached for his hand. "Were you able to rest?"

"Not really." She could tell by the look on his face that he'd been thinking of his brother. "I watched you sleep, though."

"Enlightening, I'm sure. I hope I didn't drool."

"Nope, you slept peacefully."

"That's nice to hear." Her thoughts were interrupted as the flight attendant moved about the cabin, cleaning away the empty cans, coffee cups, and what not. "How far of a drive is it to your parents'?"

"It all depends. I'd say about an hour or so."

"I can't wait to meet your family."

"I can't either. One thing's for sure, I don't think you'll get the grilling like I did with Rowena and Miles."

She chuckled. "They were pretty intense, that's for sure."

"They love you and want to make sure you're not involved with an ax murderer."

"Ax murderer?" She laughed. "Where did that come from?"

"First thing that entered my mind."

Hand-in-hand they left the plane and made their way to the luggage claim area. There, leaning against the wall, was Philippe. She noticed him first. "Hey, isn't that your brother?"

A shocked look crossed Ryne's face. She wasn't the least bit surprised when he pulled him into a one-armed embrace. Slapping him on the back, he asked, "What are you doing here? I rented a car."

"I thought you'd be exhausted after the party and your early morning flight, so I decided to meet you instead of worrying about you driving out to the ranch." She sensed Ryne's concern as he listened to his brother. She knew Philippe didn't want them to have an accident like he had and lose the brother that meant so much to him. She stayed back while they reconnected, then Ryne motioned to her.

She pasted a smile on her face even though she was exhausted and could barely function. She was excited to meet his family, especially Philippe, and hoped she could aid him in his recovery. "Phil, this is Jennifer Steele." He draped his arm around her. "Jen, my brother Philippe." She reached out, but instead of being the recipient of a handshake, she found herself pulled into a warm hug.

"It's nice to meet you, Philippe. I've heard so much about you."

"Not all good, I'm sure."

She giggled at his comment. "I haven't heard a bad thing other than the times you tried to out-maneuver Ryne on the pond behind your house. What was it, Ryne? He hip checked you into a snow bank."

"That was a long time ago, Jennifer. I think we got past that."

"Really now. What about your last game against the Generals? I was there and saw how you rammed your brother into the boards."

"I was showing him some brotherly love."

"That's what you call it," Ryne chimed in as he made his way to the luggage carousel to secure their bags.

"That's my story and I'm sticking with it. Here let me get that for you." Philippe took charge of her luggage, pulling it behind him while Ryne waited for his last bag.

"I'm thrilled that we're finally getting a chance to meet you. My mother is a nervous wreck."

"Nervous? Why would she be nervous?"

"Because my dear brother has never brought anyone home to the ranch. Consider yourself pretty special." She turned and caught Ryne's eye as he reached for his luggage.

"Well, he's pretty special to me too." She waited for Ryne to catch up and then followed Philippe.

Piling into his SUV, she took the back seat so the

brothers could have a chance to talk. She watched the countryside pass as they exited Calgary and made their way to the outskirts of town where she knew the ranch was located. It seemed like they drove forever before he slowed and took a right turn.

As they made their way down a dirt road, dust flew up all around, covering them in a fog of sorts. It was just as she felt with little to no sleep. He slowed the car as he approached some ruts. "We need to smooth this out while I'm home," said Ryne. "What have you been doing since the season ended? Catching flies?"

"I guess you could call it that," Philippe murmured as he drove on. She knew the anniversary of Annabelle's death was fast approaching and could only imagine the pain he must be enduring, reliving their wedding and her death. Five years of marriage was a milestone to celebrate, but unfortunately not in his case. Five years marked the beginning of his downward spiral that few knew of. Thankfully, he wasn't a drinker, according to his brother. He became reclusive and never shared his thoughts or feelings with anyone except Ryne. She hoped to be able to help him open up and begin to face his life without the love of his life. Time would tell, but deep in her heart she knew she could convince him to move on. Grief was an ugly animal and everyone handled it in their own way. Some were able to talk about their feelings while others shuffled them under the carpet and promised to face them another day; however, in many cases that day never came. It was often pushed further down the road as their recovery grew longer by the day, the year.

She was someone who knew what he was experiencing. She knew the rage she felt when she thought about her parents' accident. She knew what it was like to have your dreams crash right before your eyes, to have your world upended without notice. In the early days after their death, she'd survived, but barely, and to this day often wondered how. Some days she still missed them with every breath she took. She'd been lucky to have her grandparents by her side, but when she returned home, she often found herself rolled into a ball in a fit of tears. She questioned how she'd made it through the first few days, weeks, and, now, years.

She needed him to know that he wasn't alone in this world. He had his family and, most especially, Ryne whom he could talk to— to share his sense of loss with. This family wouldn't think any less of him— that's for sure. They were there to support him in the good times and the bad. He needed to understand that his support system wasn't going anywhere and that he should use it and not carry the burden of his loss solely on his shoulders. His family also lost an important member. She needed him to see that, but most importantly he needed to know he wasn't alone in his recovery.

They drove for what seemed like miles when Philippe slowed again and turned onto a paved drive. They passed through a massive set of gates and under a sign that read Storms Corner. She imagined that was a play on the team his father and now sons played for. They continued for what seemed like miles before she saw the roofline in the distance. They rounded a curve and came through a clearing, and there before her eyes stood Ryne's childhood home. It was gorgeous and massive; it had to be with housing seven children.

Philippe brought the car to a stop. Before anyone could utter a word, the front door flew open, and a woman dashed from the house. She guessed it was his mother by the way she ran towards the car waving her arms. She was tall and thin with dark hair that swept her shoulders. She was chockfull with energy and had a bright smile that filled her face. "That's Mom," he uttered as he opened the door.

"Ryne, dear, you made it safely."

"That we did. We have our driver here to thank for that." Jen wasn't the least bit surprised to watch the scene unfold before her eyes. His mother pulled him into her arms. Jen knew Ryne hadn't been home in some time, but the welcome he received was definitely something she wouldn't forget. It was like a long-lost child had returned to the fold.

She opened the car door and slowly stepped out, unsure what type of greeting she'd receive. She soon felt Philippe's hand on her arm as he led her to his mother. Ryne reached for her. With her back to his chest, he placed his hands on her shoulders. She felt her nerves lessen somewhat as he introduced her. "Mom, I'd like you to meet Jennifer Steele. Jen, my mom, Jacklynne." A broad smile crossed his mother's face. Jen could tell she was holding her excitement in, but that lasted for only a heartbeat.

His mother hesitated and then reached for Jen. Pulling her into a welcoming embrace, she said, "Finally, my dear. I'm so happy you were able to come to the ranch. We've been anxiously waiting to meet you." The embrace lasted all of ten seconds, but as his mother released her, she felt a sense of melancholy overcome her. She hadn't felt a mother's embrace in eight long years. Jacklynne wasn't her mother but she was Ryne's. Their first meeting was extremely special to her, and she knew she'd always remember it.

Jen looked back at Ryne as his mother wrapped her arm around her and led her into the house. In the initial moments, she felt accepted. She caught a satisfied expression on Ryne's face.

The next thing she was aware of, she was being led onto the back deck of the house where his father and siblings stood waiting. "We didn't want to overwhelm you at the door," Jacklynne said as she escorted her over to Ryne's father. "Jacques."

Jacklynne didn't get a chance to utter another word as Jen was pulled into a second welcoming embrace. "Jennifer, I am so happy to meet you. We all are." Jacques surprised her and kissed her cheek. "We've heard so much about you. It's been too long since our son told us he was dating you. I welcome you to our home." Jacques pulled away and led her towards his children.

She sought Ryne's eye and noticed how his mother was holding onto his arm. He winked at her and had a look of approval on his face as his father introduced her. She was consumed with emotion. Being an only child, she didn't know how to react. She hoped they accepted her as easily as his parents seemed to.

"Jennifer, or would you rather be called Jen," he asked.

"Either is fine with me."

"Good," he exclaimed as he smiled back at her. She realized Ryne had the same smile as his father. His eyes squinted somewhat as he smiled, and he had fine lines around his eyes too. "Jen, please meet Emma, she's our youngest." Emma was adorable as she didn't know whether to shake her hand or hug her, so instead of doing either she waved.

"Rafael is our middle child, and he plays for the Arizona Tide." He reached out and shook her hand. "Next here is Jules. Jules is a sophomore and attends Ryne's alma mater. He plays for UW."

"You're following in his footsteps."

"Trying," Jules shyly smiled.

"Olivia is our second youngest and is a sophomore in high school."

"It's a pleasure to meet you, Jen," she said as she pulled her into a hug. Jen smiled at his sister as she moved down the line.

"And last but not least is Ryne's twin, Etienne. He plays alongside Philippe for the Storm."

She caught herself as she looked into his eyes—the same exact eyes she'd stared into hundreds of times. He looked almost identical to Ryne. She really didn't know what hit her, he moved so quickly and pulled her into a hug. "Finally we meet— Ryne talks nonstop about you."

"Hey there, brother, don't get too close to my girl." Everyone laughed at Ryne's comment as he made his way to her side. She reached for him and slipped her arm around his waist.

"I'm thrilled to meet all of you. I hope there isn't a test after this." Everyone roared with laughter.

Ryne leaned over and kissed her cheek. "I think the only names I'll probably get correctly are Philippe's and of course Etienne's since you look exactly alike." She turned back to his mother. "How did you tell them apart?"

"It's my little secret." She chuckled and reached for Jen's hand. "I'm sure you're hungry. Follow me and we'll have lunch." She clasped her hand and they ambled back into the house. Surprisingly no one followed. She wasn't sure what their delay was.

"Jen, I just want to say one thing. You must be a very special person to my Ryne. He's never brought anyone home before. In fact, outside of high school, I've never met any of his girlfriends. I'm not going to inundate you with questions, but what I would like to do while you're here is have a nice chat. I want to get to know you, and I want you to know me."

"Thank you," she said as she hugged his mother. "That means an awfully lot to me."

Before she knew it, the sun was setting on her first day on the ranch. After lunch, Ryne had forced her to take a nap. He led her upstairs to the guest room. Philippe had already delivered her luggage there. "If you need me, I'm right across the hall. I think I'll take a nap too. I don't think I slept a minute on the plane."

She reached up and caressed his face. "You do look tired."

"Thanks.'

"I'm not going to lie, you do." She leaned up and kissed him. "Just for the record, I love your family. I feel so welcomed."

"No inquisition for you."

"Thankfully, no." She tried to suppress a yawn.

"Go to bed and I'll see you in a little while." She hugged him one last time and closed the door. *So far, so good. I'm really liking his family.*

She took a short nap and when she awakened, the sun sat low on the horizon. It was much later than she expected. She jumped from bed, ran her fingers through her hair, and rushed from her room right into Ryne's arms.

"I was just coming to check on you. I was getting worried. It's almost eight."

"Eight at night?" He nodded. "I slept a lot longer than I intended." She reached up and smoothed her hand along his jaw. "What about you, did you get any sleep?" She noticed the dark circles under his eyes but decided not to comment.

"I tried, but I couldn't, so instead I went for a ride with Philippe."

"And?"

"He's doing okay."

"I still want to talk to him."

"I know and I hope that you'll find the right time and place. Come on, I'd like to show you around a little. Mom's planning a late dinner."

"I hope not on account of me."

"No, we tend to eat late during the summer months since daylight is on our side." He grabbed ahold of her hand and led her down the stairs and out the back door.

"Don't we need to tell your mom we're leaving?"

"Nah, I already told her." He pulled her close as he led her down a path behind the house. She was in awe of the beauty that surrounded her. The grasses blew in the light breeze. They'd walked for about fifteen minutes when they came upon the pond he'd told her about.

"So this is where you learned that infamous slap shot of yours?"

"I wouldn't call it infamous, but yeah. We came out here every day after school and spent a good part of our weekends when we weren't practicing or playing a game. Fun times."

"I would think so." He led her towards a bench that sat beside the water's edge. Several Canada geese swam across the water, causing a beautiful ripple as the last rays of sun gleamed across it. She took a deep breath of the fresh air.

"It's beautiful here. I can see why you love it so."

"I do and I miss it when I'm not here."

"How often do you come home?"

"Not as often as I like. I always spend several weeks during the summer helping out. With training and all, it's difficult, but I work it in. Sometimes during the holidays, we have a stretch of off games and we get time to be with our families. I always take advantage of it although oftentimes Philippe, Etienne, and Rafael may not be here. Right now, Jules gets time off, but when he reaches the NHL, my mom will have one less mouth to feed during that time."

"I'm sure she misses all of you being together. You seem pretty close."

"We are close. We joke around a lot, but at the end of the day we're all here for one another. I know it's hard on my mom because she wants us all home during the holidays, but oftentimes it's just not meant to be."

She reached for his hand. "What have you told your parents about me?"

"What do you mean?"

"Do they know about my parents?"

"No, I haven't told them. We've never really talked in detail about us. I've told them about the fundraiser and that you're a teacher, but other than that I didn't think it was necessary."

"Aren't they curious about my upbringing?"

"If they are, they'll ask. I wouldn't worry about it. When the time is right they'll know." She rested her head on his shoulder. "Tomorrow I'd like to take you for ride if you're up for it."

"That sounds nice. I'll bring my camera."

They sat in quiet, enjoying the last rays of light as the sun drifted off the horizon. He tipped his head at her. "I guess we should go back. I'm sure dinner's about ready."

Arm-in-arm, they walked back to the house. She definitely could get used to this setting. It was so quiet and peaceful. She knew she could get lost with her camera in the beauty that surrounded her.

The next day it rained. So instead of their horse-back ride, they watched a marathon of movies. Jacklynne kept them all supplied with popcorn, and at the end of the day Jen felt more a part of the family. They'd accepted her with open arms and the more she was around them, the more she learned.

Emma, being the baby of the family, was just that— the baby. She was pretty much spoiled and got everything and anything she wanted. Jen came to that conclusion when it came to choosing what they wanted to watch. After much conversation, they agreed to a Scooby-Doo marathon. It brought the adults in the room back to their childhood and everyone, including Philippe, seemed to enjoy it.

After a while, they switched on the NHL channel and watched a replay of the Stanley Cup finals. Even though they knew the outcome, everyone got into the action including Jacklynne. She was a huge hockey fan. After driving the boys around for practices and games, she wasn't tired of the sport. She thrived on it and relished in the start of the new season.

At dinner, the conversation shifted to Ryne. "Son, how's the rehab going?"

She'd been holding his hand under the dinner table and felt the tension as he squeezed it harder than he intended. When she whimpered, he realized how tightly he was holding it and released it. Instead he placed his hand on her thigh. It didn't matter if they were holding hands or not, she knew Jacques had hit a sore spot. She'd known he was still having issues with his hip, and he definitely didn't like discussing it.

"It's coming along, Dad."

"What does that mean?"

"Just what I said. It's a work in process."

"What do the doctors say?" He remained quiet. "Ryne?"

"I haven't told them." He pushed his chair back from the table and with it removed his hand from her leg. "I have more good days than bad. I guess my hip's just slower to recover this time. You know,

I am getting older."

She could tell by the look on Jacques' face that he wasn't happy with his son's answer but knew not to press it further. Ryne had a little more than three months until training camp started. She hoped he'd get it under control by then.

That evening the boys played cards while the girls decided to watch a chick flick. As she watched the movie, she realized how easily she fit into his family. The thought took her breath away momentarily as she wished she'd have had this time with her mom. She would have loved Ryne and his family, most especially Jacklynne.

Their time sped by and each and every day she grew closer to everyone. On the Friday before they were scheduled to return home, the boys rode out to help their father with the cattle while Olivia and Emma went to see a movie. Jen and Jacklynne were alone in the house, and that's when his mom suggested they sit on the back porch and enjoy the afternoon.

It was a pleasant day. The sun was out and the temperature was perfect. Jacklynne poured them both a glass of iced tea, and they watched the horses graze. She was a tad bit nervous, unsure what his mother wanted to discuss, but she also knew that their conversation would be nothing like the one Ryne had endured with her grandparents.

"I love this time of day. I often come out on the porch and either read or needlepoint. I use it as my down time before I have to worry about dinner or run the girls somewhere."

"I can't imagine what life was like carting the boys

around for hockey practice and then adding games on top of it. You must have been going in all directions. And you did it all by yourself when Jacques was still playing."

"I did and I loved every minute of it. Look at where my children are today. Four of the five boys are in the NHL with the fifth heading there in the coming years. The girls are doing well. I'm so proud of them." She sighed. "I'll admit it was hectic at times, but it meant everything to me to see my children as they advanced. I watched them go from barely able to stand on skates to launching a hundred-plus mile an hour slap shot. Have you seen Ryne's shot?"

"I have. I have season tickets to the Generals' games. My dad's best friend is the owner."

"Ed something, right?"

"Yeah, Ed Talent. He's like a dad to me."

"Speaking of parents, you haven't told me their names or anything about them."

Ta da…The question. She knew it was only a matter of time. She averted her eyes and swallowed deeply. She didn't think she'd have such a problem telling her that her parents were dead and had been for eight long years. She's been thinking of them a lot since learning of Annabelle's death. But she was wrong. Tears swelled in her eyes. She tried to stop them but she couldn't. One fell and then the next. She swiped at them but they wouldn't stop falling. The next thing she was aware of, she was being pulled into his mother's arms. "Honey, oh please, talk to me. What's the matter?" She felt Jacklynne's hand running up and down her back as she tried to soothe her, from what she didn't know.

Finally, after a few minutes, the tears waned and Jen pulled away. "Jacklynne, my parents are both dead. They died the night of my high school graduation."

"Oh no, honey. I'm so sorry." Jacklynne pulled her back into her arms and held her then eased back and brushed the hair from Jen's eyes. "Would you like to talk about it? It's okay if you don't."

She took a few moments to calm herself and nodded. "It's been eight years. They were on the way to my graduation and were involved in a car accident. I had gone ahead for pictures and wasn't in the car with them."

"Oh sweetie, I'm so sorry."

"Thanks," she murmured. "I appreciate it. I'm an only child, and I have my grandparents. They're the only family I have left living."

"I'm sure you have friends and colleagues from school."

"I do but it's just not the same. My dad was a well-known photographer, and I was going to follow him into the business— take it over when he retired. That all changed when he died."

"Surely you can't walk away from that kind of passion. From what my son tells me, you have an eye. He's amazed with your photographs. Since time has passed, do you think you might want to try again? Maybe take that chance on the career you gave up on?"

She reached for her glass and took a long swallow. "I've thought about it a lot lately. My boss has asked me and Ryne to head up the school fundraiser."

"I heard about that."

"Part of the fundraiser is a gallery showing of my work. He was insistent on me taking pictures of the Generals' players and various other athletes in the area. He thinks we'll raise a lot of money off my photographs."

"Ryne believes you will. You need to have faith in yourself, your abilities. What's it going to cost you? Did you ever think about taking a sabbatical from teaching? I'm sure your boss would hold open your position for you. If it didn't work out, you could go back to teaching. It's just a thought."

"One I've been having a lot of lately. Except I wasn't thinking about going down the sabbatical route. I was just going to quit. Open a studio and try to make a go of it. I have all of my dad's contacts."

"Honey, why don't you give it a go?"

"Because I'm scared. Scared of failing."

"If you're as good as Ryne says, you won't fail. You'll shine."

"Thank you for your support. I hope to make a decision after the fundraiser. I want Johnston, my boss, to have ample time to find a replacement. I'd finish out the school year, but I don't want my quitting to be a burden on him. He's been there for me, and I don't want to disappoint him."

"I don't think you'll be disappointing him. In fact, you're doing him a favor by telling him early."

"I realize that."

"Jen, thank you."

"For what?"

"For telling me about your parents. When Ryne

said he was coming to visit and told me he was bringing you, I decided I wasn't going to be the mother from hell. I wasn't going to inundate you with questions. I wanted to get to know you in our own time and place. I've enjoyed your stay and I hope you'll return—of course, with my son."

"I'd like that too." She was pulled into a loving embrace.

"No matter what happens with you and my son, I want you to know that I'll always be there for you. Call me anytime."

"Thank you. I appreciate your saying that." Before she could add to her comments, they heard the boys. Etienne was jabbering at Ryne about something. She watched as his mother took in her sons. She saw the love splashed across her face. Jacklynne was a remarkable woman, and Jen appreciated how she opened her arms and took her into her family. She hoped that she'd stay there and one day become a part of it.

Chapter Twenty-One

SATURDAY MORNING THEY WENT FOR a ride. She hadn't been on horseback in years and wasn't looking forward to the soreness, but she wanted to see the parts of the ranch she hadn't had the chance to explore.

They saddled up and headed out after breakfast. Ryne expertly maneuvered them along the trails. She'd brought her camera and clicked away as they rode through the tall grasses and flowers. In the distance, she was able to frame a cow standing amidst the grasses that were swaying in the gentle breeze. She took frame after frame as they rode along.

They came upon a copse of trees and saw a hawk hanging precariously from one of its upper branches. She zoomed in and caught what appeared to be a mouse clasped in its beak. Clicking away, she caught the eye of the bird as though it were looking directly at her through the lens of the camera.

The sky was bluer than blue with cirrocumulus clouds swirling above. She knew the clouds alone would greatly impact the depth of her shots. Ryne stopped and she clicked a picture of his back, tall grasses surrounded him and his horse with the blue skies above, adding to the element of the photo. She thought she'd title it: A cowboy making the rounds.

They rode for almost an hour before he stopped at a nearby stream. He jumped off his horse and helped her down. "I think the horses need a break." He led them to the stream so they could drink the cool waters.

She made her way to a large rock that sat along the bank. She eased herself down as her muscles began to stiffen up. "Sore?"

"A little. It's been a long time since I've ridden."

"When we get back, I'll fix you up. My mom's got some ointment you can apply." He joined her on the rock and stretched his arm behind her. "Lean on my arm." She leaned against him as they watched the water swirl around the larger stones in the stream.

"It's an absolutely gorgeous day out here. I hate to go home tomorrow."

"I know, but you need to get back, and I have to ramp up my training."

"Speaking of training, and please be honest with me, how is your hip? I've noticed you flinch on occasion, and I can't believe riding a horse is helping much."

"Actually, it's improved since we've been here. Don't ask me why, but it has." He leaned over her shoulder, looking her in the eyes, "I promise to have it checked out if it keeps acting up. I don't want to lose my career over something stupid like this."

"You took a hard hit. It wasn't a stupid injury."

"Yeah, well I probably could have prevented it somehow." He kissed her cheek and moved. He straddled her from behind so she could lean against his chest. "Better?"

"Much."

She seemed relaxed as he ran his hand up and down her arm trying to find the words that he wanted to say. He'd thought about her career often since they'd been traveling and believed now was the time to discuss it. "Did you get many photos today? I heard you clicking away."

"I got a few. Actually, some good ones, I think."

"I'll have to bring you out here during the winter. If you think it's beautiful now, wait until you see the ranch covered in snow."

"Maybe one day I'll see it."

"Not maybe, I'm sure you will." He pulled her closer and nuzzled her cheek. "Honey, you know how much I love you."

"I love you too."

"Then please listen to what I have to say, okay? Don't judge me. I want you to know that I'm looking out for your best interests."

She tentatively uttered, "Okay."

He wasn't sure where to begin so he stated the obvious. "What I've noticed is the smile on your face, the gleam of your eyes, and the sense of calm you exude when you have your camera in hand. You're happy, at peace. You're in a world all of your own, in a zone where no one and nothing seems to bother you. You're at your happiest." She nodded as she listened.

"Then, when I see you at school, you're tense, unsettled. You don't seem to smile, and when you do it doesn't show through to your eyes. You seem unhappy— like you're just going through the motions to make it through the day. I know you're one hell of a teacher, but in all honesty, I don't think you're happy teaching. I know you love the children, but where I see you the happiest is behind the lens of a camera. I've seen such a change in you in the little time I've known you. I think you should consider returning full time to photography. Open that studio and reclaim the dreams you had before your dad died. I believe it's where your heart is."

The entire time he spoke she never said a word. He wasn't sure if she was still listening. He leaned up and noticed the stream of tears falling from her eyes.

"Hey, I didn't mean for you to cry. I just wanted you to know what I saw. I want you happy and not sad. So please stop crying."

She turned in his arms and placed her hands on either side of his face. Smiling at him through her tears, she told him what she'd been contemplating.

"Did you speak with your mom?"

"No, why? Should I have?"

"No, forget about it." She brushed aside her tears, "You know me too well. I've been having those same thoughts of late myself. Since Johnston asked me to have a showing, I've felt renewed and more at peace. I can't deny that I've had my days, more so of late, thinking about my parents, what my life may have looked like if they hadn't died. Then, I contemplate what my future could be. You? Your family? Photography? My life seems more enriched with you in it. I love your family; they've made me feel so at home— like I'm already one of them. And, yes, photography has been a big part of my life— a life I don't know how I lived without for so long.

"I've decided to see how the gallery showing goes. If I do well and my photographs are accepted, then I've decided that I'm going to take that chance. I'm going to resign my position at Lakeview at the end of the school year and open a studio."

"Oh honey, that's fabulous news. I'm so proud of you." He leaned in and kissed her. "Now, one more thing."

"What's that," she said dejectedly.

"I think you should add sports photography to your arsenal. The images you've taken of the players on the ice are remarkable. I still can't get over the picture of Derrick and the ice spraying up all around him. That'll catch a huge price, I'm sure of it."

"Glad you liked it."

"No, seriously, you need to think about it. What-ever you decide, I'll support you one hundred and ten percent. You've got the talent, now all you need to do is showcase it."

He felt her relax. She rested her head against his chest as they sat watching the stream flow in front of them. In the distance they heard the mooing of the cattle and the whinnying of their horses. Life was good and he was ever thankful that he got through that conversation. He hadn't been sure how she'd take his remarks and instead was pleasantly surprised. He wasn't sure what to make of the comment she made about his mother. He made a mental note to speak with her when they returned to the house.

When his stomach began to rumble, he noticed the time. "Hungry?"

"I am."

"Let's head back. I'm starved." He slid off the rock and reached for her. Hand-in-hand they returned to the horses and in what seemed a much shorter trip, reached home. Jacklynne met them on the porch.

"I've been waiting on you to serve lunch."

"Sorry about that," Jen shyly said. "Ryne was showing me the parts of the ranch I hadn't seen yet. It's so beautiful out there. I can see where one could easily get lost in thought."

"Is that what happened?" She chuckled.

"In fact, it is, Mother." He watched as Jen hobbled into the house. "She's definitely going to be sore."

"I'll fix her up."

"I'm sure you will. Hey, Mom, I need to ask you a question."

"Sure, Son."

"Have you and Jen had a chat since she's been here?"

"We did. She told me about her parents. Poor dear, my heart went out to her. She was so young to have gone through that."

"Did you discuss anything else?" He watched as she contemplated his question. "Mom?"

"In fact, we did. We discussed her career. She told me what she'd given up, and I encouraged her to reclaim her dream. Something wrong with that?"

"No." He ran his hand across his jaw. "That's why we were running late. I was talking to her about the same thing, more or less."

"What did she say?"

"If the showing goes well, she's going to give it a shot." Sighing he said, "I'm glad she made that decision without my influence. I've wanted to talk to her about her career for weeks. I was waiting for the right time."

His mother approached, placing her hand on his forearm. "Honey, what did you see?"

"As soon as she picked up her camera, I saw a happy Jen. I told her how happy she seems with her camera in hand. She's more relaxed and comfortable with everything. I've seen her in the classroom and she's tense and doesn't smile. Like she doesn't want to be there and doesn't know how to leave. I realize she needed to take the time and grieve her parents. The memories may have been too close to her, and she probably did need to distance herself from it for a while, but now I see she needs it to survive. I feel she was living just to live. She wasn't enjoying her life. I've seen a huge difference in her since we came here. With camera in hand, she seems alive, and that's where I want her to be. Happy and loving life."

"Could you possibly be a part of why she's happy now?"

"Maybe, I don't know." He paused and smirked at his mother. "What I do know is I love her with every breath I take. I want to see her happy, and I'm going to do everything in my power to ensure that she is." His mom leaned in and kissed his cheek.

"Come on, everyone's waiting to eat."

He walked beside his mother and realized how lucky he was to have her in his life. She'd quickly recognized Jen's unhappiness, as that's what he liked to call it, and spoke to her about it. Just as a mother would. He was ever-thankful that their stay had gone as well as it had.

After they ate, Jacklynne checked on Jen who had gone to lie down for a bit. She knocked on her bedroom door and heard a whisper of a response. She cracked open the door and found her sprawled across the bed. "How are you honey?"

"I'm okay."

"Sore?"

"Yeah, I am. I haven't used those muscles in forever. Guess I'll have to work on strengthening my core for my next visit."

She approached her and sat down on the edge of the bed. "I brought you some ointment for the pain. I'll leave it here and you can apply it."

"Thanks."

She reached for her hand and patted it lightly. "Honey, I'm so glad we've had this time. I'd like to invite you for the holidays. I know this is a little premature, but I'd love it if you could return with or without Ryne. As far as I'm concerned, you're now a part of this family."

"I appreciate the offer, but I wouldn't feel right not coming with Ryne."

"Let's play it by ear. Maybe he'll have some time off and you can come together. I'd love to share the holidays with you."

Jacklynne watched the emotions cross her face. She smiled at first and then she saw the pain and the tears form. "Don't cry. Oh my, I didn't want to upset you with my invitation. I did it because I love you, sweetie, and I know you love my son.

I'd hoped to convey our acceptance of you into the family."

"You did. I apologize for being a tad bit emotional. I seem to have been that way all day." She played with the comforter, straightening it and patting her hand along the edges. She rolled her lips as she tried to contain her emotions. Looking back up at Jacklynne, "I've really enjoyed my stay. I love you and Jacques and everyone. From the moment I got out of the car, I felt like I was accepted into your family. I have to admit, I was a tad bit nervous meeting everyone. I didn't think I'd remember everyone's names— I mean, I knew the names but I wasn't sure I'd get the name with the face." She laughed at her statement.

"But then, I felt like I'd known you forever. I feel so comfortable here. I can be myself and not worry about saying or doing something wrong. And Ryne, he's been wonderful. When we first met, it wasn't under the best of circumstances, but he forgave me for almost running him down, and we've been together pretty much ever since."

"I heard about your first meeting. That will definitely be something your children will get a kick out of. Mom almost ran Dad down." She noticed the look on her face. "I'm sorry, honey. I don't want to imply anything."

"I understand but it is a pretty funny story." Jen sat up and swung her legs over the edge of the bed. Jacklynne slipped her arm around her. "I love him."

"Oh, honey, I know you do. I took one look at you when you got out of the car and I knew. He can't take his eyes off of you and vice versa."

"Sometimes I get this overwhelming feeling like it can't be. How can I be this lucky to have found him?"

"Sweetheart, I don't understand."

"Nothing good happens to me."

"Oh, honey," she pulled her into her arms. "Don't think like that."

"I can't help it. My parents died and I lost my way." She took a deep breath. "But now, I think I've found it. You and Ryne have seen something in me that I didn't. You both knew how photography impacted my life and how much I need it." She pulled away from her. "Jacklynne, you've filled my heart. I can't replace my mom, but..."

Jacklynne's eye rounded in alarm. "Oh, honey, no, I wouldn't expect you to."

"I just want to say that you are important to me. I know I can't see the future, and I definitely can't see whether Ryne and I will make it or not, but what I do know is you've become very important to me, and I hope we can stay in touch."

Jacklynne tucked a wisp of hair behind Jen's ear and patted her shoulder. "Sweetheart, of course."

They were interrupted by the ringing of the phone. "I should get that as we're the only ones in the house, and I always worry about the boys when they're on the range."

Jacklynne hurried from the room. Jen knew she could never replace her mother, but if she could, this woman would be the perfect choice. She groaned as she stood.

Instead of applying the ointment, Jen decided instead to take a walk. She wanted to visit the pond one more time before leaving. She wasn't exactly sure where Ryne was but that was okay. She felt at home and comfortable enough taking a stroll.

Her back seemed tight as she threw on her shoes and headed out the door. She hoped her walk loosened up her sore muscles. She wasn't sure where Jacklynne was, so she left her a note telling her she was heading out to the pond. Camera in hand she strolled down the trail. She stopped when she saw a rabbit nibbling on the grass. Next, she caught a butterfly as it fluttered through the flowers. *So beautiful. I'm going to miss it out here.*

She neared the pond and sat down on the bench that sat along the edge. She was lost in thought when a shadow crossed her path. Before she could react, a hand grasped her shoulder. "Hey, you okay?"

She turned her head and was surprised to see Philippe standing beside her. "Hi."

"Are you okay? I called your name several times and you didn't answer. I didn't want to frighten you."

"You didn't. I was daydreaming. I've fallen in love with the ranch. I don't want to go home."

"Then stay."

"I wish I could, but I can't. Ryne can't either."

"Yeah, I know, but I could hope."

She patted the seat next to her which he took. "I know how close you and Ryne are."

"He's my brother."

"I realize but it's more than that."

He hung his head low over his bent knees and shook it. He glanced at her out of the corner of his left eye. "You're right it is." He sat up and leaned his head back, closing his eyes. She reached for his hand. She could tell he fought his emotions; the muscle in his cheek throbbed as he clenched his teeth.

Except for the sound of a chirping bird, they sat in silence. She didn't know how to approach the subject. And then, she started. "Ryne told me about Annabelle. I'm sorry for your loss." As her words registered, his eyes flew open.

"He did?"

"Yeah, he did."

"It's been five years. Five long years. I don't know how I've survived without her. She was my life. I loved her since high school." She saw the flood of emotions as he warded off his tears. "I never imagined my life without her. I still can't."

"I understand."

"How can you? You're not married. You didn't lose someone close to you."

"That's where you're wrong. I did. I lost both of my parents in one senseless car accident the evening of my high school graduation. One which I didn't attend since my grandparents informed me of their deaths shortly before I was to enter the auditorium. So yes, I do know a loss. A huge loss— one that's affected me every day for eight years."

She turned slightly so she could see his face. His eyes were clenched shut, and his muscles had tensed. "Philippe, or can I call you Phil?"

"Phil works."

"Great! Phil it is then." She caught the glimmer of a smile from him. "Phil, I know what you're going through. Granted, I didn't lose the love of my life, but where you're wrong is they were my life. I'm an only child. I grew up in a world where they took care of my every need. They provided for me. I was going to take over my dad's business when he retired. But in a blink of an eye, everything was taken from me. I had to learn how to care for myself. Yes, my parents had provided for me in their deaths, but I still had to learn how to manage my money. Manage a household that I'd never had to before. I had my grandparents to support me but that was it. When I went home, I was alone. No one was there to hold me. No one was there to comfort me when I couldn't see my way.

"I had many sleepless nights wondering how I would go on. How I would survive. Was it hard for me? Damn right it was and it still is to this day. Do I have good days? Yes, I have good days, but I also have bad ones. Ones where I can't breathe and wonder how I can go on. And then I look at their picture and know that they'd want me to carry on with my life. They'd want me to enjoy it and go on in their absence, and they'd want me to be happy.

"Only recently did I realize that I wasn't as happy as I could be. Ryne and I are involved with a fund-raiser at the school where I teach. My boss knew my father and knew that I was once a photographer. That was what I was going to be when I got through school. Anyway, he asked me to have a showing of my work and use it as a fundraiser for the school. I hadn't picked up a camera in almost eight years.

The feeling I had when I opened my camera case overwhelmed me. I cried for hours. And then I realized I needed to do this for the school but also for me. I thought it would maybe help me heal."

"And has it?"

"Yeah, but your brother has also helped. Ryne came along and changed my life. He made me see that I'd given up on my career way too soon. He helped me realize that I needed it to survive. And the funny thing is I thought I'd survived and moved on. But I was wrong. Your brother—and, I have to say, your mom too—have helped me see that I can't turn my back on what was supposed to be my life. I need it. It helps me breathe, and your brother helped me see that I wasn't breathing and that I hadn't been happy in a long, long time."

Phil seemed to relax as he listened. With a half-smile he said, "He loves you, you know."

"Yeah, I know and I love him too. And I also love you and your family. Your mom and I had a discussion right before I took my walk today. She has such insight into things. She knew I wasn't happy and talked to me about it." She smiled at him. "Have you shared your grief with her?" He shook his head. "I think you should talk to her. I know that you already speak with Ryne, but maybe her perspective will help guide you as well. I know she loved Annabelle too. In fact, I'm sure she was loved by your entire family. Don't push them aside. Listen to what they have to say and maybe their one word, one phrase, may help you through the day. I know how easy it is to bury your feelings. During hockey season that's it for you. Train, practice, play a game, travel. It's all too consuming and leaves you little time to think about what you're feeling and what you've gone through."

He leaned back against the bench and crossed his arms. "It's times like this— the off season when the memories all come rushing back," she urged. "Use your family and if you need to, seek a grief counselor." He nodded. "For me, I was enmeshed in school. I took as many credit hours as I could. I thought if I kept busy studying, I could bury my grief and forget about the accident. Except, I couldn't. At the oddest of times, my grief would overcome me, and I'd be so affected by it I'd miss days of school."

She turned toward him. "After a while, my grandparents knew what set me off: birthdays, anniversaries, and my birthday. They did their best to keep me busy and my mind off it, but it didn't work. Just know that you are going to have those days but don't wallow in your grief. Seek someone. Let them help you. When I started to do that, things improved." She squeezed his hands.

"Let your family in. Don't try and bury her. Let her live on, keep the memories but also go on with your life. I'm sure Annabelle would want you to find someone. She would want you to have a family."

He threw his head back and breathed deeply. A tear escaped his eye and trickled down his cheek. He looked into her eyes. "Thank you, Jen. I appreciate your talking to me. I am so sorry for what you've gone through. I'm just happy that you found my brother and he's making you happy."

"He is and I know he wants to see you happy too." She reached over and pulled him into her arms. She'd done what she set out to do; now it was up to Philippe.

"Uh huh, what's going on here?" She released her hold on Philippe and turned towards the voice.

"Ryne, what are you doing here?"

"I came to find you."

"How did you know where to find me?"

He pulled her note from his pocket.

"Oh yeah, I did leave your mother a note."

"Everything okay here?" He looked at his brother.

"Yeah.   All's good." Philippe leaned over and kissed her cheek. "You've got a special lady here. Don't mess up a good thing." He stood and started back towards the house.   Turning back added, "Thanks, Jen, and welcome to the family."

Ryne joined her on the bench as they watched his brother amble down the path towards the house. "You okay?" She nodded. "I gather you spoke with him about Annabelle." She nodded again. "And?"

"And I think he's going to be okay, at least I hope so.   He doesn't want to move on and leave her.   I told him he needs to talk to your mom.   She has such an insight on things.   And I also suggested a grief counselor.   I hope he listened to what I had to say.   At least, I think he did."

He pulled her into his arms.   "You're a special person, Jennifer Steele.   The luckiest day in my life was the day you almost took me out with your car.   I love you so much.   Thank you for seeking him out."

"Actually, I didn't.   He found me." He raised his eyebrow at her.   "I was sitting here daydreaming, and he found me. I'm glad it happened this way, that I didn't proactively seek him out. I wonder if Annabelle sent him my way. Whatever, it all worked out, and I think I gave him something to think about."

They spent another half hour enjoying their view and then returned to the house. They had another early morning flight the next day, and she wanted to pack and get some sleep before heading home.

Chapter Twenty-Two

THE REMAINDER OF THE SUMMER flew by, and before they knew it the fundraiser was almost upon them. Ryne had worked hard with his training and rehab of his hip. He was feeling good and was excited to get back into his daily hockey routine.

Jen spent the weeks leading up to the event photographing everything and anything she could. She was pleased with her results and anticipated raising a lot of money for Lakeview.

She'd made her decision about her future, and she'd elected to no longer tie it to the success of the fundraiser. And since making her choice, she'd been happier than she'd been in a long time. She owed it not only to the resurgence in her desire to be a photographer but also the love of a man that she'd never expected to have in her life.

Ryne was her everything. Since their meeting, he'd become her rock. He was there for her constantly, supporting her decisions and making her feel worthwhile again.

Whether he believed it or not, he taught her to believe in herself and seek her own happiness— not the happiness that others thought she needed.

A week before the fundraiser, she was working in

her home studio. She'd just finished selecting the final photographs for the showing and finalizing the website where patrons could order prints.

As she studied a photo in front of her, she remembered the exact moment she'd clicked the shutter on the image. It was near sunset and Ryne was on horseback in front of her. His image, along with his horse's, was silhouetted with the sunset in the background. The reds and oranges were strewn across the sky along with the puffy cumulous clouds. It was surreal. A strong man sitting proudly on horseback as he scoured the land before him.

She closed her eyes and recalled the night. It was their last evening on the ranch. She was sorer than all get out from the previous day's ride, but she wanted to see the land one more time before leaving. That afternoon she'd had her conversation with Philippe. Ryne had known how much it had affected her and suggested the ride. As he'd ridden in front of her, she realized how far she'd come since meeting him. She realized what it felt to be a part of a family again and how much she'd enjoyed every minute of her time with the Fergusons. His mom had made her yearn for her mother, but at the same time, she'd made a friend in her— one she hoped to have for a long time to come.

From the moment she'd walked onto the deck the day of their arrival, Jacques had made her feel at home. He was a fun-loving man and a jokester. From the little she'd seen of him, he was a definite role model to his children—guiding them along the path as they made their way through life's choices. She'd listened to him counsel Emma on a friendship that had gone awry and as he advised Etienne on his contract with the Storm. He reminded her of her own dad and it comforted her. She'd also developed a unique relationship with Philippe. They had something in common that no one should ever have to endure— the death of a loved one.

She was lost in thought and didn't hear Ryne enter. He'd come over earlier in the day and had taken a call from Adam that had gone on longer than he expected. In fact, one she'd forgotten about as she lost herself in her work as he'd taken the call in her kitchen. She felt his hand on her shoulder and jumped. "Sorry, I startled you. Where were you?"

"Just remembering."

"May I ask what?"

She pointed to the photo in front of her. "I had a clear image of the moment I snapped this." She ran her finger across it. "I remember looking at you and thinking how lucky I was to find you and your family. Your mom is remarkable. Having practically raised you boys by herself while your dad was still playing. I can't image her having to cart you all around town. And your dad." She paused as tears filled her eyes. Blinking past them, she continued. "He so reminds me of my dad. When I heard how he spoke to Emma about losing her best friend." She placed her hand over her heart. "It was so...I can't find the words. I listened to him speak with Etienne, advising him as a former player but more importantly as a father." She swiped at the tear she wasn't able to prevent from falling. "I'm so lucky to have fallen into your world."

She looked up into his loving eyes and knew that

he was hers forever. He was her everything, and she prayed nothing would take him from her world.

The evening of the fundraiser was finally upon them. It had been months since Johnston had first suggested it. Ryne had just been traded to the Generals. And now, fall was here and training camp was underway. Outside of his time rehabbing and training, they had spent almost every waking moment together since returning from Calgary. Every day she fell more in love with him. She often found herself daydreaming about them and where their lives were headed. She didn't want to get ahead of herself. She'd get through tonight and see where their future was headed.

It was a black-tie affair held in one of the prestigious hotels in downtown St. Louis. Johnston had given her the day off before the Saturday evening soiree. The silent auction had been assembled in the back of the ballroom. She'd skillfully set up the gallery in a special room that she and Ryne had agreed upon to showcase her photos.

The morning of the party, Jen woke with a blistering headache. She assumed it was a combination of nerves and lack of sleep. She'd been a frazzled mess since putting the finishing touches together. She prayed she hadn't been too confident in her abilities. All four of her grandparents were attending, and she couldn't wait to see Rowena and Miles. They'd spoken several times a week since her visit in June. She wasn't sure if Ryne was as excited but knew he'd make the best of their stay.

It had taken her weeks to find her dress. She wanted to feel comfortable and not confined as she moved about the evening. She'd chosen a sleeveless ankle-length rose colored A-line dress with an asymmetric hemline. It flowed freely around her and gave her the room she needed.

She knew she looked good when she answered the door, and Ryne's eyes practically popped out of his head. He was speechless as he leaned in to kiss her cheek. It took him a moment to get his bearings and then he ran his hand along her cheek. "You look stunning. I'm going to be the luckiest man there. I'm escorting the most beautiful woman in the world, and I can say she's all mine."

Shyly she looked at him, still unused to his compliments. Every time they were together, he told her how beautiful she was or how lucky he was she was in his life. It never got old.

"Did Rowena and Miles get in okay?"

"They did and they can't wait to see you."

"Ughh. Thanks. I certainly hope they behave themselves at least while they're at the fundraiser. I don't need them questioning my motives." He chuckled and reached for her wrap securing it around her shoulders. "Ready, love?"

She nodded and as she started to pull away from his arms, he pulled her in closer. "Will you promise me something tonight?"

"Sure, anything as long as it won't get me into trouble." She giggled.

"Trouble? I thought you were a saint and never lost your way."

"Sweetheart, that's where you're definitely wrong. I'd been lost for so long, but I didn't realize it until you entered my life."

"I hope I helped you find your way." She nodded again. "Promise me you'll enjoy every minute of this fundraiser. Put all your worries aside because there's not a thing we can do to fix it." He ran his hand along her back. "Well, maybe we can fix some things, but…" He looked into her eyes holding her gaze. "I'm so proud of you. So proud of your work. And don't let anyone ruin your happiness tonight, okay?" He kissed the tip of her nose. "One last thing."

"What?"

"Know how much I love you. I thank God every day that you were behind the wheel that night. My life hasn't been the same with you in it. I've found peace, happiness, and more importantly, love. Whatever you decide, know that I'll support you one hundred percent. Whether you remain teaching or reclaim photography, it doesn't matter to me. Just be happy."

She wrapped her arms around his neck and ran her fingers through his hair. "Ryne, thank you for helping me find myself again. I hadn't realized I was lost, but I was. I feel freer than I've felt since that awful night. I love you so much. Thank you for taking a chance on me. As it was, you really didn't know who that madwoman was that almost ran you down." He grinned at the reference she made to herself. "I want to tell you I've made my decision."

"I'm glad to hear that. I know it wasn't easy for you."

"I've certainly struggled deciding the right thing to do, but what I learned from you and your family is I need to take that chance. Spread my wings again. I may fail but at least, for the moment, I have you in my life." As she said those words, she conveyed to him her decision. "I'm going to resign at the end of the year."

"I know it was a hard choice for you to make, but I believe it's what you need at this point in your life. Honey, whatever happens remember you've got me forever." He leaned in and placed a soft, lingering kiss on her lips.

They arrived at the hotel an hour before the scheduled start. She ran through her exhibit one last time while Ryne checked with the hotel's event coordinator. Everything was good to go. They were just waiting on their guests.

Ryne also had a huge surprise for her and he wanted her to discover it all on her own.

While he stood at the entrance to the ballroom, he realized the change in her. She exuded a confidence he hadn't seen before. He was proud of her decision. Since returning from Canada, he knew she'd struggled with her future plans. He never pressed her or gave his opinion knowing she had to come to her own conclusion.

He looked up and saw five people coming his way. He was excited he'd been able to pull off his surprise with none the wiser. He welcomed his guests and motioned towards the gallery where he'd seen Jen moments ago. She was in there, alone. He hoped his surprise would calm her nerves. He couldn't wait to see her face when they greeted her.

He neared the doorway and motioned for his surprise to stand outside her vision. He entered and took in her beauty as she straightened one of her photos. He was so proud of her. "Jen, I've got some guests that would like to meet you."

"Ah sure, hold on a minute." He waved the five into the room.

"Okay, Ryne, I think it looks good." When she turned and saw the visitors, the sheer joy that radiated from her face made his surprise all worthwhile.

"Oh my God," she screamed as she ran towards Jacklynne's outstretched arms. Not only had she come to the fundraiser but also Jacques, Philippe, Etienne, and Rafael. "I can't believe you came," she uttered as she continued to hug his mother.

"Of course we came. We couldn't not support you and Ryne on this endeavor."

She moved away from his mother and then found herself enveloped in Jacques' warm embrace.

"Jen, you're a part of the family. Sorry, the girls and Jules couldn't make it."

"I'm just surprised you're all here." She hugged both Etienne and Rafael.

Philippe was the last in line to congratulate her. He had a blank expression on his face as he drew her into his arms. "We wouldn't miss this event."

"But how? How were you able to leave training camp?" she said addressing his brothers.

"We worked it out in advance. This event is important to you and Ryne, so it's important to us too."

"I'm so shocked." She made her way to Ryne's open arms. "I can't believe you did this for me. Thank you." She found herself enveloped in another embrace as he kissed her cheek.

"Sweetheart, anything for you. I knew you'd love it if we could all support your showing."

"No matter what happens tonight, you've made my day. I'm overwhelmed." Out of the corner of his eye he caught sight of some people as they neared the entrance to the room. His heart dropped only because he wasn't sure what to expect.

"Jennifer?" He watched as her head spun towards the doorway and the familiar voice. There stood the rest of her family. Miles and Rowena along with Wilford and Rose were dressed in their finest. He watched as an expression of love filled her face as she approached her grandparents.

He went to her side as she welcomed her family. Leaning in, he kissed both Rowena's and Rose's cheeks. "Thanks for coming. It's so nice to see you again." He then reached out his hand to shake both Miles's and Wilford's.

"I hope we're not interrupting something important," Wilford said as he surveyed the crowd.

"You're not. In fact, it's perfect timing," she said. Ryne moved aside so she could lead them into the room. "I'd like to introduce Ryne's family. His mom, Jacklynne; his father, Jacques; and his brothers Philippe, Etienne, and Rafael. His brother Jules and sisters, Olivia and Emma, weren't able to attend."

Ryne wasn't the least bit surprised when Rowena rushed towards his parents. "It's a pleasure to meet all of you," she said as she waved her arm about. She took a closer look at Etienne and shook her head. "Are you twins?"

"Yep, we are," Etienne commented and approached Rowena. "It's nice to meet you. We've heard a lot about you."

"That doesn't sound good," Rowena commented as she glanced towards Ryne, quirking her brow.

"Don't take that the wrong way," Etienne said, back peddling. "Jen spoke about you when she visited us this past summer."

"That sounds better." She harrumphed. "I'm pleased to meet you. Did you come all the way from Winnipeg?"

"No, Grandma Ro. They live in Calgary."

"That's right. I knew they came from somewhere north of the border."

Ryne took control and introduced her grandparents to his family. He sighed and sidled up next to Jen. "I hope they'll get along."

"They will. Rowena was just testing the waters. You know what she's like."

"That I do." He wrapped his arm about her and watched as they discussed Jen's photos.

"Is this you, Ryne?" Rose asked as she pointed to the last photo she'd added to the collection.

"That's me."

"I love it! Jen, I have to have a copy of this." He wasn't the least bit surprised with how her work was received by not only their family but, later, by everyone who attended the gala.

At the end of the night, Ryne dropped onto a chair just inside the ballroom. They were the last ones remaining, outside of the cleaning crew. He reached out and guided her onto his lap. "I'd say this was a huge success, thanks to your photography."

"It wasn't just my photos. It was everything. From that to the auction, to the dinner, and then the dancing. Everyone seemed to have a phenomenal time. I know I sure did, that is, when I could take it all in." He squeezed his arms around her.

"One thing we didn't get a chance to do."

"What's that?"

He eased her off his lap and held out his hand. "Shall we have this dance?"

"What about the music?"

"I think we can manage." He wrapped his arms around her, and she swayed along with him. It didn't matter that the band had stopped playing for the night. He had a tune that'd been playing in his head all day long and that's what he danced to.

Almost instantly he felt her relax as she settled into his arms. The stress of the evening was over. Their event was a huge success, and Johnston had already begun to talk about it becoming an annual event. As he'd listened to Johnston's excitement, he knew that more than likely, Jen and he wouldn't be a part of it.

He had a lot on his agenda in the coming months. With training camp fully underway, he'd spoken to Adam about his options and how he wanted to proceed with his career. For the first time in several years, he'd be able to spend a portion of the holidays with his family. He knew what he wanted to do, and he just needed to convince Jen to join him.

He could see she was exhausted. They'd promised both of their families that they'd meet for brunch the following morning. "Let's get you home," he whispered as they swayed about. He felt her nod against his chest. He grasped her hand and guided her to the main hallway of the hotel. Looking back towards the ballroom he murmured, "We did it, Jen."

"We did and I'm glad it's over. Now, I have to break the news to Johnston."

"You have plenty of time to do that. You'll know when the time is right."

He escorted her out the door and to the garage. He knew how tired she was, so he helped her into the car, then reached for her seatbelt and clicked it into place. He hadn't even made his way out of the garage when he heard her even breathing. She'd fallen asleep. She was spent with the worry and hours she'd put into the event. Now it was over and they could concentrate even more on their relationship. He had plans and he couldn't wait to share them with her.

The next morning, they met their families for brunch.

When he arrived at her house shortly before nine to pick her up, he'd knew she was running behind because she flew open the door and all he saw was a blur as she ran back up the stairs. He heard her yell that she'd be a minute. She was longer than her promised minute, and he could see how tired she was. Her eyes were puffy and with dark circles. One look at her red-rimmed eyes and he wondered whether she'd gotten any sleep.

He was waiting for her at the bottom of the stairs. She'd stopped one step above him and looked him squarely in the eyes. "Did you sleep okay?" he asked.

"I did," she claimed as she eased her arms around his neck. Brushing a kiss to his cheek, she said, "We need to go. You know how I hate to be late."

"Yeah, I do," but he refused to move. He brushed his hand across her face securing her hair behind her ear. "Let's be honest here. Did you sleep?"

"I did, but I also had dreams." He watched her closely as she told him about her dream. "We were in the room where the gallery showing was held last night. I heard a muffled voice and I turned. There standing before me was my father. I can remember the smile he had on his face." She looked away from him. "He told me how proud he was of me and my decision to go back into the business. I reached my hand out to him, and he started to come towards me. And then, he faded away. His last words were, 'I love you my sweet princess. Never forget that.' Before I could say another word, he was gone."

"Ah honey..."

"I kept calling out his name and he never came back." Tears started to form and fall from her eyes. "I kept calling for him and calling and then I woke up." He swiped the tears from her face.

"Sweetheart, he was telling you he approved of your decision. I know he's proud of you and what you accomplished. I'm sure when the time is right he'll seek you out again."

"I hope so. It was so good to hear his voice, if only for that brief snippet in time." He grabbed ahold of her fingers and motioned for her to follow.

He snatched her coat and shepherded her out the door.

They were the last to arrive at the restaurant. As they walked into the room, she turned to him. "You know I hate being late."

"We're not late, they're just early," he chuckled. "Look at my watch, dear. We're right on time." She playfully slapped at his chest. "Come on, let's join everyone."

He noticed that Rafael was missing. "Where's Rafael?" he asked his father.

"He had an early flight. He was sorry he didn't get a chance to say goodbye."

"I'm sorry too. I'll text him later." He made his way to his mom and kissed her cheek. "What time is your flight?"

"Early afternoon. Don't worry about us. We've got a car already scheduled to pick us up." He glanced at Etienne who was enmeshed in a conversation with Rowena.

"Poor Et," he said to his parents. "I see Rowena's got him cornered."

"Yeah, she does. She's taken with the two of you being twins. He's doing his best to appease her. I think he's done a pretty good job."

He whispered in his mother's ears, "At least he's keeping her out of my hair. I think I'll buy him a case of beer in thanksgiving." He watched his mom's expression.

"She's not that bad, Ryne. She's concerned about Jennifer. What grandparent wouldn't be especially since she's alone."

"I get it, I do, but I thought I'd vetted myself with

her. I'll have to try a little harder, I guess."

Ryne looked up and saw Philippe approach Jen.
For the first time in quite some time, he seemed
at ease. He'd carried a blank expression the night
before, but today he seemed more himself, relaxed.
His brother hugged Jen, kissing her cheek. He knew
they'd developed a special bond after their conversation. He was grateful to her for helping. In the
time his family had been in St. Louis, he'd noticed
glimpses of the old Philippe, seen life in his eyes,
and actually heard his laughter on occasion. Jen was
a godsend to both of them, and he hoped that she
continued to forge her relationship with his brother.

They were close enough that Ryne could hear
their greeting.

"I'm sorry we didn't have a chance to talk last
night," Philippe said to Jen.

"Phil, did you forget I was a tad bit busy."

"I didn't. I need to tell you this before I have to
go."

"What is it?"

"Thank you. Thank you for our talk this summer and also for our ongoing conversations. You've
helped me put perspective on my situation. I'm seeing things clearer lately, and I just wanted you to
know that." He leaned in and kissed her cheek.
"You're good for my brother."

"He's good for me, too, Phil." On that note,
Ryne joined them. "Oh hey, there honey," she said.
"Phil and Etienne have to leave in a little bit. We
need to get started on breakfast. And I also want to
share my news with everyone."

Ryne spoke up getting everyone's attention. "Let's

eat. But first, Jen has an announcement to make."

"I wonder if they're getting married." He caught Rowena's comment. If she thought she'd been whispering, she hadn't. He whispered in her ear, "Nope, not yet." He knew she'd been so focused on Jen that Rowena hadn't heard his approach. "You'll be one of the first to know, that's for sure."

All eyes were on Jen. He was so proud of her. "I want to thank you all for coming to last night's event. I'm so happy that you could share our night with us. It meant the world that you were here," she motioned to his family. "It was so unexpected and I know how difficult it was for Philippe, Rafael, and Etienne to get the time away. I'll always remember that. I think, no I know, we had a successful fund-raiser. I won't know the totals for a while, but I do know the gallery showing was successful. I'll be processing prints for weeks to come.

"But what I really wanted to share with you is I made a decision on my future." She reached for Ryne's hand. "I haven't been happy for a long time, and I didn't realize it until this wonderful man helped me see that. I've been going through the motions on a daily basis but when I picked up my camera again, I felt like I could breathe. I hadn't realized how much I missed it until I was forced into this fundraiser."

"Forced?" asked Wilford.

"Well, I was. But with Ryne's guidance and sup-port, I realized that what was a gentle prodding from Johnston to oversee this affair became a godsend. I've found my way again. So without further ado, I've decided to resign my position at Lakeview at the close of the school year. I'm reopening Steele's Photography."

"Oh dear," Rowena said as she placed her hand over her heart. "Your father would be so proud of you."

"I hope so. I want to also thank you, Jacklynne. You helped me see the forest through the trees. I appreciate your support, and I hope to make all of you proud of my decision. Because if I fail, I'm going to need a lot of support to pick myself up again."

"Honey, you're not going to fail. In fact, I see you soaring." Jacklynne wrapped her in her arms.

Before they knew it, it was time for Ryne's family to go. Philippe and Etienne had left moments ago. Jen said her goodbyes to Jacques and turned to Jacklynne. "Thank you so much for coming. It was the best of surprises."

"Thank Ryne, he arranged it."

"I will."

"Come here, dear. Let me give you one last hug." Jacklynne embraced her one last time. "I hope you'll come for the holidays."

"I'm not sure about that."

"Talk to my son. I'm sure you'll find a way."

"Honey, the car's here," Jacques called.

"Coming, dear," she called in return. "Jen, please try and come. You know how much we'd love to have you."

"I know. I'll call you soon."

Ryne draped his arm around her as his parents got into their car. Rolling down the window, Jacques said, "We'll see you soon. We love you."

"Love you too," Ryne shouted back. He turned and looked at the love of his life. "You know he included you in that comment."

"I know," she shyly said. It felt good to have his parents in her life. For some reason, she felt like they were her parents too. Although they'd never replace her mom and dad, it was good to have someone else that she could refer to as Mom and Dad. She hoped that one day she'd be able to call them that.

Chapter Twenty-Three

AFTER MUCH THOUGHT, JEN DECIDED to hold off informing Johnston of her plans until the new year.

Since making her decision, a huge weight had lifted from her shoulders. She and Ryne were in a good place. She missed him when he was on the road and was always ecstatic with his return. She and Lauren attended every home game, and she'd watch him fly down the ice, in awe that he was hers. When he had away games, her heart ached with how much she missed him.

Ryne had been on the road for the last ten days. His first game back would be against the Storm. He'd phoned the night before he was scheduled to return home.

"You realize your first game home is against your brothers."

"I do."

"Let's plan something."

"Dinner?'" he suggested.

"Sounds great. I'll make reservations." She paused. "I miss you. It seems like forever since I last saw you."

"You have no clue how much I miss you. I hate these road trips. They're too long."

"Yeah, ten days is a long time to be away from the ones you love." She sighed.

"You have no idea. I can't wait to hold you, kiss your sweet lips. Jen, you're my everything."

"I feel the same way."

They spoke a few minutes longer when his phone beeped an incoming call. "Hey Jen, I'd better take this, it's my mom."

"Okay. Love you. Say hi to Jacklynne."

"Love you too."

She made reservations at Lucerne's. It was a higher end restaurant located in the hotel where the Storm players were staying. She wanted them to have as much anonymity as possible and secured a private table.

At the last minute, she decided to invite Lauren. She wanted her best friend to get to know Ryne better but also wanted to introduce her to his brothers. She'd spoken with Etienne when they first arrived. He seemed weary and was thankful they were able to remain at the hotel. The season was still young and she worried about all of the Ferguson's.

She knew Ryne would be cutting their dinner reservation close since his flight from the West Coast wasn't scheduled to land until five-thirty, so she'd arranged to meet him at the restaurant. She'd been unsettled since speaking with Etienne. Since their plane had arrived that morning, instead of going home, she headed over to the hotel.

Thankfully, Etienne had texted their room numbers in case she needed to get ahold of them. Since she hadn't spoken with Philippe, she chose to visit his room. Knocking on the door, she heard him call out and then the door flew open. He was shirtless. His face reddened and his head ducked when he discovered it was her. "Oh, hi there, Jen. Come on in while I grab a shirt. Sorry about that."

He grabbed a dress shirt from the closet and threw it on. "I didn't expect you for a while. Isn't dinner at seven?"

"Yep, but I wanted to visit with you and Etienne. You've got to be lonely traveling all the time, never seeing your friends or family." She paused. "Not that you don't see your brother, and I'm sure you consider your teammates family."

He ran his hand through his short-clipped hair. "I understand what you mean." He walked towards the phone. "Shall we phone Et? I'm sure he's just lounging about waiting for dinner."

"Sure, but I have a question for you first. Is he okay?"

"Why do you ask?"

"He didn't seem like himself when we spoke earlier. I'm concerned."

He contemplated his words before admitting, "He had a rough game last night. Took a pretty hard hit and ended up on the ice for a few minutes. I think the wind got knocked out of him. Other than that, I'm sure he's fine." She questioned whether he was telling her the truth to prevent her from worrying. "I haven't seen him since we arrived." He grabbed the phone and dialed. It seemed like it took forever for him to answer. Maybe he'd gone out. Just as Philippe was ready to hang up Etienne answered.

"Hey, where were you?" She knew he was waiting for a response. "Jen's here. Why don't you come down and we can hang out before dinner?" She tried not to listen to Philippe's portion of the conversation but it was hard not to. Her back was to him when she heard him set the phone down. "He'll be here in a little while."

She believed Philippe knew more about his brother's condition than he was telling her. About a half hour later, a soft knock came. He didn't even check to see who it was before he opened the door and Etienne strolled in. Unless her imagination played games on her, Etienne was moving slowly. She looked into his eyes and saw pain.

She rushed to his side. "Etienne, what's wrong? You look like you're hurting."

"I must look pretty bad," he said.

"What happened to you?"

"Jen, I play hockey— that's what happened."

"Philippe told me about your hit last night."

"Hit. It was more like a bulldozer ran over me. Thankfully, I don't have a concussion, but I am pretty sore. I don't remember it. What I do remember is waking up on the ice with my brother hovering over me, asking if I was okay."

"I was concerned," Philippe added as he ran his hand across his face. "You weren't moving."

"I'm not moving very well right now, either." He chuckled as he eased himself down on the bed. "Enough about me, what's new with you? Have you found a space for your studio?"

"Actually, I still have my father's. He owned the building, and we rented out a portion of it. But I left his studio intact. I couldn't let it go." She paced about the room. "I guess my subconscious knew that someday I'd return. I can still remember the day I closed the door on it for the last time. My grandfather Wilford manages the building for me, so he takes care of everything."

"I'm glad you don't have to worry about it."

"So am I. Oh, by the way, I asked my best friend to join us tonight for dinner. Her name is Lauren Masters and she's a tax attorney."

"I never heard how the fundraiser turned out." said Philippe. Etienne sat hunched over on the bed.

"We did better that I ever expected. We raised over five hundred thousand dollars."

A loud whistle pierced the room. "Wow! I'd say you made the right decision to return to photography."

"It wasn't all from my sales. Don't forget there was a silent auction. The dinner was also underwritten. I'm thrilled with the results." She tapped her hand on her forehead. "Etienne, I forgot your picture."

She could tell he wasn't paying attention to their conversation as he seemed lost in his thoughts. "Et, did you hear Jen?"

"Huh, ah no, I'm sorry. I checked out there for a second. What did you say?"

"It doesn't matter. Are you sure you're okay?"

"Yeah, I'm fine."

Out of the blue, Etienne asked, "So, how's Rowena?"

"She's doing great, thanks for asking." Sitting down on the bed beside him, Jen said, "She asks about you all the time. I think she's in love with you."

Philippe burst out in laughter. "I think she likes

you because you're not dating her granddaughter."

"Thanks, bro. I thought she liked me for my good looks."

"That, too," she added. "She definitely grilled Ryne when he met her in June. I felt sorry for him, but he made it through, and it's behind him—at least for now."

"Only because he hasn't seen her in some time. I bet she'll be on his six when he sees her next."

"Glad it's him and not me," Philippe added. "I had it lucky with Annabelle's family. We grew up together and everyone got along."

"You also had a set of parents to watch out for you."

"That, too. She just has your best interest at heart."

"I know and so does Ryne," Jen said. "Hey, it's getting late. Let's head down to the restaurant. Lauren should be here shortly."

As they made their way towards Lucerne's, Jen caught sight of Lauren. She waved and walked over.

Reaching her hand to Etienne, Lauren said, "I gather you're Etienne. You and Ryne look exactly alike."

"We are twins," he scoffed.

"That you are, with the same sense of humor." Jen shook her head at her friend.

"Bad day at the office?"

"Isn't it always?"

Just as the hostess began to seat them, Ryne appeared. She smiled as he slapped his brothers on their backs in a welcoming way, and then he kissed her softly on the lips. She was ready to point out Lauren when he saw her standing on the sidelines.

"Lauren, I didn't know you were joining us. It's so good to see you." He drew her friend into a warm embrace. "Have you met my brothers?"

"Yeah, Jen just introduced us."

On one side of her sat Ryne and the other was Etienne. Seated next to one another and across the table from her were Philippe and Lauren. The brothers immediately started talking hockey. She imagined the dinner table while they were growing up was just like this. She knew Lauren was enjoying listening to the anecdotes about their road trips. Their late nights and travel delays on top of the game. Jen sat back, enjoying the scene before her.

The conversation shifted. Etienne had asked what Ryne's schedule looked like during the holidays. While she listened to Ryne rant over the Generals' upcoming road trips, she was surprised to see Lauren and Philippe engaged in conversation. Philippe seemed more at ease since their talk in June, and she hoped that she'd contributed to it.

"Jen?" She felt Ryne wrap his arm around her shoulder. "Did you hear me?"

"Umm."

"You didn't, did you?" She didn't have a clue what he'd asked. "Et wants to know when you get out of school for the holidays."

"You know, I haven't checked yet. I've been so busy finishing up orders from the fundraiser."

"Don't worry about it," Et replied. "Just let Ryne know so we can figure out our arrangements."

"What are you talking about?"

"Nothing, dear. I'll fill you in later."

The remainder of their night flew by and before

she knew it she was saying goodbye to his brothers. "I'll see you on the ice," Ryne called out as he headed toward the lobby with her. Lauren had left a few minutes earlier. Jen was glad she came and seemed to enjoy sitting next to Philippe and that made her happy.

"Watch your back," Philippe added as they headed in opposite directions.

"That was fun," Jen said as they made their way to her car. Ryne had taken a cab from the Generaldome.

"It was and I think Lauren and Philippe enjoyed themselves."

"I noticed that."

"Was that your plan?"

"No," she sheepishly replied.

"Sure about that?" She knew he didn't believe her but was glad that their evening turned out the way it did.

At the beginning of the season Ryne leased a townhouse. It wasn't far from her home, and she thought it suited him. She'd listened to him go on and on about owning a sizeable piece of property in Calgary not far from his parents. He liked the freedom of the ranch and hoped to own something similar. Even though she knew he wanted to own a house, leasing one at this time was so much easier especially if he were traded again.

As they drove along, she thought about his brother. "Do you think Etienne is feeling okay? He didn't seem himself."

His delay in answering spoke volumes. "He's injured, isn't he?" When he didn't answer her, she knew. "Ryne?"

"Yeah, he is. He called me earlier today after he spoke with you. He knew you'd figured it out." Right then, she pulled up at his home.

"How?"

"Just by the way you kept asking him questions." She hadn't realized she'd done that but when she replayed the conversation in her mind, she guessed she had.

"What's wrong with him?"

"He tweaked his back."

"He said he didn't have a concussion."

"He doesn't, but like me, it's a nagging injury he's been dealing with the last several years. He hoped it would go away, but they encountered a lot of turbulence coming into town and on top of his hit last night, it flared up again."

"Phil said he took a nasty hit and ended up on the ice for several minutes."

"That too."

Turning to her he cupped her jaw, leaned in and kissed her. "You need to stop worrying. We're used to injuries. It's a part of the game."

"I realize that."

"Come up for a minute. I have something I want to discuss with you." He sounded serious, and it triggered red flags that sent a shockwave scorching through her system.

Hand in hand they walked up the sidewalk, all the while Jen wondering what he wanted to speak to her about.

He threw open the door and she walked inside. She became even more unsettled by the look on his

face. With his past injuries and now Etienne's...
She gnawed on her lower lip as she waited for him
to close the door. He placed his hand on her lower
back to move her towards the sofa when she spun
around and looked deeply into his eyes. He hadn't
said a word since they arrived and it worried her.
She didn't know what to say or do, so she waited
for him.

"What's wrong, why are you so tense all of a sudden?"

"It's nothing," Avoiding the sofa, she made her
way to the French doors that led onto the balcony.
She clasped and unclasped her hands, waiting and
wondering. She watched in the glass as he moved
his hand around his neck as though he were searching for words. Her heart dropped. They hadn't
been in a fight, their dinner went well, at least she
thought it had. *What did I do? What's wrong? Is he
going to break up with me?* Those questions might
have answers she didn't want to hear. She closed her
eyes and held her breath, waiting for the inevitable.
She loved him. He said he loved her but what was
wrong, what had she done? Was she overreacting?

Then he tightened his arms around her waist
and pulled her against him. "Breathe, Jen," he
whispered. "Just breathe." She took that breath
she'd been holding and felt his lips along her neck.
"What's wrong? What did I do?"

"N-n-nothing," she stammered.

"Then why have you gone so cold all of a sudden?
Come on, let's sit down." He reached for her hand
and guided her to the sofa— the same one she'd
tried to avoid. She was afraid to sit. Afraid of what

he wanted to tell her.

She eased herself down and kept her eyes averted and her hands clasped in her lap. For the first time in a long time, she was scared. She didn't understand where her fears came from. From nowhere she'd lost her sense of confidence.

"Sweetheart, what's wrong? Why are you so tense?" He massaged her neck. "Didn't you have a good time tonight? I did. I love having the chance to meet-up with my brothers during the season. Thank you for arranging our dinner. I'm sorry I couldn't have been there earlier."

She tried to find comfort in his touch. "It was fantastic seeing Lauren again. I loved the way she and Philippe interacted. He seemed good tonight. I wonder if he took your advice and if he's seeing a counselor? Whatever, he seemed much more relaxed. It was good to see, that's for sure."

"Yeah, it was." She took another deep breath. She waited and waited.

He grabbed ahold of her hands. "Honey, what is it? Did I do something to upset you? Please, let me in— tell me what's wrong."

"I'm fine."

"No you're not. I can see it in your eyes, in your mannerisms. What have I done?"

In a wobbly voice she asked, "What did you want to speak to me about?"

She knew he'd figure out something was wrong. She was scared. Scared of the unknown. She felt his warm embrace and relaxed. "Hey there," he placed his finger under her chin and raised it. She focused her eyes on him. "What's this about? Why the sad look?"

"I…"

"Are you worried about what I have to say?" He played with her hair pushing it behind her ear. "Honey, you have nothing to worry about."

"But…"

"Sweetheart, I love you. Did I do something to make you think otherwise?" She shook her head. "I wanted to talk to you about the holidays." *The holidays? What about them?* She watched his face as he stroked her jawline. When he kissed her, she felt her confidence start to return. She wasn't sure why it had flown the coop but it had, if only for that brief moment in time.

"We had a team meeting on the plane coming home. Since we have a tiny break in our schedule, Trevor has decided to give us that time off. No practice, no meetings, nothing. He believes we need to spend time with our friends and family. It will help us regroup and recharge. So…" He ran his fingertip along her lips. "I was wondering if you'd come home with me. Home to Calgary. Spend the holidays with me and my family." She was flabbergasted. She hadn't expected that from his request to speak with her. After their dinner conversation, she should have speculated that he'd have time off but didn't put two and two together. She assumed professional hockey players spent those few off days practicing.

"I'm sure you want to spend time with your grandparents. We'd leave Christmas day so you could spend a part of it with Wilford and Rose. I'd have to go on to Chicago myself for our next game on the thirtieth. I'd love to fly you from Calgary to meet with Rowena and Miles for the New Year and then back home in time to return to school. What about it? Will you come with me?"

She gnawed on her lower lip chastising herself for doubting their relationship. Maybe the sense of doom stemmed from his long road trip and missing him. He'd been gone for ten long days, and she knew he was tired exhibited by the dark circles that rimmed his eyes. She'd overreacted.

"So what do you say, huh?"

"Isn't your last game before the holidays on the twenty-second?"

"Yeah, so?"

"Don't you want to be home with your family on Christmas?"

"I would but it's more important to me that you spend that day or at least a part of it with your family. So will you come home with me?"

She nodded. "I'd love to spend the holidays with you." She leaned in and pressed her lips to his wondering why she'd become so insecure.

"Are we good now?" He held her against his chest. "You had me worried there for a few minutes. You know how much I love you, right?" She'd developed a huge lump in her throat as she held back her tears. She dipped her head, afraid to speak. It took her a few moments to get her emotions under control. He kissed her forehead. "Okay, now?"

"I am. You had me worried there for a minute. I thought you wanted to break up with me."

"Where did you get that idea? I love you with all my heart."

She shrugged her shoulders. "Overactive imagination?"

"Let's put that imagination of yours to bed for the night."

"Sounds like a plan to me." She sat in his arms and just as he was about to fall asleep leaned over and kissed him one more time. "I'm going to go. You're tired and I have an early morning meeting. I'll see you after the game."

As she drove home, she had a good talk with herself. She realized she needed not to worry so much. All was good between her and Ryne. She couldn't let her imagination run wild because she possibly heard something in his voice that wasn't there. She should have realized how tired he was after his long road trip and not jumped to conclusions. Tomorrow would be a better day. She said a silent prayer for not only Etienne but that all three would come out of the game unscathed.

Their game the following night was definitely a barn burner. She and Lauren sat in their seats, gnawing on their nails as they watched the play move from end to end. She often wondered how they were able to skate practically nonstop for an hour.

No sooner would Philippe clear the puck out of their end, Ryne would come rushing back with it. This back and forth continued well into the second period when Ryne scored the first goal of the game with twelve minutes remaining in the period. She smiled as he received high fives from his teammates and a disgusted look from his brother Etienne. She was surprised his brother was in the line-up, as bad as his back had been the day before. She imagined he'd undergone a good session with their trainer that enabled him to play.

She was glad when Ryne came off the ice for a breather. Her eyes were glued to him as he sat on the bench, then he jumped over the boards and back into the game. His skates hit the ice at the most opportune time as the puck careened off the boards right onto his stick. He skated, weaving in and out of traffic past the blue line and wound his way around the back of the net, casting spray as his skates cut through the ice. Philippe was right there with him. He ran him into the boards where Ryne lost his balance and fell on top of the puck. Play was called.

A faceoff was held which Derrick won. He passed the puck back to Ryne, who with his masterful slap shot, raised his stick and took a shot at the puck. Everyone in the arena heard the crack of the puck as it ricocheted off the crossbar. He was lucky enough to retrieve his own rebound. The goalie slid about the crease, trying to prevent the puck from entering the goal, but Ryne snuck it underneath his pads for another score. A lot was going on in front of the net right before Ryne scored. Etienne had dug his skate into the ice which propelled him as he tried to prevent Ryne's shot. He couldn't stop his forward motion and at the end of the play, Etienne rushed Ryne from behind pushing him hard into the boards where Ryne slumped. In a heartbeat, he'd scored a point, and Etienne had received a major penalty for boarding.

Ryne's skate had plowed into the boards, ramming

his knee and then his hip. She gasped and threw her hands over her mouth as he fell. He wasn't moving. Stafford rushed onto the ice. He leaned over Ryne, and assessed his injury. She felt Lauren wrap her arm around her.

She had a difficult time watching him lie there. Circling around him at a distance were his brothers. She knew Etienne must feel remorseful, seeing him lying on the ice, knowing he'd been the one to cause him going down. It seemed forever before Ryne moved again. She worried about his hip; he'd worked so hard to return to playing form.

When he'd started to move, both Philippe and Etienne inched closer. She could tell by the look on Etienne's face how badly he felt. In fact, when Ryne was finally able to get to his feet, his brothers skated alongside him where Stafford took over and with assistance helped him from the ice.

Jen's heart beat wildly; she didn't know what to do or where to go. She needed to get to him. She grabbed her coat and purse and hurried from the arena with Lauren right by her side. She said prayer after prayer as she made her way down the corridor to the trainer's room where she waited anxiously for word on his condition.

As the minutes passed, she heard the buzzer announcing the end of the period. His fall happened towards the first half. She looked at her watch. It felt like time had stood still, but it hadn't. Almost forty-five minutes had elapsed, and she hadn't a clue as to his status. After pacing for an eternity, she noticed the door to Stafford's office crack open with Stafford peeking out. Clearing his throat, he motioned to her. Rushing to the door, her voice wavered, "How is he?"

"Shaken up. He's going to sit out the rest of the game."

"Can I see him?"

"Yeah, he sent me to look for you."

He motioned her through the door while Lauren waited. "Jen, he's going to be fine. I'm just holding him out as a precaution."

"It's his hip, isn't it?" She could tell by the look on his face she was right. He led her around a corner and right to Ryne. His eyes were closed and his cheek pulsating. One look and she knew he was in pain.

She approached his side and ran her hand softly over his forehead, brushing his damp hair from his face. "How's it going?"

He opened his eyes and smiled wryly. "I'm fine. There's no need to worry."

Her fingers trembled as she held her hand to her lips. She didn't believe him. She rested her forehead against his, and held onto him.

"I know what you're thinking," he said.

"How can you know when I don't even know?" She ran her hand over his jersey. He was so much larger with all of the pads and protective gear. How with all of the equipment he wore could he get injured? She spun away and clasped her arms about herself. "Stafford told me they're holding you out for the rest of the game."

"Jen, it's just precautionary." She returned to his side and leaned against the table. "I can't believe my own brother took me out like that." He chuckled.

"I'm going to have to have a little discussion with my twin."

"I know he got a boarding call for it, but to me it looked accidental."

"I'm sure it was but the ref had to call what he thought he saw—even though he is my brother."

She clasped his hand. "You'd tell me if you were really injured, right?"

"Yeah, I would." He ran his hand along her brow. "I wish you'd stop fretting. Other than being a little shaken up, I'm fine. Now, tomorrow may be another story." Her head shot up with a look of concern. "I was joking, but in all honesty and with full disclosure, I'll probably be sore tomorrow. It wouldn't surprise me if I become a healthy scratch for our next game. I'm being completely truthful with you. You know how hard we play."

"I know. I just worry."

"I realize that, but I promise not to keep anything from you. If I'm hurt, I'll let you know, okay?" He ran his hand along the side of her face. "Can I have a smile now?" She'd been holding back the tears. He pulled her in close and whispered, "I love you."

"I love you too," she said and slipped her arms around his neck. "You scared the living daylights out of me." She stroked his face. "Please, don't do that again. When you didn't move, I thought the worst."

"Let's not go there anymore. I'm going to get dressed and I'll meet you in a few. Is Lauren still here?"

"Oh my, I forgot all about her. I left her in the hallway."

"You go find her and I'll meet you out there." He brushed her hair aside and kissed her lips. He slid off the table and hobbled to the locker room.

She knew he wasn't telling her the complete truth but decided not to go there. He said he wasn't hurt and she had to believe him.

Chapter Twenty-Four

RYNE'S INJURY HAD NOT BEEN severe and he returned to play the following day. After that, the days flew by and before Jen realized it the holidays were upon them. She spoke with her grandparents, and they decided to celebrate Christmas the weekend before so she and Ryne could spend Christmas with his family.

When she told Ryne of the arrangements, he was speechless. He couldn't believe that Wilford and Rose would do that for him—for them. Now they could fly to Calgary on the twenty-third and surprise his family. In fact, for the first time in more years than he could remember, the entire family would be home for Christmas.

He and Jen spent the morning of the twenty-second with her grandparents. Rose called it brunch while Ryne thought it was a good old breakfast that she served. He wasn't sure what the lunch portion was.

While Jen and Rose put the finishing touches on their meal, he sat with her grandfather, watching some Sunday morning news program. He wasn't paying attention because he had other things on his mind.

Half-way through the show, Wilford reached for

the remote and muted the television. "Something on your mind, son?"

He glanced at Wilford and wondered how he knew what was going through his mind.

"I can tell there is," Jen's grandfather insisted. "I have never seen you quite this nervous before."

"Where do you get that I'm nervous?"

Wilford gestured to his hand. "You haven't stopped tapping that damn finger the entire time you've been sitting there. Made me lose my concentration on what they were saying."

Ryne was flummoxed.

"I wasn't aware, sir."

"Didn't I tell you not to call me sir?"

"Yes, sir you did." Wilford gave him the evil eye. "Sorry, ah, Wilford. Yes, you did." He didn't know why her grandparents always worked him into a tizzy but they did. He became brainless. If he didn't know better, he'd think he failed college and not graduated at the top of his class.

"See, you are nervous."

"I guess I am."

Ryne was flabbergasted when Wilford moved closer. In a whisper he said, "You have our blessings."

"Huh? What are you talking about?"

"I had a little conversation with someone who shall be nameless. I was told that you made an impromptu visit somewhere." Ryne's eyes got larger as Wilford spoke. "I won't go into the conversation I had with this person other than, Rose and I are on board."

"You are?"

"Well, of course we are." Before either of them

could say another word, Jen called out that brunch was served. Ryne stood and shook Wilford's hand.

"Thank you, sir. I appreciate your approval."

"Let me just say, for Rose and me that is, our dear Jen was lost in a way we weren't aware of until you entered the picture and brought her back to us. I'd forgotten how much I missed her smile. You've given that back to our dear Jen, and we're forever grateful. Promise me one thing, son."

"Anything."

"Just never hurt our girl. She's been through so much in her life, and I don't think she can take another disappointment or loss."

"I promise you I would never do anything intentionally to hurt her. I love her."

"I know you do. Enough of this conversation, let's eat!" Wilford slapped Ryne on the back as they headed off to the dining room.

That was much easier than I expected. Two down and one to go.

The next morning Ryne arrived bright and early at Jen's. The team had won the night before which made going into their holiday break even better. He practically ran to her door, taking the steps two at a time. "What's got you so excited this morning?"

"Well, of course, you, my dear."

"Yeah, right." She smiled and grabbed her suitcase sitting beside the door. "Ready?"

"Car's still running."

"You know better than to leave your car running like that. Someone could come by and steal it."

He raised his hand. "Extra set of keys."

"Now I know why I love you so much. You've got

brains." She leaned in and kissed him then stepped
out the door. Ryne took her suitcase from her and
started down the stairs while she locked up. "I'd say
you're definitely in a hurry."

He stopped dead in his tracks and waited for her to
catch up. "Sorry about that, I guess I am."

"And why's that?"

"It's Christmas and vacation all rolled into one,
that's why. Plus, I get to spend it with the woman
of my dreams and my entire family."

They arrived at the airport with plenty of time
to spare. For once in a long time, Ryne wasn't
recognized while they waited. He was able to sit
comfortably and not worry about having to take sel-
fies or explain why he'd ended up in the penalty box
the night before. He breathed a sigh of relief as their
plane was called and they stood to board. "What
was that all about?"

"For once I could people watch." She looked at
him funny. "I never get a chance to just watch people when I'm at the airport. I guess we're here so
early, my adoring fans are still fast asleep."

She shook her head at his sarcasm. "Sweetheart,
only you would say something like that."

They had a smooth flight and right before landing,
she asked, "What are your plans? You really think
your family hasn't a clue that we're coming early?"

"Nope. Not one clue. In fact, my mom thinks
we're at a holiday party today."

"We are? Where?"

"At Lakeview. I told her a wee little fib." He raised
his thumb and forefinger about an inch apart. "She
thinks we're at your Christmas party."

"But it's Monday. You think she didn't check to see when we got out of school? I thought you were the one with the brains."

"I am and I thought this was a brilliant plan. What does it matter? Phil and Et aren't coming in until late Christmas Eve. Rafael arrives later this afternoon, and I think Jules is already home. We're the ones who are going to be a complete surprise. She wanted you to come, and she got her wish, right?"

"Well, yeah, but what if she's not ready for us? We weren't supposed to arrive until Christmas Day."

"Oh, she'll be ready for us. Don't you worry your pretty little mind." He grabbed her hand and brought it to his lips. "She's going to love having you here. We're going to have to be sure and phone your grandparents on Christmas."

"Yeah."

"All of a sudden you seem sad. What's wrong?"

"Nothing."

He knew by the tone of her voice something troubled her. He turned her head so she was forced to look directly in his eyes. "Jen?"

"Don't get me wrong... I love it that I have the chance to spend some time with your family. I really do. It's just that this is the first Christmas I haven't been with my family."

"I knew we shouldn't have left early."

"I wanted to go. Your mom made the holidays sound so magical on the ranch. Plus, you never get to spend Christmas with everyone. I'm happy you asked me to join you, I really am. In all honesty, Christmas is really just another day on the calendar. What does it matter if I spent the twenty third or the twenty-fifth with my grandparents? I still spent time quality time with them celebrating the holiday."

"You're sure?"

"I am." She leaned over and kissed him. "You are who I really want to be with. It's our first Christmas together and I want to enjoy every minute of it."

"Me too."

They had left St. Louis where it was a mild, overcast day and the temperature was expected to hover around freezing. Calgary was the polar opposite. It was a cloudless day but also a winter wonderland. The day before, the area had encountered heavy snows that still weighed down the trees. By the time Ryne secured their rental car, the streets had been cleared and their drive was smooth sailing. That is, until they reached the road to the ranch.

Ryne couldn't believe his eyes when he discovered it hadn't been plowed yet. He wondered what was up with that since his dad was always on top of keeping the roads on the ranch snow free. Not wanting to take the chance of getting stuck, he pulled onto the shoulder and was about to phone his dad when they heard a loud noise. There sat his dad inside the tractor cab, pushing the plow. It wasn't a normal-sized tractor. No, it was a huge farm implement that stood well above their SUV.

Ryne backed up and out of the way as his dad bustled through the end of the lane and onto the highway.

"I don't think he saw us. Look, he's coming to check to see if we're okay."

Jacques approached. Ryne knew the moment his

father recognized him because a huge smile filled his face. Ryne jumped from the car and threw his arms around his dad.

"Son, I didn't know you were coming today."

"It was supposed to be a surprise."

"It certainly was, especially when I realized I almost ran the tractor into your car. You were obstructed by the trees laden with snow." He turned to Jen with a huge smile. "My dear, it's so good to see you again. Jacklynne is going to be speechless when she sees you."

"I don't know about speechless, Dad. I've never seen Mom unable to put a sentence together."

"That's true but I know she will definitely be elated you're here. This is going to be the best Christmas ever. All of my children and you, Jen here at one time to celebrate."

He motioned towards the road. "Follow me. I need to plow out the path one more time."

Jacques jumped up into the cab of the tractor and started his slow plow back up the drive. "Mom is going to be speechless, I'm sure of that."

"This I've got to see."

Ryne followed his dad at a safe distance, and after what seemed an eternity, they pulled up at the house. Jacques continued to the shed where he stored the tractor. "I'll get our suitcases a little later. I want to surprise Mom before Dad has the chance to tell her we're here."

"Would he do that?"

"My dad can't contain a secret for more than two seconds. Hurry, let's get to the house before he does." They scurried to the door.

Ryne and Jen walked hand in hand into the house without knocking. They came in through the mud room and removed their boots. Jen lost her balance and started to giggle when Ryne put his finger to her lips whispering, "Shh."

Jacklynne's back was to them as she stood at the sink, washing dishes. The radio blared Christmas songs and she sang along with the melodious tunes. Luck was on their side; she hadn't heard Jen's giggle.

In their stocking feet, they crept soundlessly toward her. Jen stood back as he approached his mom from behind. "Jacques, honey, did you get us plowed out?" She continued washing dishes.

Ryne leaned his head in and tapped her on the shoulder. "Hey there, Mom."

She jumped at the sound of his voice. Spinning around, she practically knocked him onto the floor. "Ryne," she yelled. She threw herself into his arms. "Honey, where did you come from?" She kissed him soundly on the cheek and then noticed Jen standing off to the side. "Jennifer," she cried and ran to her. "Honey, come here and let me give you a proper welcome."

Before Jen knew what hit her, she was encased in her arms. If he wasn't mistaken, he saw tears in Jen's eyes. His mother's welcome meant the world to her, he just knew it. Even though she said she wasn't nervous returning to the ranch, he was almost assured that she was. He could tell by the way she wrung her hands on the plane and in the car as they drove.

"Ryne, dear, why didn't you tell me you were coming in early?"

"I wanted it to be a surprise, and by the way you

reacted, I think it was."

"Come, sit, tell me what's going on in your lives since I last saw you?" He knew what his mother was inkling for, and he wasn't going to give it to her. *In time. Give me a few more days.*

"Not much since I last saw you," Jen commented. "I've decided to tell my boss that I'm leaving after the holidays. It just didn't feel right before, and in all actuality, he doesn't need to know until contracts are being negotiated."

"Most people would wait, so you're definitely doing the honorable thing here. I bet you're getting excited. Have you found a space for your studio?"

She told her about her father's building. "I'm lucky I held onto it. It shouldn't take me long to get it up and running. I need to freshen it up a bit and purchase some equipment. I haven't been in the studio since I closed it up eight years ago. It will be difficult at first, knowing my dad's not going to walk in the door." Ryne reached for her hand, offering her support. "But it's something I need to do. I can't tell you how much better I feel since I made this decision. I pray I can make a go of it."

"Dear, I don't see how you can't. Look at the showing you had."

"Yeah, but everyone knew me, and it was a fund-raiser."

"Pfst. I don't believe that for a minute. You have talent. Don't worry, you'll do well."

"I'm trying to convince her to get into sports pho-tography. I think she's perfect for it."

"Oh honey, I agree with you." Looking back to Jen, "You need to take your time and do what you are comfortable with. In time you can expand." She patted her hand. "Can I get you both something to eat or drink? How about a cup of coffee or hot chocolate?"

"Mom, you know what I prefer."

Smiling at Jacklynne, Jen said, "I'll have what he's having."

"Two hot chocolates with whipped cream and sprinkles coming right up."

"Sprinkles?"

"They're the only way to go."

It was Christmas Eve and the house was almost filled. Philippe and Etienne played an early afternoon game in Minnesota and their plane was scheduled to arrive around ten. In plenty of time for the entire house to attend midnight mass.

That morning Jen and Jacklynne, along with Emma and Olivia, made cookies for Santa Claus. Jacklynne wasn't convinced that Emma still believed in the fictional character but made the most of it just in case. She still gave all of her children presents from Santa even though Philippe was almost thirty. It kept the spirit alive, and she didn't care if the boys were old enough to have children themselves. It made her feel giddy with excitement, and more so with all of her children present this year.

Ryne was getting antsy. He'd paced back and forth so many times he lost count. He wanted, no needed, to talk to her now, right now. He'd made plans and he definitely hadn't expected his mother to have a cookie brigade on her agenda. He'd waited for this day for what seemed like an eternity. He wasn't happy that lunch wasn't served until after one-thirty and took longer than normal. He grew anxious listening to his mother go on and on about the cookies they still had left to bake.

It was already later than he expected and he needed to get Jen alone, so right after lunch he grabbed their coats and hats. He found her in the kitchen helping put the finishing touches on the sugar cookies. Practically running into the room, he called, "Come on, let's get out of here."

A look of surprise crossed her face. "Ryne, I'm helping your mom."

"Come on." He grabbed her hand, and threw her coat and hat at her. "You've been baking all day. I promised I'd show you the ranch after a snowfall, and now is the best time."

"We'll be here a few more days. Can't it wait?" Her eyes grew larger as he hurried her towards the door.

"No, it can't." He stormed out the door as she stopped to put on her coat. Jen glanced back at Jacklynne and his sisters, unsure what set him off.

"Something certainly has him in a tizzy. Go on, Jen we're almost done here. There are just a few more cookies that need icing. I'm curious to see what has got my son so upset." As Jen put her coat on, Jacklynne grabbed a bag and threw some cookies into it. "Maybe this'll help."

"Thanks." Jen reached for the bag and shook her head in disgust. "I have no idea what his problem is. He went from zero to one hundred. I guess I'll see you all later. Wish me well."

Jacklynne smirked at her as she headed out the door. He'd been in a lousy mood from the moment

they decided to bake cookies. Jen could only wonder what his little tirade was about. She hoped their
little walk would settle him down as she didn't want
him ruining their day. After all, it was Christmas
Eve.

She discovered Ryne waiting for her beside the
snowmobile. The sun was shining brightly and
there was a little chill in the air, but it wasn't too
bad. She zipped up her coat and pulled on her hat,
covering her ears. She hated when her ears got cold.
Then she remembered the ear muffs she'd tucked
inside the pocket of her coat. Pulling them out, she
set them over her hat so her ears would have extra
protection.

She took her time as she strolled over to where he
stood. She knew he wasn't happy, but she hadn't
a clue why. In fact, she'd barely seen him all day
as she'd been in the kitchen since breakfast baking. The entire time she rolled out the dough,
she thought of her mom and the times they made
Christmas cookies. It was an annual affair and she
missed it— really missed it. She hadn't made holiday
cookies since her mom died, and she realized how
ecstatic she was that Jacklynne waited to include her.
She'd been in a really good mood—that was, until
Ryne stormed in and ruined it for her.

"What is wrong with you?" she asked as she
stormed over.

"Nothing, why?"

Hands on hips, she said, "I can't believe you treated

me like you just did, especially in front of your mom and sisters."

"What did I do?" He was oblivious to how he'd acted. It was Christmas Eve and she decided not to press him. Whatever was on his mind was important to him, so she'd listen and then react. She wanted to enjoy the day and not end up in a fight. In that moment she decided to take the high road and hopefully not regret it.

He reached for her as he sat down. Wrapping her arms around him she leaned in close. "This better be good since I was having a good time with your family." She held off handing over the cookies. Instead, she tucked them into her pocket where she hoped they wouldn't get crushed. She decided she could possibly bribe him, if needed.

He revved up the motor. "Hang on!" And with that he started off in the direction of the pond. The sun was beginning to dip on the horizon. She assumed they had about another hour's worth of light. She hoped whatever he had on his mind, he'd get it over with, because she wasn't fond of being on the snowmobile when it got dark.

He stopped right at the edge of the frozen pond, stepped off the snowmobile and reached for her hand. He steadied her as she flung her leg over the edge and lost her balance in the deep snow. "Urrghh, I can't believe you interrupted my fun and brought me out here." She stomped her feet trying to get the snow off that had accumulated when she stumbled. When she got control of herself, she noticed his back was to her. He seemed out of sorts, tense, and for what she wasn't sure.

She was clueless as to why he insisted they come out here. But she remembered her pledge to herself to take the high road and reached for his hand. With a half-smile, he looked her in the eyes. "Will you forgive me?" He leaned in and swept aside the hair that had become plastered against her cheek from her hat and muffler. "I patiently waited for you for what seemed like hours while you baked cookies. I couldn't wait any longer, listening to you laugh and talk about whatever you were rambling on and on about."

She smiled up at him. "We were talking about Christmas."

"Oh. Whatever. I needed to be with you, today, right now."

"Why, what's so important that it couldn't keep?"

He grabbed her hand and led her onto the ice.

"Ryne, I'm not too sure about this." Pointing to the ice, she said, "It doesn't look too safe."

"We're fine. This pond's been frozen over for weeks." Earlier in the day while she'd been baking, he came out with the tractor and plowed the snow from the ice. He had a special purpose for that along with the fact he and his siblings could play a game of pick-up hockey the following day. *Just like we used to do.*

He needed to talk to her and wanted it to be right here. Somewhere they'd always remember. "So, I've been thinking."

"About what?"

"My future."

"What about it?"

"You know that I spoke with Adam about my

contract over the summer."

"Yeah."

"I still have a year left."

"I remember."

"After that hit I took in the game against Et and Phil, I've been wondering how long I'll be able to play at this level."

"Are you injured again? Why didn't you tell me?" She got all concerned.

"Sweetheart, I'm fine." He pulled her closer. "Please listen to what I have to say, okay?" She nodded her head and rested it against his chest. "My goal in life has always been to play for the Storm. When I went down onto the ice and lay there, I realized that my time is waning. What if I get seriously injured and can't play for Calgary? That's all that's been on my mind since that night."

"Why did you wait so long to share this with me?"

"Because, if I play for my hometown team, that means I have to relocate again. I'll be leaving St. Louis and returning home."

"I see." She remained locked in his embrace as he spoke.

"Jen, I love you and I don't want to be without you in my life. I wanted to talk to you about my dreams. Now that you are leaving teaching, you won't have to remain in St. Louis tied to a job."

"But my photography."

"Can't you do that anywhere?"

"Sure, I can, but St. Louis is where I have all of my contacts, my studio."

"Do you really have to live there to keep those relationships alive? You can build new ones. I'm sure you could find a location for a studio here in town. You have a website. Everything you produce can be uploaded there. It's not like you don't have alternative ways to sell your photographs; you do."

"But my grandparents?"

He pulled away from her setting his hands on her shoulders. Looking her directly in the eyes, "You don't see Ro and Miles that often."

She was honest. "No, I don't."

"So what's the difference? Today, you can Skype, talk long distance without complications. Your relationship with Rose and Wilford would be the same as what you already have with Ro and Miles. So what's the problem? Why couldn't you move?"

"I'm not going to upend my life just because." She pulled away and turned her back to him. "I know you have your dreams. I realize that you could be one injury away from ending your career. I get that, but why do I have to give up my life, my family, why?

She felt his hand again on her shoulder. He turned her towards him. "Because you love me."

"I do love you but why should I just leave my life? I'm just starting to get my career back on track. What is here that isn't there?"

"Me."

"And what if you don't wind up playing for the Storm, huh?"

"Then, I won't relocate. I'll stay in St. Louis."

"You make it sound so easy. Even I know that it's not."

"I know the general manager quite well. His name is Anthony Theophilos. He's known that I've wanted to play for the Storm since I was a little tyke. I've decided to contact him and see if he might have an interest in me."

"Do you think he does?"

"He'd love to have all three of us playing together. Who wouldn't want three brothers playing for the same team?"

"You can't be so sure." She sighed. "I don't understand why you're doing this. Everything is going so well. I'm happy, I thought you were happy."

"I am happy."

"Then why are you trying to change everything. Why?" She was confused.

He turned away from her and began to pace across the ice. He was going about this wrong. He'd played this conversation over and over again in his head, and it definitely hadn't gone like this. Where had he gone wrong?

"I've handled this so wrong," he muttered to himself.

"What was that?"

He shook his head not knowing what to say or do. *How can I fix this? Think, think.*

"Ryne, I don't want to argue with you. I wanted this to be a magical Christmas, and it has up until this moment. I love your mom and dad, and I've really gotten to know Olivia and Emma. I feel like they're family to me. Today when I was rolling out the cookie dough, I thought of my mom. I haven't made Christmas cookies since she died. Being here with Jacklynne has brought back so many memories of baking with my mom. It made my heart feel happy, remembering. Please, I don't want to fight.

I want to remember this trip as a happy time for you, me, and your family."

That was his lead in. He approached her. "I've handled this all wrong." With that he got down on bended knee. Her eyes grew wide, her hands began to tremble. "Jen, you are the light of my life. I think I've loved you from the moment you ran me down."

"Hey there."

"Well, it's true, isn't it?" He reached for her hand. "I brought you out here to do just this— Jennifer Steele, you are my everything. I love you more than life itself. I don't think I'd survive if anything ever happened to you— or us. I want to be by your side when you shine with your new career. I want to grow old with you, have kids that will know not to text and drive." She glared at him. "Seriously, I love you with all of my heart. You are my soul-mate. I became the luckiest man on this earth when we met on that parking lot. Will you have a family with me, grow old with me? Will you marry me?"

By the time he finished his proposal, tears were streaming down her face. He reached into his pocket and pulled out a box. Reaching out to her, he opened the lid. And there, on a bed of red vel-vet, sat the most beautiful ring she'd ever seen. In complete shock, she raised her hands to her face and blew out her breath. "Jen, will you become one with me and marry me?"

Overcome with emotion she couldn't put words to her thoughts, so instead she nodded her head.

"Honey, don't cry."

He removed her glove and slipped the ring onto

her finger, then wiped her tears. The three-carat diamond ring caught the last rays of sunlight. He ran his hand along her face and then cupped the back of her head. Leaning in he gathered her close and pressed his lips to hers. This was their time to rejoice and be happy. Just as he started to pull away his eyes caught the sunset. "Look at that," he pointed to the deep rose and orange colors as they dotted the winter sky. An airplane's contrail was streaked with the deep colors. He whipped out his cell phone and took a picture of the two of them with the sunset in the background. He never wanted to forget that moment in time.

When she was finally able to get her voice back, she said, "Ask me again?" They'd never talked about marriage *per se* and his proposal took her off guard.

"Ask you what?" She gave him the look that he'd become accustomed to over the last several months. Kneeling down again, he reached for her left hand. Brushing a kiss across the diamond, he looked at her directly. "Jen, my love, will you marry me?"

"Yes, yes, I'll marry you." She kneeled down beside him and wrapped her arms around him. "Here you planned this perfect proposal, and I almost ruined it baking cookies." He roared with laughter. "Well, I almost did ruin it." And then she remembered the cookies.

Reaching into her pocket she withdrew the bag. "Let's celebrate." She opened the bag and pulled out a sugar cookie. It was an angel that she'd cut out, baked, and decorated. For a moment she thought the angel was her mom looking down on her from heaven. It was ironic that she'd been thinking about her earlier, and Jacklynne had packed the angel cookies for them.

He took one bite of his cookie and asked, "So, when should we tell everyone?"

"Tomorrow, after all of the presents have been opened."

"Do you understand why I wanted to talk to you?"

"I do. I know you're concerned about me leaving my home, but the way I look at it, you are my family now, and I'll follow you anywhere."

Chapter Twenty-Five

ETIENNE AND PHILIPPE MADE IT home just in time to celebrate midnight mass with the family. Jacklynne insisted she was the happiest she'd been in a long time. All of her children were home safe enjoying the holidays.

Christmas morning, Jen was surprised to find Jacques in the kitchen. "You're up early," she said.

"Yep! Up with the chickens. I like to prepare Christmas breakfast for the entire family," he said. He'd just started to mix the biscuits.

"I love homemade biscuits. My mom used to make them all the time." A look of sadness crossed her face. Jacques immediately picked up on that and went to her side. He slid his arms around her. "Jen, my dear, I'm so sorry you lost your parents. I know how difficult these last years have been for you. Jacklynne and I would love it if you would consider us as your parents. We'll be here always for you, even if you and Ryne don't work out." She gazed up at him. "I don't mean it like that...I know you're going to be together, but if something happens and you don't get married..."

She chuckled. "Jacques, I think you should stop while you're ahead. I completely understand what you're saying, and I'd love to think of you as my parents too."

He kissed her forehead. "Well, now that's over with, let's knead these biscuits."

By the time the biscuits had been cut, the kitchen was filled with hungry men. Philippe, Etienne, and Rafael had joined them in the kitchen. Jules and Ryne weren't far behind. "Dad, it smells good in here."

"It does, but we can't eat until your mother and the girls come down."

"We're right here, Daddy," exclaimed Emma. "I've been up for a while. I had to make sure Santa came." Everyone howled with laughter.

"Well, did he?" asked her father.

"He did." She could hardly contain herself, hopping from one foot to the other. "So let's hurry up and eat so we can open our presents." She ran to the table and reached for the bowl of scrambled eggs.

"Em's, what did I tell you? You need to wait for everyone to sit down before you can begin eating."

"Dad, I know." She dropped her head and started to pout.

Jacklynne smiled at her daughter and shook her head, then looked at Jen. At least the girl still believed in the magic of Christmas, and Jen was happy to see it. Children grew up way too fast these days and she hated for them to lose their innocence. She knew the boys would make over their Santa gifts because it made them feel like kids.

It seemed like hours had passed since Emma first sat down at the table to eat. "Dad, are you almost done?" she whined as Jacques finished off the last of the biscuit on his plate.

"Em's, I'm still eating."

"But there's nothing on your plate."

He winked at her and reached for another biscuit.
"Dad…"

"Em's, you need to have a little patience here. You know the rules. Breakfast and then presents."

"I know…" She dropped her head into her hands. All the while Jen watched the exchange between father and daughter. She hoped that someday she'd be sitting right where Jacklynne was, watching Ryne and their daughter banter back and forth about the opening of presents. It brought a smile to her face.

With a crooked grin, Ryne leaned over and ran his hand across his face. "Whatcha smiling at?" She motioned her head towards Emma and Jacques.

"That's nothing new. According to Mom, Emma's the worst one of the bunch when it comes to opening Christmas gifts. You're lucky. This year's she's been pretty mild. Normally, she's throwing a hissy fit. I can remember quite a few years she ended up in time out, and it extended the time before we could open our gifts. It's pretty comical to think that she gets that worked up, but Santa does only come once a year, and he does bring surprise gifts."

"Surprises, huh? Do you have a surprise for me?"

"I guess you're going to have to wait and see."

"Oh boy, should I egg your dad on to get him to eat faster." He shrugged. "I guess I'd better behave or I'll end up in time out."

"Yeah, but I'm sure we could think of something to do in your time out." He waggled his eyebrows at her causing her to chuckle.

"What's up with you two," chimed in Rafael.

"You're a little cozy over there."

"We are not," Ryne said as he leaned in closer, to her laughing the entire time. "I certainly hope you're not keeping track of us. Don't you have other things to worry about?"

"Not right now I don't."

While Jacques lingered over one last piece of bacon, Jen convinced Emma to help clear the table. "Emma, since you're just sitting there, why don't you help me clear the table? I'm sure by the time we're done, your dad will have had his fill."

Emma dragged herself out of her chair and helped Jen and Olivia clear the table. Jacklynne had already started cleaning up the mess in the kitchen. By the time all of the dishes were rinsed, Jacques was on his last cup of coffee and was getting up from the table.

"Finally," Emma said marching towards the Christmas tree. "I've already gone through the presents."

"Emma."

"Well, I did. There's a stack for me, Olivia, Rafael, Philippe, Ryne, and Jules. *And* take a look at the huge one sitting here for Jen. It's so big I could hardly move it."

"What about my stack?" asked Etienne.

"Oh, yours is here somewhere."

"Well, since you know where everything is why don't you hand it all out," her mother said as she sat down beside Jacques.

"Okay…" Emma was so excited to open her gifts she practically threw everyone their presents. "I can't carry Jen's since it's soooo big."

"I'll get it," Ryne said winking at Jen.

"Now remember, we take turns opening gifts. That way we can see what everyone receives."

"That takes too long."

"Emma…" Jacques was losing his patience with his youngest.

"Alright, alright. Can I start first?" Jacques nodded. It seemed like it took hours for everyone to open their presents. Jen had mailed hers so she wouldn't have to carry them on the plane. She gave Jacklynne and Jacques the print of Ryne sitting on horseback at sunset— the one that helped her make the decision to return to photography. She'd taken photographs of Etienne and Philippe on the ice when they'd played the Generals early in the season and gave them each framed copies. She didn't have photographs of Jules and Rafael, so they received copies of her favorite prints. Jen knew Olivia and Emma liked to read, so they each got a book from their favorite series.

It was harder for her to shop for Ryne. She'd found a beautiful Irish knit sweater at one of the stores in St. Louis. She knew it would look great on him and showcase his broad chest. She couldn't wait to see him in it and loved his expression as he pulled it out of the box. He held it up and looked at it closely. "This is beautiful. I love it," he leaned over kissing her cheek.

Jen hadn't expected to receive any presents but was overjoyed when she saw the stash of gifts at her feet. She was overwhelmed by the kindness everyone had shared with her. It brought tears to her eyes, especially knowing she had gifts to share with everyone. Emma's excitement at one of her gifts sent Jen over the edge, and she jumped from her seat. "Excuse me," she said as she hurried from the room. All eyes were on Ryne. He had no idea what was going on, so he followed her.

He'd seen her hurry up the stairs and found her in the bedroom that she was using. Softly he knocked, then opened the door. Her back was to the door as she looked out the window. He knew she was crying for he saw her shoulders shaking.

"Sweetheart, what's wrong? Why the tears?" He drew her close and nuzzled her neck. She didn't say a word. "Talk to me. What's got you so upset?" She spun around, flung her arms around his waist and buried her head into his chest.

"This is all so much. Everyone has been so nice to me. All of the gifts and all— I never expected to be accepted so into your family."

"Hey there, look at me." With his index finger he raised her chin. "Of course my family accepts you. They love you. I can't wait to see how they'll react when we tell them we're engaged." His comment drew more tears. "Honey, come on now. Tell me, what's the real reason for the tears?" He ran his hand up and down her back comforting her in the only way he knew. He placed his hands on either side of her face and rested his forehead against hers. "Whatever it is, I want you to know that I'm here for you. I can't help you if you won't talk to me." She sniffled as she listened to him. "I love you and I'm here for the long haul."

In a wobbly voice, "I know and I love you, too." As she pulled away from him, she folded her arms about herself and walked across the room. She didn't know what had overcome her.

"I'm sorry I ruined the day."

"Honey, you didn't. They just thought you needed to use the restroom."

"I'm not so sure about that.' She rubbed her hands over her arms. "But you knew."

"Of course I knew something wasn't right. Out of nowhere I felt a change in you. I saw how you were fighting back the tears. Do you want to call your grandparents? Is that it?"

She shook her head. "No, that's not it at all."

"Then what's got you so upset?"

She made her way to the bed and sat down. She closed her eyes and when she opened them again found Ryne kneeling before her. He took her hands and raised them to his lips. "Are you sad because your parents aren't here to share in our day?" He hit the nail on the head as the tears started to flow again. "Honey, I don't know what to say. I wish they were here too. I really do, but they're not. Try to imagine them. I know they'd be thrilled that you're marrying me." He jokingly said and then heard a little chuckle come from her as he dried her tears. "Seriously though, my family is going to be your family soon. I know they can't replace your parents, but I hope my mom and dad can be there for you, too."

"Your dad suggested that to me today. Did you tell them we were engaged?"

"No, I didn't."

"A while ago, your mom offered to be there for me as well."

"From the moment they first laid eyes on you,

they fell in love with you." He moved from the floor and seated himself beside her. "I want to tell you something." She raised her eyes. "When I first decided to marry you, I knew I needed to ask the blessing of your family. I couldn't go to your dad, so instead I went to Wilford and Miles."

"You did? When?"

"When doesn't matter. I needed to know that they'd be comfortable having me in your life as your husband. I'll be honest. I wasn't sure whether or not I'd get their approval, but I did." He displayed the half-crooked grin she'd come to love. "In getting their approval, I feel like your dad approved too. If you're overwhelmed with emotion right now, I can't even begin to imagine how you're going to feel when we tell my family." He ran his finger over her bottom lip. "Honey, I realize this is going to be a huge change for you. Just thinking about moving away from Wilford and Rose has to be weighing on your mind. We'll have them visit often. I'll build us a huge house, maybe even a guest house, just so your grandparents can visit. I want you to be happy not sad."

"I am happy," she said smiling at him. "I don't know why I'm crying. Yesterday was the happiest day of my life. When you asked me to marry you… It was a dream come true. Ryne, you're my life." She ran her hand along the side of his face, cupping his jaw. "I couldn't sleep last night. My mind was going at warp speed, thinking about everything that I, we, are going to have to do. And then when I was able to breathe, I realized what if you don't get traded. Things would remain status quo— that is except we'd get married, live together, and maybe have a family. And then, my mind started racing all over again."

"So maybe these are happy tears."

"In all actuality, what I think is I'm dead tired, and when I get this way I just get all emotional." She ran her hands across her face. "Give me a minute and then we can go back downstairs." She kissed him, then stood and made her way to the bathroom.

He breathed a huge sigh of relief. He knew all along that spending the holidays away from her family weighed heavily on her. He knew how his family felt about her and believed their reaction to their engagement would turn her day around.

Hand-in-hand they returned to finish opening their presents. "Everything, okay?" Jacklynne asked.

"Everything's fine." Smiling at his mom, she said, "So, where did we leave off?"

"We're all done here, but Jen, you've got that huge gift over there."

"I do, that's right."

"Who's it from?"

"I don't know. There is no tag, just to Jen. I wonder who it could be from." She looked about the room and no one claimed it. "Maybe there's a clue inside." She opened the box and discovered a smaller wrapped box. Inside that box was another box. "Still no clue." She unwrapped that and found two smaller presents. She opened the first and discovered a camera lens. "Oh wow, I can really use this." She leaned over to Ryne, "I guess this present is from you since you're the only one here that knew I needed this lens."

He shrugged his shoulders. "Who knows? There still isn't a name."

"I know it's from you," she slapped at his arm.

"Open the next box."

She slipped the ends of the paper aside and discovered yet another smaller box. "Ryne, this is insane." Everyone laughed as she kept opening box after box after box. When she got down to one the size of a jeweler's box, she knew what he'd done. Ripping open the last box, she looked up at him. He reached for it and withdrew the ring box.

His family sat in awe as he dropped to his knee. "Oh my gosh, is he doing what I think he's doing," cried Jacklynne as she clapped her hands.

"I think he is," Jacques added as he watched his son.

"Mom, what's Ryne doing?" asked Emma. "Why is he on the floor?"

"Shhh," Jacklynne scowled at her daughter. "Quiet, I want to hear this."

Ryne glanced over his shoulder at his mother. He snickered at his sister's comment. "Only from the mouth of a ten-year-old," he said smiling up at his intended. The night before, he'd tried to decide the best way to tell his family they were engaged, so he came up with this elaborate gift scheme. He'd searched the house trying to find boxes of various sizes and with a stroke of luck he came across his mother's stash. Painstakingly, he wrapped box after box. He thought Jen would get a kick out of it, and after her little crying fit, he knew he'd made the right decision.

By the time he flipped open the box that held her

ring, she was laughing right along with him. When he withdrew the ring, he heard his mother's gasp. "Oh my, Jacques, look at that."

"Will you hush, Jacklynne. I want to hear him ask her."

By the time he'd begun to place the ring onto her finger, they were both doing their best to keep their laughter under control. The price of admission just to listen to his family watch this scene play out before their eyes was priceless.

"Mom."

"Will you shush Emma. Please."

"Dad, Mom told me to shush."

"I whole heartedly agree with her."

"Hmmm," Emma was not a happy camper.

"Now that we have a little bit of silence from our gawkers sweetheart, you know how much I love you." Looking across the room at his family. "And after having been through your first Christmas here, putting up with everyone's shenanigan's…"

"Will you just ask her?" Jacklynne blurted.

"Mom?"

"What, Ryne? Just ask her."

"Do you think you can put up with my family for the rest of your life?" She sheepishly smiled at him. She knew he was dragging this out just to spite his mother.

"I can't believe you just said that," Jacklynne said. "We're not *that* bad."

Ryne howled with laughter. Turning back to his mother, "Of course you're not. She loves you all and that's why she said…."

"Yes." Jen chimed in. "Yes, I'll marry you."

"But he didn't ask," Olivia added.

"Yes, I did, but for you, Olivia, I will again. Jennifer Steele, after all of this, will you marry me?"

"Yes, yes, I will." She threw her arms around his neck.

"She said yes." Olivia jumped out of her chair and ran to their side. She wrapped her arms as best as she could around the happy couple. "You're going to be my sister, right? I can't wait."

"I guess I am." She pulled away from Ryne and watched as he placed her ring back onto her hand. It was the best feeling in the world, having him glide the platinum band down her finger. She watched the diamond sparkle in the light. The night before she hadn't had time to admire the ring before they hurried back to the house. Ryne had hidden it in his pocket when they walked in the door, so no one was the wiser he'd proposed.

Jacques swept Jen into his arms. "Welcome to the family. I knew from the first moment I laid my eyes on you we'd be seeing this day."

Next to congratulate them was Jacklynne. As she kissed his cheek she uttered, "With the communicator that you are, son, I certainly thought your proposal would have been more eloquent than that."

"Jacklynne, it was the most perfect proposal a girl could ask for."

"But he barely asked you."

"Oh no, he did. It was the perfect setting, right at sunset."

"When, where? It certainly wasn't here."

"Oh, that's where you're wrong. Remember yesterday when he rushed me out of here when we were baking cookies?" Jacklynne nodded. "We went out to the pond, and he got down on bended knee with the most beautiful words I'd ever heard. In fact, Ryne took a photo marking the occasion."

"I have to see that."

He whipped out his cell and showed his mother the photo. Smiles lit their faces, and Jen had the ring proudly displayed in the picture with the brilliant sunset in the background. "Son, I'm glad you did it right. I knew I'd raised you better."

Everyone laughed at her comment. "Do you really think I'd spoil this moment with my family looking over my shoulder? I'm smarter than that and Jen deserved more than that."

"I think we need to celebrate," Etienne produced a bottle of champagne and several glasses. The cork popped and the wine bubbled up and over the rim of the bottle. "Ooops."

He poured glasses for all of the adults and then produced a bottle of sparling grape juice for Jules, Emma and Olivia. After he'd served everyone, he raised his glass. "To my twin and his fiancée. May you be as happy in fifty years as you are today. Welcome to the family, Jen. We're thrilled that you are here." He leaned in and kissed her cheek.

Next to toast the couple was Philippe. "Jen, the first time I saw you, you and Ryne were strolling through the airport. That one look told me all I needed to know— I knew my brother was head over heels in love with you. The way he looked at you, I knew right then and there you were going to become a part of this family. I'm so happy that he's found someone to share his life. Congratulations!

And to second what Etienne said, welcome to the family."

As they each sipped their wine, Ryne grabbed ahold of her hand. Her sadness from earlier had been replaced with an effervescent smile. She absolutely glowed with happiness. His focus from Jen shifted when he felt a tug on his sweater. He glanced down and discovered Emma. "Can I say something?"

"Well, sure you can," Jen said to her soon-to-be sister.

"Jen, my brother sure knows how to pick 'em." The room burst out in laughter. "What's so funny?"

"Nothing, Emma. That's so sweet of you to say." Jen stooped down to look into Emma's face.

"I'm so happy that you are going to be my sister. It'll be great having an older sister."

"Hey, what about me?" asked Olivia.

"Someone older than you." Olivia growled at her. "Sorry, Liv but that's how I feel. Jen, you've been so nice to me. You haven't treated me like a little kid and I like that."

"I'm glad that you do."

"Anyways— I was wondering..." Jen watched as she hemmed and hawed.

"Out with it, Emma," Olivia practically shouted.

"Okay, okay... I was wondering if I can be in the wedding."

Jen kneeled before Emma. "Of course you can. I wouldn't get married without you or Olivia."

Emma slapped her hand over her mouth. "Really, I can be in it?" Jen nodded her head.

"What about me?" Etienne playfully asked. "Can I be in it, too?"

"That's up to your brother."

Ryne chuckled at her response. "I'm going to have to think that one over." Etienne frowned at his brother.

"All joking aside, Jen and I haven't even begun to discuss the wedding. So don't begin to ask if we've set a date, or where it's going to be. We'll let you know all in due time."

Jacklynne took Jen's hand. "Honey, I'd like to help out anyway that I can. I don't want to overstep my bounds here, but…"

"You're not and I understand. I'd love to have your help. I can't do it all by myself."

Jacklynne pulled her into her arms. In a soft voice she whispered, "I don't want to replace your mother."

"You're not, but I'm glad to have you by my side." She pulled away and slipped her arm around Ryne. "I have to warn you. My grandmother Rowena may be a handful when she gets wind of this."

He tipped his head, grinned and said "I'd have to agree with you there, Jen. I still don't know how I made it home alive after I first met her."

"She was just doing her job."

"What does that mean?" asked Emma.

"Oh honey, Ryne was just joking."

"Have you told your grandparents yet?" Jacques asked as he sipped his champagne.

"*I* haven't."

"What does that mean?"

"From what I understand, your son here asked both of my grandfathers."

"He did, did he?"

"I did and I promised we'd phone when she said yes. So, how about it? Let's get them on the line."

While Jen and Ryne phoned her grandparents, Jacques wrapped Jacklynne in his arms. "That's sure some son we raised. To think he had the notion to ask both Wilford's and Miles' approval. We taught him well." She nodded.

"I have to say, Jen is perfect for him."

"She is. I'm just sorry her parents aren't here."

"We'll just have to make sure she doesn't miss them too much."

"You're good for her, Jacklynne."

"I hope so because I certainly love her an awfully lot. I think she'll fit right into our crazy family; in fact, she already does. Jacques, we have a wedding to prepare for."

"Jacklynne, not now. You heard Ryne. They haven't even set a date yet. Stay out of it until you're asked."

She frowned at her husband. Maybe she'd have a few more answers when they got off the phone with her grandparents. But either way, what she did know was this would be a memorable Christmas, one that would go down in the record books for all of the family to remember.

Chapter Twenty-Six

JEN SAW LITTLE OF RYNE when they went their separate ways after Christmas. The Generals were on the road for the first two weeks of the year. She spent New Year's with Rowena and Miles while he went on to Chicago. They spoke daily, sometimes several times a day, and were lucky enough to Skype as the clock struck midnight and entered the New Year.

Each morning she woke to a text from him wishing her a good day that always ended with 'I miss you and I love you'. She looked forward to her daily love notes and couldn't wait for their nightly calls. She anxiously awaited his return and counted down the days to where she could kiss him and hold him in her arms. She was thrilled when he finally knocked at her door. She threw her arms around him and didn't want to let go.

"I take it you missed me."

"I did," she broadly smiled and ran her hand down his scruffy cheek. "I like this." She grabbed his hand and dragged him inside where he pulled her into his arms and gave her a long, welcoming kiss. She knew he'd missed her just as much she did him.

"I know it's late but I needed to see you." He'd come straight from the airport.

"You look tired."

"What's new? This was one long road trip. I'm happy we'll be in town for a while."

She led him to the couch where he pulled her onto his lap. He kissed her again and then slid his lips to her neck and nuzzled. "You always smell so good. Gosh, how I missed holding you in my arms. This trip was *way* too long."

She clutched his shirt and pulled him close. She fed from the warmth of his body, his kisses. "I really, really missed you."

"I can tell," he chuckled and kissed the top of her nose.

She leaned away slightly. "Not to change the subject, but I spoke with your mom today."

"I'm sure I already know what she wanted."

She played with the hair along his nape.

"I guess we need to make a few plans, huh?"

"We do." She slid off his lap so she could focus on their conversation. "We need to decide on a date, a time, and place for the wedding, the size. And we have to decide where we plan on living...There's just so much we need to do."

"Wow. That was sure a mouthful. Would you mind taking a breath? I found myself holding mine just keeping up with you."

Playfully she slapped his chest and took a deep breath.

"That was quite a deep breath."

"Didn't you tell me to breathe?"

He chuckled. "Indeed, I did." He reached for her hand and pulled her towards him. "In all honesty, I haven't been around at all since we became engaged, but we've got a better schedule for the rest of the year. I think our longest road trip is less than four days, so that definitely should help." She played with the buttons on his shirt while listening to him. "First things first, have you told Johnston that you're leaving?"

"Ah—no, I kind of chickened out. And before you ask, I haven't told anyone other than Lauren that we're engaged."

"How come?"

Jen shrugged. "It just didn't feel right with you on the road."

"I've got an idea. Let's throw an engagement party. I'll fly my parents and siblings in, along with Rowena and Miles. We can have one big party, and that's also a good way for all of my family to meet yours. What do you say?"

"I like it. When and where should we have it?"

"I guess the question is do you want a more formal affair or relaxed? Formal, I'd say Lucerne's." He paused as he thought for a moment. "Hey, I just had a brilliant idea. Let's invite everyone to a game, rent out a suite, and have the party at Faceoff. They have a private room in the back that we can use."

Thumping her fingers on her leg, "I like it." She ran and pulled out a schedule, returning to sit beside him. "Did you realize the Storm is coming to town the end of February?"

"Don't remind me." He rolled his eyes, remembering the last time they were in town when Etienne had slammed him into the boards. He grabbed his phone and pulled up the Storm schedule. "They have the next two nights off after that, and their next game is at home. Maybe my brothers can arrange to stay and then meet up with the team in Calgary."

Ryne didn't even let her respond. He pressed a number on his phone and waited for the party to answer. "Hey, brother of mine, we've got a question for you." She knew right away who he was speaking with, Etienne.

"We? We as in Jen and I?" He smiled at her and ran his finger along her cheek. "I didn't know you had another trip to the big Lou this year. Jen and I are thinking of planning a party. Do you think you'd be able to stick around for it?" She watched his face as he listened to Etienne. "Great. We'll go ahead and plan something, and if it doesn't work out for you, we'll deal with it. We want to include as many of the family as we can."

She could tell he was trying to get rid of his brother. "I just got home a few minutes ago. It was the road trip from hell. We won all of the games, but between flight delays, injuries—you name it, it happened. I'm just glad to be back home with my gal." He grabbed her hand. "Okay I will." He ended the call. "Et says hi."

"Well? What did he say?"

"He thinks they can swing it. He needs to check in with the coach." He curled a portion of her hair around his finger. "I'll arrange the suite and Faceoff. Now we need to decide on who we're inviting."

"My grandparents, of course, and Lauren. I'd like to invite the teachers. We can't forget about Ed."

"No, we can't. I'll take care of the team and my family, too."

She ran her hand down his thigh. "You're doing

everything."

"Eh, I'm at the dome all of the time, and it makes sense for me to arrange that. You know I do have a few contacts there."

"You do, do you?" She laughed.

"I'll make an announcement to the team and post the information in the locker room. You take care of school and whoever else you think of. And that's it."

"We need to arrange the food."

"Piece of cake, too. Don't worry. It was my idea and I don't want to stress you out."

"Well, okay then. Don't forget to arrange a hotel for your parents." She paused and thought for a second. "Don't do that. They can stay with me."

"Are you sure? Since it's a Saturday night game, I'm sure they'll bring the girls, too."

Pointing to the upstairs, "And how many bedrooms do I have? I think I have plenty of room."

"That's settled then. We can check one thing off your list."

"That wasn't even on it."

He pulled her close. "When do you want to get married? I'm sure you've been pondering that some." She nodded her head. "Have you thought about where you want to get married?" She nodded again. "Would you care to share it with me?"

She'd thought of nothing else but where and when since he'd asked her to marry him. On her flight home from visiting Rowena and Miles, she came to a conclusion. It was mainly just her grandparents and Lauren who were important to her. He had a whole family. She had decided to wait until they were together again to tell him what she wanted. She grabbed for his hands. Holding them tightly, she began to gnaw on her lower lip.

"Hey there, what's got you troubled all of a sudden?"

"I just realized how much I missed you. I'm not sure why, but I started to think about Philippe and Annabelle. I don't know what I'd do if something happened to you. These last two weeks have been the longest in my entire life. I understand how lost Philippe is without her because I don't know how I'd be able to go on without you."

"Honey, you have nothing to worry about. I'm not going anywhere."

"You're sure about that?"

"Yep. As far as I know you've got me for at least another fifty years." He kissed the tip of her nose. "Now let's get you out of these doldrums...Where and when?"

She attempted to pull away from him, but he tightened his hold on her. "You're not going anywhere until you answer my question."

"I wasn't going anywhere." She smiled. "I hoped to have a better view of the man I love."

"Well, okay then," he said as he loosened his hold on her.

Turning slightly in his arms, she cupped the side of his face. "I want you to listen before you say anything." He nodded.

She ran her fingertips along his bottom lip. Brushing his scruff, she started. "When it comes to family, for the most part it's just my grandparents and me. Except for Lauren, who I plan on asking to be my maid of honor, that's it. Five people that I call family." *Where is she going with this?* He started to speak but she shushed him with her fingers. "I have a few friends at Lakeview but that's about my list of invited guests." She placed her hand on his chest. "You have this big 'ole family. Between your siblings, parents, grandparents, friends..."

"Jen, I'm kind of having a hard time following you here...can you please get to the point."

"You said you wouldn't say a word."

"I broke my promise, didn't I?" He winked at her.

She rested her head against her hand that still lay against his chest. "Sweetheart, I want to have the wedding in Calgary on the ranch."

He was stunned by her request. "You what?"

"You heard what I said. There will be fewer people to worry about needing to travel, and it feels right to me. Outside of this house, which I know more than likely I'm going to have to sell, it feels like home. I haven't spoken with your mom about it, and she might not want all the brouhaha, but I believe the ranch setting will be absolutely perfect for our wedding. You love it there, and I've grown quite fond of your country and home. So that's it. I choose the ranch."

He playfully ran his hand down her tresses and swept them behind her ear. He wanted to get a better look at her beautiful face. The face he'd soon be waking up to on a daily basis. "My mom's going to go crazy. She'll love that you want us to be married there. Now the next question...When?"

She raised her finger. "I've given that a lot of thought, too. If, and I know it's a big if... If the

Generals were to make the Stanley Cup finals." She paused as she heard him groan. "Hey, there, you've got to think positive."

"Okay, when we compete in the finals..."

"That's better, I checked the calendar and the seventh game of the series is scheduled for the middle of June. Taking that into consideration, I thought you'd need a little time to recoup. How does two weeks sound?"

"Get married in two weeks? That's impossible."

"No silly," she smiled broadly at him while she played with his shirt. "Two weeks after the Cup finals."

"Got you. I guess I got lost there for a minute." He smirked.

"You certainly did." She playfully patted his shoulder. "Now back to my suggestion. I know July first is Canada Day, and it's a national holiday. How about we get married that weekend? That way, those of your friends that have to work will have an additional day they can celebrate with us."

He startled her as he sat up quickly, practically knocking her off the couch. Placing both hands on either side of her face, he kissed her with a force she wasn't used to, and then he jumped from the couch.

"What's wrong, where are you going?"

He grabbed his phone that he'd set down on the table after speaking with Et. Checking the time, he realized it was later than he expected, but his parents stayed up later than normal during the winter because they enjoyed watching their sons' hockey games live on satellite television. Rafael had a game in Arizona and, fingers crossed, his parents were up watching.

He didn't think twice when he pulled up their number and dialed. To him it seemed like forever, but after only two rings his dad answered. "Ryne, is everything okay? You normally don't call this late."

"Everything's perfect, Dad. I need you to get Mom and put the phone on speaker."

They heard the click, then his mom's voice. "Ryne, I can't believe you're calling this late. Is something wrong, are you injured?"

"Mom, I just told Dad everything was fine." Jen snuggled him.

"That's good to hear. So why the call?"

"Hi, Jacklynne?"

"Oh Jen, is that you?"

"It's us," he said as he reached for her hand. He winked at her. "Mom, Jen has a question to ask you and Dad."

Shyly Jen started in, unsure how his parents would take her request. "Hi, Jacklynne and Jacques."

"Hello there, dear. And have you forgotten you can call us Mom and Dad now?"

"No, I haven't." She squeezed his hand, unsure how to ask them her all important question. "Ryne just got home a little while ago. I haven't seen him since Christmas."

"Oh honey, I'm sure you're happy he's home. I know how lonely it can get when he's away. I remember those days well."

"I'm sure you do." She looked at Ryne. He batted his hand at her and mouthed the words, 'ask her.' She swallowed and took the plunge. "So, we were sitting here talking about the wedding."

"Honey, what did your friends say about your engagement?"

"I haven't told them yet."

"What? Why?"

"It just didn't feel right with Ryne on the road. I wanted to wait until we could tell some of our friends together. But that's not the reason for our call. I was wondering..."

"Yes, honey, go on, what is it that you need?"

"I was hoping— no we were hoping—that if it's not too much trouble, you'd let us have the wedding at the ranch." They heard a gasp and then dead silence. "Are you still there?" She waited momentarily. "Ryne, did we lose the call?"

She heard Jacklynne as she cleared her throat. "No, sweetheart, we're still here. Are you sure you want to have the wedding here and not in St. Louis?"

"I'd really like it there. I've fallen in love with the ranch and the entire Ferguson family."

"But Jen, what about your family?" asked Jacques.

"It's really just me and my grandparents. I have a few close friends but that's it. It's easier for us to travel the distance than for you all to travel here. I hope we're not asking too much, but I'd love to have it there, especially if Calgary becomes our home."

"What's that? Ryne are you being traded?"

"Mom, not that I know of. I think what Jen is referring to is I'd like to retire there someday, and she's getting used to the fact that Calgary will eventually become our home." He raised his finger to his lips so she wouldn't contradict what he'd said.

He'd spoken again with Adam, and he hoped that

by the end of the season he'd be a member of the Calgary Storm. He didn't want to get his mother's hopes up too soon, especially if things didn't work out.

"So, what do you say? Can we get married on the ranch? I'd love nothing better than to make my future wife pretty happy right about now."

"Nothing like putting the pressure on them," Jen said in a snarky manner.

"Honey, I'm not." He pulled her close waiting for his parents' reply.

"We'd like nothing better than to host your wedding. So yes, you can have your wedding here. Have you decided on a date?"

"How does the weekend of Canada Day sound?"

"Perfect," Jacklynne said. They could hear tears in her voice. "We'll be honored to do this for you."

"Son, it's getting late for you and us. Why don't we talk in the morning?"

"Okay. Hey before we go, how's Rafael doing tonight?"

"Eh, he's had two penalties and two goals, so all in all a good night for him."

"Thanks, Mom and Dad," Ryne said as he prepared to end the call. "We love you."

"We love you both," Jacques chimed in before the call ended.

"That wasn't so bad." He again winked at her.

"It went better than I thought it would," she said.

"Jen, how can you say that? You must have known they'd say yes. They love you. You're family."

"Not yet I'm not."

"I'm not going to argue with you."

"Ryne, I'm not picking a fight with you. It's just your parents have welcomed me from the first moment they met me. It's still almost impossible for me to believe they care for me as much as they do."

Jen tightened her arms around Ryne and held on for dear life. She loved him more than words could express. He had become her rock and always seemed capable of helping her down off the mountain of doubt that seemed to pop out of nowhere.

Chapter Twenty-Seven

THE NEXT MORNING JEN WOKE bright and early. A sense of calm filled her. She'd told Ryne the evening before she was going to inform Johnston of their engagement and her decision to return to photography.

As she drove into the parking lot, she recalled the look of sheer pleasure that crossed his face when she told him of her plan. The smile and the glimmer of love in his eyes stayed with her throughout the night and lived with her in her dreams until she woke.

She'd been so caught up in her thoughts, she didn't notice Ryne's car so she didn't realize he was there until she entered the building and heard his voice. She hurried into the office and found him sitting across from Johnston, sharing a cup of coffee. "Jen, look who the cat dragged in."

Ryne stood and reached for her hand. Leaning into her, he placed a chaste kiss on her cheek and slid his hand around her waist. She knew his affection had come as a complete surprise to Johnston. Only a few people knew of their relationship and how close they'd become. With an astonished look on his face, Johnson motioned to Jen. "I see you're early today. Have a seat for a few minutes so we can chat with Ryne."

She nervously smiled at Ryne and sat in the chair beside him. She mouthed a 'thank you' to him before turning back to Johnston. "I was pleasantly surprised when Ryne walked into my office this morning." Johnston took a sip of his coffee. "So Ryne, what brings you by Lakeview this bright and early, especially on a Monday?"

Ryne looked at Jen and reached out to her. Grasping her hand tightly in his, he motioned to her to share their news.

She cleared her voice. "I've wanted to tell you this for a while now, and I realized that the time has come." She looked down at their clasped hands. She knew Ryne was aware of her nervousness and felt his thumb rub alongside her hand, providing her with the support she needed. "I wanted to give you ample opportunity..."

She turned to Ryne and demurely smiled again at him. She needed his strength to continue. Once again she felt his love as she looked into his eyes. His eyes sparkled full with the feelings he had for her. One squeeze of his supportive hand allowed her to finish.

"I want you to know this decision has been a long time in coming. Johnston, know that I appreciate everything you've done for me here at Lakeview. Last year, you presented me with an opportunity I wanted absolutely nothing to do with. The fundraiser was like a thorn in my side, especially when you asked for a gallery showing. I hadn't picked up a camera in I can't tell you when." She shook her head trying to clear the memories. "You added Ryne to the mix and I had no out. In time, he made me see that I needed to follow through with the showing and confront my past."

"That wasn't my intent, Jen. I remembered your talent and thought we'd be able capitalize on it to raise money for Lakeview."

"I understand that and I'm thankful we did. But along the way, I realized how much I missed being a photographer. Through Ryne's encouragement and with the success of the showing, I've decided I can't deny what I truly want to do with my life. Photography is my passion, and I'd thrown it all away when my parents died. Because of you and Ryne, I've decided I can't ignore my calling any longer. I want you to know that I've decided not to return to Lakeview next year. I have to follow my heart and right now that's being with Ryne and the career I've put on hold for way too long."

With that, she lifted her hand. And there, sitting on her ring finger was Ryne's engagement ring. She knew he'd been totally surprised by her first announcement but was completely thrown off guard when she raised her hand.

Shocked and almost stuttering, Johnston said, "I..I... Is that what I think it is?"

"It certainly is," chimed in Ryne. "Jen and I are engaged."

Quickly overcoming his shock, Johnston stood and practically ran to her side. He pulled her into a tight hug. "I'm so happy for you. Did this just happen? I had no idea you were even a couple."

Sheepishly she said, "No, we got engaged at Christmas."

"Christmas. How come I'm just finding out about

it?"

"Because I wanted to wait until Ryne returned from his road trip to tell everyone. He's been traveling since right before New Year's, and it didn't feel right sharing the news without him by my side."

"So when's the lucky day?"

"The first of July. We're getting married in Canada."

A perplexed look crossed his face. "Canada, why Canada?"

Again, she squeezed Ryne's hand. "Because my family's there."

"I thought your grandparents lived here and on the East Coast."

"They do."

"I don't understand."

"My family, which now includes Ryne's, is mainly from Canada. He has a gazillion siblings, and I didn't think it was right for them to have to travel all this way when I have only a few family members and friends that live here." He nodded approvingly. "Ryne and I are going to throw an engagement party here in a few weeks, and then I hope to have a little something here in St. Louis after the wedding. That way, my friends who can't come to Calgary can still celebrate with us." She looked at Ryne as she said this and discovered a supportive look cross his face. The idea came to her out of the blue when Johnston had questioned her reasoning for getting married in Canada. A party was the perfect answer, she thought.

Jen looked at the clock and jumped from her seat. It was almost time for the bell to ring, and she needed to get herself organized for the day. "I hate to hurry out of here, especially after dropping our news on you this morning, but I need to get a few things together before the day begins."

"I'm sorry I kept you, but I'm thrilled with your news. Why don't you come by my office during your morning break, and we can discuss your plans in a little more detail." She smiled and nodded. She ran her hand across Ryne's shoulder as she headed out of the room. "To say I'm surprised about you two is an understatement. How did you keep your relationship under the radar screen for so long?"

"We didn't do it intentionally," he said. "A few people knew about us. In the end, we didn't want it broadcast all over the city. It's not like we didn't go out and do things, but we also didn't make a big deal about it either."

"I completely understand wanting your anonymity when you're in public. I see what our parents here at Lakeview go through being recognized and it can be overwhelming at times."

"It can be and that's one thing that I don't want Jen to have to encounter too often. She's been really good about it so far, but sometimes it can definitely weigh on you." Ryne glanced at his watch just as the bell rang. "If it's okay with you, I'd like to stop by Jen's classroom before I go. I know she's pretty excited to share our engagement."

"Sure." Johnston stood and extended his hand to Ryne. "Your announcement threw me for a loop. I can't even remember if I said congratulations or not, but congratulations," he said shaking Ryne's hand. "You couldn't have found a better woman than Jen.

She's had a rough go of it since her parents died."

"She has. But you know what? I consider myself the lucky one. She's made such an impact on me and my family's life already, and I can't wait to see where we go in the next fifty years." He raised his hand motioning goodbye. "I'll see you soon."

By the time Ryne made his way down to her classroom, the daily announcements were being broadcast. He peeked into her room and noticed the children had all gathered around her. They were sitting in a circle towards the back of the room.

He slowly opened the door and eased in. Her back was to him, and she was so enthralled with telling them a story, she wasn't aware of his presence. As he leaned against the wall, a smile crossed his face. Even though he knew of her doubts as a teacher, she mesmerized him with her tale as she weaved her story. He listened intently and then laughed out loud at one part along with the class. No one had noticed him until they heard his guffaw, and then all eyes were upon him.

The kids were flabbergasted with his presence. Jen turned, acknowledging him. He strode to her and laid his hand on her shoulder. "I think you remember Ryne Ferguson," she said, smiling at him as she reached up to squeeze his hand.

Her students' all nodded. He felt her movement and realized she now stood at his side. He started to say something when one of her students let out a huge gasp. "Is that what I think it is, Miss Steele?" the girl sitting at her feet yelled.

He wasn't sure what she was going to say or do, but she wrapped her arm around his waist and said,

"Yes, Francine, your eyes are not deceiving you." Her hair hit the side of his face as she spun her head and looked up at him. "Ryne and I are engaged. We're getting married."

Her class broke out in whoops and screams. It got so loud that Alison came running into the room. She glanced back and forth between them and then spotted Jen's ring. Her hand flew to her mouth, and she dashed over to pull Jen into a hug. "Carson and I both saw this coming. Is it recent?" She reached for Ryne. She held on tighter than he expected, causing him to grunt. "Oh, sorry about that. I'm so excited for the two of you." She grabbed Jen's hand again, raising it to examine her ring. "When did this happen?"

Jen pulled in her lips as she gazed into Ryne's eyes. She ignored Alison and turned to her students. "Let's everyone return to your desks and grab your math books." She pulled her hand from Alison's. "How about I fill you during our break? I need to settle them down."

"Sure thing," Alison scurried from the room calling over her shoulder, "I won't tell Carson. It's my little secret, right?"

Ryne nodded. He followed Jen to her desk and whispered, "Sorry about the commotion. I thought this would have played out a little differently."

She placed her hand on his cheek. This was her first day openly wearing her engagement ring. Since returning to school, she'd worn it on a chain close to her heart. "It's alright. I didn't think I'd be able to keep it a surprise for much longer, especially with me wearing this rock on my finger." She glanced at her hand. The ring glowed brilliantly in the light and Jen raised her eyes to his — sparkling with her excitement.

She pressed her lips together to keep from smiling, but he knew she couldn't keep the effervescent smile from him. She was happy. Their announcement to her class and Johnston played out just the right way.

He chuckled at her comment. "I guess not. I'll talk to you later." He squeezed her hand once again and started out the door. Winking back at her he said, "Have a good day."

As he made his way to his car, he realized he needed to get busy arranging their party. Instead of returning home, he headed into the Generaldome where he immediately sought out Phoenix, who was in charge of the suites. "I'm sorry, Ryne, but all of the rooms are booked for that night. I wish there was something I could do."

"I understand," he said, then realized he had another avenue he could try. Ryne left Phoenix and headed up to the executive offices. He was almost assured he'd found a way to make their party happen.

He approached a closed door and rapped his knuckles against it. He heard a muffled, "Come in," then cracked open the door. He poked his head around the edge.

"Ryne, is that you? Come on in."

Ryne strode into the room and stood directly in front of Ed's desk. Ed rose and reached out his hand. "This is quite a surprise. Is there something wrong?"

"No, oh no, nothing like that." He ran his hand

through his hair. He was a tad bit nervous and didn't want to be presumptuous. Still.... "I have a favor to ask."

"Have a seat," Ed said, gesturing to the chair in front of his desk. "What's up?"

Ryne knew he needed to be upfront with him. He wasn't even sure if Ed knew he and Jen were dating, let alone serious. "Okay, here goes nothing," he mumbled to himself. "I'm not sure if you're aware of this, but Jennifer Steele and I have been dating for some time now."

"Yeah, I knew."

He blew out a breath. *At least he knows that.* "We're pretty serious…"

"Glad to hear that's she's found someone like you to date."

"Well, it's a little more than date. Jen and I are engaged."

Just as Ryne said the word engaged, Ed took a sip of water. When he heard the words, he swallowed wrong and started hacking away. Ryne jumped from his chair and started pounding Ed on the back. After a few moments, Ed said, "Ryne, quit beating me, I'm fine.

Ryne returned to his seat. "Are you sure you're alright?"

"Fine. I'm fine." He paused. "I guess congratulations are in order."

"Thank you, sir. I appreciate it."

"I'm happy for you. Outside of this news, is there something else you needed?"

"Ah, yeah there is. My brothers play for the Storm."

"I'm aware of that. In fact, wasn't it your twin who knocked you into the boards and caused your injury?"

"Yeah, that was Etienne. He says he didn't mean it... I need to get back on the subject here. The Storm is coming to town, and Jen and I wanted to have an engagement party while the team was here. I tried to book one of the boxes but they're all..."

Before he could finish his sentence, Ed said, "My suite's all yours."

"Really, just like that?"

"Jen is like a daughter to me, especially after her parents' deaths. I'd do anything for her. So, yes, you can use it."

"Thanks, Ed. That means a lot. I hated having to tell Jen our family would be scattered around the arena."

"Have you thought about using Faceoff?"

"That's where I'm headed next. Hopefully the party room is available."

"More than likely it will be. Let me know if you have any problems with that, and we'll figure something else out."

When Ryne stood, Ed said, "You're going to be good to her, right?"

"Of course."

"I have to assume you received Ro's approval."

"I did. In fact, I went to see Miles and Rowena first. I wasn't too sure, but Rowena actually likes me. At least that's what she told me."

"You must be a good man, not that I don't know you are, but Ro's a hard nut to crack."

"That she is," Ryne added as he walked to the

door. "I appreciate it Ed and I'll get back to you."

"Hey, Ryne. Is this a secret, or does everyone know?"

"Give me ten minutes and everyone here will be up to speed. I just came from Lakeview. Johnston was totally clueless to our relationship, and her class was overflowing with excitement. They were so loud; Carson's wife came running in thinking something was wrong."

"I didn't want to say anything if it was a secret. Did you just get engaged last night?"

"No. I proposed during Christmas break. I haven't seen her since, and she decided to keep it quiet until I returned from our road trip."

"That's good to know."

Ryne proceeded to the locker room where he shared the news with his teammates. Congratulations rang out from everyone. "You mean we'll have to play nice with Etienne and Philippe?" Derek asked as he slapped him across the back.

"Not during the game," Ryne said. "I plan on being my normal rough self. I definitely won't be going easy on them, especially Etienne."

Derek roared with laughter. "But after?"

"Well, they are my brothers, so I have to play nice in the sand since my family and Jen's will be there too. I need to be on my best behavior, especially around her grandparents. I won them over, and I don't want to jeopardize that."

The weeks leading up to their engagement party

were busy. Ryne had gone on two short road trips, leaving Jen to handle the nitty gritty details of planning.

While Ryne was on the second of his prolonged road trips, Jen and Lauren took the long President's Day weekend and went wedding dress shopping. Jen was unsure what she wanted in a gown, so they visited traditional wedding dress shops, wedding boutiques, and anywhere else that might have the perfect dress. Luck wasn't on her side. She was tired and cranky when she said goodbye to Lauren and stopped by her grandparents' home for dinner.

Since Wilford and Rose were expecting her, she walked right in. Her grandmother was at the stove. The smells pierced her senses as Jenn leaned over Rose's shoulder, peeking into the pot. "What smells so good?" she asked as she kissed Rose's cheek. "Ooh, looks like your special sauce."

She ran her finger along the wooden spoon Rose had used to stir the red sauce, and touched it to her tongue. "Oh my, that's good. I can't wait for dinner." The smells lifted her spirits after a depressing day of looking for dresses.

Jen grabbed a glass from the cupboard and filled it with ice cold water. Taking a sip, she lost focus and the cool water dribbled down her chin. She wiped the coolness away and strayed to the table, where she plopped into her seat.

"Rough day?"

She nodded her head. "I lost track of the number of stores we visited. I feel like we drove from one end of the city to the other, and nothing called out to me saying this is the dress."

Rose turned from the stove and walked out of the room. Momentarily she returned with a huge box. Jen could tell it was relatively old, the cellophane over it had yellowed and become brittle. Parts of it had cracked open.

"What's this?"

"See for yourself, my dear." She set the box on the table. "Open it."

Again, she asked, "Grandmother, what is this? It looks old."

Rose sat across the table gestured again for Jen to open it.

"Are you sure?"

"Dear, if I wasn't, do you think I would have struggled getting it down from the closet? Please just open it. If you don't like it, I'll have it rewrapped. In fact, by the condition of this box, I need to do that as it is."

Jen chewed on her lower lip unsure what was in the massive box. As she contemplated what to do, Wilford walked in. "Hey there, honey. I didn't know you'd arrived."

"I've only been here a few minutes." Her grandparents exchanged a look.

"What do you have there?"

"I don't know. Grandmother just gave it to me."

Wilford sat next to Rose and reached for her hand. "Why don't you go ahead and open it."

She saw a second glance exchanged between her grandparents as she pulled the box closer. Some of the cellophane crumbled. She wiped her hands together, then ran her fingernail along the edge of the box, breaking the seal. She pulled the brittle covering away, crunching it into a ball, and set it aside. Rose stood and threw it away. As she returned to her seat, she grabbed onto her husband's arm.

Both Rose and Wilford watched her lift the lid and pull aside the yellowing tissue paper. Jen gasped as soon as she realized what lay before her. Tears began to cascade down her face. She tried to brush them away but one fell right after the next. "She would want you to wear it." Jen didn't utter a word as she listened to her grandmother's voice.

A glimmer of sadness crossed Rose's face but was replaced with an expression of peacefulness. Jen's breathing slowed as she took one look at the off-white dress sitting in the box and knew she'd found her answer. She tipped her head back, closed her eyes, and ran her hand along the delicate fabric. The briefest of smiles crossed her face as she laid her hand across her heart. She knew this was right.

She gazed at her grandparents and saw the look of love on their faces as they watched her. Rose opened her arms and Jen found herself engulfed in a tight embrace. Somehow, she contained her emotions.

"I can still see your mother in this very dress walking down the aisle on your grandfather's arm. Her eyes shone brightly with unshed tears. I knew she was happy and that your father was the only man for her. They loved one another, I think, from the moment they first laid eyes on one another. Their love never waned, and I have to believe they are living happily together right now."

Rose lifted her head and grasped Jen's hand. "Jennifer, I see in you and Ryne what I saw in your parents— an all-consuming love. The way you look at him and he looks at you— I feel like I've fallen back in time and I'm witnessing your parents all over again. Stay true to that love. Never forget what you have."

Jennifer knew exactly what Rose spoke of. She clearly recalled every time her father walked into a room; her mother looked at him with the brightest of smiles. If there was one thing she'd always remember about her parents, it was the true love that always emanated when they were together. She hoped she'd forever feel the way she did right now. Ryne was her world and he meant everything to her.

"So, what about the dress? Will you wear it?"

Jen looked back at the gown. It was such a gift that her grandmother had given her. She knew by wearing it, her parents would be close to her heart on her special day— as though they were there in spirit. She lifted the dress from the box, holding up the top half. "Of course, I'll wear it. Mom and Dad will be with me as I pledge my love for Ryne." She ran her hand along what she knew were puffy sleeves. Being a dress from the 1980's, the sleeves would need to be tamed down a bit. "I think we'll need to alter these," Jen said pointing to the puffiness. Rose broke out in laughter. "Don't you think, Grandmother?"

"I'd have to say yes. Those sleeves are definitely out of date. A few alterations and it will be all yours."

Jen enjoyed the remainder of the evening. Rose's dinner was the perfect way to end the emotional rollercoaster of a day. What had been a truly stress-ful one driving around the city looking for the perfect dress turned into one filled with memories of her parents' happiness and undying love for one another. Jen was relieved when she closed the door on the last few hours. She'd found the perfect dress. Now she could move forward planning the remain-der of their special day.

Chapter Twenty-Eight

RYNE'S PARENTS AND SISTERS ARRIVED on a mid-morning flight from Calgary. Ryne was caught at an early practice, so Jen arranged a personal day to meet them. She hadn't slept the night before as she was worried about everything. From the tidiness of her house, which was spotless, to whether or not his sisters would be bored out of their minds without school or hockey practice.

Ryne had called her after his game the evening before as he waited for their plane to take off for St. Louis. They'd won their game, although it was a hard-fought battle in which he incurred two penalties. He hadn't been happy with his play and was out of sorts when they spoke. "Hey there, babe," he said. "I wasn't sure you'd answer."

"Of course, I'd answer. Don't I always?"

"You do." He could discern in the tone of her voice and the way she responded to his question that something was wrong. Ryne ran his hand through his hair as he waited for her to speak. He really wasn't in the frame of mind to carry on a conversation. He was tired, sore, and just wanted to sleep in his own bed. I'm getting too old for this, he thought as he waited for her to speak. For some reason, the traveling was getting to him this season.

Deep down, he believed it was because he always missed her with a passion and couldn't wait to return to her smiling face.

"So, what have you been up to?"

"What do you think? Come on Ryne, your family's arriving in a few short hours. I've been cleaning up a storm."

"Honey, your house is immaculate in the worst of times. You have nothing to worry about."

"You say that now. Your family is staying in my home. I have to worry about its appearance. My house reflects on me. On whether or not..."

"Will you stop it? Just stop, okay?"

"Stop?" she practically yelled into the phone.

"Jen, take a deep breath and listen to me for a minute."

"Ryne!"

He could hear the panic in her voice. He couldn't fathom why she was acting this way. It wasn't as though she'd never met his family before. She had no reason to try and impress them. They already loved her just the way she was— without having to go above and beyond the call of duty. She needed to just be the Jen that he loved and all would be well.

"Jen, you need to calm down."

"I am calm."

"Not from where I'm sitting. I can hear the panic in your voice. Look, everything is going to be just fine. Stop your worrying."

"Easier said than done."

"Ya know, I don't think we're going to see eye to eye here tonight. The plane is boarding and I need to get going. Think about what I just said. Be yourself and stop this unnecessary worrying."

"Glad you think it's unnecessary."

"I love you." When she didn't respond to his endearment he added, "Trust. You need to trust that everything will be just fine. My parents love you, my sisters love you. In fact, Emma can't wait for us to be married. You're all that she talks about. Have faith in us. Listen, I've gotta go."

With that he ended his call, grabbed his bag and boarded the plane. He felt awful with how their conversation had played out. He needed to make it right and he would just as soon as he could. He was clueless and surprised by how emotional she was. Since their engagement, she'd been in a better place and seemed less rattled by past memories.

Thankfully, the Generals had played in Chicago which was a short plane ride from St. Louis. The wheels had barely touched down at the airport, and Ryne was readying to leave the plane. In minutes from the doors' opening, he'd deplaned and hurried to his waiting car.

It was late when he pulled up at her door. The house was still ablaze with lights. He knew with her scheduled day off the following day and by the way their earlier conversation played out she was still awake. He grabbed his bag, hurried up the stairs, and rang the doorbell. He was surprised when she didn't answer. He was certain she was still awake.

He stood at her door as the cold northeast winds blew across her front porch. When she didn't come to the door, he whipped out his phone. It rang quite a few times before she answered. He thought it was heading to voice mail when he heard her voice.

Immediately, he could tell she'd been crying. His heart dropped to his stomach. He hadn't a clue what had caused her this pain. "Hey, it's me. Can you open the door?" He wearily leaned against the doorframe. He wasn't exactly sure how he was holding it together himself. They'd endured another long four-day road trip. Exhaustion had taken over as he drove to her house. He closed his eyes and waited.

"Hmm hmm," is all he heard before she opened the door. Standing before him was the love of his life. He took one look at her, dropped his bag, and drew her into his arms. He held her tightly as his own weariness increased.

He pulled away, grabbed his bag, and closed the door all the while holding her close. He led her to the family room, sat down in the curve of the couch, and reached for her. She curled up into his embrace, resting her head on his chest. He comforted her—from what he hadn't a clue.

He rested his head along the back of the couch as he stroked her back, then raised his finger to her forehead brushing aside some of her hair that had fallen from her messy bun. He leaned over and placed a soft kiss against her brow. "Feel better?"

He felt her nod as her head brushed against his chest. As he sat there with her in his arms, he grew more tired by the second. He'd taken several hard hits during their game against the Wind, and his muscles were starting to feel the strain. Out of the blue, his thigh started to seize. He'd felt the onset and tried to rub it out but his efforts didn't lessen the pain. He sucked in a deep breath when the strongest of cramps hit.

She practically jumped off his lap when she heard his gasp. "What's wrong?" He'd closed his eyes as he focused on massaging the cramp from his leg. He scrunched his eyes and as the pain lessened, he felt her hand on his. "Let me," she said and started a deep massage of his leg. He'd experienced those miracle fingers before, but this time they felt like manna from heaven. In a matter of minutes, the cramp was gone.

He pulled her up beside him and secured his arm around her shoulders. "Thanks," he mumbled. "That feels so much better." He struggled to get into a better position all the while grunting until he finally felt settled again.

"Rough night?"

"You could say that three times over." He caught her eye and raised his finger to her lips. "Don't worry about me right now. I'm okay. Just a little rough around the edges." He smoothed his hand along her cheek. "What's upset you? I know it can't be all about my parents and cleaning. There's definitely more to this picture, isn't there?"

He knew there was more than met the eye here. She seemed overwhelmed for some reason. From her shortness to him on the phone earlier, to her tears. he needed to understand what was going on, and she was the only one that could tell him.

He sat with her and almost drifted off to sleep when she grabbed onto his fingers pulling him out of his quasi nap. His eyes caught hers and then she began to softly share with him why she'd been so worked up.

Her fingers tightened around his as she snuggled

into his chest. Jen loved to latch onto his shirts and tonight was no different. He could feel her nervousness. He continued to sit there with his eyes half closed waiting for her. He wasn't a mind reader and was clueless as to what set her off. As he sat there peeking through his lids, he could see the varying emotions cross her face. "I'm sorry," she murmured. "I shouldn't have talked to you that way especially right before you boarded the plane."

"It's okay."

"No it's not." She pulled away and scooted several inches from him. "One thing I definitely learned is that you never have cross words like that and then expect someone to get on an airplane." She pulled in her trembling lips, and he watched her as she did her best to keep her tears at bay. Looking away, she murmured, "What if something happened to you?"

He reached his hand out to hers. Grasping hers tightly, he raised it to his lips and brushed a kiss against her knuckles. "Sweetheart, look at me." She gnawed on her lower lip— closing her eyes, she shook her head and then he saw her begin to relax. She released her lip and opened her eyes. She looked directly at him. "Nothing happened. I am fine albeit a little sore and tired." He chuckled at his comment and gave her a quirky half-smile.

"You can't live your life afraid that any time we have a little disagreement, and I'm not calling what we had a disagreement. But whenever that happens, you can't think that the world is going to collapse and life as you know it is coming to an end. We're going to have our little tiffs, but at the end of the day you have to know that I will always love you. I'll do my darnedest to always be by your side. You've got to stop believing that the worst is going to happen. Stop looking around every corner..."

"I realize that. I'm sorry. I know that I stressed myself over absolutely nothing. I know my house is immaculate. After all, I'm the only one who lives here. Everything is always in order." She stopped and took a deep breath. "I'm sorry that I worried you and that you came all the way over here when you should have gone home and soaked in a hot tub."

"I'm where I need to be. Got it? I've missed you. Come here," he said as he held out his arms. "I've missed holding you like this. I've got to say, these road trips of late have become harder and harder. I don't know if it's my age or just the fact that I'm in love with the most perfect woman and that I miss you when we're not together."

She toyed with his shirt as she listened to him. "Are you sure it's not something else? How's your hip?"

"Good, really good."

"You're not keeping something from me, are you?"

"No, never. When it comes down to it, I'm home-sick. I miss you so much, and I definitely can't wait until I can hold you all night long."

"What's stopping you?"

"You know the answer to that question." They'd discussed taking their relationship to the next level, but she was old fashioned in that way and wanted to wait until their wedding night to make love for the first time.

"I do."   She brushed her hand along his jaw. "Tonight, can we stay right here, wrapped in each other's arms?   I'm more than comfortable.   What about you?"

"It feels right." He pulled her in closely and closed his eyes. He made the right decision, stopping by her place. He knew why she'd acted the way she did.   When all was said and done, she'd always return to the evening of her high school graduation. The night that she walked out the door on her parents not knowing that it would be the last time she'd have the chance to tell them how much she loved them. Not remembering what her last words to them were. He knew that she never wanted to experience that again and that she always did her best to end a conversation on a good note, not like she'd done with him earlier.

The next morning Ryne was out the door bright and early. She'd kissed him goodbye and watched as he threw his bag into the car. He looked back at her and smiled once again, mouthing the words he'd last spoken right before walking down the stairs. *I love you.*

As he pulled away from the curb, she felt more at peace with herself. She still couldn't believe that he'd stopped by on his way home the night before. She knew how tired he was, but she also realized how much he truly loved her. She'd answered her phone and was surprised when she heard his voice and was even more surprised when she discovered him leaning against her front door.

When she pulled open the door and discovered the dark circles surrounding his red rimmed eyes, she fell in love with him all over again. She was loved and felt it to her core. Spending the night in his arms felt like pure heaven to her, and she couldn't wait until they were married.

When she could no longer see his taillights, she closed the door and straightened the family room where they'd spent the night. She hoped Ryne wasn't too sore after his leg cramp and sleeping the remainder of the night on the couch with her.

Two hours later, her nerves had returned to a state of frenzy as she made her way to the airport. The Fergusons' plane was due to land at eleven. Somehow, she found a parking spot in the garage right outside baggage claim. She wasn't sure how much luggage they'd have, so she snagged a luggage cart on her way into the terminal.

It was just eleven when she made her way to the waiting area. She pulled out her phone and texted Ryne. *I'm at the airport waiting for your family. See you after practice.*

She'd barely hit send when she heard a shout and a slight commotion. She looked up just in time as Emma threw herself into Jen's arms. She hadn't expected her exuberance and lost her balance, stumbling into a pillar. "Jennifer, we're here!"

Jen laughed at Emma and hugged her tightly. "Yes, you are." She brushed Emma's hair from her face and kissed her cheek. "How was your flight?"

"It was awesome," added Olivia. Emma stepped aside, allowing Olivia the chance to hug Jen. "We were in first class."

"You were?" Jen looked up at Jacklynne with a smirk on her face. Jen knew Ryne had booked first class as a surprise to his sisters. He knew they'd get a kick out of flying in style and knew they'd definitely have a story to tell when they returned home.

Next, Jen was wrapped in Jacklynne's arms. "It's so good to see you, dear," she said as she kissed Jen's cheek.

"Okay girls, you've had your chance, now let me have mine." Jacques stepped up to his soon to be daughter-in-law and reached for her hand. "Come here and give me a hug."

As soon as Jacques pulled her close, all the anxiety that had been building for days faded. Out of nowhere, a sense of calm overcame her. She felt at home in his arms. She held onto him tightly then heard Emma call out, "Dad, let her go."

Jen pulled away and placed a soft kiss on his cheek. "Thanks for that," she whispered.

Jacques winked at her and placed his hand along her cheek. "Everything will be just fine," he returned. She knew he'd sensed her anxiousness.

"They've been so excited for this trip," Jacklynne said as they waited for their luggage. She grabbed Jen's hand, "And they can't wait to call you their sister."

Jen smiled. "I can't wait for that myself. July will be here before we know it."

"Indeed, it will."

Jacklynne had finished her thoughts when Emma approached Jen and grabbed onto her hand. Smiling up at Jen, she motioned for Jen to lean over. Emma threw her arms around Jen's neck. "I love you, Jen. I'm so excited for your party."

"I am too." In those few moments she'd been in the Fergusons' presence all of her qualms about the weekend had faded. She knew everything would be just fine.

Instead of returning to her house immediately, Jen took the scenic ride home. She wanted the girls to see a little bit of the city. She exited the airport and entered the highway heading toward downtown St. Louis.

As they came around the bend into downtown, they passed the massive conference center that abutted the highway, next came the Arch, and the stadium where the Rivermen played baseball. She exited the highway.

"Are we almost there?" asked Emma.

"No honey. I thought we'd take a little detour." Right before they'd left the airport, Jen received a text from Ed. He knew, by way of Ryne, that she was in the process of picking up his family and suggested they stop by the Generaldome for a quick tour.

As she neared the arena, she could hear Olivia whispering to Emma. "This is where Ryne plays: the Generaldome."

"It is," Jen said as she pulled into the parking garage.

"I thought we were going to your house," Emma added.

"We are, but my friend Ed Talent, the owner of the team, texted me to stop by. He thought it would be a nice surprise for you to have a tour of the arena."

"This is awesome," Emma called out. "How cool is this. Jen, how do you know him? Through Ryne?"

"No honey, I've known Ed all of my life. He was my dad's best friend."

Ed was waiting for them when they entered the building. "Mr. and Mrs. Ferguson, Ed Talent. It's a pleasure to meet you." After shaking each of their hands, he welcomed Ryne's sisters. "And you must be Emma and Olivia."

Emma being Emma put out her hand. "I'm Emma," she said, "And this is Olivia."

"It's nice to meet you both. The team's just about to wrap up practice. I thought we could sneak a peek before they finish."

Ed led them into the arena. They were at Club Level just one section above the ice. The players were at the opposite end, so Ryne wasn't even aware that they had visitors, let alone his family.

Ryne took one slap shot after another. Several of his hundred mile-an hour shots ricocheted loudly off the crossbar, the shrill of the puck echoing throughout the empty arena. Emma clapped her hands as she watched her big brother take command of the ice. She reached for Jen's hand. "That's my brother. He's got a wicked slap shot, doesn't he?"

"He certainly does. One of the best in the league." Ed smiled at Emma. "Practice wraps up soon. Let's take a little tour and surprise your brother when he comes off the ice."

Ed had arranged with Trevor to hold Ryne in his office. He rapped his knuckles on the door, announcing their arrival. Trevor greeted Ed and gestured for him to enter.

"Hey Ryne, I was just watching you on the ice. The slap shot looked good."

"Thanks," Ryne grumbled.

"I brought some visitors by." Ed motioned them in. Emma was the first through the door. Full speed, she ran towards Ryne and flung her arms around his waist. Jen could tell by the look of surprise and the way he stumbled backwards that he hadn't expected to see his family.

Running his hand down her back, "Em's what are you doing here?"

"I knew Jen was picking up your family," Ed said as he watched the smile spread across Ryne's face. "I thought it would be fun if they surprised you. I have to say by the look on your face it was a surprise."

"Definitely," Ryne said as he looked directly at Jen. The love for his family shone brightly on his face. She caught his eye and he winked.

In the past twenty-four hours, she felt like her life had turned upside down. Yesterday, she'd been out of sorts and overwhelmed. Yet one look at his family and her anxiety had all but disappeared. When Jacques pulled her into his arms, his warm embrace soothed her and brought her back into the moment.

Her heart fluttered with the feelings of love that surrounded her.

She knew she'd look back on this day and remember Ryne's smile when his family entered the room. She prayed that smile would always be there. He was her rock and didn't want to ever think about never having him by her side.

She felt his peck on the cheek as he placed his arm around her waist and whispered, "You okay?" She nodded. Yes, she was fine. More than fine with her arm around the love of her life. So much had changed in such a short time. Her career was changing directions, she'd fallen in love with a kind, loving man, and she was about to become a member of his family. Life was good and she prayed that all of her hopes and dreams would continue to fall into place— and she'd remain right beside this man and have her happily ever after.

Chapter Twenty-Nine

IN THE BLINK OF AN eye, the weeks flew by. Jen had said her goodbyes to her friends at Lakeview and she was in the final preparations for becoming Ryne's wife.

As she exited the plane in Calgary, she grabbed the backpack that contained her camera. The last six months were a total blur. As she waited to cross onto the jetway, she knew life as she once knew it would never be the same. In a few short days, she would marry the love of her life. She'd never again have that feeling of being alone since she was marrying into a huge family, one comprised of the Fergusons but also Ryne's Storm hockey family as well.

Just last week, they'd received the news that he'd been dreaming of his entire life. He'd been traded from the Generals to his beloved Storm. Three Ferguson brothers would now call the Calgary Storm their home.

It was overwhelming to say the least. Not only was she in the final stages of preparing for her wedding, but she was also going to have to pack her home and relocate to a town she knew absolutely nothing about. Ryne had been her rock as she came to terms with the news.

A smile crossed her face as she started across the jetway. She recalled Ryne's first words when he shared his surprising news. He was already in Calgary preparing the ranch for the wedding while she remained in St. Louis. She'd been worried at first when he'd texted her to see if she was available to Skype. They rarely took to Skype. She knew whatever he wanted to discuss was important, so she quickly replied to his text and ran to her computer.

She was a nervous wreck while she waited for her computer to boot up and then connect. In moments she saw his handsome face all aglow. She didn't know what to expect, so she waited while he seemed to gather his thoughts.

When he sprang the news on her, the biggest smile she'd even seen crossed his face, that is, outside of when he proposed to her. She knew whatever he had to share was huge. She could feel his excitement through the screen. "You're sitting down, right?"

"What does it look like to you? Of course I am."

"Good, good."

She couldn't imagine what his news was only that it was big since he was speechless and that never happened.

She anxiously waited. "Jen, my dream, it finally came true..." She waited as he took a deep breath.

"Honey, my prayers have been answered."

"They have?" She hadn't a clue where he was going with this. Prayers?

"Adam came through. He worked his magic. He's given us the best wedding gift ever!"

"He did? What did he do?"

"You're looking at the newest member of the Calgary Storm."

She was shocked. She had given up the notion of his being traded this year. She rested her chin on her hand while Ryne continued.

"I was at the pond when my cell rang. I contemplated not answering but when I saw Adam's name pop up, I did."

She was getting breathless listening to his excitement. "Ryne, can you please stop and take a breath. I'm afraid you're going to pass out."

He chuckled. "Sorry, I'm just so excited. My dream—it came true."

"Breathe."

"Okay." He inhaled a deep breath; then exhaled. "Better?"

She smiled. "Right now, I am but please slow down a little. I was getting breathless listening to you."

"Phew. Sorry again." He ran his hand through his hair leaving it standing on end. "So."

"So? Go on," she said.

"Okay. He asked if I'd packed my bags. I thought he was referring to our honeymoon." He laughed. "I told him it was a little early since the wedding was more than a week away."

"And?"

"Then he told me. He wasn't referring to the wedding. He told me I was coming home. Home to Calgary and that's when it all began to sink in." He took another deep breath and smiled. "Jen, I can't believe it. My dreams are coming true. I'm marrying you in a few short days and I can play for my team. That's all I've ever wanted since I was three years old, watching my dad skate for the Storm."

Her stomach fell on his news. He'd been traded. Traded away from her beloved Generals and the only home she'd ever known. She knew it had been a possibility but the notion hadn't crossed her mind in months. She'd been so focused on preparing for the wedding and making the transition to a married couple that she hadn't given it a thought.

"You're sure?"

"Of course, I'm sure." He paused and raised his brow. "Do you think he was pulling my leg?" He laughed at himself. "Nah, he wouldn't do that..." He sat back. "I can't believe it. I'm going home."

Home? Home? She thought she was going to be his home. She was doing her best not to freak out but she was. She swallowed deeply and plastered a smile on her face. "I'm happy for you. I know it's been your dream."

Her heart began pounding. She felt like it was going to leap out of her chest. She raised her hand to her temple unsure what to say to him. "Wow! I can't believe Adam was able to pull this off and so close to the wedding." She was lost in thought—they had *so* much to do.

"Jen, hey, are you okay with this? I know it's a lot to take in with the wedding approaching and all."

"Yeah, it is." She sighed. "By the time we return from our honeymoon, it will be just about time for you to head off to training camp. How will we be able to accomplish everything?" She paused and smiled. "Honey, I'm thrilled, I really am. This has been your dream."

She tucked a stray hair that had fallen across her face behind her ear. "I'm thinking ahead—all we have to do. It's going to be hard enough making the transition to married life, but now we have to move. Don't take this the wrong way. I'm in complete shock." She inhaled deeply. "Wow, it's a lot to take in." She ran her hand across her face.

"Sweetheart, I understand that you are in shock. So am I. But this is a dream come true!" He paused. "I never ever believed this could happen. Never. I realize how much this is going to stress you out with the wedding and all. Remember you're not in this alone. You have me and my family."

"I realize that. But where will we live? We have only a few weeks before training camp begins."

"We'll work it out, trust me."

"I do with all of my heart."

She half-listened as he ran through his list of things to be accomplished before the wedding. She needed to end the call as she had a final dress fitting scheduled for that afternoon and she didn't want to be late. "Ryne, I hate to cut this short," she said. "Lauren, Grams, and I have our final dress fitting in less than an hour, and I need to pick up Grams."

Before ending the call, he clenched his fists and raised them in the air. "I can't believe this is really happening. My dreams have come true. I'm marrying you and going to the Storm."

She blew him a kiss, said her goodbyes. She sat for a moment and took another deep breath, realizing that her life had definitely been thrown a curve ball— one that she'd not been expecting. Married life yes but relocating right now, no.

She brushed her hand through her hair, grabbed her car keys, and headed out the door. As she approached her grandparents' house, she found her grandmother standing in the driveway waiting for her. "You're late," her grandmother goaded her as she closed the door and buckled her seatbelt. "I expected you fifteen minutes ago."

"Sorry about that." Jen pulled out of the driveway to the blaring of a car horn. Thankfully, the other driver stopped before they collided. Jen pulled back into the driveway and pounded her hand against the steering wheel.

"Honey, what's got you so upset?"

She started to tremble. "Jennifer dear," Rose said reaching for her granddaughter. "Come on, out with it. What's wrong?"

Jen had Rose's full attention, "I...I...I'm leaving."

"Oh honey, I know you are. You're leaving in a few days for Calgary. Your grandfather and I, we're coming with you."

"No..."

"No? You're not leaving, not getting married?"

"No, it's not that. I'm leaving for good."

"Jennifer, I'm not following. You need to start this conversation over."

Rose held tightly onto her hand as she told her about Ryne's trade. "But honey, that's a good thing, isn't it?" Rose brushed the wisps of hair that have fallen across Jen's face aside. "Hasn't Ryne wanted to play for the Storm since he was a child?"

Jen nodded.

"You should be happy. He faced his dreams head on and now they've come true."

Jen listened as Rose spoke. "Honey, I know how overwhelmed you are with the wedding, change in career and all, but this is a chance in a lifetime for Ryne." Rose squeezed her hand. "You'll always have your home here whether you live in the city or not. You know your grandfather and I will take care of it."

Jen sighed.

"Dear, your place is with Ryne. He's going to be your husband. Your grandfather and I will always be here for you whether we're right around the corner or two thousand miles way. And don't forget we can talk to you by Sipe."

"That's Skype, Grams," she rolled her eyes. She could never get that right.

"Yeah, okay, Skype. But dear, you need to move forward. Ryne is your future. He's going to be your husband. The one you go home to. I realize how sentimental you are, but if it makes you feel better, your grandfather and I can visit as often as you like. Just maybe not during the dire winter when it's colder than heck up there."

Rose's comments got a little chuckle out of Jen. She threw her arms around her grandmother. "Thank you for making me realize how blind I am. You're right. Ryne is my future." She paused. "It's just so hard sometimes, Grams. I miss Mom and Dad so much."

"I know you do. But look at it this way, you've got not only me and your grandfather, Rowena and Miles, but you're adding Jacques and Jacklynne and Ryne's siblings into the mix. I know how much you miss Mom and Dad, but from what I see, Jacques and Jacklynne have accepted you into their home without question. I know you'll never, ever forget your parents, but embrace Ryne's now as your own too. They love you so."

Jen nodded. "They do and I need to remember that."

She ran her hand through her hair once again and put the car in reverse. "Let's try this again," she said and headed down the street towards the dressmaker.

Jen exited the Calgary terminal into Ryne's waiting arms. He brushed a kiss across her lips and swung her around in a circle. "You're finally here."

"I am," she said as she ran her fingers along his lips. "It feels so good to be in your arms." She wrapped her arms tightly around his neck. "I can't believe our wedding is almost here."

She nuzzled his neck, oblivious to the world around them until they heard a loud noise. "Ahhem," She lifted her head from Ryne's shoulder to discover the face of her grandmother. "I guess you've already forgotten about your grandfather and me."

"Rose, I didn't see you there," Ryne said as he pulled away from Jennifer and hugged her.

"I can see you didn't," she said as she slapped at his shoulder. "You only have eyes for my granddaughter."

"That I do." He extended his hand to Wilford. "It's good to see you, sir."

Wilford gave him the look that he'd been accustomed to when he referred to him as sir. "Sorry about that, sir...I mean, Wilford. Maybe I'll get it right someday."

They all laughed. "Come on, let's go fetch your bags, and then we can grab something to eat before heading out to the ranch."

Ryne discreetly texted his mother when they left the restaurant to expect them within the hour. When they drove through the clearing of trees, he wasn't disappointed. Standing on the driveway, was his entire family. Emma was bouncing from foot to foot. Ryne threw his head back in laughter as he stopped the car.

"What's so funny, Ryne?" Wilford asked.

"Take a look at Emma. She's so excited she can't contain herself."

And with that, she sprang from the sidelines, throwing open Jen's car door. "Jen, I can't believe you're finally here. I've been waiting forever."

"Emma," Jacklynne chastised her.

"It's okay, Jacklynne. I'm just as excited to see Em as she is to see me."

Ryne couldn't take his eyes off of her as she exited the car. In a few short days she would be his wife. Words could not express his thoughts. His dreams of having a family of his own were coming true along with his ultimate dream of becoming a member of the Calgary Storm. Life was good and would only get better in a few days when he heard the words, 'I do' coming from Jen's lips.

Chapter Thirty

IT WAS LATE WHEN EVERYONE called it a night on the wedding rehearsal festivities. Ryne didn't want the evening to end so he grabbed Jen's hand and led her to one of the ATV's kept in the garage.

From the moment he'd picked her and her grandparents up at the airport, he had a sense that all wasn't completely right. He wasn't exactly sure what was troubling her, but he wanted to hash it out before they said their *I do's*. He knew she loved him and he loved her so much that his heart ached when they weren't together. He needed to put his qualms to bed and fully enjoy his wedding without any reservations on her part to speak of.

"Where are you taking me?"

"I'm sure you can guess." He pulled her beside him, revved up the ATV, and backed out of the garage. He took the long way around the ranch to their special place. The place where he'd asked her to marry him and where they were scheduled to be married in a few short hours.

He slowed the vehicle and eased himself from the seat. He grabbed her hand and pulled her along to the exact location he'd proposed. He knew where it was because there was a little dip in the hillside beside the pond.

Ryne raised his hand to her hair, smoothing it behind her ear. He ran his fingertip alongside her face and rested it against her lips. She started to speak but he pressed his finger against her, shushing her voice.

"I love you," he said. "I want to spend the rest of my life with you." He looked longingly into her eyes. "You are my life, Jen." He removed his finger from her lips and laid his hand against her heart. "You've brought so much love and joy into my heart. When I am away from you, I physically ache."

He dropped his hand and pulled away. "I need to make sure you're doing what you want to do, and if you say no, then I'll have to deal with it in my own way." He cleared his throat unsure how she would take his next words. "I think I've loved you since the moment you ran into me."

"Ryne."

"Shh, listen to what I have to say first, and then you can speak." She nodded.

"I know this is a huge adjustment for you. Marrying me and relocating to Canada." He paused before asking her the question that had been on his mind for days now. "Are you sure you want to do that? Do you really want to marry me?"

She gasped. "Of course, I want to marry you. Why do you think I don't?"

"I just want to be one hundred percent sure before tomorrow. I plan to only get married once in my lifetime and that's to you. So if you have any doubts…"

"Why would you think I have doubts? I love you

with all of my heart."

"I know you say you do, but then I see the sadness in your eyes. When I told you about my trade, I saw the uncertainty fall across your face. The Storm is my dream, and I just want to make sure that it's yours too. I get the feeling it's not."

She wrung her hands together, and he could feel her nervousness. She stood slightly turned away from him, gazing across the horizon. "If you want to call it off, let's do it right here and right now," he said.

"I don't," she whispered.

He reached for her hand and cupped the side of her face. "Then please, tell me what's troubling you."

She raised her eyes to his. Holding back tears, she shared with him her conversation with her grandmother shortly after discovering his trade. "Grandmother helped me see the light. I'll be honest; at first, I was unsure about the trade. In fact, I am still a little overwhelmed with everything. But then I see your loving face and know that I made the right decision when you asked me to be your wife.

"I love you so much that I'm oftentimes consumed with my love for you. I think of you from the moment I wake until I go to sleep. Will this move be difficult for me? Of course it will. But then, I recall Emma when we arrived the other day, and I realize that I'm not losing my family. I'm gaining so much more: You, your parents, your brothers, Olivia, Emma and of course, your Storm family. My life is going to be so full of family." She smiled.

He chuckled as she described her newfound family. "My life is so much fuller with all of the Fergusons.

As Grams reminded me…She can always visit us as often as I wish…"

Ryne groaned.

"Hey, come on."

"Just kidding. I love Rose and Wilford. They're welcome anytime."

She grabbed ahold of his hand. "Once I came to grips with the fact that I wasn't losing my family, only gaining one, I was okay. I just ask you one thing."

"And that is…"

"Please have patience with me. I know this is going to be a difficult adjustment for me. I'm going to have to get used to the fact that I can't visit my grandparents on a whim. I'll have to set aside quality time for them. I don't want to lose them."

"Honey, you won't. I won't let you. They'll always be there for you although just a little further away. They won't be there to put that physical bandage on your wound, but they'll always be there by your side, albeit just not around the corner."

"If you call eighteen hundred miles around the corner."

"You're sure?"

"Absolutely." She inched closer to him and then brushed her fingertips against his lips. "I have to be completely honest with you, though." She raised her fingers along his brow and chuckled at his expression. "Stop worrying, will you."

He focused on her every word. "I have to admit I am a tad nervous," she said.

"Just a tad?"

"Maybe more than a tad. I'm joining your family in just a few short hours, and I have to say it's a little daunting. I'll be going from living basically alone to sharing my entire life with you; being able to call Jacques and Jacklynne Mom and Dad. Add in your brothers, Olivia and Emma, and I'm just a little overwrought. Please forgive me if I made you believe that I didn't want to marry you.

"Marrying you is what's keeping me sane these days. You've guided me to the realization that I needed to refocus my career and live my life doing what I'd originally planned." She ran her finger along his brow. "Just have patience with me. Be there on those days that I can't seem to see straight. Hold me when I'm overcome with homesickness."

He laughed at that.

"No. I'm serious. I know I'm going to have good and bad days as I work through the adjustment to being married and moving away from the only home I've ever known. Promise me one thing."

He nodded as he waited on her.

"Promise that you'll never give up on me or us. I need you more than anything. You're my lifeline, and I don't know what I'd do if you ever gave up on us."

"Never. I've waited a long time to find you. In the one moment when my life flashed before me and I looked into your eyes, I knew you were the one. We were meant to find one another that night on the parking lot. Fate brought us together, and love will keep us together.

"I have to be honest that being a hockey wife isn't all that it's cracked up to be. I'm on the road at least three months of the year. I get banged up a lot."

"Like I haven't noticed."

"Seriously, it's a rough sport. So what comes around goes around. I'll be there for you when you're experiencing one of your lows, but I expect you to be there on the nights I can barely get off the couch."

He placed his hands on either side of her face. "We're in this together. The good and the bad. The ups and downs. That's what married life is all about, and I can't wait to experience what life's got to throw at me. With you by my side..."

She leaned in and gave him a soft kiss on the lips. "Together we'll survive...one day at a time."

He held her close. "This time tomorrow you'll be my wife. I can't wait to call you my wife— Mrs. Ryne Ferguson."

"And I can't wait to call you my husband."

The wedding was everything she imagined. She'd considered both of her grandfathers to escort her down the aisle but instead chose Ed. He was the closest thing to a father she had—being her dad's best friend. He'd been there since she was a little girl, and after her parents' deaths, she often sought him out for advice.

When she came down the stairs and met him in the foyer, she noticed the tears in his eyes. "My dear, your father would be so proud of you. You are marrying a wonderful man. He loves you very much."

"I know and I love him with all of my heart. I'm

sorry my parents aren't here to witness me marrying Ryne, but I am ever thankful that I have you in my life. Getting married has made me realize that even though I haven't said it, I consider you a second father. You've been with me every step of the way since Mom and Dad died. I want you to know how much I love and appreciate you. I'll never forget what you've done for me, and I'm ever thankful for the trade you orchestrated bringing Ryne to the Generals. I owe this day to you. I would have never found Ryne if it weren't for you. Thank you, Ed. You've given me so much."

"Oh sweetheart. I didn't do a thing. What I see is that fate sealed this day for you. You were meant to run down Ryne on the parking lot, and fall hopelessly in love with him."

"Neither of you are ever going to let me live that little faux pas down, are you?"

"I don't see how we can. I can hear it now. I met Mommy when she almost ran me over in the parking lot. What a fantastic story you'll be able to share with your children. Now, let's get this show on the road." Ed pulled her into his arms and kissed her brow. "I can feel your parents here today. They are watching you and smiling, knowing that Ryne is the perfect man for you. This day is going to fly by in the blink of an eye. Take in everything you can."

On that note, the carriage appeared that would take them out to the pond where she and Ryne would exchange their vows. As promised, the hillsides surrounding the ranch were filled with a multitude of colors as the flowers were at their peak.

As they neared the fabric runner that would lead

her to Ryne, she took a deep breath. Her life was about to change. She closed her eyes committing to memory the beauty that surrounded her. The cumulus clouds that blanketed the sky reminded her of her favorite Florida sky. The perfect day all around. When she reopened them, she saw Ryne, dressed in a formal black tux, standing at the end of the white runner. He shifted from foot to foot as he waited for her.

Ed assisted her from the carriage and Lauren straightened her mother's eight-foot train adorned with hand sewn Swarovski crystals.

As the girls prepared to head down the aisle, Jen was overwhelmed with feelings. In a few short minutes, they would be her sisters, and she couldn't be happier. When the music began, Emma took one last look at Jen, flashed a bright smile, and winked. Only Emma, Jen thought.

Emma started down the aisle followed by Olivia. Right before Lauren proceeded down the aisle, she turned back to her lifelong friend and whispered, "Be happy." Jen was more nervous than she'd even been in her entire life. She reached for Ed's arm and he patted her hand in place, giving her the reassurance that she needed.

As Jen began her way towards her future, she heard the oohs and aahs as everyone recognized the beauty of her dress. The fabric was a gorgeous color of ivory silver lace on ivory tulle and moscato royal organza beaded with the same Swarovski crystals.

The lace detail not only surrounded the skirt just above the hem, but also mirrored the lace edges of the sparkling bodice. Wide straps came across the back, forming an elegant keyhole opening. She looked like a princess in her mother's dress.

As she moved down the aisle, the sun was at the perfect angle and her dress glittered brightly with each step she took, creating a magical moment. Her whole dress shimmered in the sunshine. As she approached Ryne, she knew he was doing his best to contain his emotions as he gnawed on his lower lip.

Ryne met her and Ed. With tears in her eyes, she brushed a kiss on Ed's cheek and reached for her future. She clasped Ryne's hand and gazed into his eyes. The smile that she'd come to love shone brightly on his face. She winked at Ryne, and they turned towards the minister.

As they stood preparing to say their vows, the sun went behind the clouds casting a shadow on the horizon.

She curled her fingers around his hand and tightly held on. When the minister asked 'Who giveth this woman all eyes turned to Ed.

"Her parents, grandparents, and I," he responded.

Wilford and Miles stood on either side of Ed. It was definitely a difficult time remembering Jen's parents. Even though they weren't present in mind and body, they weren't forgotten.

As they recited their vows, Ryne became emotional. She knew how much he loved her especially as she watched this proud, powerful center iceman weep at his own wedding.

She cried right alongside Ryne. Once they completed their vows, the clouds parted and the sky was filled with the most beautiful sunbeams she'd ever seen. She squeezed Ryne's hand and smiled. She felt at peace. All the apprehension that she felt only moments ago had disappeared.

As they started down the aisle, she could finally breathe again. Her life as she once knew it, in so many words, had ceased to exist. Her life now was filled with a family she'd never once turn her back on.

As they neared the carriage that would take them to the barn where the reception was being held, she took one last look back towards the pond. There, flying low across the water, were two Canada Geese. They landed at the water's edge. Facing them they each lowered their heads almost as a sign to Jen that her parents were nearby.

A tear escaped and ran down her cheek. "Hey, I thought your tears were over."

"They were, but look." She pointed at the geese. "Look where they landed...Right in our spot where you asked me to marry you."

"I see that."

"Do you think it's a coincidence?" He looked at her questioningly. "Never mind. It's just my imagination playing tricks on me."

In her heart she knew the geese represented her parents.

As the wedding guests made their way to the barn, Ryne and Jen rode around the ranch in the horse drawn carriage. "I wanted to tell you this when you came down the aisle, but I was speechless. Sweetheart, you look absolutely beautiful."

"Thank you and you look quite handsome yourself."

She rested her head on his shoulder as the sun

began to sink along the horizon. "I was shocked with how emotional Ed seemed. I've never seen him like that. Even when my parents died, he was stoic and never showed one ounce of emotion."

"He was. I have to believe he knew he needed to be strong for you. It was a nice gesture that he included your parents and grandparents in the ceremony."

She nodded. "It was and I know they were there in spirit. I could feel them and I know the others did too."

Throughout the evening friends and family took to the microphone, offering the couple words of wisdom. When dinner was over, Emma decided she needed to say something. Jen watched as Jacques tried to discourage it, but Jacklynne encouraged her since she was over-the-top excited to have Jen as her sister.

Jen wound her fingers through Ryne's as they listened to Emma.

"Hi! I'm Emma Ferguson and Ryne is my older brother." Jen looked up at Ryne and burst out laughing.

"Hey, Em's, I think they know I'm your brother," Ryne yelled from the table.

"I wasn't sure," she added staring her brother down. "Jen, I am so excited to be able to call you my sister. I've always wanted an older sister."

"Hey, what about me," cried Olivia.

"I said older!"

"I am older."

"By what, five years? I said older and I mean older—older like Jen older." Everyone laughed at the exchange between Emma and Olivia. "I'm so happy you are moving here. We can go shopping, have sleepovers…"

"Sleepovers?" Ryne whispered. "What about me?"

"Shhh. You know what she means," Jen said, elbowing him in the ribs. "Stop so we can hear what she says."

"Well, that's all I wanted to say. I love you Jen, and I'm so glad you married my brother."

Jen pulled away from Ryne and stood as Emma ran towards her. She enveloped her arms around Emma. "Oh Emma. Thank you for that. I love you too! I'm so glad I can call you and Oliva my sisters." She kissed Emma on the cheek; then Ryne reached for Emma as well, planting a kiss on her forehead.

"Thanks for accepting Jen, Emma. It means a lot to me."

"You're welcome. Oh and I forgot while I was up there," she said pointing to the microphone. "I love you too, Ryne."

"Right back at you, Em's."

Next up to the microphone was Rowena. Jen had been so focused on Emma and Ryne's conversation that she missed her grandmother moving to the stage. As soon as she heard her voice, she groaned, unsure what she was about to say.

"For those of you that don't know me, I'm Rowena Steele. Jennifer is my granddaughter. I'm not very good at this, but I feel I must say a few words in the absence of her father." Miles stood beside Rowena as she began her toast or rather speech that she'd all planned out and was reading from.

"Jennifer is my only grandchild. I'm sure most, if not all of you, are aware that her parents were killed the evening of her high school graduation. Jen was going to be a photographer and follow in the foot-steps of her renowned father, Marcus Steele. But that evening, she lost her way and gave up on her life's dream. I have to say that my granddaughter hasn't been the same since she lost her parents.

"Now, fast forward all these years later. She's a teacher at a Lakeview Private School where many of the students' fathers are professional athletes. Not to forget Ed here is the owner of the St. Louis Gen-erals...Jennifer was surrounded by athletes in some way.

"Then, one cold night she runs into Ryne— quite literally. Isn't that a story?"

"Ah, Rowena, I don't think we need to go there." Ryne chimed in.

"Shhh." Rowena shushed Ryne and continued with her speech. "I thought everyone knew how you two met." Everyone heard both Ryne and Jen-nifer groan. Rowena would tell the story. "So you see, fate played a part in these two meeting. I still can't believe my granddaughter almost ran the star of the team over but enough of that." Everyone chuckled.

"Miles and I didn't know Jennifer and Ryne were dating until they came out East for a Black Gold Management party honoring Tony and Ashley Regada. In fact, our family has ties to them."

"Grandmother," Jen called out.

"Okay honey, I won't go into how we know Ashley Regada other than we knew her and her first husband, Morgan Cameron. Suffice it to say, Jennifer brought Ryne to dinner." Rowena turned back to Miles. "Her grandfather and I weren't sure what she had gotten herself into. Involved with a hockey player. I thought all hockey players were mean fighting machines. It seems like we always hear of these brutal fights on the ice. Anyway, I took one look at Ryne and I knew he was different.

"For being a defenseman, he didn't seem like he had a bad bone in his body. He actually was well behaved..."

Everyone could hear Ryne clearing his throat. "If I may Ro, I'm a center iceman not a defenseman."

She glared at him as he corrected her. "You're a hockey player, that's about all I know. Anyway, where was I?" She looked at her notes clearing her throat. "Well, you were well behaved, that's what I know, and even enjoyed my cooking."

"Which is very good," he added.

"See why I like him?" The crowd burst out laughing. "Now to get to my point. Even though I gave Ryne a little bit of trouble, I knew he was the perfect match for our Jennifer. I felt like the Jennifer of old had returned. She was smiling, laughing, and seemed happy. The happiest I'd seen since the day before her high school graduation.

"During dinner, I discovered that she'd returned to photography. I know she was somewhat forced into it because of the fundraiser she was put in charge of, but she was doing what she was meant to do. Not only was she taking the pictures she loved to take, Ryne had talked her into taking sports photographs. From what I've seen, you're going to be quite the sought-after sports photographer, but I digress there.

"In the last year, Miles and I have witnessed the return of our beloved granddaughter. I know, Ryne, you were a little apprehensive about me." Everyone saw Ryne nod his head in agreement. "And you should have been. I did ask a lot of questions."

"That you did," Jen called out.

"I did that because I needed to know what type of man you were involved with. Ryne, dear, you are a perfect gentleman. You are going to be the perfect husband for my granddaughter. I am thrilled to be standing here at your wedding. The one thing I'm not too keen about is your forcing her to move so damn far away from me and Miles, Wilford and Rose. But I guess that's what a guest room is for, right Jennifer?"

Everyone saw Jennifer roll her eyes. "Now dear, don't roll your eyes at me." Again laughter rang out.

"Are you almost done?"

"Almost, dear. Almost. Your grandfather and I will always be here for you if you need us. We're all proud of you. And most of all, your parents are too." Rowena reached for the glass that sat in front of her. "So let's everyone raise your glass in a toast to our couple. To Ryne and Jennifer: May your life be filled with happiness but most of all, love."

By the time Rowena finished her speech, the tears Jen had been holding at bay let loose and cascaded down her cheek. No matter what happened in her life, Jennifer would always have her grandparents by her side, cheering her on.

Ryne and Jennifer made their way to Rowena
where Ryne pulled Rowena into a hug. "Thanks,
Rowena. I'm glad you like me so much."

Rowena slapped him on the shoulder. "Do you
think I'd have given you permission to marry her if
I didn't?"

"No, you definitely wouldn't."

"Just be true to her. Keep her happy and when
she's sad because she's missing St. Louis, be an understanding ear to her. That's all I ask. I know how
much you love one another." Rowena kissed Ryne
on the cheek and then hugged her granddaughter.

"Jennifer, be happy. Just be happy. That's all I
want."

"I am, Grandmother Rowena. I am."

The rest of the reception was filled with more
toasts and dancing. It was late when Ryne and Jennifer snuck away. They'd enjoyed every minute of
the day and looked forward to what the future had
to offer. Most especially his move to the Storm and
his chance at finally becoming a Stanley Cup winner.

Chapter Thirty-One

WITH RYNE'S TRADE HAPPENING SO close to the wedding and the beginning of the preseason, they had little time to pack and find a home. Still, they wanted a wedding trip. The day after the wedding, they flew to Alaska where they cruised the inside passage and took a road trip around the state exploring the vast nature Alaska offers.

Their honeymoon afforded them the time to relax before having to pack up Jen's house, and for Ryne to begin the preseason. Their trip went according to plan up until they arrived at the airport to return home. Their schedule was tight as it was, having to travel to St. Louis, but at Anchorage's airport, they discovered a delay. There was no flight out that day.

Both were annoyed but they decided it wouldn't put a damper on their special trip.

They contacted Philippe since he was scheduled to be their chauffeur.

"Heads-up, Dad wants to talk to you as soon as you get home."

"Wonder what he wants?"

"Haven't a clue. Maybe you should reach out to him."

"Sounds good," replied Ryne. "See you tomorrow."

"What's wrong?" Jen asked when he ended the call. "Did something happen?"

Ryne shrugged. "I don't know, but I'm going to find out."

He dialed his father. "Dad, our flight's delayed and we can't get out until tomorrow. Philippe said you needed to speak to me."

"Sorry to hear about that. How was your trip?"

"We had a great time. Oh, and Jen says hi." She gave him a thumbs up.

"Dad, what's up?

"It can wait until tomorrow. Enjoy your last day of freedom. You've got a lot on the horizon with packing up Jen and the start of training camp."

"You're sure?"

"Yep. Nothing to worry about."

Thankfully their flight was on time and when they pulled up at the house, Jacques and Jacklynne greeted them with open arms.

"Welcome home. You look so happy and relaxed," Jacklynne exclaimed as she hugged Jen.

"We had the best time," Jen said. "And I feel relaxed and rested although I'm not looking forward to packing."

Jacques motioned to Ryne.

"Honey, I'm going to have that chat with my dad." He brushed a kiss to her cheek. "Why don't you and Mom catch up?" He smiled and leaned back for another kiss.

"Don't worry, Ryne. I'll take good care of her," Jacklynne said as she slipped her arm through Jen's and led her to the house.

"Your mom missed her along with Emma. She can't wait to see her."

"I guess I'm old meat, huh?" he said, rolling his eyes.

Jacques laughed. "I wouldn't say that but you're definitely not the new kid on the block."

"I understand."

Jacques led him across the yard where they hopped on the ATV and drove off towards the opposite side of the ranch.

"So, you had a good trip." Jacques asked as they drove along.

"Yeah, we did. It was nice and relaxing." Ryne ran his hand through his hair. "Now the tough part. We need to find a place to live, pack, and then move, all within a few weeks' time. It's definitely going to be a huge adjustment for Jen, especially with me starting training camp. Luckily, it's being held at the Sauderhouse Arena and not in some far away hole-in-the-wall town."

"I remember our training camps were held out of town, making the season seem that much longer. Since they built Sauderhouse, the team has everything at their fingertips. Why travel out of town and have to pack and haul all of the equipment? It makes perfect sense to me."

"It does. But don't get me wrong, Dad. I am ever thankful for this trade. I don't know how it happened so fast. I approached Adam a while ago, but I didn't think it would come until my contract expired. I have to believe Adam spoke with Ed who made it happen.

"Two years ago, when Anthony moved into the

general manger role for the Storm, I even spoke with him, letting him know that I wanted to come home." He stopped and looked across the fields still full of summer color. "Maybe in Anthony's own way, it was a wedding gift to us." He shrugged. "All I know is that I need to stop by his office before training camp begins and thank him— that's for sure. He made my dream come true. Now we just have to win that Stanley Cup, right?" He paused shaking his head. "Gosh, I hate thinking about moving again. I was just getting settled."

"About that, son." As they drove along, Jacques shared with him an idea that he'd been pondering since he discovered Ryne had been traded.

"I know how hard it is with just getting married. It's going to be a huge adjustment for both of you but especially Jennifer. I have a temporary solution for you." He stopped and turned to Ryne. "We have the cabin."

"Yeah, and?"

"And, I've fixed it up. I put in all new appliances, added a new furnace. We even painted. What about you and Jen moving in there while you take time to find a place to live? That way, you're not being pressured into making a decision you're not ready to make. The cabin's far enough away from the main house that Emma shouldn't bother Jennifer *too* much. And Jennifer will be close enough that if she gets lonely, she can come visit us. Plus, we'll be close by if she needs anything. We're not her grandparents, but we are her family now. So, what do you think?"

"Wow, Dad," he ran his hand along his whiskered

jaw pausing in thought. "Thanks for offering it to us. Of course we'll take you up on it."

"Don't you think you should ask your wife?"

"Yeah, definitely, but I don't think she'll have to think twice. I know she'll say yes."

"Good," Jacques added.

"Have you completed all of the upgrades that I can take Jen by right now?"

"Yep, it's all ready for you."

"Thanks, Dad. This really means a lot. I know how difficult a transition this is going to be for Jen. Being away from the only home she's ever known, living in a country and a climate that can be brutal during the winter. She's definitely going to need family, especially when I'm on the road. I love you, Dad." Ryne threw his arm around Jacques neck and hugged him.

"Thank your Mom. It was really her idea."

"I will. Mom is going to be the best thing for Jen. I know how much she misses her own, but she's really come to love you and Mom a great deal. You'll both look out for her. I love her so much but I worry that all of these changes are going to be unsettling for her, and I won't be there quite as much as I should."

"We'll take care of her, don't you worry, son."

They made their way back to the house and found both Jacklynne and Jennifer deep in conversation. They'd already finished a glass of iced tea, and Jen was pouring a second when Ryne and Jacques walked in the door.

Ryne kissed his mom on the cheek and turned to Jen. "Do you think I can steal my wife for a little while?"

Jacques winked at Jacklynne.

"Of course, you can." Jacklynne reached for her glass with a broad smile plastered across her face.

Ryne led Jen from the house. "Is everything alright?" she asked as he guided her to the ATV.

"Of course, why do you ask?"

"I don't know. You're acting strangely."

"Come on. I need to show you something."

Ryne led her to the garage and helped her into the ATV. He revved the engine and backed out.

"Where are we going?"

Ryne grinned at her and drove along. "Did you have a good time catching up with Mom?"

"I did. According to her, Emma was bummed out that she and Olivia wouldn't be here when we arrived. They're at some hockey clinic." She placed her hand on his forearm. "Oh, by the way, your parents want to have a meeting with Emma." Ryne cocked his brow. "Emma won't like it but I think it makes sense with how excited she is with our relocating to Calgary."

He cast a sideways glance at her. "What's this all about?"

She hemmed and hawed and then admitted they wanted to lay down some strict rules concerning Emma.

"Jen, they need to let Emma just be. She's ten years old. She has an exuberant personality."

"I realize that but your mom wants to do this for *us*. Emma needs to learn to respect our privacy and not bother us all the time."

They drove along for a few minutes when he

stopped. He reached into his pocket and pulled out a handkerchief. "Close your eyes and just to make sure you're not cheating; I'm going to cover them."

"Ryne, what are you up to?"

"It's not what I'm up to but what my parents are up to." He covered her eyes and restarted the engine. They bumped along and then he stopped. "Hold on a second," he said as he jumped from the vehicle. "I'm going to help you. And keep that blindfold on."

"Yes, sir," she snapped back.

He reached for her hand and aided her from the vehicle. "Hold onto me and you shouldn't have any problems." They took a few steps. "Okay, now there are a few stairs ahead. I'll lead you." He gripped her hand and helped her onto the porch. He turned the doorknob and pushed the door inward. He led her inside, turned, and placed his hands on her shoulders.

"I'm going to take off your blindfold, but keep your eyes closed until I tell you to open them." He untied his handkerchief. "Okay, open your eyes."

He stepped aside and watched her face as she opened her eyes. They grew as big as saucers. "Where are we?"

"Do you like it?" He watched her as she spun around, taking in the cabin. She made her way farther into the large, expansive room, immediately falling in love with the stone fireplace, the vaulted ceiling, and the multitude of windows that stretched along the back wall. She ran her hand over the back of the couch and strolled towards the opening that led to the kitchen. He heard her gasp when she noticed the new appliances and fully stocked kitchen.

"I don't understand. Where are we?"

"Our temporary home, if you like it."

"Like it, I love it. But…"

"Mom and Dad knew how stressed our life is going to be with getting married and having to relocate. They decided to help us out a little, so they redid the cabin for us. We can live here until we have the time to find a place of our own. That way, we won't be forced into buying something we're not ready for."

"I can't believe they did this for us. I'm…."

"Honey, they wanted to make this transition easier for you. We'll have our privacy here, but we'll always be welcome at the house. And if I know Emma, this will be her home away from home."

"Yeah, probably."

"And don't you let her live here. She's going to need to learn her place, and in time, she will. You being here will become old school soon enough… At least I hope so." He reached for her fingers. "When I'm gone, you won't be alone or isolated somewhere especially if we have bad weather. Mom and Dad will always be available so don't be shy. Reach out to them if you need it."

"I will. Wow. I can't believe they did this. I'm speechless."

"They don't expect anything other than a simple thank you." He pulled her into his arms. "Come on, let me show you your new home." He brushed her brow with a kiss then took her on a tour of the cabin.

It really wasn't a cabin in her terms. It was a

house that contained three bedrooms, an oversized remodeled kitchen, two bathrooms, a laundry, and even a detached garage. "Let me ask, how do we get here?"

"There's a separate driveway, and we can come and go as we please without bothering anyone. We're kind of off the beaten path as we're past my parents' place, so they'd have to drive out here to even determine if we we're home."

She ran her hand along the granite countertop in the kitchen. "We need to do something special for them. They've helped us so much. Between the wedding and this house...I have to say finding a place was a weight on our shoulders that they've removed. I feel so much better. I wasn't looking forward to finding something in a short amount of time."

"They understood our predicament and wanted to lessen our burden. My dad realizes what it's like to marry and head off to training camp. At least the Storm train at the Sauderhouse Arena and not some far away small-town rink in a remote area. I can come home every night, and it will help us as we ease into married life before the season takes over our lives."

As they neared the house, Jen pulled out her phone. "Who are you calling now? Not Lauren again."

She raised her brow.

"Well, didn't you just speak with her on the drive from the airport?"

"I did and what's it to you…"

He looked at her as a smile broke out across her lips. "Just so you know, I'm phoning your mom to see if the girls are home." While she dialed, he placed his hand on her thigh. She glanced his way when Jacklynne answered.

"Are the girls home?" She waited for her response.

"We're on our way."

He turned to her. "And when is this so-called meeting?"

She gnawed on her lower lip and raised her brow. "When we get there."

"Be prepared for a pouty Emma. Not sure how she'll react to these restrictions. You are her 'older' sister and I'm sure she's going to want an all-access pass."

"Maybe we should rethink this. I don't want her upset with me."

He shook his head. "If my parents think this is best, then I agree. They're *never* wrong."

Changing the subject, Jen slapped at his hand and looked across the horizon. "I can't believe the flowers are still in bloom," she sighed. "It is so beautiful here."

"So you're okay with moving here?"

"Absolutely. I'd follow you anywhere. I'm not going to say this will be easy, but with you and your family by my side, I think it will be a piece of cake."

"I like that attitude."

She reached for his hand as they entered the

kitchen.

"I told Emma in a few minutes we were having a family meeting. Are you okay with that?" Jacklynne asked as she wiped down the counter.

"We are," Ryne said as he grabbed a cookie from the cookie jar. "In fact, I think it's a fantastic idea to set ground rules with Emma especially since we'll be living right down the road."

They gathered as a family: Jacklynne, Jacques, Ryne, Jen, Emma and Olivia.

Jacques led off the discussion. "Your mother and I wanted to set some ground rules now that Ryne and Jen are moving home."

"Ground rules?"

"That's right, Emma." Emma's eyes grew large and she pushed out her lower lip.

"Jen and Ryne are moving to the ranch."

Excitedly, Emma clapped her hands. "Really? You're staying here at the house?"

"No."

"But where?"

"The cabin," Jacques added.

Emma raised her brows. "The cabin? Why would you go there? It's old and dirty. The heat doesn't even work."

Everyone laughed at her comment. "Well, it doesn't."

"It does now," Jacques chimed in.

"So, here's the deal," said Jacklynne. "You can't just go over there on a whim. You must call in advance and if Jen says it isn't a good time, you must respect her. She and Ryne need their privacy and you won't always be welcome."

She rolled her eyes. "I get it. I won't bother you."

"It's not that they don't want you to bother them. She and Ryne have their own life now. Just because they're living close by doesn't mean you can disturb them whenever you want. You need to treat it…"

"I know, Dad, I understand. I just love Jen so much." She paused and added, "Can I have a sleepover?"

Jacklynne chuckled. "We'll have to talk about that, Emma."

"I love you as well, Emma." Jen said as she pulled Emma into a hug.

"I get it, Jen. I promise not to bother you and my brother." As Jen pulled away Emma added, "But can I help you get settled?"

They all laughed. Only Emma, who could be taken full circle through a lesson, would ask such a silly question. "Not right now, Em's but maybe you can come by later on. Jen and I need to figure out a few things first."

"Will we see you for dinner?" Jacklynne asked.

"You bet," Jen said as she headed out the door.

As they drove the rest of the way to their new home, Jen took in the beauty of the ranch. The last of the flowers were blooming, and she knew all too soon winter would be upon them.

She reached for his hand. "Thank you," she said as she squeezed it. "Thank you for allowing me to become a part of your family. After today, I certainly know what it's like to have a sister."

She knew her life wasn't going to be easy, but what she hadn't expected was being able to really feel the closeness of family. Their family meeting brought it all together for her. Before today, she'd felt like a member of the Ferguson family, but now she realized that she was really a part of it.

Chapter Thirty-Two

THEY SPENT A FEW DAYS in Calgary before heading back to St. Louis to begin the packing process. After much thought, she and Ryne decided not to put her house on the market. They would use it when they visited during the summer months. Worst case, they would rent it and use it as investment income.

Ryne, who had pretty much packed his place before the wedding, helped Jen choose what she wanted to move. For the time being, she boxed-up her winter attire and a few spring things. She rationalized that she could always buy new clothes if she needed them.

She chose a few pieces of furniture along with all of her camera equipment. Her father's studio would remain intact—she'd use it when she was in St. Louis.

The night before they were scheduled to put their belongings on the moving van and head north, they had dinner with Rose and Wilford.

On the drive to their house, Ryne noticed her quietness. He knew how difficult this evening would be for her. Outside of her visits to Rowena and Miles' home and the few vacations she'd taken over the years, Jen saw her grandparents several times a week. She'd still be able to visit with them via Skype, but he also knew it wouldn't be the same.

He reached for her hand, lacing their fingers together he rested them atop his thigh. Squeezing, he asked, "You okay?"

She nodded. He raised their interlocked hands placing a soft kiss on the back of hers. "You're not leaving forever."

"I know. I worry about them. They're not getting any younger."

"No, they're not."

"What if something happens to them?"

"You'll be there just as always."

"But Ryne?"

"Honey, you'll always be there for Rose and Wilford but just at a greater distance. They know that you need to move on with your life. They don't expect you to always be there holding their hand. They love you and want to see you happy. You are, aren't you?"

"What?"

"Happy?"

"Of course, I am. I love you."

"That's good to know." He glanced her way with a half-smile. "All kidding aside, if something were to happen to any of your grandparents, you could be there in a matter of hours. No, it may not be in a matter of minutes like today, but you'll be there for them." He kissed her hand again. "Now, let's see a smile on your face. You don't need to upset Rose any more than she already is. Remember you're not alone. We're in this together, okay?"

In his periphery, he saw her nod. They'd get

through the evening. Then they'd load the moving van tomorrow, jump into his car, and head north, stopping off to visit Miles and Rowena before trekking across Canada to their new home.

Wilford threw open the door as they hit the porch. "Jen, Ryne, come on in," he said in a booming voice. He kissed Jen's cheek and shook Ryne's hand.

"You all packed and ready to move?"

"We are, sir. The movers are supposed to come at eight." Wilford quirked his brow at Ryne. "Ah, am I ever going to get that right. Sorry, Wilford. Maybe one day I'll forget the 'sir.'"

"I guess in the next hundred years, right?" Wilford laughed and led them into the family room. "Your grandmother's in the kitchen, finishing up."

"I'll join her," Jen said as she placed a soft kiss against her grandfather's forehead.

"This is going to be a difficult transition for her. Are you prepared?"

Ryne sat beside Wilford on the couch. He leaned over his knees, wringing his hands together, then turned to Wilford. "I know this is hard on her. You and Rose along with Rowena and Miles have been her backbone since her parents died. I keep telling her that's not going away. But..."

"She has you now, Ryne. Rose and I are getting older, and we're not always going to be here for her. In fact, I think her moving to the wilds of Canada is the best thing for her. In time, she'll learn to adjust to us not being around all the time. And when something happens to us or Miles and Rowena, it won't hurt quite as much. Now, don't get me wrong, I know Jennifer and I know how she is. Just be there for her, son. Love her, support her, and keep her happy. Promise me that you'll do that. You are her life now. We're just a bunch of supporting characters, wanting to see her happy."

"Wilford, you know I'll do whatever's in my power to keep her happy. She's my life and I can't imagine her not in it."

Somehow, they made it through dinner without tears. Rose seemed upbeat to Ryne. In fact, when Jen excused herself from the table to use the bathroom, she leaned over, patted his hand and whispered, "She's going to be fine. Stop your worrying."

"I'm…"

"Dear, I've known you long enough to know how worried you are about our Jennifer. She'll be just fine. I am excited for the next chapter in her life. Will I miss her? Of course I will, but it's not like I won't talk to her or see her again. Now about that Skype…"

Rose stopped talking when she noticed the bathroom door reopen. "No more talk, okay. Wilford and I will figure it out."

"What did you say, Grandmother?"

"Nothing, dear. I was just asking Ryne if he was ready for dessert."

"He is, isn't he? I can't wait for a piece of your coconut cake. It's my favorite."

"That's why I made it." Rose's her eyes filled with tears as she hurried from the room.

Ryne reached for Jen's hand and smiled. "Before we leave we need to show Wilford again how to access Skype."

"Ryne, I think I have it down. I've been practicing. We've been Skyping with Rowena since you showed us. Whoever invented that was a genius. In fact, we've had a virtual tour of their house. I thought they downsized."

Ryne burst out laughing. "They have a few less trees."

"That's what Ro said. I don't consider that downsizing, do you? A few less bedrooms yes, but trees?"

"I thought the same thing when we visited the first time. You know Grandmother Rowena."

"I do and I love her just the same."

When the time came to leave, Ryne stepped onto the porch while she said her final goodbye.

"I'm going to miss you both," she told her grandparents. Her voice wobbled.

"Honey, it's not like we're going anywhere," Rose said. "We're always going to be here for you— just not around the corner. We love you, but you're married now. You have Ryne to look out for you. He has your best interest at heart."

"I know he does, it's just…"

"Sweetheart, I know you'll never forget that night. It will always be with you. You've come so far, don't let it pull you back under. We're not going to disappear. You'll see our bright and shining faces on Skype as often as you like. We can talk daily, just like we always did. Nothing's going to change."

"I know. It's just so hard. I'm going to miss you so."

"We realize that," Wilford said. "It's time for you to break free and fly. You'll never forget that night, but you can't let it consume you either. Your husband loves you so much. You have his family you can now call your own. Enjoy that, but know if you ever need us, we'll be there for you."

Wilford pulled Jennifer into his arms. "I love you, Jennifer. Never forget that."

Ryne looked back through the door and caught Rose pulling Jennifer into her arms for the last time. "Enjoy your new life. I love you dear, with all of my being. You'll never be far from my thoughts, but it's time for you to make a life of your own. Start the family you've dreamed about since you were a little girl. Ryne's dream of returning to Calgary has come true— now set about making your dream come true. Your grandfather and I will always be here, and we can't wait to meet the next Steele."

Wiping her eyes, she smiled at Rose. "You mean the next Ferguson."

Laughing she said, "I'm getting as bad as your husband. He keeps forgetting and refers to Wilford as sir, and I still can't remember that you're a Ferguson now."

"Deep down, I'll always be a Steele."

"I know dear, but now you have a new family. Get to know them and embrace the future."

Ryne smiled at Rose's last words. "Embrace the future." That's what they needed to do and they would.

Moments later, Jen emerged from the house, followed by Rose and Wilford. "We'll call you from Rowena's," Ryne said as he reached for Jen's hand.

"Call? Why not Skype?"

Jen had to laugh at her grandmother. As they walked down the steps to embrace their future, they turned back and waved goodbye. Ryne knew it wasn't a goodbye to the past, they were moving forward to a future filled with hope and dreams.

★★★★★

Wilford and Rose surprised them as they were closing the door on her past and walking towards their future. Jennifer had just locked the door when she heard a car door slam. She turned and discovered her grandparents waiting at the curb. "We couldn't let you leave today without saying goodbye."

Jen ran to her grandmother and threw her arms around her neck. "Thank you, Grams. This means so much."

"Dear, I thought you two might need this." Rose pulled away and reached for the grocery bag that Wilford held. "Just a few snacks for the road." She passed them to Ryne.

"What's in here?" Ryne spoke as his head went into the bag.

"All of my granddaughter's favorites, including another slice of my coconut cake."

"Only one slice?"

"There's enough for you too." Rose reached for Ryne. "Come here son and give me a hug."

Ryne hugged Rose, kissing her on the cheek. "Thank you," he murmured.

Rose reached up and patted his cheek. "Anytime."

Ryne had phoned Rose when Jen had been in the shower that morning, requesting they come and say a final goodbye. He believed that it would ease Jen's fears of leaving them when they finally pulled away from her home.

They said their farewells and hopped into Ryne's

car. He knew he'd made the right decision with his early morning phone call as the tears he'd expected never materialized. She smiled and waved profusely at her grandparents as they drove down the street towards their new life.

After a quick visit with Rowena and Miles, they started on their long journey from Greenwich, Connecticut, to Calgary. They drove through Pennsylvania and Ohio, Indiana and around Chicago, through Wisconsin and Minnesota then finally North Dakota before they hit the border and entered Canada.

When they finally arrived at the ranch, they couldn't wait to get settled. The movers had delivered their things and placed the furniture in the exact locations that Jen had instructed Jacklynne. Only a few boxes sat unopened in the family room.

Jacklynne had seen to unpacking the majority of their boxes. Jen knew immediately how much care she'd had taken to make the move as painless as possible for them.

"I can't believe your mother did all of this for us," Jen said as she swept her arm in front of her. "She unpacked our clothes, organized the kitchen..."

"She wanted to. And I'm sure she had a little help," Ryne said as he discovered a note on the coffee table.

Dear Jen and Ryne,

I hope we didn't make a mess of things. We did our best to put things away, but I'm sure you'll find a better spot to put your kitchen utensils.

Take your time settling in and we'll see you when we see you!

Much love, Mom

Jen handed the note to Ryne. "That was so kind of her. She didn't have to unpack for us."

"As I said, she wanted to and I'm sure she also had some help."

"Yeah, I gather that as she referred to 'we.'"

"Come on, it's late. I'm sure you're just about as tired as I am," Ryne said as he reached for her. "We can unpack the car tomorrow." He draped his arm around her shoulders and led her off to their bedroom. It was the first night in their new home, and all he wanted to do was wrap his arms around her and sleep.

Jen spent the next few weeks settling in unpacking and arranging things to her liking. They'd both been surprised how little they'd seen of Emma. They assumed she'd taken her parents warning to heart.

When Ryne wasn't training for the start of the season, he was out on the range helping his dad maintain fence lines and cutting hay that would be used to supplement the cattle feed during the winter months.

The day before training camp was officially set to begin, Jacklynne had a family dinner. Everyone was there. Philippe, Ryne, and Etienne didn't have a far commute the next day, while Rafael couldn't linger long after dinner as he was taking a red-eye flight back to Arizona where his training camp was set to launch on Tuesday.

Jules, on the other hand, had flown home for the weekend, surprising even his mother. He'd been back in Madison for the new semester, but decided to return home to share the weekend with his brothers. For the first time in what seemed like forever, the family was together before the all-important beginning to the new season.

"Mom, can you hurry up...I need to leave for the airport."

"Jules, I still don't understand why you came home. You're here for less than forty-eight hours."

"Yeah, I know but it was important for me to be here." He looked up at his brothers. "I still can't believe you're all playing for the Storm. Who'd have thought?"

"I did," Ryne stated as he reached for Jen's hand. "Even before I met Jen, I knew I wanted to end my career here."

"Are you thinking about retirement, son?"

"No, Dad, not really. I'm just being realistic here. I'm not sure how long my hip's going to hold out."

"Is it bothering you?" Jacques asked with a quirk to his brow. "If it is..."

"It's not, Dad. You know what my dreams always were. I was disappointed when they didn't draft me, but all along my heart has been with the Storm." Looking at his brothers, "Look at us, the three amigos..."

"Don't start there," Etienne said.

"Well, it's true. Anyway, look what we can accomplish. Three brothers taking a team that was once led by their father to the Stanley Cup finals."

"Don't you think you're taking this a little far?"

Philippe asked as he stood and reached for the tray Jacklynne had carried into the room.

"No, I don't. In fact, I think we're going to go all the way. Right here, right now, with our talent, I predict we're going to win the Stanley Cup this year. No ifs, ands, or buts about it."

"Ahh, big brother…I think I have something to say about that," Rafael said. "We have a decent team too. I believe the Tide could go all the way."

"Is that a bet little brother?"

"No, Ryne, it's not. I'm not betting on who goes to the Cup. What I'm hoping for is that none of us gets seriously injured and that includes you, Ryne. So quit thinking about that hip of yours. I foresee you being a member of the Storm for many years to come."

"We can only hope," Jen quietly spoke. "I have to agree with Rafael. Here's to a safe season filled with much success and no serious injuries." She leaned over, kissing Ryne's cheek.

Jules and Rafael lingered as long as they could before leaving for the airport. As he headed out the door, Jules turned back to Ryne. "Stay safe, big brother. I don't want to hear about you getting injured again."

"I'll do my best. And while you're at it, bring another championship to UW."

"Like you, I'll do my best." With that, Jules headed out the door.

Jen stood in the background watching the interaction between brothers. She still couldn't believe that she was married, and was entrenched in this family.

She hadn't heard Emma approach until she felt a hand brush hers. "Jen, are you okay?"

"Of course, I am."

"You had a funny look on your face. You seemed far away and didn't hear me when I called your name."

"Em's, I was just enjoying the view."

"Huh?"

"Oh nothing. I was having fun recalling your brothers' argument over who was going to win the Stanley Cup."

"You're sure that's all?"

She was looking forward to the hockey season. It was her favorite sport and for the first time ever, she would be seeing it from the inside.

She knew life would be different. She was doing her best to embrace all of the changes. And family would definitely be the key in surviving her first year as a hockey player's wife.

"Yep, all is good." Jen slid her arm around Emma's shoulder. All was good in her opinion. She'd settled into life in her new home, had a family that she could call her own, and was married to wonderful man.

Chapter Thirty-Three

TRAINING CAMP FLEW BY AND, thankfully, Ryne's worries about his hip were in the past as they rolled through the preseason, winning seven out of eight games.

He was definitely on a high, playing well, when he was called into the coach's office. For the first time in his career, he was a little apprehensive. In his opinion, his preseason had been the best of his career. His thoughts had been all over the place when Raymond Oldsman, the coach of the Storm, asked to see him before leaving the facility for the day. "Hey, Ferguson," Ray had called out after practice. Ryne, Etienne, and Philippe all turned their heads. "I need to see you—Ryne—after practice. Meet me in my office after you've showered and changed."

"I wonder what that's about," Etienne said as he skated alongside his brother.

"I haven't a clue," Ryne responded.

He made his way down the tunnel towards the showers and tried his best not to question the meaning behind the meeting. When he reached his locker, he stored his equipment and walked straight towards the showers. Normally, he would take his time changing but not today. He didn't want to keep Ray waiting.

After a quick shower, Ryne threw on his street clothes.

As he approached the closed door, he found his heart rate increasing and actually felt sweat running down his back. If he didn't count meeting Rowena and his wedding, he hadn't been this nervous in a long time. He pulled in his lips and knocked on the door, unsure what the future held in store.

He was surprised when Anthony Theophilos, the Storm's general manger, opened the door. Ryne thought he'd been nervous before; his heart rate escalated even more when his eyes landed on Anthony.

Anthony reached out his hand. "Hey there, Ryne. Come on in."

Ryne eased his way through the door, his senses on high alert. His eyes immediately sought out Ray along with Assistant Coach Ty Randspeed. His eyes scanned the room further, landing on Head Trainer Oscar Tomas. He couldn't imagine what he'd done. His thoughts were all over the place. *Why are they all here? I thought I was meeting with Ray only. Am I playing that badly?*

Ryne grew tenser as he took in the scene before him. "Have a seat, Ryne." *Have a seat? Maybe I should just stand. If I'm being traded again? What will Dad think? What about Mom? And Jen? She's just getting settled.*

"We wanted to touch base with you before our opening game tomorrow night."

"Okay?" he said questioningly as he ran his finger along the neck of his shirt. He was getting hotter by the second. *I'm going to let them do all of the talking. I'll sit here and see exactly what they want.* And then he thought even further. *Adam's not here. Maybe I'm not being traded.*

All four men were staring at him. "You can breathe, Ryne. We aren't the firing squad." Ray stated. Ryne knew he must look a sight. He took a breath as instructed.

"And stop worrying. You're not being traded," Anthony chimed in right behind Ray. "In fact, there are a few things we'd like to speak to you about, and one of them is your contract. But you and I can have that discussion after we're done here," Anthony added as he reached for a bottle of water that sat on the table behind him. "You look warm," he said as he handed it to Ryne.

Ryne unscrewed the cap and took a long swallow of the cold water. It felt like heaven going down his throat. *At least I'm not being traded. He wants to talk about my contract. That's good, I think.*

"So...we decided to have a sit down with you since the preseason is over." Ryne listened to Anthony. "I have to say we're impressed with what we've seen so far. You definitely came prepared to play."

"I trained hard this offseason."

"It shows," Ray spoke up. "I like what I see out there, Ryne. I've looked at game footage from your past preseasons, and I have to say I think this is your best yet. You're really on your game."

Ryne nodded as he listened to Ray. "Your hip doesn't seem to be bothering you."

"It's good, really good. I haven't felt this good in a very long time." Ryne looked towards Oscar, hoping for some added support.

"Just keep doing what you're doing and hopefully you'll stay out of my office," Oscar commented with a half-smile.

"It seems married life agrees with you."

Ryne smiled broadly back at Anthony. "It certainly does and I think Jen is adjusting well with the move and all."

"Glad to hear," Anthony added.

"Putting all pleasantries aside." Ryne turned towards Ray. He held his breath again unsure what to expect. *Now what? He's going to drop the hammer. I'm not being traded...what else could it be?*

"So the real reason why I, better we, brought you in here was this..."

Ryne looked Ray directly in the eye. He realized he could take whatever he threw at him— good or bad. "Didn't I just tell you to breathe?" Ray asked.

"You did."

"Well, do it. Haven't you figured out by now we're not the firing squad?"

"I have."

"Then what's got you so nervous? You look like you could keel over?"

"Ahh, I'd have to say I've never had a meeting like this before. Being new and all..."

"Stop fretting, will you? The main reason we called you in here was to touch base with you, see how you're feeling, how you're adjusting to the team and all. But most of all, we want you to wear an 'A' on your jersey and be one of the alternate captains on the team."

Ryne almost jumped from his seat. He was taken

aback by the leadership role they wanted to give him. He was new. His brothers had been here forever and were alternate captains too. "So what do you have to say?"

"I'm surprised. I'm the new guy."

"Yeah, you're the new guy with loads of experience. We haven't forgotten your past leadership roles. You played a significant role on the Eagles and the Generals, and we need that leadership here. We have a team that can go all the way. You are a team player and role model for all. We need your guidance to take us there. The question is are you up for the challenge?"

Ryne was speechless. He was blown away with the confidence they had in his abilities.

"Well, cat got your tongue? What do you say? How do you feel about being a team captain?"

Ryne ran his tongue across his lips. It was rare that he'd be asked to fulfill this role in his first year with the team. He believed he needed to gain the trust with his teammates, but he also realized that management had seen something in him that convinced them he could do the job.

"I'd be honored to be a team captain. I've already told my family that this is our year to win the Stanley Cup. Thank you for the confidence you've shown me. I'll do my best to make this a reality."

Ryne stood and shook hands with them. "Again, thank you for this opportunity."

"I guess we had you going there for a minute—with all of us practically ganging up on you."

Ryne swallowed the rest of his water. "You certainly did, Anthony. I wasn't sure what I was in for when I saw the four of you. I'd have to say I was a tad nervous."

"You have nothing to be nervous about. We all know how much you want to be here playing for the Storm. I know it's been your lifelong dream. You never gave up, and I have to say I respect you for reaching out to both me and Adam. Plus, you had Ed in your corner. He loves Jen and wants her to be happy. It's a win all the way around. Now, go out there and be the player we know you can be. Lead us on to becoming the next champions of the NHL."

Ryne clasped Anthony's hand and walked out the door feeling energized. He'd just been given the title of alternate captain for his team. He was elated and couldn't wait to share the news with Jen. But first, Ray had called a team meeting where his brothers would be the first to learn his news.

He knew his brothers would be excited for him. The three of them would do a hell of a job leading the team along with Team Captain Josh Ulteria.

Ray led the charge into the locker room where all of the players sat listening to loud music, waiting for the meeting to begin.

Ryne caught his brothers' eyes as he followed Ray into the room. Etienne quirked his brow at his twin while Philippe shook his head. His brothers were as clueless as he'd been just moments earlier.

The meeting was short by Ray's standards. He reiterated the team goals for the year, discussed the game plan for their opening game, and introduced Ryne as one of the alternate captains. All of his teammates seemed overjoyed that he'd been chosen

as a team leader and role model. He had a phenomenal reputation in the league and everyone, including
his brothers, respected his game.

Etienne was the first to congratulate Ryne. "Hey
little brother, congrats." Ryne always hated it when
he referred to him like that. They were twins for
god's sake.

"Etienne, you're only five minutes older than me,
not years like you let everyone believe."

"Stop it you two." Philippe slapped Ryne on the
back. "What an honor. We're in the best of company with you wearing an 'A' too. Who'd have
thought— all three of us being alternate captains?"

"I have to say I was taken by surprise. Let's just
say I was a little concerned when Ray asked to meet
with me." He ran his hand along his jaw. "When I
was greeted at the door by Anthony, I was sure I was
being traded again."

"You need to put those thoughts out of your mind.
You're here for the long haul."

"Phil, I think I am," he smiled broadly. "Plus,
Anthony wants to talk contract so hopefully that
means an extension."

"Sounds that way to me, little brother," Etienne
said laughingly. "It's all going to work out. Just
keep playing like you have and all will be good."

Ryne couldn't wait to meet up with Jen. She'd
come to town with him, dropped him off at the
arena, and shopped while he was practicing. Ryne
texted her that he was done for the day, and minutes
later she met him at the player's entrance.

She pulled to the curb and he hopped into the
car. He couldn't wipe the smile off his face. "Good

practice?" she asked as she leaned over kissing his cheek.

"The best. You'll never guess what happened."

"You upended Etienne?"

Ryne burst out laughing. "Ah, no. Why would I do that to my brother?"

"Pay back maybe?"

"We're well past that although I wish he'd quit referring to me as his little brother."

"Well you are, aren't you?"

"Why do you keep taking his side?"

"I wasn't aware that I was…"

He was in too good a mood to fight over Etienne. He placed his hand on her leg. "Changing subjects," he said as he squeezed her thigh. "I have some good news, great news if I have to say so myself."

"Out with it then."

"I was called into a meeting with Ray, Anthony, Ty, and Oscar."

"That sounds serious."

"I was a little concerned, especially when Anthony opened the door. I have to say I haven't been that nervous since our wedding."

"I didn't think you were nervous," she said in jest. "You told me you weren't nervous at all."

"Well, I was. So anyway, they started questioning me. I thought for sure I was going to be traded again and then they asked me…"

"Asked you what?" She turned in her seat and rested her hand on his arm.

"To be an alternate captain."

"You get to wear an "A?"

"Yep, I do."

"Ryne, that's awesome." She flung her arms around his neck and planted a loud kiss against his cheek. "But you're new to the team."

"I know. I was totally flabbergasted when they suggested it. They're impressed with my background and my play during the preseason. They want me to be a role model."

"Wow. That's fabulous." She brushed her hand along his arm.

"And I have even better news." Ryne grabbed ahold of her hand. "Anthony wants to talk contract. I'm hoping for an extension. I've got to call Adam. I wonder if he knows about all of this."

"Probably not or he would have forewarned you."

"Jen, if I get an extension...That would be icing on the cake. I can finish my career in Calgary."

"Don't go jumping to conclusions until you speak with Anthony. But, yeah, it does sound good."

"Baby, they want me to lead the Storm to the Championship. Bring a Stanley Cup to the team. Do you know what that means to me?"

"I think I do." She leaned over and pulled him into a hug. "I'm so proud of you. I think this trade was meant to be." She planted a kiss on his cheek. "Come on, let's go celebrate."

Chapter Thirty-Four

THE SEASON WAS MOVING ALONG quite nicely. The holidays were nearing and the Storm was leading the Western Division by twelve points. The entire team was riding a high. They were at the end of a long, five game road trip that ended right before Christmas.

Jen had flown home a few days after the team left on that trip. With the Storm's last game before the holiday break being in St. Louis, she and Ryne decided to spend a few days with Rose and Wilford and then fly on to Greenwich and see Miles and Rowena before returning to Calgary.

Jen was thrilled to return home. She'd only been to St. Louis once since moving. She'd been commissioned for a photo shoot that would showcase the St. Louis area. She was slowly building the career her father would be proud of.

Jen had a rough go of it. She'd overslept and barely made her flight. When she boarded the plane, she'd felt fine until they were airborne, and then she became nauseated. As soon as the doors opened, she deplaned and hurried to the nearest restroom when she became ill.

She hadn't a clue what was wrong. She'd felt fine when she left the house. She guessed she'd eaten something that upset her stomach.

With carryon in hand, she went straight home. Thankfully, she had a closet full of clothes and was able to avoid baggage claim.

The night before she'd missed Ryne's phone message. She'd been exhausted with preparing for her trip and slept through his call.

She heard the frustration in his voice. Not only had she seen the first period of their game against the San Francisco Otters, she knew Ryne had incurred two penalties losing in a shut out 6-0.

The team had lost their last two games, and he hadn't been happy with his play. He blamed the loss on himself. "I don't know what happened," he said, "but I royally messed up. I know my mistakes cost us two maybe three goals. I don't know what's wrong with me. I'm supposed to be a team leader, but by the looks of my play I wasn't one tonight."

He went on complaining about their losing streak, and he worried they wouldn't make the playoffs. Jen knew he was blowing this way out of proportion since they'd barely played a third of the season, but she could also understand his frustration.

Ryne had taken his role of alternate captain seriously and since being given the opportunity, he'd placed an inordinate amount of pressure on himself. When the team did well he was happy, elated, but when they were on a losing streak such as they were, he was almost a bear to live with. She knew winning a Stanley Cup was important to him but wondered at what cost.

By the time she got home, she barely had enough strength to make her way from the car to the house, let alone phone Ryne. She threw her carryon over her shoulder, stumbled up the stairs, fumbled with her key, dropping it as she tried to place it in the lock. She brushed her hair aside as she bent down to grab her key. She became lightheaded and threw her hand against the door which prevented her from collapsing onto the porch.

She steadied herself and reached for the key. Rising ever so slowly, she slipped it into the lock and pushed opened the door. Somehow, and she didn't know how, she made her way inside. With a thud, her bag fell from her shoulder and she leaned against the closed door.

She stood there for a few seconds as she caught her breath. *What's wrong with me? I feel like I've been hit by a Mack truck.* Ever so slowly, she practically crawled to the sofa. Her purse and cell phone lay right inside the door.

Before she knew it, she was sound asleep.

Jen was startled with an incessant pounding and the ringing of her doorbell. She scrubbed her hand across her face, unsure where the sound was coming from when she realized her phone was ringing, someone was pounding on her door, and her doorbell was continually chiming.

"Uh," she groaned. The room had grown dark and she'd lost complete sense of time. She eased herself up, threw on the lights, and walked to the door.

"Jen, Jen are you in there...Jen." She recognized the voice and opened the door.

"Oh my God, Jen are you okay? Ryne and I have been trying all afternoon to get ahold of you." Lauren rushed through the door.

Dazed, Jen watched Lauren hurry past. She closed the door and leaned against it, and that's when she noticed her purse lying on the floor beside her carryon. Again, as she reached down, she became lightheaded and crashed against the door, causing Lauren to turn around.

Before she knew what had hit her, Lauren was at her side leading her back to the couch. "You look awful. Are you sick?"

"I think so. Can you get my purse for me? I need to check my phone."

Lauren grabbed not only her purse but her carryon and set it on the couch beside Jen. "I don't know what happened. I felt fine when I left this morning, but I started feeling ill on the plane. I don't even remember driving home…"

Jen pulled her phone from her bag. She had twelve missed calls. Ten of them were from Ryne, one from Lauren and the last from Jacklynne.

"Ryne's been trying to reach you all day."

"I can see that. I missed ten calls from him."

"I had quite a few myself. I was in a deposition and forgot my phone. By the time I was able to get back to him, he was frantic with worry. He said he'd left a message for you last night, and you never called him back."

"Yeah, I was pretty tired and missed his call. I overslept this morning and was lucky to get to my flight."

She flung her hand across her eyes and then looked at her friend. "I'm exhausted. I hope after a good night's sleep I'll feel better."

She glanced at her watch. "Thanks for checking on me. I'd better call Ryne."

"Yeah, you'd better. I'd stay a bit longer but I have a dinner meeting. How about I drop by tomorrow and pick you up for the game?"

"Great idea. And then we can catch up." Jen walked Lauren to the door and pulled her into a tight hug. "Thanks for stopping by. I'm sorry Ryne made you come over."

"He was worried. In fact, he told me that was the last time he was trying me and then he was calling the police. At least you got me and not the police."

"I'd much rather see you, my friend." Jen said her goodbye and then made her way to the kitchen. It was nearly six o'clock and she was starved. She grabbed a can of soup and while she waited for it to warm phoned Ryne.

The Storm was playing in Chicago and then he was coming to St. Louis to play the Generals. She couldn't wait to see him. This had been one of the longest road trips of the season. She missed him, especially at night when he wasn't there to hold her in his arms. She'd become accustomed to sleeping with her head on his chest. The strong beating of his heart seemed to lull her to sleep.

She knew she was taking a chance calling his phone as the Wind's games usually began at seven thirty. She was almost sure he was on the ice warming up but tried his number anyway.

She stirred her soup waiting for the call to go through. She felt much better since Lauren had arrived. *I guess it's just a little bug but I think I'm over it.*

Jen expected the call to go to voice mail when an

unexpected voice answered. "Jen, is that you?"

"Yeah, it's me, Philippe. Where's Ryne and why are you answering his phone?"

"He's on the ice right now and asked me to listen for it. He's been worried sick since he wasn't able to get ahold of you. All I could think about was Annabelle…"

"Philippe, I'm sorry to have caused you such grief. I apologize. I wasn't feeling well and came home and took a nap. I dropped my purse at the door, and didn't hear my phone."

"You're sure that's it?"

"Yep, I'm fine. By the way, how is my dear husband? He seemed a little stressed in the message he left me last night. I saw the first period. What was up with those penalties?"

"Yeah, I don't know. Ryne's been a little off this trip. Hopefully tonight he'll be more in the zone, and if he is, maybe we'll catch a win."

"Philippe, he needs to settle down. He's so consumed with being a role model. I'm happy he was chosen as an alternate captain, but I think he's taking the responsibility way too seriously. All he talks about is going to the playoffs and winning the Cup. He needs to calm down and enjoy his time on the ice."

"I know. Etienne and I had a long talk with him this afternoon when he became unglued and couldn't locate you. I had my worries, of course, but I put those thoughts aside as we tried to calm him down. Et and I believe he feels like he has to justify being traded to the Storm on top of being selected to wear the 'A'. We've noticed how hard he is on himself when he falters on the ice. I told him he needs to play *his* game and not worry about everything. The rookies will follow his lead..."

"You know more about it than I do, but yes, he leads by example. He needs to forget about this Cup. It's consuming him." She sighed. "Philippe, you don't think he's hiding an injury, do you?"

"Physically I think he's fine. Right now it's all emotional with him. I'm betting once he gets his arms around you he'll be one hundred percent again. He misses you. I remember what those days are like. Annabelle and I were together a long time. I know what he's going through being so much in love. I also know what he went through today when he couldn't reach you. I think his finger was on redial all day."

"It was. I have ten missed calls, and I haven't the faintest idea how many voice mails he left me. I just picked up my phone and called after Lauren left."

"Yeah, he was frantic to reach her too."

"She was in a deposition."

"That's what Ryne said. I'm glad you're okay. Here he comes."

Jen briefly closed her eyes and stretched out her neck waiting for him. Then, she heard the voice she'd needed to hear.

"Jen, are you okay? I've been trying all day to reach you."

"I'm fine. Sorry about that. I almost missed my flight and by the time I got home I was exhausted. I took a nap and didn't hear my phone."

"That's alright. I was worried something happened."

"Nope, all's well. Shouldn't you be on the ice warming up?"

"I was but I came back in to put on a different jersey. I'd asked Philippe to listen for my phone."

"Isn't he playing tonight?"

"No, he's a healthy scratch. Ray thought he needed a night off. He was pretty busy last night killing off all of my penalties."

"I saw the first period."

"That wasn't pretty and neither was the rest of the game. I lost count with how many penalties I incurred. In fact, I'm surprised I'm playing tonight with as badly as I played."

"You're entitled to an off night."

"Not really. We need to take every game seriously, every game counts."

"They do but you need to stop being so hard on yourself."

"I'm the only one that can be accountable for me. If I don't hold myself to those standards, who will?"

"Ah—Adam, Ray, Anthony...They will."

"Enough of this. So what's new? Have you seen Rose and Wilford yet?"

"No. Like I said I came home and took a nap. I don't know why but I'm so tired. I guess I haven't been sleeping too well. I miss you."

"Likewise. Hey, I need to go. I'll phone after the game. I love you."

"I love you too." She stared at her soup as she stirred it, watching it swirl in the pot. She knew he wasn't himself. The way he spoke, the words he chose...it seemed almost like he was keeping something from her. She knew he was upset with himself, but there was something in the tone of his voice that made her suspicious. She would wait until they had a few days to themselves and maybe she'd discover what was bothering him.

After eating, she phoned her grandparents and went straight to bed, again missing Ryne's call. When she woke the next morning she was still tired but felt better. She checked her phone and listened to Ryne's message. "We won," she heard him say. She could see the smile on his face as he spoke. "It was a good game. Thankfully, I stayed away from the penalty box. We're going to have a morning skate here before coming down to St. Louis. I should see you around two. Love you."

She smiled at the phone as she stretched and made her way to the shower. She couldn't wait to see him.

She showered, dressed, and headed off to the grocery store. She needed a few things as they weren't going to be in town very long. She stopped by her grandparents on the way to say a quick hello.

"Oh my, Wilford, look who's here," Rose called out as she drew Jen into her arms.

"Grams, it's so good to see you." She pulled away and saw a look of concern on her face.

"Dear, are you feeling alright? You have such dark circles under your eyes."

"I think I have a virus. I've been so tired. Yesterday, I even got sick at the airport when I arrived. I came home and collapsed and barely heard Lauren when she woke me pounding on the door."

"Heavens, dear, why was she pounding on the door?"

"Because Ryne couldn't get ahold of me. I was

asleep and my cell was right inside the door. I didn't even hear it ring."

"I guess you needed your rest then. Are you feeling better?"

"I am. I think I needed a good night's sleep." She spent about a half hour with her grandparents. "I need to head out, Grams. Ryne will be here soon, and I want to be home when he gets there."

"Okay, dear. Don't forget dinner tomorrow night."

"I won't. Ryne's looking forward to it."

She kissed her grandparent's goodbye and ran by the store. Just those few errands caused the little energy she had to wane. She dragged herself back home, put away the few groceries she'd purchased, and dozed off waiting for Ryne.

The next thing she knew, she felt something— a whisper touch against her forehead. She fought to open her eyes and there, standing before her, was her handsome husband. "You looked so peaceful lying there. Did I wake you? I hope not."

He slid down beside her on the bed and pulled her into his arms. He brushed a feather kiss across her brow. "This feels good," he said before he leaned over and brushed his lips against hers. "It seems like an eternity since I last held you in my arms."

"You've got that right. This road trip seems like it's lasted a month instead of a week."

"I can't agree with you more." He moved closer to her, snuggling her neck. "I'd love to stay here with you, but I need to head back to the arena soon."

"I know. By the way, Ed texted me and asked if I would sit in his box tonight. I hope that's okay."

"Why wouldn't it be? After all, he is like a father to you."

"I just thought I needed to be…"

"Honey, we're not in Calgary and this is your hometown."

"I know…"

"Enough. Let's take a quick nap before I need to go. Then, in a few short hours, we'll have some quality time to ourselves. Did you see Rose?"

"I did and she told me to remind you about dinner."

"I haven't forgotten. I look forward to it." She nestled deeper into his embrace and drifted back to sleep.

She slept so soundly that she didn't hear him leave. She was startled awake when she heard her phone and answered. "Hi, Lauren."

"Are you almost ready?"

"Ahh, I'm just waking from a nap. Give me twenty minutes and I'll be ready."

"Another nap."

"I know. I think I'm fighting some kind of virus or something. I need to go if I'm going to be ready when you arrive."

Jen rushed to dress and got to the living room only moments before Lauren rang the doorbell. "You still look tired," Lauren squawked at her as she made her way inside.

"I am. Maybe I need to get used to the time change."

"Jen, it's not like you traveled from New York to California. You're only dealing with an hour's difference."

"I know." She reached for her purse. "Come on, I have a surprise for you."

"A surprise? I love surprises."

"I think you're really going to like this one. We're sitting in Ed's box."

Lauren's eyes grew wide, "I love this surprise."

"Thought you would."

They arrived at their usual time and instead of going to Faceoff's before the game, they made their way to the Storm's locker room.

As they strolled down the hallway, she ran into Ray.

"Hey there, Jen, Ryne's suiting up."

"I came to see Etienne and Philippe."

"Not your husband?"

"Him too, but I've already seen him today. I haven't seen my brothers-in-law yet."

"Wait here and I'll send them out."

A few moments later, Philippe came bustling through the doorway. "Oh hi, Jen," He pulled her into his arms. "I bet you're glad to be home."

"It's nice, yes, and I get to visit with my grandparents so that makes it even better." As he released her from his embrace, he noticed Lauren.

"Lauren, I didn't see you standing there." He leaned over and kissed her cheek. "It's so good to see you again."

Before Philippe could carry on his conversation, he was interrupted by Etienne. "Looky here, Ryne," he called over his shoulder. "Your wife is here." He became aware of Lauren and added, "Lauren's here too." Etienne welcomed Jen in the same manner as Philippe, pulling her into a tight embrace and kissing her cheek. "You look tired. Everything okay?"

"I missed my husband," she stated. "But you wouldn't know what that's like, would you?"

"What a low blow," he clamored as he reached Lauren and pulled her into hug. "I'm not sure I can forgive you for that..."

"Forgive who," Ryne asked as he made his way into the hallway, reaching for Jen. He dropped a kiss on her cheek and pulled her near.

"Don't worry about it," Jen added as she leaned into Ryne. "Lauren and I decided to stop by and give you our well wishes before the game. Plus, I haven't seen those two scallywags in a while." She gestured to his brothers. "How about coming over after the game?"

"We can't," Philippe stated. "We're scheduled to fly home with the team. Ryne here's the only one not traveling home with us."

"Then I consider myself lucky," Jen tightened her arm around Ryne.

"Aren't you having dinner with Rowena this trip?" Lauren asked as she smiled at Philippe.

Ryne groaned. "After Christmas we're heading up to Greenwich. We have dinner plans with Rose and Wilford tomorrow night, right honey?"

"We do." She looked at her friend and noticed Lauren only had eyes for Philippe. *What's up with that?* In that moment, she decided to commit that look to memory. Maybe she could become a match-maker to her two friends. Philippe needed to find someone to share his life with, and Lauren needed to *get* a life. She definitely worked way too hard. *My New Year's resolution...Find a way to set these two up!*

They didn't have much time to visit before Oscar stuck his head out looking for his missing players. He always did a quick assessment to make sure they were game ready. "Sorry about the interruption but we do have a game to prepare for."

"Yeah, yeah," Etienne said as he quickly hugged Jen goodbye. "We'll see you back home."

"Have a good Christmas," Philippe softly spoke to Lauren as he reached for her hand, squeezing it before saying a final goodbye to Jen.

"Stay safe," he called back over his shoulder to Jen as he made his way into the locker room.

Jen reached up kissed Ryne and patted him on the chest. "Play your best and I'll be waiting right here when the game's over."

Ryne squeezed her one more time, raised his hand in a farewell to Lauren, and proceeded back through the door, closing it behind him.

Jen turned to her friend with a broad smile. "What's the look for?" Lauren questioned.

"Ahh, nothing." Jen had seen the way Philippe squeezed Lauren's hand. She felt a good vibe between them and needed to figure out a way to bring them together for an extended period of time. She couldn't easily arrange a date. Philippe lived in Calgary year-round and Lauren in St. Louis. It would take some creative planning on her part but she would find a way.

Chapter Thirty-Five

A FTER SAYING THEIR GOODBYE, JEN and Lauren went directly to Ed's box. She was excited to see him and practically ran into his arms. They generally spoke weekly but with the season in full swing he'd been hard to get ahold of.

They lost track of time and almost missed the player introductions. She stood at the edge of the box and waved at Ryne and his brothers when their names were announced.

She was thrilled to be back in the Generaldome. Although her allegiance was now with the Storm, the Generals still held a special place in her heart.

As the players stood on the ice during the National Anthems, she couldn't help but notice Lauren's eyes focused solely on Philippe. As Philippe made his way to the bench, he raised his stick and motioned in their direction.

"What's that all about?" Jen giggled and turned to her friend.

"I guess he was saying hi."

"If that's what you want to believe, okay. I think it's a little more meaningful."

"I don't know what you're implying…"

Before she could finish her thought, the fans were on their feet cheering as the players retook the ice.

Ed's box was close to the *Hockey Tonight* crew. She could hear Kelly Rhodes and Ted Jackson getting ready to call the game.

"Ted, this is a big night for Ryne Ferguson. He's returning to the Generaldome for the first time since being traded."

"You're right, Kelly. The two teams played earlier this year in Calgary and it was a pretty tame game. I expect it to be a little more physical tonight especially with the Generals' losing streak. They're going to come out fighting. Ferguson's having a stellar year— the best of his career although the last couple of games have been a little shaky for him. I have to wonder if he's got an injury."

"You never know. These hockey players are tough as nails and play under extreme conditions. Time will tell."

"Okay, here's the lineup for the game..." Jen tuned out the rest of their spiel as she watched Ryne head towards the faceoff circle.

Since becoming involved with Ryne, Jen was a nervous fan. She worried the entire game that he would get injured. As the players lined up around the faceoff circle, she raised her fingers to her mouth. She had a nervous habit of chewing on them at the outset of the game and tonight was no different.

Ryne stood in the circle ready to face-off against Derek. She'd noticed they'd spoken during the warm-ups. They were no longer friends on the ice, they were rivals. The Storm was on a one game winning streak while the Generals had lost four of their last five. Jen knew Ryne felt good going into the game.

Nervously, she watched as the referee prepared to drop the puck. As a visitor, Ryne was the first to place his stick on the ice. She held her breath waiting for the puck to drop. In a blink of an eye, the puck was on the ice, and Ryne took control. The puck moved to Josh's stick as he crossed the blue line.

Ryne circled behind the net, waiting for a pass. Ice sprayed along the boards as his skates cut through the rink's surface. He stopped at the side of the net waiting for Philippe to pass him the puck. His stick lay flush against the ice, waiting, anticipating Philippe's next move. And then the whistle blew. Less than a minute into the game, Etienne was involved in a skirmish. She was surprised by the quickness of the fight and wondered what led to gloves being dropped and Etienne's head in a head lock.

"Wow, this game is starting out intense. Tucker jumped right on Etienne Ferguson. This is going to be a physical game, Ted." Jen caught Kelly Rhodes' voice as he described the fight on the ice.

"The fight didn't last long, that's for sure, Kelly."

"No, it didn't. It looks like the officials are going to have to be on their toes tonight." Kelly added as the players were escorted directly to the penalty box.

Both players were sent off the ice with fighting penalties and wouldn't be seen again for five minutes. Ryne shook his head at his brother, seemingly disgusted that he took a penalty so early in the game.

Derek won the faceoff after the penalty. Ryne hurried down the ice to help defend his goal. Philippe somehow intercepted an errant pass and sent it across the ice to Ryne who raced down the rink. He crossed the blue line, and carried the puck behind the goal. He spun around, still in control, and flipped the puck towards the net. It bounced on the ice and skipped by the Generals' goalie. The blue light lit and Ryne had his first goal of the game.

Jen exhaled the breath she'd been holding and felt relieved. Ryne seemed like he was on his game, playing with a high level of intensity. Ray pulled his line and Ryne sat leaning over the boards, waiting, ready to return to the ice. She kept one eye on the penalty clock and the other on Ryne. In her gut she knew he was going to return to the ice shortly and he did. Vladamir Pantengelo stole the puck from one of the Generals' players. Just as he started up ice, Ryne flew over the side of the boards. His skates had barely touched the ice when he received a pass directly onto his stick from Vlad.

"Look at Ferguson go," Ted announced to the Hockey Today audience. "I haven't seen him skate this fast in a long time."

"You're right, Ted," Kelly stated as they looked on. "He's in phenomenal shape."

Ryne sped down the ice towards the Generals' goal. As long as Jen followed hockey, she'd never seen a slap shot like her husband's. Ryne's was the best in the NHL, averaging more than one hundred miles an hour. She felt the play setting-up and wasn't surprised when he stopped on a dime, raised his stick and slapped at the puck. It flew over the goalie's shoulder into the net. The blue light went off again. In a matter of minutes, Ryne had scored his second goal of the game and the Storm led 2-0.

"Look at that— two goals in less than five minutes. I have to wonder why we traded him." Ted seemed to shout above the boos coming from the sellout crowd.

Jen was beside herself with excitement.   She high-fived Lauren and turned to Ed who shook his head. "Who do you think I'm rooting for? Not the Storm." They all burst out laughing at Ed's comment. His team was losing.

Ryne's line was again pulled from the ice to catch a breather. "There goes Ryne Ferguson off the ice. He's deserving of this little breather," Ted stated.

"He definitely is," responded Kelly. "There's five seconds left in Etienne Ferguson's penalty. And here goes his brother, Ryne, back onto the ice."

Just as Etienne was returning to the ice, Ryne pitched over the boards, catching another pass from Vlad. Ryne, in turn, shot the pass onto Etienne's stick. He rushed in behind the play hoping his brother would shoot the puck along the boards.

Etienne seemed to read his mind. He ran the puck along the boards hitting Ryne's stick square in the middle of his blade. He eased along the boards coming out to the post. He faked a slap shot, instead passing the puck back to Josh. He, in turn, directed the puck back to Ryne. Ryne expected the pass and raised his stick and struck the puck. A loud clang rang out as it deflected off the crossbar. The crowd oohed in the background thankful of the missed shot.

"Did you see that slap shot?" Kelly practically screamed.

"He's a powerhouse."

"That he is, Ted," Kelly stated.

Ryne circled back around again, apparently hoping Josh would send it back his way. Josh lost control and turned it over to Derek who shot the puck down the length of the ice.

"That's icing to stop the play," Ted called as the official grabbed the puck from the ice.

Play returned to the Generals' end of the ice. Ryne was again in the faceoff circle against Derek.

When the puck was dropped, Ryne handily won control.

"Ferguson's in control again, Kelly. Can he make it a hat trick?"

"Only time will tell, Ted."

Ryne passed the puck to Vlad who spun around and sent it back to Ryne. Ryne had a clear shot. He raised his stick and smacked the puck. This time it soared over the shoulder of the Generals' goalie. The blue light lit a third time. Ryne had a hat trick. All three goals were scored within the first nine minutes of play.

"Can you believe it, we're still in what I call the opening minutes of the first period and Ryne Ferguson has another hat trick. He's on fire tonight," said Ted.

"That he is," Jen heard Kelly Rhodes say as hats flew onto the ice. Ryne was still respected by the St. Louis fans, and she was excited to see how they responded to his achievement.

Ryne's celebration lasted only a moment when after the next faceoff things got rough. The Generals were frustrated with their play and the play of their friend. From that moment everything went downhill.

The Generals won the faceoff and headed to the Storm's end of the ice. Ryne skated hard and did his best to defend. The puck was being played along the boards, and Ryne rushed to try and kick it out. Instead of fighting for the puck, he was upended from behind. He crashed hard to the ice falling directly onto his hip.

"Ferguson's down; he appears injured." Kelly Rhodes said as the crowd looked on.

Ryne was surrounded by his brothers. As soon as he hit the ice, the crowd grew quiet. Philippe knelt beside him as they waited for Oscar to rush onto the ice.

He lay on the ice for several minutes before Etienne and Philippe helped him stand. With their support, they skated alongside him until he reached the boards where Oscar and Ty escorted him to the locker room.

Jen winced when Ryne fell so hard. She held her breath, waiting and watching as Etienne and Philippe helped him from the ice. She couldn't take her eyes off her husband as he lay writhing in pain. She knew instantly what was wrong and feared his season was in jeopardy yet again and even possibly his career.

She didn't know what to do. She was shaking. Her worst fears were unfolding right before her eyes. Ryne was hurt again. She knew it wasn't good by the way he fell.

Lauren draped her arm around her. "He's going to be alright."

"It's his hip," she whispered.

"What did you say?"

"I'm sure it's his hip. He's been so worried about reinjuring it."

"Don't jump to conclusions, Jen," Ed said as he reached for her. "We have the best of doctors. We'll check him out."

"Thanks, Ed. I know that. I should go to him."

"Just wait here and we'll get word on his condition."

Lauren led Jen to a nearby chair, then grabbed a bottle of water and handed it to her.

Jen couldn't focus. She was a mess. Her hands were trembling so badly she couldn't hold onto the water bottle. As she set it down, she began to break out in a cold sweat. All of a sudden the nausea that had subsided had returned. *I can't get sick. I can't.* No sooner had those thoughts crossed her mind, she jumped from her seat and ran to the bathroom, practically slamming the door behind her.

She was breathless. She leaned over the sink and ran cold water over her wrists, hoping that would calm her. She dropped her head to her chest and gnawed on her lower lip—anything to prevent herself from being ill.

She reached for a paper towel and wet it, then applied the coolness to her neck, thinking about her husband and praying she wouldn't get sick.

Several minutes passed before she heard a soft knock on the door. "Jen, are you okay?"

"Give me a minute, Lauren."

"Take all the time you need."

Jen leaned against the door. Her nausea had given way to tears. He has to be alright; he just has to. The tears fell one right after the other. She swiped at them but that didn't do any good. They kept coming and along with the tears came sobs.

She knew Lauren heard her crying because the door handle turned, and she soon found herself in her best friend's arms. "He's strong. He'll be fine."

"You don't know that. Lauren, his hip...his hip." She hiccupped as the tears began to lessen. "He's been worried all year that he'd reinjure it. It was bad last year and I hope..."

"You can't speculate until he's examined. Don't go there, Jen. You need to stay strong. Come on, let's see if we can find out how he is."

Jen blew her nose and wiped her eyes once again before she left the bathroom. She was feeling better. She had the support of her best friend and Ed and that's what mattered.

When they entered the room, Ed was on the phone. He raised his hand stopping them from leaving. Jen clung onto Lauren as Ed ended his call.

"Here's the deal...They're taking him to the hospital..."

Jen gasped. "Now don't go there, Jen. It's precautionary. They're going to run an MRI, take some X-rays, and then more than likely send him home. In all honesty, I don't think they think it's too serious."

"But Ed..."

"Stop worrying until you need to, okay? The ambulance has already left for the hospital. I have my car waiting. Let's go and maybe you can see him before he starts in with his tests."

Jen found herself in Ed's arms. A father's embrace, she thought. He would stay by her side until they knew what they were dealing with.

"Lauren, why don't you go home? I know you have a deposition tomorrow. Ed will take good care of me." She did her best to smile.

"Call me when you know anything."

"I will." Jen drew her friend into a tight hug. "Thanks for being here for me. You're one in a million."

"Ed, you make sure she takes care of herself."

"Oh, I will. I won't let her out of my sight until I know Ryne's going to be alright."

As promised, Ed's car was waiting. As they drove to the hospital, Jen reached for his hand. "I just know it's his hip. And if it is, I don't know if he has it in him to rehab it again."

"Let's cross that bridge when we need to." He squeezed her hand. "Ryne is old school. He's not going to let this injury send him to the woodpile. He has a lot of good years left in his career. Stop fretting until you need to. You need to be strong for him."

"I will."

In a matter of minutes, they were walking through the doors to the Emergency Room. Jen approached the receptionist. "My husband, Ryne Ferguson, was just brought in. He's a hockey player."

"Oh yes, he's in X-ray right now. Have a seat and we'll call you when he returns," a nurse interjected. Jen smiled and thanked the nurse. She reached for

Ed's arm and he guided her to a quiet corner.

She didn't know what else to do so she closed her eyes and said a prayer. She knew how much this season meant to him: being traded to the Storm and vying for the Stanley Cup. Those were his dreams. He'd faced the first— that of being traded home to Calgary. His dream of winning a Stanley Cup was still alive, and she needed to find a way to allow him to achieve it. Whether she sat listening to him blow off steam because of his injury or holding his hand through the pain of rehab. Whatever it took, she'd remain by his side. She loved him more than she ever imagined loving anyone.

She pulled herself out of her thoughts. "I better call Jacques and Jacklynne. I'm sure they were watching *Hockey Tonight* and saw him go down. Jacklynne must be frantic."

"Why not wait until you know what he's facing?"

"I should but my heart tells me I need to call her. I need to hear her voice."

Jen patted Ed's arms and walked from the room. She started down a long hallway and noticed an empty waiting room. Visiting hours at the hospital were over and it was quiet. She made her way into the darkened room. There was a dim light lit on the corner table. She sat and phoned Ryne's parents.

Jacklynne was quick to answer the phone. "How is he? How's my son?"

As soon as she'd heard Jacklynne's voice, she became emotional. And then the dam burst. She knew Jacklynne would hear her crying and held the phone away from her face, pausing before speaking. "I don't know," she sniffled as she wiped the tears from her eyes. "He's at the hospital and they're X-raying him and then he's going to have an MRI. I haven't seen him, Jacklynne."

"I certainly hope you're not alone."

"No, Ed's with me." She hesitated afraid to voice aloud her fears. "Jacklynne, I think it's his hip. I don't know what he'll do if he's injured it again."

"He'll do what's he's done in the past— rehab it. Ah honey, I know how upset you are, but Ryne's tough. He'll recover just like he has in the past."

"But…"

"No but's, dear. You can't get upset until we know what we're dealing with. He's strong and so are you. You'll get through this together, and before you know it he'll be back on the ice, ripping a slap shot and celebrating another hat trick.

"I know this is hard but you may be worrying over nothing. I've seen my children take enough jaw-dropping spills during their careers. Over time, you learn to develop a thick skin. He may be a little beat up but he'll be just fine. You know Ryne; he's going to want to be in that Stanley Cup final game. He'll do anything to come out on the other side of any injury as long as he can fulfill that dream."

"You're right," she chuckled. "I don't know why I got so upset. It's not like I haven't seen him take a hard spill before and need to be helped from the ice."

"That's it, my dear. Positive thoughts."

"Yes, positive thoughts. Thank you Jacklynne— Mom. It means a lot to me." It was one of the first time's she'd called Jacklynne Mom and it felt right. She needed her 'Mom' and she needed Jacklynne.

"Honey, you have a special place in my heart. Now, go take care of my son. Call me when you know more. I love you, Jen."

"I love you too." Jen ended the call and sat in the quiet of the darkened room and didn't hear Ed as he approached. He sat down beside her and pulled her close.

"Everything okay?"

"Yeah. Jacklynne helped me see things a little more clearly."

"Glad to hear. Now, would you like to see your husband? He's back and they're waiting on the results."

With Ed's arm draped around her shoulders, they returned to the ER. As they approached the waiting room, she heard a commotion and discovered Etienne and Philippe standing just inside the doors.

Jen moved out of Ed's embrace and right into the arms of Philippe. "Jen, he's going to be just fine. You know Ryne."

"He's strong. We won't let this injury sideline him," Etienne said as he reached to give her a hug.

"I thought you were flying out with the team."

"We wanted to be here so you wouldn't be alone. Good to see you, Ed," Philippe said as he reached to shake his hand. "How's Ryne?"

"We were on our way to find out. He's just back from an MRI. I think he's waiting on the results."

Etienne wrapped his arm around her. "We'll be here," he said motioning to the waiting room.

Jen kissed both of her brothers-in-law on their cheeks.

A nurse had been patiently waiting to take her to

Ryne. She smiled at Jen and said, "Follow me."

Jen walked alongside the nurse as she led the way to Ryne. She approached his bedside and laid her hand on his leg. His eyes immediately popped open. She knew she looked a fright. Her eyelids were swollen from crying, her nose was red. It wasn't as though he hadn't seen her upset before. She looked a mess and really couldn't have cared less. Her main focus was on Ryne: his pain and injury.

She swept her hand along his forehead dropping a kiss on his brow. She grabbed his hand and squeezed it tightly. "Have you seen a doctor yet? Do you have your test results? When can you go home?"

"Sweetheart, please one question at a time, okay? I'm not thinking too clearly right now..."

"Alright."   She grabbed the nearby chair and brought it to his bedside and dropped onto it. Exhaustion was starting to claim her. She needed answers, now. She wasn't thinking clearly either. She just wanted to know what was going on.

"To answer your questions...One: yes, I've seen a doctor. In fact, he's pretty good. I really like him. Too bad he's an ER doctor."

"Ryne, can you just give me the answers I'm searching for."

"Wow, what's gotten into you?"

"Do you have to ask? I'm worried about you, I'm about ready to drop with exhaustion. Do I need to explain any further?"

"No, you don't." He reached for her hand and drew her into his arms. She knew he was in pain although she was sure it had been lessened with a pain killer. She wasn't sure how she ended up in bed with him but one pull of his hand and she was lying next to him. She cuddled up beside him, and nestled her head against his chest.

"So what's this with you being so tired? I thought you took a nap today."

"I did," she said as she ran her hand along his chest. "Ever since I got on the plane yesterday I haven't felt myself. I guess I have a bug of some kind." She smoothed the hair away from his eyes. "Please tell me what the doctor had to say." She drew in her lips. "I'm scared, Ryne, really scared for you."

This was the first time she'd been in this position. Ryne was her husband, and she didn't want to see him in pain. She didn't want to see him upset. She didn't want him questioning his future.

"I'm sure you've already guessed it's my hip. The hit came out of nowhere. I was blindsided and when my feet were taken out from under me, I couldn't do a thing. I went down like a ton of bricks. So much for my new hip pads.

"Anyway, I'm back to the drawing board. They don't think my injury is quite as bad as last year's but time will tell. Of course, I'm going on the injured reserve. I'll be out at least a month, maybe longer."

She ran her hand along his jaw as she looked into his eyes.

"I guess it could be worse, right? It's not like I haven't been down this road before. Maybe this time, I can get through rehab more quickly. After all, I have the best wife in the world to take care of me, right?" She nodded at his comment. "I guess the bright side of this whole situation is that we can spend a little more time visiting your grandparents.

I'll be on crutches for a while, and when the pain is manageable, I'll start therapy. So that's it in a nutshell. Are you sure you want to stay married to me? It seems like I'm a walking injury lately."

She rolled her eyes and playfully slapped her hand against his chest. "Why would you even ask me that? I love you. And did we not vow to stand by each other in sickness and health…Well, I'm standing by my man."

Ryne chuckled at her comment and tightened his hold on her. "I love you so much. Jen, I'm sorry."

"Sorry for what?"

"What do you think? Getting injured…Not being able to play and help my team make the playoffs and, most of all, letting my teammates down."

"Ryne, you can't help that you took a cheap shot." She felt him flinch with her comment and raised her hand defending herself. "I don't care what you think— it was a cheap shot. Just because you're out for a few weeks doesn't mean the Storm isn't going to make the playoffs. Heck, you're leading the league in points. The finals are over four months in the future. There's plenty of time for you to get back in the game and be there when the team goes all the way."

She reached up and patted his cheek. "Now let's see about getting you out of here. I think we may have a few additional houseguests. Your brothers are waiting outside to hear what kind of damage you sustained. In fact, I'll go get them and Ed and bring them back."

"Ed's here?"

"He drove me." She started out the door and

turned. "I hope the doctors allow a party in your room because I'm bringing them all back." She blew him a kiss as she left.

As she made her way to the waiting room, she sighed. He'd be okay. She'd be right there beside him throughout his recovery. He was her life and she'd do everything in her power so he could return to the game he loved.

Chapter Thirty-Six

A T TWO THAT MORNING, RYNE was discharged from the hospital. Ed, Philippe and Etienne all remained by her side.

While Ed got the car, Jen helped Ryne get dressed. His brothers had been able to retrieve their suitcases before the team left for Calgary. Since he and Etienne wore the same size, Ryne found suitable attire to wear home.

Everyone was thoroughly exhausted by the time they traipsed into the house. With his brothers on either side to help, Ryne negotiated the stairs to the bedroom. Even though he had quite a bit of experience on crutches, he was having difficulty maneuvering the steps.

Jen followed, praying the entire way he'd make it to their bedroom without incident. She breathed easier once he plopped onto the bed, but winced when he called out in pain.

She was instantly by his side but he shooed her away. "Etienne, will help me," he gruffly said, easing against the headboard. "You need to check on their rooms. We're all tired, and I'm ready to get some rest."

She didn't like the tone of his voice but chalked it up to the pain killers.

She hurried, gathering towels and extra blankets. When she placed the towels on the dresser in one of the guest bedrooms, she ran her hand through her hair and took a deep breath. And that's when she felt a hand glide across her shoulders.

"He didn't mean that back there. He's frustrated, tired, you name it. He loves you."

"I know." She turned around and Philippe pulled her in a comforting hug. "He's got a lot going on up here." He tapped his head. "I believe in the back of his mind he fears his career is on a downward spiral. But it's not. You and I both heard the doctor. It's not as bad as last time. He needs time to recover, heal."

"I realize that. Philippe, I hope that's all it is."

She'd barely finished her thought when Etienne joined them. "He's tucked in and by now, probably fast asleep. Those are some pretty strong painkillers, and they definitely throw him for a loop."

"I'm well aware how they affect him. I've seen it firsthand."

"If you'd show us where you want us, we'll get out of your way. By the way, we're on an early afternoon flight. We'll make sure you're both settled and then we need to head out," Etienne added.

"Thanks, Et, for all you and Philippe have done for us. I really appreciate you staying behind."

"No thanks are necessary. You're family. I'm just thankful we're off for a few days, otherwise we might not have been able to skip the flight." Philippe kissed her brow. "Positive thoughts, Jen, that's what he needs. I'm going to grab our bags."

It was close to three when she finally settled into

bed. Ryne was fast asleep and she lay there, watching him breathe in and out. Even in sleep she could tell he was in pain.

She dozed off and was awakened when the bed shook. She almost jumped out of bed fearful that he'd fallen only to discover he sat precariously along the edge of the mattress. "You okay?" She ran her hand along his back.

"What do you think? I can't even stand."

"I'll help you. Where are you going?"

"The bathroom."

"Okay then." She reached for the crutches, handed them to him, eased her arms around his waist, and helped him stand.

"I'm not an invalid. I can use crutches."

Her head popped up. He'd never spoken to her in this manner before, ever. Again she was going to chalk it all up to the painkillers. She stepped away and he hobbled to the bathroom.

She covered her face with her hands and rubbed her eyes. She was doing her best to prevent tears. She always became emotional when she lacked sleep, so these feelings were nothing new. That is until she became lightheaded, that was then followed by her need to hurl.

Ryne was in their bathroom so she flung open their bedroom door banging it loudly against the wall and staggered as fast as she could to the nearest bathroom. She realized she must have made a huge commotion because when she stumbled from the bathroom, she was greeted by Philippe.

"Jen, are you okay? Your face is as pale as that wall."

Leaning against the wall, she sighed. "I'm fine. I've been fighting a virus since I left Calgary. I'm okay now." *At least I think I am.* "I'm going to check on Ryne and then I'll make breakfast."

As she passed Philippe, she ran her hand along his arm. "Just so you know, he's still in a foul mood."

When she returned to their bedroom, Ryne was stretched on the bed with his arm thrown over his eyes. She didn't bother him, dressed, and hurried from the room. She knew the next few days would be trying and would do her best to accept whatever he threw at her. He wasn't himself but hoped that *her* Ryne would return sooner rather than later.

They spent an uneventful Christmas at home with Rose and Wilford, but now that it was over, she was ready to head home. But first they had a stopover in Greenwich to visit Rowena and Miles.

Ryne had been a bear to live with. Between his pain meds and his wanting to start therapy, she was ready to pull her hair out.

She still wasn't feeling the best. She continued to fight fatigue and daily bouts with nausea. She chalked it all up to the upheaval they'd experienced. She hadn't slept well, and she constantly worried that Ryne was going to overdo it.

They'd gotten into several arguments: she wanted him to rest while he wanted to work out. The latest brouhaha had her throwing down the book she'd been trying to read and running off to their bedroom in tears. She curled up into a tight ball and cried herself to sleep.

When she woke, she found herself snuggled against Ryne as he rested. As she lay there, she felt the odd, now familiar, feeling that had started less than a week ago. She bolted from the bed and ran to the bathroom. After she was done being sick, she rolled into a ball, and that's where Ryne found her.

She'd been lying in the same position for almost ten minutes when she heard the thump, thump, thump of Ryne's crutches as he neared the doorway. She didn't think she had it in her for another argument. She just wanted to lie there and feel better.

"Jen, hey there, are you okay?" He placed his hand on her back as she lay on the floor. She'd been crying, unsure what was wrong with her, afraid to even move, because every time she tried to stand she became sick all over again.

"Can you stand?" he asked with a worried look on his face.

"I don't know." She slowly sat up and clutched the sides of the toilet. She got to her knees without another sign of nausea, pulled herself up, and sat on the lid of the toilet. She ran a tired hand through her hair and breathed deeply. She believed the nausea had passed. Wearily she looked up at Ryne. She knew by the way he leaned over his crutches that he was worried about her. She took another deep breath, clasped the edge of the sink as she got her balance, and stood.

"Why didn't you tell me you weren't feeling well?" She shrugged. "I took a pain pill and laid down. I didn't even realize you'd gotten out of bed. You know how out of it I am when I take those pills."

"I do."

"You should have called out to me. I would have helped you."

"Helped me how? Thrown up for me?"

He ignored her question. "I could have at least held your hair, ran a cool cloth against your neck... Held you when you were too weak to kneel." He reached for her hand. "What's wrong? The flu?"

Tiredly she stated, "I think I have a virus. It started when I got on the plane. It's gradually gotten worse since I've been here. I'm just so worried about you, I think that's got my stomach all in a knot. I'll be okay. I just need to rest.

"Tomorrow we'll see Rowena and Miles, and then we can go home." She looked at him with the saddest of eyes.

"Honey, I'm sorry I've been such a bear. I don't like getting into stupid arguments with you. My behavior of late is unforgivable. You know that's not the man I am. I love you and I'm sorry if I've hurt you in any way. This injury has definitely thrown a curve into my season. I promise to do my best to be the man you married. Forgive me?"

"There's nothing to forgive. I understand your fears. One of your dreams finally came true and you realize that winning the cup may not happen. You've set your sights on a goal that may be out of reach. I get it, I really do, but Ryne, you also need to realize that life happens. Things occur that you can't control. You couldn't control what happened the other night, and you can't control where the season's going to end.

"You need to focus on you. Take the time you

need to heal, focus on your mental strength. It will all come together. Give it the time it needs."

"When did you get to be so intuitive?"

She shrugged.

"I wish I could carry you back to bed," he pointed to his crutches, "but I can't. Let's take it slow and easy, okay?"

She reached for his outstretched hand. He waited while she ambled from the bathroom, making her way towards the bed. By the time she had lain down, he was sitting on the bed. He reached out to her. She scooted over and laid her head on his shoulder.

She felt loved and protected. "I love you," she whispered as she drifted off to sleep.

The next morning they were both in a better frame of mind. She added a few outfits to her carry-on and was packed in a matter of minutes. Ryne hadn't even opened his suitcase, so they were ready to go early. Thankfully, her stomach had settled and they made it to the airport with plenty of time to spare. Their flight was on time and they were moments away from landing.

Ryne reached for her hand and looked her in the eyes. "Just think, tomorrow this time we should be home."

"Yep, home." She smiled as the flight attendant came by cleaning up the cabin. "I can't wait."

They were at Rowena and Miles's before noon. Jen hadn't seen them since the wedding and was looking forward to catching up. They were aware of Ryne's predicament and had arranged for a first-floor bedroom, so he wouldn't have to negotiate stairs.

Ryne groaned as usual when it came to Rowena. She was standing under the portico when the cab came to a stop. "Does she have radar or what?"

"You seem to forget we did pass through the front gate."

"Yeah and it was open."

"And it has a buzzer too. She knew we were approaching."

Before he could say a word, Rowena pulled open the door, and that's when he noticed the wheelchair. "Oh my dear, Ryne, do you need help? Here, I've got a wheelchair for you."

"I don't need a wheelchair, Rowena, my crutches work just fine."

"Are you sure?"

"Yep, I'm sure." He glanced over his shoulder at Jen. She knew what was going through his mind. *One night, that's all we need to get through. One night.*

With all the fuss Rowena made, they somehow made it inside and were met by Miles. "I didn't know you'd arrived."

"Well, Rowena certainly did," Ryne stated. "I don't know why she thought I needed a wheelchair."

"You know Ro, always prepared." Miles slapped Ryne on the back. "How goes it, feeling any better?"

Jen knew he didn't want to rehash his injury. In all honesty he wanted to forget all about it. "Grandfather, the house looks beautiful."

"Ro did all of the decorating herself. You know what a control freak she can be."

"Miles, how dare you say that."

"It's true, isn't it?"

"Well...yes, but let's not go there. Come on in and we'll settle in the conservatory. I have some cool drinks waiting."

Jen looked over her shoulder as she followed Rowena. Ryne followed suit at a much slower pace.

He sat beside Jen while Rowena served drinks and finger sandwiches. Out of the corner of his eye he caught Jen raise her hand to her lips as the color drained from her face and in an instant, she bolted from the couch.

"Oh dear, is something wrong?" Rowena asked with a concerned look on her face.

"I'm not sure. Jen hasn't been feeling well for a few days. She chalked it all up to my injury—nerves and all. Let's give her a minute."

A minute turned into twenty. Ryne hobbled to the powder room he'd seen Jen run into. He knocked on the door and heard her groan. Opening the door, he found her in a familiar place, sprawled on the floor with her head resting on the toilet. He closed the door so Ro couldn't overhear their conversation.

"Did you get sick?" She didn't answer only nodded her head. And then, she got sick again and again. She couldn't stop throwing up. She had nothing left in her stomach and was onto dry heaves.

"This has got to stop. I'm taking you to the ER."

"I'll be fine."

"That's what you said last night. This has been going on too long, and it seems like it's getting worse." She nodded.

"Can you stand?"   He could tell how weak she

seemed. He was concerned she was dehydrated. "I'm sure you need fluids. I'm going to see if Miles can drive us."

"Let's not trouble them. Just get a cab."

When Ryne informed Rowena that he was taking Jen to the hospital, she reached for her purse. "Come on, I'm driving." With a look of determination, Rowena headed to the garage. "I'm pulling the car around to the front. Meet me under the portico."

Ryne knew not to question Rowena. Miles helped Jen stand and aided her to the car, hopping into the passenger's seat. Knowing Rowena had taken charge of the situation, he didn't argue with her. Ryne slipped in beside Jen and held her close. She was pale. Dark circles rimmed her eyes. He knew they needed to get to the bottom of her illness and soon.

He'd barely snapped their seatbelts in place when Rowena accelerated. Practically on two wheels, she flew out of the driveway, cutting off a driver in her race to the hospital. Luckily, they were only minutes from the largest ER in the area. As she approached an intersection, she blared her horn and flew right through. Ryne held his breath until they were safely on the other side. Thankfully, no police were in sight.

"Don't you think you could slow down a tad?" questioned Ryne.

"Indeed not," she exclaimed as she squealed her tires, rounding the corner leading to the hospital entrance.

Ryne was forced to hold onto the door handle as

she took the corner into the driveway of the hospital. She threw on the brakes, practically laying a tire
patch in the driveway. They all pitched forward as
the car came to an abrupt stop.

"Thank God we're here," he mumbled.

"What did you say?"

"Ah, nothing, Rowena. Miles, can you grab a
wheelchair for her. I don't think she's strong enough
to walk, and I'm definitely no help."

Miles hurried inside while Ryne unbuckled Jen's
seatbelt and stumbled from the car, his crutches sav-
ing him from falling. "I'll help her," Rowena stated
as she leaned into the backseat. Ryne felt absolutely
helpless, watching them help Jen into the wheelchair.

Rowena took charge, pushing Jen while Miles
went to park the car. Ryne hobbled up to the
receptionist and informed her of Jen's condition.
Somehow they were lucky and Jen was immediately
taken to a room. As Ryne started to follow, Rowena
stopped him. She placed a comforting hand on his
arm. "She's going to be just fine." He simply nodded and swung down the hallway.

Ryne listened as Jen described her symptoms. He
was shocked to hear how long she'd been suffering.
The night before she'd told him she hadn't felt right
since boarding the plane, but he never believed she'd
been as ill as she had.

In all actuality, he'd thought her stomach issues
resulted from upset over his injury until he learned
she'd been ill since leaving Calgary. He was stunned.
He didn't understand why she hadn't told him, and
then he realized that she'd put her sickness aside to

support him with his injury. Then he recalled how he'd treated her. He'd been heartless, the way he spoke to her, and she'd put up with that along with the nausea she'd been fighting. He was ashamed because he'd focused solely on himself and never took her into account.

Ryne stepped out as she was examined. When he returned, a surge of pain coursed through his hip. He gasped as he sat. Even though he did his best to hide it, he knew she was cognizant of his pain. "Ryne, have you taken your meds?"

He shook his head. "I forgot. I've been too worried about you." He grabbed her hand and held it against his chest. "When I found you on the floor today looking the way you did, for once in the last few days I forgot about myself. You are my focus right now. I'll deal with my hip later."

"But Ryne, you need to take it."

"I can't be falling asleep while you're lying here in the ER. You come first right now. Got it?" He kissed her fingers. "I'm sorry how I've treated you."

"You've already apologized."

"I know but I also should have been more aware of you. You're my wife. I should have known you weren't right. And you should have felt like you could've told me too. I realize I've been a little standoffish, and I'm giving you my solemn promise. From this moment on, I'll stop feeling sorry for myself. As you said, life is what it is. If the Stanley Cup is in my future so be it and if it's not, well it wasn't meant to be. I need to focus on you— us— and not let my damn career interfere.

"Hockey is hockey but there will be a time when

I'll have to retire. Maybe sooner rather than later, but what I will always have after the game that has meant so much to me is you. You, Jennifer Steele Ferguson. You are my life and I need to show you how much you mean to me."

Before Ryne could continue blabbering, the doctor reentered the room. "Are you feeling any better, Mrs. Ferguson?"

She shrugged. "A little I guess." She looked at the IV attached to her arm. "I guess I was a tad bit dehydrated."

"That you were." He glanced down at his hand. "I have your results here."

Ryne clasped her hand tightly as they waited for her diagnosis. "I have a question for you two…"

Ryne wasn't sure if he liked this doctor. A question? Ryne looked at Jen unsure where this was going.

"My question is…what are you doing in, say, June, July?"

"I hope to be playing in the Stanley Cup finals, why?"

"And you?" he asked Jen.

"I'll be right by his side, cheering him on, why?"

The doctor chuckled at her comment. "I hope you're not cheering too much."

"Why, what's wrong with my wife? Just tell us."

"Impatient are we?"

"No, I just want her feeling better and soon."

"I'm not sure how long it will take…days, weeks, maybe even months…"

He was speaking in riddles. Ryne was getting more impatient by the second. On top of this crazy doctor, his hip was throbbing. "Would you please tell us what's wrong with her?"

"Congratulations, you're pregnant."

They were stunned. "We're what?" they said in unison.

Wide-eyed she asked, "Pregnant?"

"How can that be?" Ryne asked looking at Jen.

"I don't know. I guess I lost track…With the start of the season…moving, a whole host of things. I didn't even consider that I could be pregnant."

"You are. I believe you also have hyperemesis gravidarum. Less than one percent of women experience this. It's characterized with severe nausea, vomiting, possibly dehydration."

"Check, check, check," Ryne said as he ticked off the complications on one hand.

"Often times the symptoms improve after the twentieth week but can last the duration of the pregnancy. I suggest you go home and make an appointment with your doctor. You need to stay hydrated. Drink as much as possible. I'll be honest, you may need additional IV's, so do your best to stay hydrated. Your doctor will have a better idea of how to treat you.

"If you're feeling better, I'll release you as soon as your IV's done. The nurse will be in with your discharge instructions. Again, congratulations."

The doctor shook both of their hands and walked from the room. Ryne ran his hand through his hair. "Did you hear what he said?"

Wide-eyed, she said, "How could I have not?"

"We're pregnant, you're pregnant. I can't believe it." He laid his hand on her stomach. "I can't believe you're—we're going to have a baby. Jen, I'm thrilled, excited. I can't…"

She placed both hands on either side of his face. "I gather you're happy."

"Happy? After I got over being speechless…"

"That you were."

"You were too."

"I have to admit it's quite a surprise. Being pregnant didn't cross my mind. We've barely been married six months. And now a baby's on the way. I'd say I'm a little overwhelmed right now."

He drew her close. "I'm just glad it's nothing more serious. You have to decide if you want to wait to tell everyone."

"If we were by ourselves, I'd say wait, but my grandparents are with us."

"Can Rowena keep a secret?"

"I'll bribe her," Jen said with a straight face. "Although I'm sure she'll be right on the phone with Grams as soon as we leave tomorrow."

"Let's tell your grandparents. We'll Skype in Rose and Wilford and break the news to them all at once. We can hold off telling my family…"

"If my family knows, so will yours." He leaned over and kissed her. With those two words, you're pregnant, their lives were about to change. They'd talked about having children but hoped to hold off for at least a year or two.

"The best laid plans…"

"Can be changed, Ryne. My being pregnant right now happened for a reason. Consider it a gift from God."

"I do, honey, I do."

In just under an hour, they were headed back to Chez Steele. This time Miles was behind the wheel, driving much slower. They'd told her grandparents that she would be fine in time. Just a virus.

When they arrived at the house, Ryne suggested she take a nap. While napping, he phoned Rose and Wilford and set up a time for their Skype. He decided not to let Rowena in on his planned conversation until after dinner.

Jen was still on the pale side during dinner. Ryne had clued her in on their planned call. "How about we take dessert in the conservatory?"

"Great idea, Rowena," Ryne stated.

Miles helped Rowena clear the table and swooshed them into the sunroom. "Relax for a bit, and I'll be right in with dessert."

While Rowena and Miles were cleaning up, Ryne retrieved his laptop. He called her grandparents, giving them the ten-minute warning.

"What's this?" Rowena asked when she saw Ryne's laptop booted up and sitting on the coffee table.

"I thought it would be fun to Skype with Rose and Wilford. They said they hadn't spoken to you both in a while."

"When was the last time we spoke, Miles?"

Miles shook his head. "I don't know. I thought you kept track of all that."

"Miles," she chastised him.

"Well, don't you?"

Ryne was ready to connect and moments later,

Rose and Wilford were on the screen.

After the perfunctory introductions, Ryne cleared his throat. "So the real reason why I called this little soiree…"

"I didn't realize we were celebrating," Rowena chimed in.

"Grandmother Rowena, can you please stop and let Ryne speak."

Rowena pulled her lips in seemingly angry at her granddaughter. "Sorry about that, dear. Ryne please go ahead with why you called us all here other than to wish Rose and Wilford happy holidays."

Rose stepped in. "Honey, how are you feeling? You look a little pale."

"That's what this call is all about. We had to rush Jen to the ER today."

"Oh honey, what's happened?"

"She was violently ill. We thought it was the flu but it turns out…" Ryne clasped her hand and with a half-smile nodded at her.

"I'm pregnant."

"You're pregnant?" Rowena asked.

She nodded.

"I knew it." Rowena leaned into Miles. "See, I told you so."

"How did you guess?" Jen asked.

"I'm definitely not blind. I knew it the minute you walked through the doors." Rowena smiled broadly at Jen. "I am so happy for you."

"We were a little surprised. I didn't give it a thought when I started getting sick a few days ago. Each day it got worse and today…Let's say I hope I don't have a repeat. But…"

"But what, honey?" asked Rose.

"The doctor thinks I may have hyperemesis grav-idarum. It's a severe type of morning sickness. He was being nice, but he prepared me that this could last longer than I'd like. He's concerned about dehydration so I have to be careful. I've already called my doctor and have an appointment for the day after tomorrow."

"You need to take care of yourself and not overdo it."

"I'll make sure she doesn't," Ryne said. "I'll be home rehabbing for at least a month, so I'll be watching her closely."

They spent a few more minutes discussing the baby, Ryne's hip, and the holidays. By the time they headed off to bed, both were whipped with exhaustion. "I can't wait to get home."

"Neither can I," Ryne said as he pulled her close.

What had started out with a tragedy of sorts had turned into a miracle. Jen was expecting her first child. She was excited and scared all at the same time. Deep down, she wanted her mother by her side during her pregnancy, but she had the next best thing, Jacklynne.

Chapter Thirty-Seven

ONCE AGAIN PHILIPPE WAS WAITING for them at the airport. Ryne had phoned him the day before, requesting that he pick them up. For some reason, he wanted his brother to learn about the baby before the rest of the family, including his parents.

Philippe met them right outside the terminal. They'd avoided baggage claim and were happy to be home. They'd secured a wheelchair for Ryne since it had been a long flight, and he hadn't wanted to overdo it with the crutches.

Philippe leaned against the wall, waiting. He noticed Ryne first because of the wheelchair. When his eyes found Jen, he did a double take. She looked sicker than all get out. She was pale and appeared absolutely exhausted. If he wasn't mistaken she'd lost weight too. He was taken aback as he'd just seen her a few days ago.

As they approached, he couldn't stop himself from asking, "Jen, are you sick? You look like you don't feel well."

"About that," Ryne stated. He stood, thanking the attendant for the wheelchair, then steadied himself with his crutches. Philippe took his suitcase and flung Jen's carryon over his shoulder. "Can you wait till we get to the car, and we'll fill you in?"

"Sure thing."

Philippe had been lucky and had found a parking place close to the doors. They waited while he went for the car. "Are you sure you're okay with telling Philippe first?"

"Definitely. I know he's come a long way, but I want him to know first. Don't ask me why but I just do."

Ryne and Jen settled into the backseat of the car. "So, I guess I'm the chauffeur?" Philippe chuckled. "At least that's how I feel."

"So Mr. Chauffeur, we'd like to stop and get something to eat before going home. Are you okay with that?"

"I am if you are."

Philippe jumped onto the interstate and headed towards the ranch. A few exits before he turned off for home, they stopped at a local family-style restaurant. It was relatively empty, and they asked for a table towards the back where no one would overhear them.

The waitress delivered their drinks and while they waited for their meals, Philippe asked, "So what's this about? I take it you don't want anyone to hear us."

"Right on." Ryne took a sip of his coffee, cleared his throat and shared their news. "We wanted you to know before anyone else…"

"Know what?"

"We're pregnant."

"What? You are? Congratulations," he high fived his brother.

"Thanks, Philippe," Jen added.

"I'm a little surprised, though. Were you trying?"

"Ah, no, not really," Jen spoke. "But we're thrilled just the same."

"Of course you are. Am I the only one who knows?"

Ryne went on to describe the events from the prior day. "So no you're not. Jen's family knows. We haven't decided when we'll tell Mom and Dad and everyone else."

"I think you better as soon as you can. Don't take this the wrong way, Jen, but I have to be honest. You look like you've been through the wringer."

She ran her hand across her forehead. "I know I don't look too good. This morning sickness is a bear. I was lucky not to get sick on the plane today and I'm not sure how."

"But you're feeling better."

"I am for the moment and I can't wait to eat. Hopefully, I'll be able to keep it down. We're not too far from home, are we?"

"Only a few exits."

"Good."

They finished their meal which Jen relished. She felt a bit better but didn't want to think too positively, or her luck might run out. And it did. On the way home, not fifteen minutes later, she asked for Philippe to pull over. She practically ran into the hollow alongside the road where she got sick.

She eased her way into the backseat beside Ryne, resting her head against him. "Feeling better?" he asked.

"Um hmm," she sighed and snuggled closer.

Philippe drove them directly to their house and carried their bags inside. Jen kissed Philippe's cheek and thanked him, then headed to the bedroom. "She looks like hell, Ryne."

"I know. I'm really concerned. The doctor said she could fight this her entire pregnancy, and I'm not sure how much more she can take. She's been sick morning, noon, and night. She's lost weight, and I'm concerned that she's heading towards dehydration again."

"Didn't you say she has a doctor's appointment tomorrow?"

"Yeah."

"I'll take you."

"Thanks, Phil. I know that would mean a lot to Jen."

"I'm going to head out. If you need anything let me know. By the way, Mom hasn't a clue that you're home today. Last time I talked to her she seemed confused as to when you were returning. Just so you know, I didn't tell her."

Philippe gave his brother a quick hug and walked out the door. He was happy for them but was also concerned about Jen. He appreciated being one of the first to find out. He and Annabelle had planned on starting a family right away. His thoughts went to her. He still thought of her daily, but he wasn't as sad as he once was. Jen had helped him turn the corner on his grief, and every day he fought that battle. Now he had something else to be happy about. He was going to become an uncle, and he was thrilled beyond words.

Jen pretty much slept the rest of the day. Ryne checked on her hourly. He tried to take her something to eat, but it was a lost cause. A cup of soup and crutches definitely didn't mix. He became frustrated that he couldn't take care of her in the way she deserved. The best he could do was hold her and that was about it.

Philippe checked in that evening. "How's it going?"

"She's slept most of the day. I tried to take her a cup of soup, and I'm sure you can imagine how that turned out."

"Yeah, on the floor."

"Good guess. Phil, I wish I could do more for her."

"You're doing your best. I'm sure as soon as Mom finds out, she'll be whisking you both up to the house."

"More than likely, yes, but I don't think Jen will go for that. She likes to be independent although I'm sure she'll want Mom's help at some point. She's going to need her advice, that's for sure."

"You know Mom will be over the moon about this baby, don't you?"

"Yeah, I know. I just hope Jen starts feeling better soon. It's so hard to see her lying on the bathroom floor."

"I'm sure it is. How about I stop by tomorrow morning and check on the both of you. I can even do shopping if you need it."

"Thanks, Phil. You're a lifesaver. And thanks again for picking us up at the airport."

"Not a problem. Try and get some sleep."

Ryne thanked his brother again. He sat on the couch, contemplating what the best thing for both of them would be. Maybe they should move to the big house temporarily. That way, his mother could take extra good care of Jen.

With that in mind, he decided they'd tell his parents about the baby.

Ryne phoned his Mom early the next morning. "Hey Mom, how are you?"

"I'm good. Where are you? Are you still in Greenwich?"

"No, we came home yesterday."

"Yesterday? How come you didn't stop by?"

"That's what I'm calling about." He knew he probably scared his mother and added, "Everything's alright but could you and Dad come by around ten? Jen and I need to talk to you."

"Oookay," she said drawing out the word.

"It's nothing serious, but we don't want little ears overhearing our conversation just yet."

"Gotcha."

He'd just hung up when Jen appeared. She had a tad more color in her face. "Feeling better?"

"Don't jinx me but I am for the moment."

"Good. I just spoke to Mom and asked that she and Dad come by around ten. I thought we'd tell them here without having to worry about Emma interrupting us."

She sighed deeply as she nestled into his side. "I'm glad. You know I love Em to death, but I don't think I could take her exuberance right now."

"I understand and that's why I arranged it. Philippe's coming by in a little bit, so if you need anything from the store write it down."

"You've thought of everything."

"Not really. He's the one who offered."

"He's a good brother. I think he took our news pretty well, don't you?"

"I do. I also think he appreciates that we told him first. It allowed him to digest it without hearing the congratulations and having tons of eyes on him. He and Annabelle were planning to start a family right away. I'm sure the news hit home, but I also think he handled it well."

"He did. He seems to be dealing with his grief a little better. I'm going to take a shower and dress before your parents come by."

"Call if you need me. I'll be right here although I'm not sure how much help I'll be."

"Just knowing you're here is all I need." She kissed him softly and headed off to their bedroom.

She'd barely left the room when Philippe knocked. "Come in," Ryne called, knowing it was his brother.

Philippe came in carrying a tray from the local bakery. He had hot coffees, bagels and cream cheese. "I thought I'd bring these by as I wasn't sure what you had around here."

"Thanks, Phil. That coffee smells out of this world." Phil handed him a cup, grabbed one for himself, and set Jen's on the counter along with the bag of goodies. "So, how's my favorite sister-in-law feeling this morning?"

"I think better. She definitely doesn't look like

death warmed over. She had a little color in her face. She's in the shower right now. Mom and Dad are coming over in a little while."

"Then I'd better scamper out of here. I don't want her knowing that I know you're home."

"She knows we came home yesterday."

"And she wasn't upset not knowing?"

"I think she was perplexed, but I told her we'd explain when she got here."

"You know she's probably getting all upset wondering what's up."

"Probably, but isn't that what moms do?"

"I guess you're right. On that note, I'm going to head on out of here. Text me what you need, and I'll run to the store."

"Thanks again, Philippe. I owe you one."

"Just get better and take care of your lovely wife. You know she's one of a kind."

"I do and I'm the lucky one. She's certainly changed my life."

Not a half hour after Philippe left, his parents knocked. It didn't surprise him that they were a half hour early. He knew his mother wanted answers. He grabbed his crutches and hobbled to the door. He also wasn't surprised by the look on his mother's face. "Oh dear, you're on crutches. Ryne, how are you making it?"

Before Ryne could speak, Jen entered the room. "Jacklynne, Jacques, come on in. Would you like something to drink?"

"We didn't come for social hour, my dear. We're here for answers, such as why you didn't let us know you came home yesterday."

Ryne was taken aback with his mother's tone. His dad raised his eyebrows as Jacklynne sat down. Jacques slipped his arm around his son. "Ryne, how's the hip? It seems your mother forgot to ask that all-important question instead focusing on why her married son neglected to tell her he'd come home." Jacques eyed Jacklynne, putting her in her place.

"It's getting better every day."

"That's good to know." Jacques sat down beside his wife. Ryne settled in the oversized chair adjacent to the couch, and Jen perched on the arm of his chair.

"So what did you want to speak to us about?" Jacklynne asked. "Is your injury more severe than you thought?"

"It's not that, Mom." He reached for Jen's hand and laced their fingers. He looked up into her eyes not sure exactly who should share the news. Since he'd called this meeting, he took the lead.

"So, we came home yesterday as we intended. We wanted to be here to celebrate New Year's."

"I certainly thought you would have stopped by especially since you weren't here to celebrate Christmas with us."

"That was our plan originally but..."

"What changed?" Jacques asked.

Ryne grappled with his thoughts. Sharing the news with Philippe had been much easier. He didn't know why he couldn't formulate the words. He cleared his throat and Jen tightened her grip on his hand.

"The reason we came straight home is because Jen

was sick."

"Oh honey, are you feeling better? You do look a little pale and have you lost weight?"

"Mom, Jen's pregnant."

"Pregnant?"

"That's what I said," he glanced up at Jen. "And she has severe morning sickness."

"Oh honey, I'm sorry to hear that."

"Yeah, the ER doctor thinks I have hyperemesis gravidarum."

"ER doctor?" Jacques interjected.

"Ryne took me to the hospital when I couldn't stop getting sick."

"Isn't that pretty serious?" Jacklynne stated with concern in her voice.

"It can be, Mom. We have an appointment this afternoon with her doctor. I think one of the main concerns is dehydration. She's already had one IV plus I assume there's a whole host of other things we need to be concerned about as well."

Jacklynne looked at her husband and then back at Ryne and Jen. "I think you should move up to the house for a little while— at least until you're more mobile, Ryne. You can't cook and clean on crutches and…"

"I was hoping you'd insist on that," Ryne said interrupting his mother. He glanced back at Jen and noticed a look of relief cross her face. "I, we, appreciate it."

"Think nothing of it. We need to make sure you're both being taken care of." Jacklynne hopped off the couch and went to Jen, pulling her into a congratulatory hug. "I'm sorry dear, I didn't congratulate you. I am so excited for you." She looked at Jacques, beaming and said, "We're going to be grandparents."

"Sounds like it," Jacques replied and joined Jacklynne in congratulating them.

They arranged for them to move up to the house later in the afternoon after her doctor's appointment. "Would you like me to drive you?" Jacklynne asked.

"I've got that covered. Philippe is already on chauffeur duty."

"So he already knows."

"Yeah. We thought it would be a good idea to tell him first. He took it well and seems happy for us."

"Your brother's come a long way in the last year. I hope he decides to take a chance and find someone to spend the rest of his life with."

"So, do we," Jen added. "Now let's discuss why we're moving up to the house. I don't want to tell the rest of the family about the baby for a little while. I think we can use the excuse that Ryne's having difficulties navigating the stairs, and we're going to use the first-floor guest room."

"I think that sounds reasonable." Jacklynne reached for both of their hands. "I need to apologize for the way I spoke to you, son. I had no idea what you were going through. Just know we'll keep a good eye on Jen and you. I promise not to coddle you. When you need something, just ask. We'll focus on Ryne and not Jen, or else Emma will get wind that something's afoot. You know how relentless she can be when she feels left out."

Jen stood and wrapped her arms around Jacklynne. "We know you have our best interests at heart. Depending on what the doctor says, we'll decide when to tell the rest of the family."

"Does your family know?"

"They do since my grandmother drove us to the hospital."

"She did? What about Miles?"

"Mom, that's a whole other story that I think we'll save for another day. Let's just say, I had no idea Rowena had it in her."

They all laughed at his comment. "Ro is something else."

"Yes, she is, Jacklynne. She's the best."

Jen's doctor's appointment went well and she and Ryne received more than enough literature on how to combat hyperemesis gravidarum. They returned home relieved. Jacklynne and Jacques had announced they were moving up to the big house to help with Ryne's recovery. Everyone took the news in stride and thankfully Emma didn't question the story as she knew it was best for her brother. In fact, she'd been a little reserved with the news which was a change for Emma.

That evening Philippe moved their essentials and helped settle them into the guest room. "Let me know if you need anything else," Philippe said as he carried Ryne's suitcase into the room.

"I think we're good, Phil. We appreciate everything you've done."

"Not a problem. I gather Jen's appointment went well."

"Yeah," Ryne ran his hand along his jawline. "She needs to be cautious and keep the doctor informed. We hope she won't need another IV."

"Did he say how long this is going to last?"

"Nope. He said the majority of his patients with hyperemesis gravidarum have it through the third month, but in all reality she could experience it her entire pregnancy."

"Let's hope for it ending soon. I have to say I took one look at her yesterday, and I thought she looked like death warmed over. I was concerned."

"I was and still am. At least we're home and she's close to her doctor. That's what matters."

"What about you?"

"What about me?"

"Are you happy?"

"I am. We didn't plan this pregnancy, but I'm excited."

"What about your hip?"

"I've been in quite a bit of pain, but I'm doing my best not to take anything. I need to be focused on Jen and not me."

"I understand what you're saying, but you need to take it easy and not overdo it. You want to return to the ice sooner rather than later."

"That I do."

They chatted for a few minutes before Philippe decided to leave. "I'll let you get some rest. Last I saw Jen she was watching a movie with the girls."

"I know. I just hope Emma doesn't bother her too much especially when she's not feeling well. You know how our sister can be."

"I think she's happy to have her nearby. I've seen a

change in Emma since you got married. She seems
to have settled down a bit. Now that Jen's nearby
she doesn't get worked up anticipating her visit. I
hate to say this but Jen's become old hat."

"That she has."

"Get some rest," Philippe said. "I'm glad everything's alright with Jen."

"At least for the time being." Ryne raised his hand
in goodbye. It felt good to lie back and relax, at least
for the moment. Jen seemed good and for the first
time since he'd been injured, he felt at peace.

Chapter Thirty-Eight

THEY WAITED UNTIL JEN WAS well into her second trimester to tell the rest of the family about the baby. Jen's morning sickness had all but disappeared and Ryne hoped to return to the ice in a matter of days.

On the day they were scheduled to move back to their house, Jen called a family meeting. Earlier in the day, they had phoned both Rafael and Jules, sharing the news with them. Both of his brothers were thrilled. "So you're going to be a dad," Jules stated. "I'm really happy for you. When's the baby due?"

"The last week of June."

"I hope she doesn't have it early. With the Cup finals and all."

"The doctor said most first pregnancies are late, so I think we'll be okay."

"Let's hope so," said Rafael. "Wouldn't it be something if you went into labor during one of the games?" He laughed.

"I don't think that's funny, Rafael," Jen said.

"Just teasing," he responded.

When the time came to tell the rest of the family, her nausea had returned. She'd been feeling pretty good up until they gathered everyone. Just as Ryne began to speak, she ran from the room. She knew the color had drained from her face as she saw the look of trepidation on Ryne's face.

"Is Jen okay?" a concerned Olivia asked.

"I'm sure she is but I'll go check on her." As Ryne walked from the room, he noticed an anxious look cross Philippe's face as well as those of his parents.

Ryne found her rinsing out her mouth. "Sorry about that," she said "I've been feeling good all day. Maybe it was something I ate." She looked at him with sadness as she'd convinced herself the worst of her morning sickness was over. "I guess everyone's wondering what happened."

"Olivia just happened to be standing right inside the doorway when you ran past, so I know she's worried. And Philippe and my parents all shot me a troubling look as I left the room. I'm not sure if anyone else noticed."

"That's good." She reached for his hand, "Let's do this."

He leaned over and kissed her forehead. "And when we're through, we're headed home. I can't wait to spend the night in our bed."

Ryne led her down the hallway and back to the family room. She ran her hand along Olivia's shoulder smiling as she reentered and took a seat on the couch. Ryne sat beside her and grabbed ahold of her hand. She nodded her head and grinned at him as he began to speak.

"Jen and I are moving back home tonight. I'm comfortable taking the stairs and Jen— well she's got something to say."

She was hoping he'd share the news but instead

passed the baton to her. "I need to apologize for rushing out of here a few minutes ago." She glanced back at Ryne, squeezed his hand and smiled. "We need to thank you for letting us stay here while Ryne and I recuperated."

"I didn't know you weren't feeling well," Emma said.

"Yeah, well, I need to explain that…I've been suffering from hyperemesis gravidarum."

"What's that?" Emma asked as she scrunched up her face.

"It's a severe case of morning sickness." Emma didn't catch on at first but Olivia and Etienne did.

"Oh my, you're having a baby," Olivia shrieked.

"A baby… Is Olivia right? Is it true?" Emma jumped up and ran towards Jen. She threw her arms around her. "Does that mean I'm going to have a new cousin?"

"Not a cousin, Em. You're going to be an aunt," Etienne spoke.

She grinned. "You mean I'm going to be an aunt?"

"You are," Ryne said as she turned to hug her brother.

"Congratulations, you two," Etienne said as he hugged her. "Sorry to hear you haven't been feeling well."

"I guess it goes with the territory. At least now, Ryne can fend for himself in case I'm under the weather."

Philippe approached as everyone sat around speculating on whether they were having a boy or a girl. "You sure you're up to returning home?"

"Yeah. I'm good, getting stronger every day, and Jen's much improved from when we first came home."

"It didn't look that way a few minutes ago."

"Take it from me, Philippe, I'm feeling much better," she said. "I'm not sure what caused me to get sick this time, maybe I ate something that didn't agree with me."

"I hope that's all it is. Changing subjects, do you need help taking your things back to your house?"

"An extra pair of hands would be great. I don't want him overdoing things," she said as she placed her hand on Ryne's forearm. "He needs to get back on that ice soon…"

"Honey, I'm headed there. Give me another week or so, and I'll be out there skating like a rookie."

"That's all I want to hear. When you're happy, I'm happy and right now I'm happy to be going home."

"On that note, let me grab your suitcases and I'll take you home."

Jen and Ryne hugged his parent's goodbye. "Don't be strangers, you two."

"We won't, I promise," Jen said as she reached for Ryne's hand. "In fact you may just get tired of seeing me, since I don't plan on going too far from the ranch."

"Never. We'll never get tired of seeing your bright and shiny face. Call if you need anything."

"We will," Ryne said as he pulled Jen out the door.

He spent one game with the Storm's minor league

affiliate before being recalled home.

Practice had already started when he arrived at the Sauderhouse Arena. He'd driven straight from the airport, so he exchanged his street clothes for his pads and jersey. He was wearing a new pair of pants that were reinforced with special padding that would hopefully protect his hip from further injury.

His brothers were standing along the boards when he entered the arena. No one was aware of his return to the team except Ray, who stood near the blue line. His brothers were shocked and skated over to him. "What's this?" Etienne asked as he slapped Ryne on the back. "I can't believe you're back already. I thought they'd have made you play the maximum number of games after being on the long-term injured reserve list."

"I did too," Philippe added. "I sure thought we wouldn't see you for a week."

"Oscar gave me the okay and Ray knew he needed my expertise to lead this team to the Cup."

Etienne cleared his throat. "When did you get such a big head? I think we did pretty well in your absence, didn't we, Phil?"

"We did but it sure is good to have you back."

"Okay, boys, it's time to break up the welcoming committee. Show us I didn't make a mistake in authorizing your return."

"Yes, sir," Ryne shouted to Ray as he started warming up.

"I'm glad he's back," Phil said, turning to Etienne as they watched Ryne fly around the ice.

"Yeah, I was a little worried there. Two hip injuries in a short amount of time."

"We're not going to think along those lines. He's back and that's what matters." Phil jumped onto the ice and took a pass from Ryne. In a moment's time they were back in the groove. Three brothers skating around the rink they called home.

Ryne's return to the team fueled an energy that at times was lacking in his absence. They were still in first place but had lost their momentum when he'd gone down with his injury. They were leading the standings by one point against Ryne's former Eagles team.

There were two weeks left in the regular season. Ryne had returned to the ice three weeks earlier and had played well. Jen's morning sickness had settled down, and she was enjoying her pregnancy. During Ryne's first road trip after returning to the team, she stayed up at the big house. They'd been expecting snow and Ryne had been concerned with her being alone.

When Jacklynne had called insisting that she stay with them, she refused at first and then rethought her decision. Five minutes after refusing, she packed her things and before she knew it, Jacques was knocking on her door.

When she opened it, he took one look at her and pulled her into his arms. "I'm so happy you took Jacklynne up on her offer. She was worried sick with you out here by yourself."

"It's not like I'm that far from the house."

"She knows but, in all honesty, she's missed you.

We've hardly seen you or my son since you moved home."

"Sorry about that. In all actuality, I've hardly gone out. I've been to the doctor, and Ryne pretty much does the shopping. I've been hibernating."

"Honey, you still should be out amongst people."

"I realize that. In fact, I'm glad Jacklynne phoned. You're right. It's time for me to get out and about." She turned to grab her bag, but Jacques beat her to it.

"I've got this," he said. He closed the door, locking it behind her.

Jacklynne was waiting for them in the kitchen, steeping a pot of tea, and welcomed Jen with a kiss on the cheek. "With as cold as it is out there, I thought I'd fix tea. Would you like a cup?"

"That sounds delightful," Jen said as she rubbed her hands together. "I wonder, will I ever get warm again?"

"Come May maybe." Jacques chuckled. "Let's sit by the fire," he added as he led the way to the family room.

"How are the girls?" Jen asked as she sipped her tea.

"Good, really good. Emma has a game tonight. Would you like to go?"

"I'd love to. I'm sorry I haven't attended her earlier games."

"Both she and Olivia understand why you've been absent of late. They can't imagine what you were going through with your morning sickness. That's all pretty much passed, hasn't it?"

Jen nodded. "I've been holding my breath the last

couple of weeks, but I have to say yes, I think I'm finally over it. I don't know how women experience that level of sickness throughout their entire pregnancy. It was stressful, tiring… I never knew if I could leave the house. I was fearful I'd be on the road in the middle of nowhere and have to pull over. That's one of the main reasons I've stayed home."

"Maybe we'll see a little more of you then?" Jacklynne added. "I've missed you and I know the girls have too."

"Let's put an end to that starting today."

And that's what Jen did. She started going out again and visiting with Jacklynne while the girls were in school. She asked for her advice when she began shopping for the nursery. She needed a woman's touch. Lauren and her grandmothers were too far away. Jacklynne became the ear that Jen needed. She sought her out for answers when she was unsure of what she was feeling as her pregnancy progressed. Jacklynne had given birth six times with a set of twins. If she didn't have the answers, then who would?

With the remaining games in the season upon them, Ryne's stress levels increased. Jen could tell by his level of play he was pushing himself. His hip was holding up, but the number of minutes he found himself in the penalty box was on the rise.

Jacques box was near the *Hockey Tonight* play-by-play announcers. Jen overheard them host their pregame segment before the start of the game.

"We've got two weeks left in the season. The Storm is leading the Western Conference. They've already secured a spot in the playoffs."

"That's right, Kelly." Ted stated. "The team seems more focused since Ryne Ferguson returned."

"They do. He's definitely a leader."

"You're right about that except he's spent a lot of time in the penalty box of late."

"He has, Kelly. It's important that he keeps himself in check tonight. The Eagles are knocking on the Storm's heels to win the division. They've won four of their last five while the Storm has lost the last two games."

"Ted, I have to wonder why Ryne has incurred so many penalties since returning from his injury."

"Yeah, you have to wonder if he's one hundred percent healthy."

Jen was tired of listening to them talk about her husband. She knew he was healthy. She knew what was driving him. It was his need to see the team win the Cup. He would do everything in his power to make that happen. If he incurred a few penalties along the way, so be it. Ryne was focused solely on seeing his dream become a reality, and he wasn't going to let anything come between him and that Cup.

Within minutes of the puck being dropped, Ryne found himself in the penalty box. Jen shook her head at her husband's stupid trip of his good friend Wiley that led to the penalty. He shook his head as he poured water into his mouth. She knew by his expression that he was madder than heck at himself. Tripping, she thought. Stupid penalty all the way around.

In the middle of the second period, Ryne led a two-on-one break down center ice with Philippe as his wingman. He passed the puck to his brother as he skated behind the goalie. Philippe controlled the puck and moved out to the point. Ryne slapped his stick on the ice signaling he was open at the side of the net.

Philippe passed the puck sharply to him as he skated out from the side of the net. Spinning and spraying ice as his skates cut through the surface, Ryne turned on a dime and came out on the other side of the net. He faked a pass to Etienne and pushed the puck around the side of the net. The blue light went on. Ryne had scored his first goal in six games.

She felt like she could breathe again. He'd scored a goal that she hoped would settle him down for the remainder of the game.

Her wishes extended well into the third period. With less than five minutes left to play, the Storm was losing by one goal.

Ryne's line was sitting on the bench catching a breather when Vlad took a pass from Heinrich. His skate was just over the blue line when he accepted the pass and off sides was called.

Ray took advantage of the stop in play and redeployed Ryne's line. Ryne won the faceoff and tipped the puck to Josh who sped behind the net. Ryne stood out by the point waiting for Josh to pass the puck. He drifted towards center ice when he caught the pass. He faked a slap shot and skated along the blue line. Josh yelled at him. He raised his stick and let off his infamous slap shot. The puck flew right over the goalie's shoulder. Ryne had scored his second goal of the night but also ended up flat on the ice. One of the Eagles players had run smack into him.

Jen was excited by the goal until she saw Ryne lying on the ice. Her thoughts immediately went to his hip, but then she saw him moving around. She imagined he was stunned by the hit and held her breath as he stood and made his way to the bench. Then he turned towards the exit to the locker room. Her heart beat wildly, fearful of another injury but then looked at the clock. There was less than three minutes left in the period. It was a tie game, and she prayed he was just getting an extra breather before overtime began.

Thankfully, the Eagles had incurred a penalty on the cheap shot to Ryne which the Storm converted into another goal before time expired. They'd won and didn't have to worry about an overtime period.

They'd barely made it to the locker room when Ryne came through the door, showered and dressed. Jen ran to his side. "You're okay?"

"Why wouldn't I be?"

"That hit, you lying on the ice, and then leaving the game."

"Oh that. Ray was giving me a few extra minutes before the end of the period. Etienne's line was playing better than mine, and he wanted them to finish out the game."

"That's good to know. I was worried."

"Jen you can't get all bent out of shape when I fall to the ice. It's a part of the game."

"I realize that."

"Stop fretting. I'm fine. Now let's go home and get you to bed." Ryne slipped his arm around her shoulders. As they walked along Ryne recounted the game with Jacques.

"Dad, did you see that slap shot?"

"See it? I felt it all the way up in my box." Jacques grinned at him. "You're playing well, son. Keep it up and you'll be parading that Cup around town before you know it."

Chapter Thirty-Nine

SPRING HAD SPRUNG IN CALGARY. The temperatures were warming as April brought about the end to the regular season with the Storm riding on a high, winning their last three games.

As the temperatures rose, Jen was excited about the baby, especially as she entered her third trimester. She was feeling much better as she'd been sticking close to the foods her doctor recommended and had gained hardly any weight which she was thankful for. In the last couple of days, she was just beginning to really show. She finally needed maternity clothes and asked Jacklynne to accompany her to the store to choose a few outfits.

On the way home from their shopping spree, they stopped at a bakery that served sandwiches along with pastries. "Thank you for asking me go with you today," Jacklynne said as she took a sip of her coffee.

"You're welcome although I should have asked you sooner."

"You were getting along just fine with what you had until a few days ago. I think you really popped out since just yesterday," Jacklynne said as she placed her hand on Jen's stomach.

"I have," she smiled at her mother-in-law. "It

feels more real everyday as I feel her move around. She's keeping me up at night."

"So it's a she?"

"We decided not to find out. Ryne and I want it to be a surprise."

"I thought you were going to find out at your last visit."

"I did but he wants to be surprised so we waited."

"Jacques and I never knew what we were having."

"Did you at least know you were expecting twins?"

"That we did. I was as big as house when I had Ryne and Etienne. In fact, I didn't think I wanted any more children after them."

"And what? You had four more?"

"We did." Jacklynne took a bite of her sandwich. "Have you chosen names yet?"

"We've thrown a few around but nothing for sure yet. I think I want to wait until I see his or her, face. I think that will help us name him. It's a hard decision. How did you choose?"

They enjoyed the rest of their lunch discussing how Jacques and she had chosen names. As they got in the car to return home, Jen turned to Jacklynne, "Thanks for coming out with me, Mom."

Jacklynne's head spun when Jen referred to her as Mom. "I hardly call you that, but I am going to do my best going forward to refer to you as Mom." Jen reached for Jacklynne's hand. "You've been there for me since we discovered I was pregnant. You've passed along a wealth of knowledge to me, more than my mother ever could have. I miss my mom every day, but I feel like I have a mom in you that

I can go to for advice, support or just an ear when I'm having a questioning thought about the baby. I was sure lucky when I married Ryne. I've got an amazing husband but I also have a family now. I've missed having a mom and dad, but to me you and Jacques are my parents now. So I want to thank you from the bottom of my heart."

"Oh honey, you don't need to thank me for anything. Jacques and I have loved you from the very first minute Ryne brought you out to the ranch. You're a daughter to us. Whether you refer to us as Mom and Dad or Jacques and Jacklynne, it doesn't matter. Family is what matters and you're a part of our family." Jacklynne reached over and pulled Jen into her arms. "I love you."

"I love you too, Mom."

Later that afternoon, Ryne returned home from practice. Their first playoff game was scheduled the following evening. He was all worked up as the Storm won the President's Trophy for having the most points in the league during the regular season. Jen knew he carried the weight of the trophy on his shoulder knowing they needed to earn it by winning the Stanley Cup.

She could feel the high level of stress he carried through the door. From the way he stood in the kitchen as he watched her prepare dinner, to the way he continually kept tapping his finger against the counter. She found herself out of breath from breathing to the beat of his finger.

She knew she needed to do something to ease the tension. She walked around the counter and laid her finger over his. At first he wasn't aware of what she was doing until she got up in his face and glared at him.

"What?" he asked. "Is something wrong?"

"You bet there is. Can you stop what you're doing?"

"What am I doing? I'm just standing here looking at my beautiful wife."

She latched onto his finger and raised it to her lips. Kissing it, she said, "This finger needs to be put out of commission." He continued to look at her strangely. "Were you not aware that you've been tapping your finger against the counter since you walked into the room?"

"I was? I wasn't aware..."

She grabbed his hand and led him to a chair where he sat then pulled her onto his lap. "Honey, you're a tangled mess. I can feel the tension radiating off of you. I was breathless trying to breathe to the beat of your finger. You haven't even started the playoffs and you're this way. How will you be if you make it to the finals?"

"Worse." He chortled. "Sorry about that, I didn't mean to get you all stressed out." As he laid his hand atop her stomach, he felt the baby move. He moved his finger about, caressing his child. "I can't wait for this little one. Sorry if I'm upsetting you and the baby. I'm excited, anxious, all rolled up into one. We're so close and yet so far away."

"Take it one day and one game at a time. Play your game, the game that helped you lead the Storm to the President's Trophy. That's all you need to do. In the end you'll either win or lose, but in your heart, you'll know you gave it your best shot. I know it's been hard since your injury. You tried to make up the games you missed, and it almost backfired on you. Between the stupid, and I mean stupid, penalties you incurred along with the fights you engaged in— that's not you Ryne." She cupped his cheek.

"Play the game you've always played, don't change it up or I'm afraid you'll regret it. Don't get yourself drawn into a fight that only hurts the team." She brushed her lips against his. "I love you. I believe in you and I know your teammates believe in you."

"It's just…"

"Listen to me. You have nothing to prove. You made it to the team you've dreamed of playing for. You've helped them make it to the playoffs, and you'll be there when you win. Relax and enjoy the rest of the season. Because if you don't, I'm afraid you'll regret it twenty years down the road when you can't remember what you were feeling when you hit the ice for your run to the Cup. You'll also regret if you do something stupid that causes you to lose your dream. Keep your head about yourself. And no matter what happens, the baby and I will always be here for you. Your family will be here for you. Got it?"

"Yeah. Thanks for screwing my head back on straight again."

"I needed to set you right or else I wouldn't be able to sleep or eat around you. You were stressing me out just watching you."

Ryne leaned in and kissed her. "I love you so much. Everyday I'm thankful that I found you. I'd be lost without you."

"I don't think you'd be lost, maybe a little challenged."

She laid her head on his shoulder. "You know the next few weeks are going to fly by." She felt him nod. "I hope you realize that this little one is going to be here soon, and if he or she is early could arrive during the Cup finals."

She heard him nervously swallow. "I'm not trying to add any more weight onto your shoulders, but I wanted to remind you."

"I realize that." He stroked her stomach. "Whenever this little one decides to make his grand entrance will be the happiest day of my life." He pulled her close. "I can't wait for our baby to join our little family. I'd put you both in front of playing in the seventh game of the Stanley Cup any day. Yes, that's been my dream since I first stood on skates on the backyard pond, but you are my reality. Dreams may or may not come true, but you're also my dream. I've wanted a family that I can call my own and now I have it. Either way, I'm already a winner. I won your hand and I'm thankful every day I was traded to the Generals. If Ed hadn't traded for me, I would have never met you, and I wouldn't be sitting here holding you and our future on my lap. Fate played a role that day, and I will never forget it."

She felt a calmness overcome him. The tension drained from his shoulders. His eyes were more focused, and he was no longer tapping his finger. Life was good and she knew it would only get better in the weeks to come.

The Storm easily won their conference quarterfinal round against the Otters in a blowout, winning all four games played. Their semifinal triumph against the Oregon Diamonds came almost as easily, taking the series three games in a row. Each series so far had its moments of scare for the Ferguson family.

Etienne was upended and ran into the boards during the final minutes of play in the conference quarterfinal win. He'd slammed his shoulder into the glass and went down hard. He didn't return to the bench but headed straight to the locker room where he was met by Oscar. Thankfully it was just a bruise, and since they'd swept the series, he was able to recover before the start of the next round.

Philippe, on the other hand, wasn't as lucky. He was involved in an altercation with Yevgeni Vasilev, one of the Diamonds' hard fighting defensemen. Within moments of the opening faceoff, gloves were dropped and punches exchanged. Yevgeni walked away with a bloody nose while Philippe jammed his thumb. Yevgeni went to the bench while Philippe went straight to the locker room. He was out the remainder of the game and was day to day the rest of the series.

Again, the Storm was lucky with their series ending in five games. They were off almost a week before the conference final series began. By the time they were ready to drop the opening puck, the entire Storm team was healthy, including Etienne and Philippe.

They had home ice advantage against the Eagles, so when the conference finals began the entire Ferguson clan was in attendance. The Tide had lost their series. If they'd won, the final series would have put all four Ferguson brothers against one another. Now, three of the four brothers had the opportunity.

Jules had completed his semester at UW and had returned home. The entire family stood along the wall of Jacques' box watching the Storm warm up. As they departed the ice, Ryne, Philippe, and Etienne raised their sticks and gestured towards the family.

Ryne was all pumped up to begin this series. In the last few weeks, Jen's pregnancy had advanced. The weight she'd held off gaining crept on. She definitely looked pregnant, and Ryne knew she was starting to feel the effects.

Between the swollen ankles and feet, she couldn't wait for the baby to be born. The evening before the start of the conference finals, she experienced Braxton Hicks contractions while Ryne was home. It freaked out not only her, but also Ryne as these had been the most intense yet. He wanted to jump in the car and rush her to the hospital, fearing that she'd gone into labor.

That afternoon, they'd taken a long walk. She'd hoped that it would de-stress Ryne and help him focus better. After their walk, he attended practice and when he returned found her stretched out on the couch clutching her abdomen.

"What's wrong," he called out as he dropped to

the floor beside her.

"I've had a few pains." Just as she said that another sharp pain shot along the sides of her abdomen. She smoothed her hand over the area.

"Where's your suitcase," he asked as he grabbed ahold of her hand. At the same time, he grabbed his phone and started to make a call.

"Who are you calling?"

"Your doctor."

"Why are you calling him?"

"You're in labor. We need to get to the hospital." Jen grabbed his phone.

"What are you doing?"

"Stopping you from doing something stupid."

"But you're in pain. The baby…"

"Ryne, can you please stop for a second? I'm fine. It's just Braxton Hicks contractions. I've been getting them on and off for a while now."

"You didn't tell me."

"Because it's nothing to worry about." She took a deep breath. She supported her stomach and sat up. "I just need to change positions, that's all." She patted the sofa beside her. "Sit," she instructed him.

Ryne pulled himself from the floor and sat beside her. "You're sure you're okay."

"Yep, never better." She gave him a sideways glance. "Except for the swollen feet, ankles, sleepless nights…"

"Okay, I get it. I have to believe you're not in labor…" He reached for her hand and raised it to his lips. He smirked. "You will tell me when you're in labor, right?"

"Definitely." She wrapped her arms around his

neck. "You'll be the first to know." She laid her head on his shoulder. "So how was practice?"

"Great. I think we're going to win the series."

"Don't be too cocky. After all, it is the Eagles that you're playing."

"I realize that. In fact, I ran into Beck Randolph as I was leaving the arena tonight."

"Huh, what did he have to say?"

"That he wished he hadn't traded me to the Generals."

"And what did you say?"

"I thanked him."

"You did?"

"Of course I did. I thanked him for leading me to you. I also told him we're expecting any minute now."

"Ryne, we still have at least six weeks."

"To me that's any minute." She laughed at his description.

He ran his hand along her stomach. He saw what could have been an elbow or foot. He was in total amazement. "I can't get enough of watching the baby move. It's unbelievable to think that soon we'll be holding him…or her. I can't wait."

"I can't wait to see your face when you hold him for the first time."

"I'll be happy when the baby's here and I know that you're both safe and healthy. I have to be honest; I'm not looking forward to seeing you in pain."

"That's a part of having a baby."

"I know but I don't have to like that part, do I?"

"You'd think you were the one in labor."

"No, I'll just be the one hoping my hands make it

through…"

"Your hands?"

"Yeah, I'm sure you'll be clutching onto one or both of them."

"I think you can handle me holding your hand."

"Not from what I hear. Jim told me when Holly had their kids, his hands hurt for days after the children were born."

"Maybe he's just a wimp."

"Who, Jim? Never." He guffawed then smiled. "Yeah, maybe he is a weakling. After all, I am pretty strong." He raised his arms and flexed his biceps.

She ran her hand along his muscle. "I guess you're strong."

"You guess?" he said reaching out to tickle her.

After a few moments rolling around laughing another pain hit her. She grabbed her side. "Enough, okay? I don't need any more of these Braxton Hicks. I'm getting tired as it is. I'm going to take a warm bath. That usually helps relieve them." She kissed him on the forehead and headed off to the bathroom. She hoped their exchange settled him down. He needed to be as relaxed as possible as they began the conference finals.

Relaxed was not the word to use for Ryne as he skated back onto the ice to take the opening faceoff. After the national anthem, he made his way to the circle. He eyed his friend Wiley and then the puck was dropped.

As soon as he won that opening faceoff, he put his

nervousness aside and skated for the team. Ryne scored a hat trick in that first game and led the team in overall points for the series. He scored nine goals as the Storm surprised the Eagles, winning the series in four games.

When the buzzer sounded to end the series, Ryne threw his arms over his head and fell to his knees in jubilation. Philippe and Etienne rushed him as did the rest of the team. The Storm was headed to the Stanley Cup finals. The long road with all of its twists and turns had been reached. Ryne's dream had come true. Now all he needed to do was help his team win one more series, and they'd be champions of the NHL.

Ryne said a silent prayer as he kneeled on the ice, then stood and motioned with his stick towards Jen. He saw her clapping away and then she threw him a kiss. He raised his hand, as if catching it and placed his hand over his heart and nodded to her. He couldn't wait to hold her and the baby. He needed to tell her how important she'd been to him as he reached this milestone. He'd done it for himself but also their family. If not for her, he wasn't sure he'd have returned from his latest injury.

He'd watched her as she suffered through her bouts of morning sickness and knew if she could make it through that, he could persevere through his rehab. She'd been his rock when he needed it, egging him on to keep focused so he could return to the ice.

In Ryne's estimation, the team's celebration and reporter interviews lasted way too long. He needed to get to Jen. Almost an hour after the buzzer rang ending the game, he departed the locker room and walked right into her arms.

"Gosh, I love you," he said as he swept her hair to the side of her face. "It's all because of you that I'm standing right here, right now." He brushed a soft kiss onto her lips. "You made me believe that I could still play."

She smiled at him. "I didn't do anything. You were the one to push through the long hours in rehab."

"You were right there beside me."

"Yeah, throwing up."

He chuckled at her response. "But you were there when you didn't feel like doing anything but crawling back into bed. He laid his hand over the baby as he moved. "We're going all the way, and then before we know it, this little one will be in our arms. What a way to end a magical season." He hugged her tightly, reached for her hand, and pulled her out the door.

The Stanley Cup finals would begin in a matter of days; their opponent had yet to be determined. The Generals were playing in the conference finals as well. They were fighting a good fight, and he hoped they'd be matched against them.

Chapter Forty

THE DAY RYNE HAD DREAMED of his entire life finally arrived. The Stanley Cup finals. Not only did he have an early morning skate, Jen also had a doctor's appointment. He woke early and rolled over in bed. He lay there and watched her sleep. She'd had a rough night. He heard her up at least four maybe five times to use the bathroom, and each time she returned to bed, she groaned as she tried to get comfortable.

He pulled her close. He helped her settle a pillow underneath her stomach and between her legs. When she sighed, he knew she'd finally received some ease. "Comfortable?"

"It's as good as it's going to get."

He settled his hand across her stomach. "It's going to be a big day. Try and get some sleep." She nodded. "If I'm not here when you wake-up, I'll see you at your appointment. Mom said she was going to take you."

"Yeah, she is." She yawned and laced her fingers through his. "I love you, Ryne."

"I love you too, honey. Try and get some sleep." He lay there listening to her breathe and knew the moment she fell asleep. He continued to hold her and felt the baby move continually as she slept. *I don't know how she can sleep, as active as you are. No wonder she's exhausted.*

Ryne finally dozed off and woke with a start. It was time to get up. He needed to be at the rink in a little more than an hour. He lightly kissed Jen's brow as he slid out of bed.

He was worried about her. She was getting less and less sleep, and he thought she'd looked tired the day before. He took a quick shower and a grabbed something to eat as he hurried out the door.

As he drove to the rink, he phoned his mom. "Hey, Mom, I wanted to remind you to take Jen to the doctor."

"Ryne, do you think I'd forget something that important? Don't concern yourself with me. You need to worry about getting safely to practice. I'll see you later at her appointment."

"Thanks, Mom," he said in a shaky voice.

"Son, stop fretting. I'm sure she's just fine. It's getting close. She has four weeks left."

"She's having problems sleeping."

"That's to be expected." Jacklynne reminded him he needed to concentrate on his morning skate and she'd see him later.

His skate went well and so did Jen's doctor's appointment. He discussed his concern about her Braxton Hicks contractions with the doctor along with her sleeplessness. The doctor put him at ease, but he knew he'd regain his feelings of helplessness when he watched her toss and turn and suffer through her false labor.

On the way home, they grabbed a quick bite to eat; then Ryne headed off for a power nap. He wanted to arrive at the arena early so he could take his time with his pregame warm-up.

As he sat beside his locker at Sauderhouse Arena, the importance of the night hit him hard. *This is it. The Stanley Cup finals.* Ryne was doing his best to stay calm, but it wasn't working. His career played out before his eyes. From his time at UW, winning all of the awards he did, until his trade to the Storm, he'd experienced it all. Yet now he was playing in the series that held the key to his heart. He'd dreamed of being where he was right here today—on home ice skating for the ultimate trophy. He didn't want to disappoint his parents nor family nor the fans of Calgary, but mostly he didn't want to disappoint himself. He'd been dreaming of this night since he was three years old and watched his father play. He'd trained hard and had discovered the importance of perseverance. He'd beaten the odds with his injuries and now look at himself. He wanted to make Jen proud. She'd been there by his side during the good and bad times of late. She'd seen him at the lowest of lows as he battled back from his hip injuries. Tonight, when his skates hit the ice and he heard his blades slice along, he knew his nerves would disappear and he'd get into his game. The game he'd been playing for so long. He was a winner, and he wanted to bring this all-important title to Calgary.

Before he knew it, he was standing at center ice ready to take the opening faceoff against his good friend, Derek. The Generals had won the seventh game of their series in a shootout.

Ryne took a deep, calming breath as he leaned

over waiting for the referee to drop the puck. Before he knew it the game had begun and he was winding his way down the ice. He fought for the puck against the boards and heard Etienne yell his name. He passed the puck to his brother who attempted a wrist shot, but it was deflected by a Generals player before it neared the net.

He skated end to end, fighting his way to gain control of the puck, losing it every time he neared the net. His legs were feeling the back-and-forth play when Ray motioned for his line to take a rest.

It was scoreless with just two minutes left in the game. Ryne was running on nervous energy. He'd had more than enough attempts to push the puck past the Generals goaltender and had been stopped each time.

As the clock counted down to overtime, Ryne caught a breakaway pass from Josh. He was alone as he entered the Generals' zone. He was moving so quickly he couldn't get a good shot off so he circled behind the net. By the time he came around the other side, Vlad was waiting. Ryne flicked the puck to Vlad and moved towards the front of the net. Vlad passed the puck back to Ryne who turned quickly and stuffed the puck behind the Generals' goalie. The blue light lit just as the buzzer rang to end the game. The Storm had won the first game of the series.

Ryne raised his arms and was immediately surrounded by his teammates. It had been a well fought game, and thankfully, the Storm had won.

By the time Ryne arrived home, he knew Jen was most assuredly exhausted. His parents had taken her home when he'd been barraged by reporters for interviews after his last-second goal. He knew she'd screamed the entire game because during lapses in the action, he could hear her voice all the way down to the ice. He wasn't sure how because it had been louder than heck in the arena, but for some reason it stood out to him. He was almost certain she'd lost her voice.

Ryne found her lying in bed curled up on her side. He sat on the edge of the mattress and laid his hand on her stomach. Lately, he couldn't get enough of touching her and the baby. It seemed like her abdomen had tightened when he placed his hand on her, and then he looked at her face. He could tell she was in pain. "More Braxton Hicks?"

In a gravelly voice, she said, "Yeah."

"Lost your voice, didn't you?" She nodded her head. "I could hear you all the way down on the ice." She moved her hands up and down the sides of her stomach, and almost immediately he noticed a relaxed expression cross her face.

"Better?" She nodded her head avoiding speaking. "Maybe you should stay home and watch the games on television. I think it's too stressful on you, and I don't want something to happen to you or the baby."

"Really? How would that look?" she whispered. "Ryne Ferguson's wife stays home, isn't present when her husband scores one of the most important goals of his career? I can see the headlines now." She tried clearing her throat.

"It's not like the press isn't aware that you're nine months pregnant."

"I realize that but I need to be there to support you!"

"You're my number one supporter. The people I care about know that too."

A look of pain crossed her face again. He waited until the contraction eased. "Let's play it by ear. We're off tomorrow, then we have a travel day after our next game." He was thinking out loud. "We'll play two more in St. Louis and then go back and forth between the cities for the last three games."

"I know the schedule, Ryne."

"Oh, sorry, was I talking out loud?"

"You were."

"I thought I was going through the schedule in my head. Anyway, you will not be traveling to St. Louis. You're too close, and I'm sure no one would want you to go into labor on the flight."

"But Ryne..."

"No buts, and anyway, the airline won't let you fly, so there." He stuck out his lip and nodded at her.

"What if you win in St. Louis? I won't be there to celebrate."

"Well, I guess I'll have one hell of a welcome home." He winked at her. "Jen, you need to do what's best for you and the baby and keep me out of the equation. I know you want to be there supporting me, supporting us, but your health and the baby's is more important."

"I know," she faintly uttered.

Ryne leaned over and laid his head on her shoulder. "I know you mean well and I love you for it. Mom promised me she'd stay home and wants you to move up to the house when we're in St. Louis."

"She asked me this morning, and I already told her I would."

"What? You mean you put me through this exchange only to have already made plans?"

She smiled. "I did and I enjoyed every minute watching you try and convince me to stay home. Ryne, I'm not stupid. This baby means the world to me. I know you understand and would never want to put us in danger." She ran her hand up and down his back. "I just had to have fun with you, especially after tonight's game. That was pretty intense."

"It was. I was lucky at the end there. I was sure we were headed for overtime." He lay down next to her and held her until she fell asleep. He was wide awake and didn't want to disturb her. Just as he tried to ease out of bed, she mumbled something in her sleep. Instead of heading off to watch a little television, he snuggled in deeply at her side and rehashed the game in his head.

In all, he'd played an average game. He knew he could have scored on several of his breakaways and wished he had. The finish wouldn't have been so intense. And if he had scored, maybe Jen wouldn't have been so stressed out at the end.

He berated himself. He knew he could have played much better. He vowed he would play harder in the next outing. He wouldn't allow errant passes, he'd stay out of the penalty box, and he would win each and every faceoff he took. The rush to the finish line was on, and he was going to see that they were the first to cross it.

But in the second game, even though Ryne had committed to not making the same errors, he didn't live up to his own promises. Instead, he ended up taking a major penalty when he was involved in a fight that led to a goal.

Philippe had also scored a goal to tie the game, but it was waved off because of Ryne's reckless high stick. He was furious with himself, especially when they lost.

Ryne wasn't in the best frame of mind when he returned home to find his mother and Jen watching highlights from the game. When he saw what was on the television, he grabbed the remote from the coffee table and shut it off. "I'd say he's not in a pleasant mood." Jen turned to Jacklynne and shrugged.

"I'd say not." Jacklynne leaned over and kissed Jen on the cheek. "I'm going to head on home and leave you with Mr. Grumpy." Her purse was lying on the table. As she reached for it, she squeezed her son's shoulder. "You'll get 'em next game." With that, she left the house.

Ryne took his mother's seat and stared straight ahead. "I really messed up tonight. I should have never gotten involved in that fight."

"Then why did you?"

"Because he tripped me up a few minutes earlier and then went after me again against the boards. I'd had enough of his play."

"So you needed to drop your gloves and duke it

out."

"Yeah, I did."

"And did you feel better when you were cussing yourself out in the penalty box?"

"No."

"Lesson learned, then. What about the high stick?"

He shook his head. "I don't know…"

"Ryne, you're doing it again. You're putting too much pressure on yourself to perform. There are twenty-one players on the team besides you. This is a team sport. You can't be everywhere on the ice. Everyone needs to step it up a little. This loss isn't yours alone. It's everyone's that put their skates on tonight. You seem to forget that you're not the only person carrying the team. Now snap out this."

"When did you get so wise?"

"I've always been this way; you just haven't listened to me when I've spoken."

"I always listen to you."

"Really, now?" She paused. "Ryne, I've told you this at least a hundred times." She turned to place her hand on his cheek. "You got to where you are by playing the game *you* play not the one you think you need to play." She rested her forehead against his. "You can't do anything else about tonight's game. It's in the books. What you can control is the next game and the game after that." She softly kissed him on the lips. "I'm ready for bed, what about you?"

He leaned over and kissed her forehead. "Go ahead and I'll be there in a minute." Ryne knew she was right, and there was absolutely nothing he could do about the game. He needed to have a positive attitude as they traveled to St. Louis.

As he skated onto the ice to begin warm-ups for the third game in the series, he glanced up to Ed's box. He didn't understand why, but he was overcome with emotion. Ed had surprised him when he stopped by his hotel room earlier that day. "We've all been busy with this series, but I needed to know how Jen's doing. I know she's not with you on this trip, but I worry about her."

"She's doing as well as can be expected. She doesn't sleep as the baby seems to decide to keep her up at night. She wanted to be here but I put my foot down."

"I know. I spoke with her when the Generals first made it into the playoffs. She was upset that she couldn't travel. She wanted to be here."

"She did but instead of her wise words, I have Rose and Wilford's."

"About that…"

"Hey, I understand. I wouldn't expect you not to invite them and Lauren to join you in your box." With a snicker he added, "We all know they're cheering for…The Storm!"

"I think not," Ed kiddingly added.

"No matter who wins, whether it's the Generals or the Storm, I'm just thankful that I've been able to play with two stellar teams." They chatted for a few more minutes then Ryne said, "Ed, thank you for being such a good friend to me and Jen. You hold a special place in her heart." They shook hands and Ryne headed off for his meeting. He'd been lucky to call Ed a friend as well.

Ryne skated off the ice. He glanced up at Ed's box and motioned a greeting with his stick to Rose, Wilford, and Lauren.

Philippe joined him on his walk back to the locker room. "Did you see Lauren in Ed's box?" Ryne asked.

"Yeah, I did. She's a traitor."

Ryne chortled as he sat beside his brother.

"I spoke with her earlier, and she informed me she's a Generals' fan at heart and wouldn't be cheering for me," Philippe said as he tightened his skate.

"So was Jen until love entered the game," Ryne added then slugged his brother in the arm. "You just need to step it up a little, big brother. She's not going to wait forever for you."

"I'm not searching for that right now. I'm still working on getting my head on straight. Give me a little more time." Time is not what Philippe needed. Ryne wanted to see his brother move past the loss of Annabelle, and he thought Lauren was the perfect choice to help him. He needed to figure out a way to put them in the same orbit, or Philippe would never see that she was the one for him.

Three hours later Ryne sat down hard in front of his locker. Shaking his head, he knew he'd truly messed up again. He couldn't understand what was wrong with him. Not only had he gotten into another fight, but he found himself in the penalty box way too many times. He rubbed his hand across his face. He was ashamed with the way he'd played, and he wouldn't blame Ray if he became a healthy scratch for the next game. They were losing the series two games to one and needed to win the next one.

They had a day off between games and he met with Rose and Wilford. They had a good visit and Rose imparted to him the same words her grand-daughter had. He needed to play his game, plain and simple.

So when Ryne took the opening faceoff in the fourth game, he recalled Rose's words. Not only did he stay penalty free, he scored a hat trick, and the Storm shut out the Generals four to nothing.

As they flew on their chartered flight back to Calgary, Ryne felt good. The series was tied at two games each. In his opinion they were starting the series from scratch.

Their plane arrived late and Ryne did his best to be as quiet as possible when he walked in the door. Jen had texted him after the game that she was going home and would be waiting for him. He found her sprawled on the couch fast asleep with the television turned on the sports channel.

He set down his bag and scooped her into his arms and carried her to bed. He jostled her slightly and she woke for but a moment but went right back to sleep. He eased into bed beside her and slipped his arms around her. On a whisper, "Daddy's home, little one," he stroked her stomach. "I'm sure glad you're allowing Mommy to get some sleep." He felt the baby move in response to his comment and drifted off to sleep.

Time seemed to stand still but also flew by. As

Ryne walked back into their home six days later, the series was tied at three games each, and a seventh game was needed to decide the winner. Ryne was tired and sore as he rubbed his hip. It had been one hell of a long season, and he was glad it was coming to an end.

He didn't think twice when he walked through the door and headed off to bed. He found Jen's eyes on him when he entered the room. Every time he looked at her he thought she was bigger. For the first six months, you wouldn't have known she was pregnant. And she still had about two weeks until her due date. He wanted the season over so he could devote his time and attention to her and the baby because before he knew it, September would again be upon them with the start of another season. "Hey there," he said as he sat down on the edge of the mattress and ran his hand down the side of her face. "How are you feeling? Is little bits behaving?"

"She wasn't until about a half hour ago. I'm afraid she's going to follow in your family's footsteps and be a hockey player." She yawned as she ran her hand along his cheek. "I watched the game. You won."

"We did and at least we're still in the hunt."

"Would you want it any differently? Sweetheart, you played one heck of a game tonight." She ran her hand along his thigh. "How's the hip? You were a little slow getting up after taking that hit from Derek. And what's up with that? I thought he was your friend."

"He is off the ice. He's in it to win too."

"I realize that but he didn't have to take your legs right out from under you."

"It's all a part of the game."

"I know." She yawned again. "Why don't you take a hot shower and come join me. I promise not to fall asleep on you."

He took a quick shower and returned to their bed where she was fast asleep. As he lay down and pulled her into his arms, he thought. *Three more days...Three more days until my dream could possibly come true.*

"Don't argue with me, Ryne. I'm coming to the game. I took a nap earlier and I feel really good." He decided it wasn't worth his effort to argue with her. She'd do what she wanted, and he couldn't do anything about it. He understood her reasoning, but the ever-protective husband he was wanted her to stay home.

Thankfully, she'd be surrounded by his family. He knew they'd watch out for her, along with Lauren, who'd flown in for the game.

Ryne arrived early and suited up, making sure his hip pads were well secured. His hip was smarting, and he just wanted to get through the game without causing further injury. He skated onto the ice. It was just him and the ice— no other players.

He slowly slid around the rink. The sound of his skates cutting through the ice had a calming effect. It reminded him of his youth when he'd skate on the pond. He'd go round and round for hours taking in the scenery and dreaming of this day that seemed so far out of reach. Yet today he was here— living the dream he'd often thought would never happen.

One step, two steps… He felt all the emotion of his career come full circle. At the end of the day, he believed his dream would be fulfilled. And then, in a few short days, he'd welcome the birth of his first child. He was anxious for it all… So much in so little time.

He skated to a halt along the boards and sprayed the ice. In front of him stood his wife. They'd practically come full circle with her watching him in this manner. He was luckier than most and had found the woman of his dreams doing what he loved most, playing hockey.

"You're awfully early. I thought you were coming with Mom and Dad."

"Lauren brought me. I knew I'd find you out here before everyone else. I wanted to watch you as you took it all in. I'll always remember the first time I watched you skate after our little incident."

He wryly smiled at her. "If that's what you want to call it."

"Well, that is what it was."

"I know that's what you want to believe…" He leaned over the boards and ran his hand along her brow. "That night changed my life forever. I found you. I don't care whether it was you watching me warm up, or meeting you at the bar, or by running into your car. I found myself that night."

"I didn't know you were missing."

"Funny," he quipped. "Anyway, you set me on this course. I'm not sure I would have pushed Adam to trade me to the Storm if it wasn't for you. I needed you to push me here. If tonight is the last game I ever play in the NHL, I will have experienced all of my dreams. I'm playing for the hometown in the seventh game of the Stanley Cup finals, and I have you and little bits right here beside me. I couldn't be happier than I am right now." He leaned over and placed a soft kiss on her lips. "I love you Jen, and I am ever thankful I found you."

She leaned into him and wrapped her arms around his neck. "I love you too." The baby took that moment to let out a swift kick. She laughed and rubbed her stomach. "And little bits loves her daddy too."

He held her for a few moments when he heard footsteps. He looked up to see Lauren standing just behind Jen.

"Sorry to interrupt..."

"Oh hi, Lauren. I didn't see you."

"I just walked up."

"I'd better go." He turned and started to skate towards the tunnel and then returned. "I expect you to behave. Don't get overly excited. I don't need you to go into labor tonight."

"I'll be good, I promise."

With that he skated away. In a few short hours, the season would be over. Only time would tell who the winner would be.

Chapter Forty-One

JEN STOOD NERVOUSLY IN JACQUES' box watching the Storm take the ice. She was surrounded by her family. She was nervous and excited all at the same time. Jacklynne had been mother hen making sure she wasn't overdoing it. In fact, she'd ordered her to sit while the team warmed up.

She watched Lauren. She knew her friend hadn't taken her eyes off of Philippe. She hoped she'd convince her to vacation with them later in the summer. Lauren's job was driving her crazy. Every time they talked Jen tried to convince her to look for a new position. The stress lately had caused Lauren some health problems. Jen kept reiterating that her health was way more important than a stupid job. She didn't need to make partner to be a successful attorney. Jen hoped Lauren would listen to her and make a change.

As she sat along the open box that overlooked the rink, she watched Ryne circle the ice. He seemed more relaxed and at peace than he had earlier. She caught a smile on his face as he ran into Etienne. Something must have been awfully funny for him to crack up the way he did. Before she knew it, the anthems were being played, and he was standing at center ice awaiting the faceoff that would ultimately bring a close to the season.

As he leaned over awaiting the puck drop, she saw him tense and knew his mood had changed from only moments ago. Jen was so familiar with the way he held himself; she hoped he got through the game in one piece.

She held her breath as the puck dropped and Ryne won the faceoff. The puck landed on Josh's stick and he headed up ice. Everyone was fresh and scurried down the ice with Josh leading the charge. He entered the Generals' zone and quickly passed the puck to Etienne who circled behind the net, spraying ice against the boards as he came around the other side.

Etienne offered a quick pass back to Josh who shot it across the ice to Ryne. Ryne faked a shot, spun around Derek Pfeil, and passed the puck back to Josh.

"They're doing an awful lot of passing," Lauren commented.

Jen nodded as her eyes never left the ice. Josh skated along the boards and was pushed up against them, momentarily losing the puck in his skates. A scuffle ensued for the puck when the linesman blew his whistle.

"That was intense," Jen stated as she watched Ryne skate off the ice for a line change. Josh took the next face off and lost it to Curt Wiles who controlled the puck as he skated up ice. Quickly he crossed the blue line, catching Jorge off guard with a wrist shot, scoring the first goal.

Jen's eyes sought out Ryne who'd been sitting on the bench, awaiting another line change. She witnessed the frustration on his face as he slapped his gloved hand against the wall. She knew he wished he'd been the one to take that faceoff.

By the end of the first period, the Storm was losing by one goal. As Jen stood to take a bathroom break, she felt the baby move. It was a hard kick to the bladder. She couldn't make it fast enough to the bathroom.

When she returned, Jacklynne had taken Lauren's place. "Everything okay? You looked like you were in pain."

"Yeah, I'm fine. The baby's a little active, that's all."

Jacklynne reached over and laid her hand over the baby. "I promised my son to keep an eye on you."

"I know. I felt your glare the entire first period." She guffawed. "I think I behaved myself pretty well."

"In all honesty, dear, there wasn't anything to get overly excited about."

"You're right there. At least they're not losing too badly. They can easily make up one goal."

"They can and they will," Jacklynne commented as the players returned to the ice.

Jen's eyes scanned the ice for Ryne and she didn't see him at first. Philippe stood at center awaiting the faceoff. "I wonder where Ryne is?" she commented to Jacklynne. "Do you think he's injured?"

"There he is," Jacklynne pointed to the bench. "Maybe Ray's decided to shake up the lines."

"I hope that's all it is. This game means so much to him."

"That it does," Jacklynne said as they watched

Josh lose the opening faceoff.

The opening minutes of the period were a rush of back and forth. Ryne was just getting ready to return after a line change when Etienne broke up a Generals' pass. Ryne flew over the boards, and as his skates hit the ice the puck was on his blade. He rushed up ice and crossed the blue line. He stopped and spun around, faked a pass and flicked his wrists. The puck flew into the air, deflecting off one of the Generals' players' stick right into the net. Goal. Ryne threw his arms into the air and was immediately surrounded by his teammates. He'd tied the game.

Jen saw a look of relief cross Ryne's face. They were back to square one. She sighed loudly and watched as everyone stood cheering the goal. She remained seated, doing her best to stay calm and not get too excited.

By the end of the second period the teams were still locked in a tie. Lauren rejoined her as she'd spent the entire second period entertaining Emma and talking with Jules. "You doing okay?" she asked as she handed Jen a bottle of water.

"I am. On the outside I'm doing my best to remain calm, but on the inside I'm a basket case. When Ryne scored I wanted to scream from the rooftops, but right as the blue light lit, the baby kicked pretty hard and decided I needed to stay calm and not upset her."

"That was smart."

The third and hopefully final period began with Ryne at the helm. He took the faceoff and thankfully won control. The puck shot between his skates and Philippe fought for it, winning and shooting it into the Generals' zone. Josh skated in but lost control of the puck. Again it was end to end play. She knew Ryne had to be getting tired. Ray constantly switched up lines, but his line seemed to have the most ice time.

They'd passed the half way part of the period, and the game was still tied. The more nervous she got, the more the baby moved. She ran her hand along her belly, hoping to settle her down. Yet all of the turmoil around her didn't seem to help as she got more excited watching the play. At one point, Etienne took a shot that careened loudly off the post. Everyone thought he'd scored, and she jumped to her feet only to discover that he hadn't. They watched as the Generals flew back up ice into the Storm's end.

Ryne broke up a play and grabbed the puck only to end up along the boards, fighting hard to retain possession. Then he was slammed into the glass where he lost control of the puck and fell hard to the ice. Play continued as he slowly rose and made his way to the bench.

Her concern must have shown in her face, because Lauren said, "I'm sure he's okay." Philippe flew up the ice, passing the puck off to Etienne as Ryne moved to the bench for a breather. Off sides was immediately called as Josh stepped across the blue line before the puck.

With the stoppage in play, she certainly thought Ryne would return but he didn't. The longer he sat there, the more concerned she became. Lauren grabbed her hand. "Stop worrying. I'm sure he's fine. He's been on the ice a lot this period. I'm sure he's getting a little longer to recover."

Jen listened to her friend, never taking her eyes off her husband. With three minutes left to play, someone laid their hands on her shoulders. Jacques had positioned himself behind her. He massaged her tight shoulders and waited for play to resume. "I have a good feeling," Jacques whispered in her ear. "Ray's just resting him. I'm sure of it."

Jen reached back and clasped his fingers. "I hope so…and that it's nothing else."

Jacques stood over her shoulders as play resumed. Josh took another faceoff in the Generals' zone which he won. He rushed down the ice, losing the puck at center ice. End to end play with less than a minute to go. Ryne hadn't been on the ice for over five minutes when Etienne caught an errant pass. He looked up just as Ryne floated over the boards. He flicked the pass to his brother who flew into the Generals' zone. It seemed as though time stood still. Ryne raised his stick and, in what appeared slow motion, slapped the puck towards the Generals' goal. The goalie had committed to going down on the play when Ryne had approached, but the puck flew high over his shoulder, past the goalie into the net.

She released the breath she'd been holding as the blue light lit. Ryne had scored the tie breaking goal with five seconds to remain in the game. The crowd went wild. Jen jumped out of her seat and into Jacques arms. "Oh my gosh! Did you see that, Dad? He did it, Ryne scored the winning goal."

"Honey, there's still five seconds left to play, anything can happen."

"Not with my husband taking the faceoff," she said with confidence. The arena was the loudest she'd ever heard. The rafters were shaking as everyone stomped their feet, screamed at the top of their lungs, and clapped loudly. Jen got caught up in the excitement, jumping up and down celebrating Ryne's biggest goal of his career.

And then she felt it— a stabbing pain. She clutched her abdomen and collapsed back into her chair. Jacques immediately noticed her sign of distress and caught her as she sat. "Honey, are you okay? Is it the baby?"

Through clenched teeth she nodded her head. "Let me sit here a minute, okay. I'm sure it's just a Braxton Hicks." Clutching her hands against her belly, she watched the time tick down on the clock. Five…four…three…two…one…

The cheers rang out and the Storm players gathered at center ice, out of control with excitement. They'd done it. Ryne had scored the game-winning goal with five seconds to remain in the game of his life. He'd won the Stanley Cup for his hometown team. When she looked back at the rink, the players had collapsed onto the ice. Ryne was at the center of their celebration.

Next she felt Lauren's arms surrounding her, cheering the Storm's win. "Ah, did you just change alliances," she quipped at her friend.

"No, absolutely not," she adamantly said. "I'm just happy for my friends."

Jen caught Lauren smiling wryly at her.

The entire family was in celebration mode, high

fiving and hugging each other. She leaned against the wall watching the fans cheering their hometown team. Ryne was surrounded by reporters. He'd already thrown on a ball cap and a new t-shirt proclaiming they were Stanley Cup champions. She watched his interview on the television monitor in their box. The smile on his face shone brightly.

"I haven't seen him happier since your wedding. Look at that smile," Jacklynne stated as she wrapped her arm around Jen. They continued their celebration in Jacques' box and took in Ryne's interview before the players headed off to the locker room. Ryne's last words in his interview were priceless to her.

"This is for you, Jen. I love you and can't wait for the next chapter in our lives."

Tears welled in her eyes. She raised her hand to her lips to stave them off, but wasn't successful. She turned to Jacklynne as a lone tear slid down her face. "He did it, Mom. His dream came true."

"That he did, honey. Now, let's go congratulate the boys."

She reached for Jacklynne's hand and was caught off guard again by a searing pain. She was sure it was just a Braxton Hicks as she'd overextended herself with excitement. She clenched Jacklynne's hand, took a deep breath, and eased it out slowly.

"Honey, are you okay? Shall we sit for a minute?"

"I'm okay. Let's get this reunion over with so we can go home. I think I need to lie down."

The entire family along with Lauren took a private elevator, and Jacques led them down a series of corridors to the locker room. She was ever thankful they arrived as quickly as they did. She didn't want to put a damper on Ryne's celebration, but she needed to get home.

They'd waited for only a few moments when Ryne appeared. She opened her arms and he hugged her tightly. "You did it!"

"Yeah, we did," he said as he looked her squarely in the eye. As he ran his hand along her cheek, she knew he knew something was wrong.

She leaned in and kissed him. "I'm so proud of you. Are you okay after that fall?"

He ignored her comment as he placed his hand on her stomach. "I'm alright but are you?"

"Of course, I am. Your parents are going to take me home so you can bask in the glory of this win, okay?"

"Let me change and I'll take you home."

"Ryne, no! You need to celebrate with the team. I'll be just fine. Your parents will make sure."

"I've had my celebration. Give me a few minutes to shower and I'll be right out." Just as he leaned in to kiss her, she crumbled in his arms clutching her stomach.

"Jen, hey, what's wrong? Is it the baby?"

His parents surrounded them immediately. Before she could utter a word, she felt a warm trickle of fluid run down her legs. "Ryne," she said nervously. "I just think my water broke."

"What? Are you in labor?"

She nodded her head. "I think I am."

Jacques took over. "Ryne, go shower and change. I'll get the car, and Jacklynne can help Jen to the players' entrance."

She took one look at Ryne. She knew he was just as scared and nervous as she was. He kissed her cheek and hurried back to the locker room. "I'll be right back. Wait here."

In less than five minutes, Ryne was by her side. He tightened his arm around her and guided her to the back doors. Just as they reached the entrance, she clutched his hand. "Are you having a contraction?"

"I think so."

Jacklynne grabbed ahold on her hand. "Breathe, Jen. Don't forget to breathe."

When the contraction had ended, they hurried out the door. Jules waited with Lauren, Emma, and Oliva for Philippe and Etienne. Jules would go home with the girls while Etienne, Philippe, and Lauren decided to follow them to the hospital.

Less than three hours later, Jen and Ryne welcomed their bundle of joy— a baby girl. The Braxton Hicks contractions she thought she'd had for hours were in fact real, and she'd been in labor a good portion of the day.

Tears of joy ran down not only her but Ryne's face as well. She clutched her precious little girl to her chest.

"Look at her Jen, she's perfect." Ryne ran his hand lightly against his daughter's hair. He leaned his head against Jen's and cried. It had been a truly emotional day for them. He still hadn't fully come to terms with winning the Stanley Cup, but add in the birth of his daughter, and this was a day he'd never ever forget. Who could imagine? All of his dreams had come to fruition. He had fulfilled his career goals, just had his first child, and he had a beautiful wife.

"Ryne, hey, you okay?"

He sniffled. "Yeah. It's been one hell of a day." He brushed the tears from his eyes. "I still can't believe it. Who would have thought when I woke up that I would achieve all of my goals in one day? Never in my wildest of dreams. Never." He leaned over, brushing a kiss on the baby's head and Jen's brow. "I love you so much, Jen."

She smiled up at him and clasped his cheek. "I love you too." She nuzzled his neck as he wrapped his family in the first of what he knew would be many hugs.

"We need to name her," she said now through her own tears.

"Let's enjoy this moment. We have time."

Epilogue

TWO DAYS LATER JEN AND the baby came home. They stopped off at the big house before heading to their own place for some much-needed rest. Ryne had gone home only long enough to change clothes and gather Jen's suitcase, spending the remaining time at the hospital.

They decided on a name for their daughter, Jacklynne Rose. It was Jen's idea to name her after his mother, the mother who now meant the world to her. She chose her mother's and grandmother's name of Rose as her middle name. They hadn't told anyone about her name; they'd chosen it just that morning before they were released from the hospital.

For the first time, they pulled up to the ranch as a family. She felt like she had when she first arrived two years earlier as only Jacques and Jacklynne were waiting for them on the porch. "I gather everyone else is inside."

"Probably. I'm sure Mom didn't want to overwhelm you and Jacklynne."

"I remember the first time you brought me here. So much has happened since that summer day."

"You're so right."

Ryne parked the car and came around to help Jen

before opening the door and gathering Jacklynne. Jen watched as he carefully removed the car seat. Thankfully, Jacklynne had fallen asleep on her first car ride, and he was doing his best to keep it that way.

He guided her towards the steps. "Where is everyone?" she asked as she found herself wrapped in her mother-in-law's arms.

"On the deck waiting for you and... Do we have a name?"

"We do," Ryne said with a smile on his face. "Let's join the rest of the family, and we'll share it with everyone."

Jacques took a quick peek at his adorable granddaughter. He brushed a sweet kiss on Jen's cheek. "How are you feeling, my dear?"

"I'm doing pretty well as long as this little lady keeps taking a nap." She chuckled. "I'll be glad to go home and sleep in our own bed."

"I'm sure you will. Let's make this a short visit; we don't want to tire you out."

They gathered on the deck. All of the Fergusons were present along with Lauren. She'd held off returning to St. Louis until Jen came home from the hospital.

As Jen came through the French doors onto the deck, she saw her friend off to the side speaking with Philippe. She noticed Lauren's smile and focus on him as he spoke. Lauren looked better than when she had first arrived. Jen was concerned for her friend and hoped that she'd return to Calgary later in the summer.

"Look who's here," Jacques spoke as he reached for

the car seat. He set it down on the patio table. "She looks like you did when you were a baby," Jacques indicated to Ryne. "Look at her nose and hands. A Ferguson through and through."

Jen smiled up at Ryne. She knew how much Ryne loved his daughter and was ever thankful the season was over. After Jacklynne was born, she noticed a grimace on his face. He'd kept it from her while she'd been in labor, but he'd reinjured his hip when he took the hard fall to the ice. It wasn't serious and she was thankful the season had ended so he could get much needed rest. He'd decided to take some time off from his training to let his hip heal and spend the summer with his family.

"So, do we have a name?" Emma cheerfully asked at a decibel level higher than they expected. Jacklynne jumped in her sleep and settled back down.

"Emma, you need to tone it down a little now that Jacklynne is here."

Ryne had slipped in her name wondering if his mother would pick up on it. It took her a second before the baby's name registered. "Ryne, did you say what I think you said?"

He nodded. Both a smile and tears broke out on his mother's face. "Jen and I would like to introduce Jacklynne Rose to everyone."

As soon as Jacques heard the first mention of the baby's name, he'd draped his arm around his wife. "Jacques, did you hear that? They named her Jacklynne."

"I heard, dear."

"And Rose is for my mother."

"Oh sweetheart, it's such an honor for you to have

named her after me."

"As far as I'm concerned you're my mom now, so why wouldn't we?"

Jacklynne walked out of her husband's arms into Jen's. "I'll never forget the day Ryne brought you into our lives. I've loved you from that very moment."

Jacklynne had woken, so Olivia and Emma got the chance to hold her. While they were ogling over their niece, Jen and Ryne took in the scene before them. Philippe and Lauren were still enmeshed in their conversation. "I hope he does something about that."

"I do too, Ryne. I think he's finally moved on."

"I hope so. He seems happy now, and I think Lauren's a part of it."

Ryne grabbed Jen's hand and looked her in the eyes. "Sweetheart, I can't believe we're standing here today, happily married, with our daughter. So much has happened since our first meeting." He ran his finger down her cheek and smiled. "I still can't believe I was traded to the Storm, and soon I'll be parading the Stanley Cup down Main Street with you on my arm."

He brushed an errant strand of hair from her face. "It took you and my love of this city to get me here. For a long time, I was facing what I like to refer to as Calgary's Dream, but you made it come true. I've come to the team I love, faced my dream of winning the Stanley Cup, and fulfilled the ultimate dream of having a family. You and Jacklynne are my family. I don't know what I'd do without you in my life."

"As far as I'm concerned I hope you'll never have

to face that day."

He pulled her into a tight embrace.

"I love you, Ryne, and this moment will forever be etched into my memory. I'm wrapped in the arms of the man I love, and I've finally found my family."

She glanced at Lauren and Philippe. "We can only hope and pray that our luck rubs off on them." With that he kissed her then reached for Jacklynne's car seat.

"We're going to head home now." He picked up his daughter and clasped Jen's hand. Ryne's life was complete. They were heading home. Home to a place both of them had longed for.

Jen's life had come full circle since losing her parents. She'd recaptured the career of her dreams, discovered the love of her life, and finally found a family she could call her own. Nothing could be sweeter then what stood before her eyes. She'd dreamed of this day forever. One filled with love, hope, and a happily ever after. Her dream had become a reality, and she was ever thankful for that slip of fate when she practically ran Ryne over in the Generals' parking lot. Her life had changed that day, and she'd always look back on it as the day she found herself.

Author's Note

Thank you so much for reading Facing Calgary's Dream. For news and updates from Anne Stone, subscribe to her newsletter. You'll be treated to sneak peeks, giveaways, free books and bonus material just for signing up.

If you enjoyed reading Facing Calgary's Dream, please consider leaving a review. Reviews are always appreciated!

Connect with Anne online:

Follow Anne on BookBub:
Anne Stone Author

Follow Anne on Facebook at:
Anne Stone Author

Follow Anne on Goodreads:
Anne_Stone

Email:
Anne@Annestoneauthor.com

About the Author

Anne Stone was born and raised in St. Louis, Missouri but now lives in the cold state of Wisconsin with her faithful Cavalier King Charles Spaniel. She writes heartfelt sweet contemporary romance and is the author of the following series: Black Gold Management Agency, The Show Me, and Williams & Company. She loves to tell a story and that's what you'll definitely get in an Anne Stone novel.

Anne's degree is in education but she has worked in the corporate sector managing a large number of staff. Now, she works from home where part of her day is still spent in the corporate world and the other part is dreaming of her heroes and heroines.

Learn more about Anne by visiting *www.AnneStoneAuthor.com*.

Also by Anne Stone

The Show Me Series:
Book 1:Life's Second Chances
Book 2: Life's Gateway to Happiness
Book 3: Life's Turned Upside Down
Book 4: Life's Second Journey
The Show Me Series Boxed Set: Volume 1
(Books 1-3)

Williams & Company:
Never Lose Hope

Black Gold Management Agency:
Book 1: Love's Final Match

**Black Gold Management Agency:
The Ferguson's**
Book 1: Facing Calgary's Dream

www.ingramcontent.com/pod-product-compliance
Lightning Source LLC
Chambersburg PA
CBHW030538020726
47494CB00005B/1416